# WOLFPACK

## A DCI TYLER THRILLER

### MARK ROMAIN

*I hope you have as much fun sailing in IONA as I did!!*

*Romain.*

Copyright © 2024 Mark Romain.
All rights reserved.
ISBN-13: 979-8-8794-7639-2

The right of Mark Romain to be identified as author of this work has been asserted by him in accordance with sections 77 and 78 of the copyright, designs and patents act 1988. This book is a work of fiction and any resemblance to actual persons, living or dead, is purely coincidental.

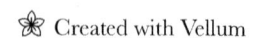

❦ Created with Vellum

# THE DCI TYLER THRILLERS

TURF WAR

JACK'S BACK

THE HUNT FOR CHEN

UNLAWFULLY AT LARGE

THE CANDY KILLER

DIAMONDS AND DEATH

WOLFPACK

# DEDICATION

For Jane and Flora, and all the other readers who told me I left it far too long between books…

I promise to try harder next time!

# READER ADVISORIES

### Content

This book deals with the highly emotive subjects of child abduction and paedophilia. Readers may find some of the scenes and situations described disturbing, and reader discretion is strongly advised.

### Language and opinions

The DCI Tyler Thrillers are set in the late nineties and early noughties, which means most of the detectives they feature would have joined the police in the eighties. In the interests of realism, the books contain language and opinions that were commonplace and acceptable at the time, but which would now be considered inappropriate and offensive.

### Spelling and Grammar

Please note that this book is written in British (UK) English, and that many spellings in the UK differ from those in the USA.

# PROLOGUE

King's Lynn, August 1976

It was a stiflingly hot night in rural Norfolk, with the UK experiencing its hottest summer in over 350 years. The air was still and heavy, silent apart from chirping crickets, the occasional howls of an amorous fox, and the irritated screeching of a distant barn owl.

The sky was cloudless; a velvety blue backdrop peppered by a million faraway stars, all shimmering in the darkness like tiny diamonds. It was the third and final night of the full moon, and visibility was so good that the craters of Tycho and Copernicus could be seen in stunning detail with the naked eye.

The campsite was in complete darkness, its patrons having long since retired to their tents and their caravans. Every now and then, for those lucky enough to have pitches facing the coastline, a gentle breeze would blow in from the sea, bringing with it a temporary respite from the oppressive heat.

Had anyone still been awake, they might have heard the

distressed noises the small boy was making as he was dragged from his tent by two masked men. His name was Robbie Diggle, and until a few moments ago he had been enjoying a carefree summer holiday with his parents and twin brother, Phillip.

Like grave robbers making off with a freshly dug up corpse, the darkly dressed men carried the struggling child across the field. He was bucking and twisting, arching his back in a concerted effort to break free, but he was too small to cause them any real problems.

"Stop wriggling you little brat," the man in the blue ski mask hissed. Holding Robbie under his armpits, he was panting heavily from the sustained effort of supporting the boy's weight as he ran.

The one holding Robbie's ankles wore a red ski mask, and he was breathing just as heavily.

Before dragging him from the tent, Blue Ski Mask had rammed a dirty sock deep into Robbie's mouth, choking him to the point where he could barely breathe, let alone alert anyone to his fate.

When he heard gravel crunching underfoot, Robbie realised that they had reached the end of the field and were now on the winding track that led up to the road.

Twisting his head sideways, Robbie caught a brief glimpse of a waiting van up ahead. It was either a Leyland DAF or a Ford Transit, he couldn't be sure. A thick plume of white spewed from the exhaust pipe as it stood there, engine running, lights out.

A third man waited anxiously by the back doors. Like the others, he wore dark clothing and a ski mask, his being green in colour. He hurriedly opened the rear doors, then stood aside as they chucked Robbie into the back as callously as if he were a sack of potatoes.

Robbie landed heavily on his left side and rolled twice before colliding with a protruding wheel arch. The impact bought him to a jarring halt. He attempted to stand, but Red Ski Mask leapt upon him, pinning him down and pressing his head into the van's floor.

"Don't get any clever ideas," he sneered. "You ain't going nowhere."

Green Ski Mask was peering into the back of the van. "What does he look like?" he asked, in a voice full of sexual tension. "Let me see his face."

Red Ski Mask obligingly grabbed a handful of Robbie's hair, and twisted his head sideways until it was facing towards the rear doors.

"Very nice," Green Ski Mask said, leering in at him.

The strange glint in his eyes sent a shudder down Robbie's spine.

Blue Ski Mask appeared by his side. "Shut up and get back behind the wheel," he growled, giving the other man a hard shove. "We need to be on our way before anyone clocks us."

"Alright, keep your hair on," the chastised driver complained, but his tone was deferential.

Climbing into the back, Blue Ski Mask slammed the door in his face without replying.

Robbie was beyond terrified. His heart was thudding so painfully against his chest cavity that he was finding it difficult to breathe.

Why had they taken him away from his family?

What were they going to do with him?

He had watched helplessly as one of these monsters strangled his brother. Tears prickled his eyes as he wondered whether Phillip was still alive or–

Robbie was hauled into a sitting position, breaking his train of thought.

Red Ski Mask placed a gloved hand on either side of Robbie's head, painfully compressing his temples until he could no longer move. Then Blue Ski Mask stuck two fingers in Robbie's mouth, making him gag as the sock was removed.

Laughing at his discomfort, Blue Ski Mask grabbed a duffle bag from behind the driver's seat. He rummaged around inside it for a few seconds, removing a small metal flask. Unscrewing it, he held it up to Robbie's face.

"Drink this," he instructed.

Robbie instinctively tried to pull away, violently twisting his head from side to side.

With a savage curse, Red Ski Mask tightened his grip, making Robbie squeal in pain.

"Do as you're told and drink it," he ordered, yanking Robbie's head so far back that he was afraid his neck would snap.

Before Robbie could scream, Blue Ski Mask grabbed his chin and began pouring the liquid into his open mouth.

As the tangy substance flowed down his throat, Robbie coughed and spluttered, doing his best not to choke. Unable to breathe, he felt as though he were drowning. He reached up in panic, frantically clawing at the hand holding the flask, trying to drag it away from his mouth.

Blue Ski Mask viciously slapped his hands away. "Stop it," he snarled, shoving the displaced flask back into Robbie's mouth with such force that it smashed into his teeth.

Robbie yelped with pain.

Glug, glug, glug…

His eyes bulged.

He was choking…

He was going to die!

Suddenly, the flask was yanked away, and Robbie found he could breathe again.

Hot tears cascaded down the terrified boy's face.

A soon as Red Ski Mask stopped squeezing his skull, Robbie's head sagged onto his chest.

Head spinning, he sucked in air hungrily.

"Good lad," Blue Ski Mask said, ruffling his hair. After returning the flask to the duffle bag, he sat down beside Robbie. His eyes were bloodshot and veiny, like one of those scary monsters from Dr Who, and his breath smelled like rotting garbage. Robbie almost gagged when he caught a whiff of it.

"You'll fall asleep soon, and when you wake up, we can all have some fun together," Blue Ski Mask said, cheerily.

Red Ski Mask nudged his companion's shoulder and sniggered nastily. There was an ugly wart-like thing attached to his lower left eyelid, and the sight of it bobbing up and down when he blinked made Robbie feel sick.

"We're going to have *lots* of fun," Red Ski Mask added, emphasising the word in a sinister way that made Robbie think it wouldn't be fun at all.

Robbie didn't like him; he didn't like any of them, and he certainly didn't want to have 'fun' with them. The only thing he wanted was for these scary men to take him back to his loving family.

An image of Phillip popped into his mind, lying on the floor of their tent, having been left for dead.

Robbie was beginning to feel dizzy, disorientated; his vision was starting to blur, and he was struggling to think clearly.

Was he dying?

Had they poisoned him?

There was a harsh grinding of gears, and the van suddenly lurched forward.

"Careful, you Muppet," Blue Ski Mask scolded the driver.

"Not my fault, Benny," the man responded, churlishly. "The gearbox is on its way out."

"Don't use my fucking name, you idiot!" Blue Ski Mask snapped, leaning forward to slap the driver across the back of his head.

He needn't have worried; the powerful sedative was already taking effect.

Overcome by a warm fuzzy sensation, Robbie suddenly found himself too tired to struggle; too tired to worry about Phillip or the disturbing possibility that his captors had just poisoned him. Slumping against the side of the van, he toppled sideways, onto the vibrating floor of the moving van.

He was vaguely aware of Blue Ski Mask draping a heavy blanket over him, covering him from head to toe. Robbie wanted to protest that he was far too hot to be wrapped up like that, but before he could utter a single word, he was sound asleep.

---

The van drove for the best part of two hours, initially winding its way through the country lanes surrounding the campsite, then joining the busy A11. After leaving Norfolk, it briefly passed through Cambridgeshire before entering Essex, where it took the southbound M11 towards London.

Exiting the motorway at Saffron Walden, the van took to the quieter rural roads once more, venturing deep into the countryside. It eventually glided to a halt beside a dilapidated single-axle caravan in an otherwise deserted field on the outskirts of an abandoned farm.

When the engine died, the three men wearily climbed out and stretched their legs, leaving the boy in the back, where he remained in a drug-induced sleep.

The only noise to be heard was a soft ticking coming from the van's exhaust as it cooled and contracted now that the engine was off.

"Are you sure no one will bother us out here, Benny?" the man who had worn the green ski mask asked their leader, who was trying to locate the lock on the caravan's door, but struggling in the darkness.

"Shut up Angus, and give me some light," Benny hissed.

Removing a disposable cigarette lighter from his pocket, Angus thumbed the friction wheel several times before a spark ignited the butane gas and a weak flame sprung into life. Cupping the lighter to prevent the warm breeze extinguishing it, Angus dutifully held the flickering glow up to the door so that Benny could find the lock.

"Don't get too close," Benny snapped, feeling crowded.

Angus sighed. "I just can't win with you, can I?" He was a tall man, with a long, horse-like face, and when he wasn't snatching children with the others, he worked as a ride attendant and rigger for a travelling funfair.

The four-berth caravan was a battered Sprite Major that was riddled with rust and ready for the scrap heap.

Mo, the man who had worn the red mask, cupped his hands against one of the filthy windows and peered in, squinting at the grubby interior. The front seating area had been converted into a double bed, and there was a small kitchenette, which looked absolutely filthy.

"It looks like a bit of a shithole to me," he said, unimpressed.

"It is," Benny agreed. "But it's a shithole in the middle of nowhere, so we won't have to worry about anyone disturbing us while we're partying with the boy."

Angus was sent to fetch the child while the other two prepared the caravan.

After turning the lights on, Benny carefully draped a plastic sheet over the double bed, while Mo rushed around the van, opening all the windows and pulling the blinds down.

"Christ! This place smells even worse than you do," Mo complained.

He was always whinging about something or other, so Benny ignored him.

Angus appeared in the doorway, carrying the drowsy child, who was weeping and begging them to release him.

Benny didn't like it when they whined; it ruined the atmosphere. "Give him some more sedative," he instructed, nodding towards the duffle bag he had left on the wobbly dining table. "That'll shut him up, but don't give him too much; I want him to be awake for this."

Removing a second flask from inside the duffle bag, Mo made the struggling boy take a couple of large gulps, ignoring his feeble protests.

"That should do the trick."

They waited a couple of minutes, until the boy was groggy enough to be pliable, at which point Mo carefully removed his pyjamas and laid him on his back, while Benny removed a tube of KY jelly from the duffle bag. The boy immediately rolled over and curled into a foetal position, crinkling the plastic sheet beneath his sun-kissed body.

"I do believe he's ready," Angus announced with a sadistic grin. He was already unbuttoning his trousers.

They took turns raping him, with Benny going first, as was his prerogative as the wolfpack's leader.

When they had all finished, Benny told the others to grab their clothes and wait outside for him while he tidied up.

They complied wordlessly, leaving Benny to do the dirty deed that neither of them had the stomach for. Now that the boy had served his purpose, he couldn't be allowed to tell the tale. He would be dead and buried before the authorities even started looking for him.

As soon as the other two had left the caravan, Benny quietly closed the door and sat down beside the broken boy. The brutally violated child was lying on the crumpled bed, with his back to the paedophile, making soft sobbing sounds.

"You did good," Benny said, feeling the familiar stirring in his loins as he studied the boy's naked body. After a moment's contemplation, he reached out and caressed his head. "Perhaps there's time for you and me to have one more dalliance before you leave us."

# 1

## WEDNESDAY 31ST OCTOBER 2001

*It could certainly do with a little TLC*

Detective Chief Inspector Bartholomew Craddock was the on-call Senior Investigating Officer for Norfolk Constabulary's Major Investigation Team. In that capacity, he walked along the shingled driveway towards the small cottage that sat in isolation upon an elevated stretch of land overlooking Caister beach.

Craddock loved the Norfolk coastline, and regularly enjoyed taking long afternoon strolls along its beautiful beaches during his days off. He found the sea air invigorating, and the calming sound of the waves, as they gently lapped against the shore, never failed to sooth his soul or clear his head when he had things on his mind. Today though, the weather was bleak and foreboding. The waves crashed into the beach with primal force, and the wind was blowing up a sandstorm.

Trudging along beside him, and constantly plucking at the tight-fitting material digging into his crotch, newly promoted DS Frank

Stebbins was complaining that the all-in-one Tyvek forensic oversuit he had just slipped into was too small for him.

"Perhaps you ought to go on a diet then, young Frank," Craddock suggested, raising his voice to be heard above the howling wind.

That shut Stebbins up, as he'd known it would.

The cottage was old and uncared for; its exterior walls cracked and weather-stained, its sagging roof looking like it was about to fold in on itself.

"It could certainly do with a little TLC," Craddock observed, sadly. He loved the quaint period properties that overlooked the sea, and hated to see them going to ruin.

Stebbins clearly didn't share his enthusiasm. "It could do with being torn down and rebuilt," he said, turning his nose up at the old place.

The small lawn to the front of the cottage was overrun with moss and weeds, giving them the impression that it hadn't been tended to in years.

"Morning, Brian," Craddock acknowledged the uniform PC who was standing guard at the door, and looking very sorry for himself for being stuck out in the cold.

"M–morning sir," PC Brian Parsons replied, teeth chattering.

Craddock noticed that the door frame was badly splintered by the lock, presumably from where someone had hoofed it open. From the rotting state of the woodwork, he doubted it would have taken much force.

The biting wind was gusting around the sides of the cottage and, despite his Gore-Tex coat, gloves and scarf, poor PC Parsons was shivering. Unfolding the scene log that had been tucked under his arm, he noted down the two detectives' names and promptly stepped aside to admit them to the crime scene.

"D–do you think I'll be s–stuck here long, sir?" he enquired. "Only I c–can't feel my toes anymore."

Taking pity on him, Craddock told him to go and sit in his patrol car, which was parked in front of the cottage gate, and warm himself up.

Stebbins shook his head as the grateful constable scurried off. "You're far too soft, you know that, don't you?" he reproached his boss.

They were met in the dingy hallway by the Crime Scene Manager, a slim woman who, like them, was dressed from head to toe in barrier clothing, including a forensic face mask and protective overshoes.

"Morning, Stella," Craddock said with a grim smile. "What have we got?"

"Bit of a strange one," Stella Bridlington said, consulting the notes on her clipboard as she spoke. "The victim's an elderly white male called Angus Clifford. He's a recluse who's lived here for the past five years. Judging by all the medication I found in his bedroom, I'd say he wasn't in very good health." She nodded at two walking sticks leaning against the wall by the street door. "It looks like he had mobility issues and needed those to get about. Clifford hadn't been down to the post office to collect his pension for three weeks, which is apparently very unusual for him, so the Postmaster asked the local beat bobby to pop in on his travels and make sure that Clifford was okay."

"What time did the beat bobby get here?" Stebbins asked, notebook at the ready.

"PC Cornwallis arrived at 09:30 hours, but got no reply. When he peered in through the kitchen window, he saw the victim slumped in a chair with his back to the window. Cornwallis thought he might've suffered a heart attack, so he forced entry. From the decomposed state of his body, I'd say Clifford's been dead for between two and three weeks, which fits in perfectly with the last reported sighting."

"Cause of death?" Craddock enquired, raising a bushy red eyebrow.

"Exsanguination." Stella replied, as casually as if she were telling him the time. "He was tied to the chair Cornwallis found him in. Someone had slit his throat from ear to ear, but before doing that, they had cut off his wedding tackle and stuffed it into his mouth."

Both men winced.

"Well, that gives new meaning to the expression, dickhead," Stebbins said, masking his revulsion behind a joke.

"You say Cornwallis forced entry?" Craddock queried. "I take it that when he arrived, the place was otherwise secure, and there was nothing to suggest that anyone had previously broken in?"

Stella nodded, sombrely. "That's right. The only damage to the property we've found was caused by PC Cornwallis' size ten boot when he forced entry."

"Where is Cornwallis?" Craddock asked, looking around. "I didn't see him outside."

"He was pretty shaken up, so I sent him back to the station for a cup of tea as soon as PC Parsons arrived," Stella said.

Stebbins shook his head, reproachfully. "You're as soft as he is," he said, nodding at Craddock.

"I think the word you're looking for, young Frank, is kind." Craddock corrected him.

Stebbins scratched his head through his Tyvek hood. "If the killer didn't force entry, then how did he get in?"

Stella shrugged. "The most likely scenario is that the victim knew his attacker and let him in."

Stebbins grunted. "Do we know if anything's been stolen?" he asked, tugging irritably at the crotch of his oversuit.

"Are you okay down there?" Stella queried, raising an eyebrow in amusement.

"He needs to lose some weight," Craddock said, getting in before his bagman could.

"I do not!" Stebbins spluttered, indignantly. "I just picked up the wrong sized oversuit by mistake."

Stella didn't really care one way or another. "In answer to your question, Frank, it doesn't look like anything's been stolen." She pointed back along the hall, towards the kitchen. "The victim's wallet is lying on the kitchen table in plain sight, and it still has money in it, plus he's wearing an expensive looking gold chain around his neck, so I don't think this was an aggravated burglary gone wrong."

Craddock sighed. "Might have been easier for us to solve if it had been," he said, wistfully. This murder was beginning to feel like a deeply personal act to him. "Come on then," he said, gesturing for her to lead the way. "We'd better take a gander at the victim."

---

Two hours later, Craddock walked into the incident room at police headquarters. The first thing he did after removing his overcoat, scarf and gloves was send DC Yvonne Granger down to the control room to run a PNC check on the victim, requesting that she obtain a printout of his offending history, if he had one.

Strolling through to his high ceilinged office, with Stebbins trailing behind, Craddock stood with his back to the radiator and began massaging his buttocks to restore some warmth to them. He was a large man in his mid-fifties, with flame red hair and the weathered complexion of an outdoorsman. Clad in his habitual three-piece tweed suit, he more closely resembled a successful farmer than a senior detective. Over the years, many people had made the costly mistake of underestimating Craddock when they first heard his thick Norfolk burr, wrongly assuming that he was a harmless country yokel and therefore no threat to them. They soon discovered that Craddock was anything but simple; he had two degrees to his name, both obtained with honours, and an IQ that had earned him a membership of Mensa.

"I've called the team in for a briefing," Stebbins said, rubbing his hands together to warm them up.

Grunting his approval, Craddock turned to stare out of the window, which afforded him a view of the car park down below. "Good, good," he said, his mind elsewhere.

"What's your take on this one?" Stebbins asked.

Craddock had hardly said a word during the journey back from the crime scene.

"It's certainly an interesting case," Craddock mused. When he turned to face Stebbins, his eyes were twinkling. "I think we've been presented with a rather tricky puzzle to solve, young Frank," he said, sounding as though he was relishing the challenge.

Stebbins expression became even more dour than usual. "You make it sound like that's a good thing," he protested. "Personally, I would have preferred a simpler case, with the solution handed to us on a plate."

Craddock tutted his exasperation. "And where would the challenge be in that?" he demanded.

Before Stebbins could respond, DC Granger entered the room. In addition to the PNC report Craddock had requested, she was carrying a tray containing three cups of steaming hot tea and a small plate of Rich Tea biscuits. "Thought you might be in need of some refreshments after being stuck down at that crime scene for so long," she told Craddock with a fond smile.

His face lit up. "Yvonne, my dear, you are far too good to me," he said, helping himself to one of the biscuits.

"And here's the PNC printout you requested for the victim," she said, handing it over.

Stebbins noticed that this was received with considerably less enthusiasm than the tea and biscuits.

"Thank you, Yvonne," Craddock said, inviting her to take a seat while he flicked through the report. "Hmmm, very interesting," he said as he passed it across to Stebbins. "It seems our victim has form for molesting young children."

Stebbins was working his way through the printout. "There are two previous convictions for indecent assault," he read aloud, "and a further charge he was acquitted of on a technicality when he was younger." Stebbins looked up; his eyes alight with a theory. "Do you think someone could have killed him because he's been interfering with their kid? That would make a bloody good motive, wouldn't it?"

Craddock tugged at his lower lip. "From what Stella told us, the victim was old and frail, and in poor health, so I doubt he was physically capable of sexually assaulting anyone."

"But if the crime wasn't committed for monetary gain, and he wasn't killed because he was a nonce, what was the motive?"

Craddock smiled, encouragingly. "Come on, Frank, think! Give that underdeveloped brain of yours a proper workout."

Craddock studied Stebbins' bemused expression in amusement, thinking that his sergeant was a good copper, but he was also a bit of a plodder.

"What if the killer was sexually abused by Clifford when he was a child?" Granger offered, earning a look of fierce resentment from Stebbins for coming up with a plausible alternative before he could.

Craddock beamed at her. "Excellent!" he said, applauding her effort.

"I was just about to suggest something very similar," Stebbins said, convincing no one.

Craddock crossed to his desk. Sitting down, he took a brand-new daybook from his top drawer. "That scenario would certainly tick a lot of boxes."

"But, if that's the case, why did the killer wait all that time before striking?" Stebbins asked.

"Excellent question," Craddock applauded. He looked at Granger, a bushy eyebrow arching upwards in encouragement. "Do you want to take a crack at the answer, Yvonne, or would you prefer to leave that to me?"

"I'll take a shot at it," she said, eagerly.

Stebbins bridled at her childlike enthusiasm but said nothing.

"Maybe…" she began, deliberately drawing the word out to buy herself a few extra seconds of thinking time. "Maybe, the victim only moved to the area recently." Her face became more animated as she developed the idea. "Yes, that would make perfect sense. The killer sees him, recognises him, and decides to kill him because of the terrible abuse he suffered at Clifford's hands as a child."

"Nice try, Sherlock," Stebbins scoffed. "But Angus Clifford's lived in the area for over five years. Why would the killer wait that long to knock him off?"

Granger was momentarily at a loss to explain that one away, but then inspiration struck and her face lit up again. "The victim might've lived here for five years, but what if the killer only moved to the area recently?"

Stebbins opened his mouth, intending to pour scorn over the suggestion, but then realised it actually made sense. He glanced across at Craddock, trying to gauge his reaction before responding.

"I suppose that could work," he allowed when he saw that Craddock was nodding.

"It's a pity Mr Clifford's cottage is situated in such a remote location," Craddock said, stroking his chin thoughtfully. "It almost certainly means there won't be any CCTV covering the approach route."

"And it doesn't look like there were any witnesses either," Stebbins added, sullenly. "So, I guess the case is going to hinge on forensics."

"Not necessarily," Craddock said. "We know that Clifford was a recluse who only went out once or twice a week, so his movements shouldn't be too difficult to establish. Let's start by obtaining CCTV from the post office and corner shop he regularly visited, and any local authority footage from cameras in the surrounding streets. You never know, a review of that might highlight a potential suspect."

"What about Clifford's phone?" Granger asked. "Shouldn't we get that downloaded, in case there's anything on it to give us a steer? I mean, he might have been in contact with his killer for all we know."

Stebbins sighed. "There wasn't a landline at the cottage, and I didn't see a mobile anywhere, did you, sir?"

"No," Craddock admitted, "but it hasn't been searched properly yet, so let's wait and see what turns up. In the meantime, Frank, can you arrange for the victim's injuries to be run through method index on the PNC. I'd be very interested to know if there are any similar offences on record. I mean, I don't imagine it's a common way to die, do you?"

## 2

## SATURDAY 3RD NOVEMBER 2001

An early bonfire night

The cramped alcove at the rear of the Incident Room served as the team's designated CCTV viewing area, and it had become Yvonne Granger's home from home for the past couple of days. Sitting down at a table that was only just about wide enough to house the monitor atop it, she stifled a yawn and steeled herself for another gruelling day of watching boring footage.

Her shift had only started fifteen minutes earlier, yet she was already struggling to stay awake. Like everyone else in the team, she had been working twelve hour stints since the murder enquiry was launched on Wednesday morning. They were still no closer to solving it though, and DCI Craddock had cancelled everyone's leave for the weekend. While she couldn't deny it was nice to be earning the overtime, Granger felt so utterly knackered that she would have gladly traded every penny for a couple of hours of extra kip that morning.

Granger inserted the VHS tape and pressed the play button.

Today, she was going to be viewing CCTV footage from Mr Khan's post office, which she had collected the previous evening. She had already viewed the relevant footage from both convenience stores the victim was known to frequent, an experience that had been marginally less fun than watching paint dry and had yielded nothing of interest.

"God, this is so dull," she mumbled, resting her chin in the palm of her hand with an exaggerated huff.

"Sometimes dull solves murders," Craddock gently admonished, materialising beside her like a ghostly apparition.

"Sweet Jesus!" she gasped, almost jumping out of her seat. "I didn't hear you coming."

Craddock chuckled. "Not many people do, Yvonne," he said with pride.

The DCI was always the first to arrive at the office and the last to leave, yet he invariably looked as fresh as a daisy and never seemed to tire. Granger didn't know how he did it; she was half his age, but he was putting her to shame. And not just her, she thought. Frank Stebbins had dozed off during the morning briefing, and had she been forced to elbow him in the ribs when he started snoring.

"How are you getting on?" Craddock asked, peering over her shoulder.

Granger wrinkled her nose. "To be honest, not very well. I spent all day yesterday watching CCTV from the Londis shop. I know the layout so well now that I could probably tell you which shelf every item they sell is kept on."

Craddock chuckled.

"The victim hasn't gone there in three weeks," she continued. "But, before that, he went in twice a week, as regular as clockwork. Always on the same days – Monday and Friday – and always at the same time – between three and four o'clock. He shuffled around on his crutches, filled up his basket, paid with cash and then left. He never socialised with any of the staff or other customers, not that there were ever many customers around when he went in."

Craddock frowned. "Have you been able to identify any of the other customers?"

"No, but it's never the same people, and none of them look like a crazed killer, except for Mrs Warrington, the manager there. She's a two-faced cow if ever I've seen one, always smiling and joking with the customers, but as soon as the shop is empty, she immediately turns into Attila the Hun, ordering the staff about like they're her personal slaves. And she's aways shouting at them." Granger shuddered. "I wouldn't last a week working for her."

"We need to identify the people who were in the shop with Clifford," Craddock said. "Print out some stills, and I'll raise an action for someone to show them to Atilla the Hun. Let's see if she, or any of her minions, recognise them."

Granger nodded. "Will do," she said, smiling up at him. "I'll show them to the local beat bobby, too. If they live locally, he might be able to identify them."

Craddock beamed at her. "What a good idea," he said, approvingly. "See, that's why I made you the CCTV co-ordinator for this job." He gave her a wink, then lumbered off towards his office.

---

"Now, don't forget what I've told you, Peter," Alison Musgrove instructed her son as she helped him slide into his parka. "Go straight to Gavin's house. Be careful crossing the roads on the way there. Don't get too near the fireworks and remember to do exactly what his parents tell you when you get to the funfair. Is that clear?"

Peter responded with a weary nod, as he did with all her boring safety lectures.

She fixed him with an iron stare, her speckled brown eyes narrowing to emphasise the importance of her words. "Is that clear, Mister?" she repeated, doing her best Sergeant Major impression, but sounding more Asian than American.

He rolled his eyes at the terrible accent. "Yes, mum."

"Good," she said, appeased. "Tell Gavin's parents that I'll swing by and pick you up at ten o'clock, sharp."

Peter bridled at the suggestion. He found her constant need to hold his hand incredibly frustrating. "But mum, I *can* walk home on my own," he protested, fiercely.

He was nine years old now, and he played out by himself all the time, so he certainly didn't need to be told how to cross a road, or have her come and collect him from his friend's house, which was only a few streets away.

"That's not the point," Alison countered, wagging a manicured finger at him. "I will not have my son roaming the streets alone at that time of night."

"I'm not a little baby anymore, mum," he insisted.

"You'll always be my little baby, even when you're all grown up with kids of your own."

Peter grimaced. That would involve marrying a girl; he didn't even like playing with them, and the thought of having to live with one was just too gross to contemplate.

"Stop pulling faces," Alison chastised him. "If the wind changes, you'll be stuck looking like that!"

Peter responded by poking his tongue out at her, but he was smiling playfully as he did so. As much as her overprotectiveness annoyed him, he knew it came from a good place; he just wished that she wouldn't mollycoddle him all the time, especially when his friends or classmates were around.

It was just *so* embarrassing!

Yesterday evening was a prime example; after dropping him off at their local McDonald's restaurant for Martha Brownlow's tenth birthday party, his mum had made a big show of blowing kisses at him as she left. With his cheeks glowing bright red, he had stood there, cringing in humiliation. And, as he'd known they would, his classmates had ribbed him mercilessly afterwards. Tommy Evans, who never missed an opportunity to poke fun at Peter, had called him a 'mummy's boy' and a 'pansy'.

Alison dropped to one knee and began zipping the front of his coat up for him.

"Leave it out, mum," Peter said, pushing her hands away in exasperation. "I can do it myself."

Alison stood up, stung by the rebuff but trying not to show it. "I know you can, sweetie," she said in a brittle voice.

She waited patiently for him to yank the zip all the way up to his chin, then ruffled his hair.

"Don't do that," Peter complained, ducking out of her reach.

He *hated* the way she still treated him like he was three; the way she smothered him all the time, but no matter how many times he pleaded with her to stop, she just kept on doing it.

"Sorry," she said, lamely.

He continued to scowl at her as he brushed his unruly mop of blonde hair back into place, just to make sure she got the message. After checking his reflection in the hall mirror, a feat he could only achieve by going up on tiptoe, he stomped off towards the street door, pulling his mittens on as he went.

"Have you got your mobile phone with you?" Alison called after him.

Groaning in irritation, he theatrically patted the pocket containing the phone. "Yes, mum."

"Good boy," she said, sounding relieved. "I don't ever want you going out without that."

Peter decided that the next time he left the house, he would leave it in his room, just to spite her.

"Bye, mum. See you later."

As he opened the door, struggling to turn the latch in his cumbersome mittens, Alison flapped a hand in the air to attract his attention. "Hang on, Peter," she said, crossing the hallway in a fluster.

Peter paused, halfway out the door. He looked at her warily, expecting another lecture on road safety and not talking to strangers. Not a single day passed without one of those.

Dropping to one knee, Alison exhaled noisily. "Look, I know I go on a bit," she confessed with a conciliatory smile, "but that's only because I love you so much."

Despite his resolve to be angry with her, Peter's face softened. "I know you do, Mum," he said, staring at her earnestly, "but I'm not a baby, and I don't want my mates thinking I'm a mummy's boy."

Alison's smile faltered for a moment, but then it was back in place, brighter than ever. "In that case, I'll try not to overdo it in front of them in future," she promised. "As long as I can still make a big fuss of you when we're all alone."

He considered this for a moment, then nodded, seemingly satisfied by the compromise. "I guess that would be okay," he conceded. "See you later."

"Have a lovely time," she called, seeing him off with an overly cheery wave. "And don't eat too much candy floss at the fair. The last time you did that, you ended up with a stomach ache."

---

After he'd gone, Alison retired to the kitchen to prepare dinner for her and Ciaron. It was getting on for six o'clock, and he would be arriving home from football any minute now. He had left orders for his dinner to be on the table at half past, and he would be angry if it was late. He would also be angry if the O's had lost, which they usually did – at least that was the impression she got from the way he constantly complained about Leyton Orient Football Club to his fellow supporters. She really didn't understand men and their stupid obsession with football. If the club he supported was that bad, why didn't he just change his allegiance to a better team?

Although she tried not to fret, she couldn't help but worry about her precious little Peter as he made his way to Gavin's house in the dark. She had been sorely tempted to throw on her coat and follow him, just to make sure he got there safely, but knowing how much that would have upset him, she had stopped herself – just.

Alison experienced acute separation anxiety every time Peter went out without her. Giving him a mobile phone had gone some way towards alleviating this, because it meant that she could check in with him whenever she wanted. More importantly, it meant that Peter could call her straight away if – heaven forbid – there was ever an emergency.

The very thought sent a shudder through her.

Alison accepted that her paranoia was completely irrational, but after everything she had been through, who could possibly blame her?

She had miscarried eight months into her first pregnancy, resulting in her perfectly formed baby being delivered stillborn. He had looked so beautiful and peaceful as she cradled him in her arms. They had named him Andrew, after her maternal grandfather.

A year later, they had tried again.

Following a textbook pregnancy, Alison had given birth to a healthy baby boy. Overjoyed by his safe arrival, they had christened him Luke, in honour of the dashing young doctor who delivered him. Even though Alison felt permanently tired during the months that followed Luke's birth, she had never been happier. But then, tragedy struck a second time. One morning, when Alison went into the nursery to give Luke his early morning feed, she found him lying face down in his cot, tangled in his blanket. He had been suffering from a cold for a couple of days, and although he had gone to bed with a mild temperature, he had otherwise seemed reasonably well.

Alison blamed herself for Luke's death. He had been unwell, and she should have stayed with him that fateful night. If she had, he might still be alive.

Afterwards, Alison was put in touch with an organisation that provided advice and support for bereaved families. She spoke to specially trained counsellors, and went to several meetings with other families who had gone through similar experiences. Finding them beneficial, she tried to drag Ciaron along, but he was having none of it. His coping mechanism for dealing with Luke's death was to bury his grief and repress any outward displays of emotion. He expected her to do likewise. At his insistence, Alison reluctantly stopped attending the meetings. She tried to bottle her emotions up inside her the way he did, but this had a detrimental effect on her mental health.

Her doctor prescribed anti-depressants, but they did little to dull the pain or dispel the sense of loss and desolation that made her feel so alone. There were several occasions during the dark days between Luke's death and Peter's conception when Alison was so consumed by grief that she seriously considered washing a bottle of sleeping pills down with a litre of whisky.

Everything changed when Peter was born.

His arrival rekindled Alison's waning belief in the existence of a higher authority, and the moment she laid eyes on his angelic face, she knew that he was a gift from God. Peter gave Alison unbridled joy and a reason to smile again, something she hadn't done for a very long time.

Having already buried two children, and knowing that she wouldn't survive losing a third, Alison became utterly obsessed with keeping Peter safe. Unfortunately, Peter had other ideas; he was strong willed and fiercely independent, with a thirst for excitement and adventure. He didn't seem to be afraid of anything, and this gave her constant nightmares because he was so small and frail for his age. Their relationship had become a constant battle of wills, with her wanting to wrap him up in cotton wool and protect him from danger, and him rebelling against what he perceived to be her stifling overprotectiveness.

She glanced down the hallway at the telephone on the small rectangular table opposite the lounge door. Maybe she should give it a couple of minutes and ring him, just to make sure that he had arrived at Gavin's without incident?

---

Gavin Grant's parents, Tom and Margo, had purchased a huge box of commercial grade fireworks, and Peter was utterly thrilled to have been invited around to watch them being set off.

He and Gavin were the best of friends. They were as different as chalk and cheese, but they had clicked from the first moment they met at pre-school nursery, and they had been inseparable ever since.

Margo had prepared food for the occasion, which consisted of hot dogs in long, slim buns, accompanied by a mountain of French fries. After smothering their dogs in long criss-crossed squirts of tomato sauce and mustard, the boys hungrily devoured them in the rear garden, while watching the impressively loud fireworks explode high above their heads.

It was a bitterly cold night. Frost was already starting to settle on the grass, and their breath formed hazy white halos around their smiling faces every time they exhaled.

Peter adored fireworks, but his dad had always refused to take him to any of the local authority displays, claiming that he didn't like large crowds. That hadn't put him off going to see Leyton Orient play football at their home ground every other weekend, Peter had once pointed out, only to earn himself a clip around the ear and a reprimand for being rude.

The Grants weren't the only family in the street holding a firework party that evening. An impressive assortment of rockets, roman candles, and other exotically named fireworks lit up the night sky around them, the myriad of colours accompanied by a cacophony of high-pitched screeching sounds and loud explosions.

Margo ensured that the two boys constantly had sparklers on the go, and these were being waved around with great gusto.

"Careful, you two," she cautioned when they started having an impromptu sword fight with them.

Tom quickly retreated from a humungous rocket that he had just lit, giggling like a naughty schoolboy as he ran. "This one should be really good," he said, placing an affectionate arm around each boy's shoulder as they eagerly awaited its take-off.

A moment later, with the touch paper glowing bright red, the rocket burst from the milk bottle it had been placed in and zoomed into the night sky, screaming as it climbed to meet its inevitable doom. It exploded with a solid bang that reverberated through Peter's chest, then produced a succession of dazzlingly bright colours before finally burning itself out.

"See, I told you," Tom beamed at each of them in turn.

Peter grinned back, thinking that Tom was enjoying the fireworks even more than they were. He was always struck by the marked difference between the overly enthusiastic Tom Grant and his own dad, who was a bit of a killjoy when it came to having fun.

Next, they set off a fountain firework that spewed plumes of lava into the air like an erupting volcano.

Tom handed out more sparklers, on the strict proviso that there was no more sword fighting, and Peter gratefully accepted two, holding one in each hand.

As a special treat, the boys were allowed to light the final two fireworks themselves, under Tom's watchful supervision, of course.

"Better not tell your parents I let you do that," he told Peter, with a conspiratorial wink. "They might not approve."

They all cheered and clapped as the rockets exploded above them, signalling the end of the display.

As they headed back inside, Peter was grinning from ear to ear, thinking that it had been a wonderful evening. And the good news was, it wasn't over yet!

"Right," Margo said, rubbing her hands together in eager anticipation. "Who fancies a trip to the funfair?"

The boys yelped with delight and thrust their hands into the air, but Tom had already beaten them to it. "Me! Me! Me!" he shouted, jumping up and down and making them all laugh at his silly antics.

---

The funfair had been set up on a stretch of common land in nearby Rangers Road, on the edge of Epping Forest. As they crossed the road, Peter caught a fleeting glimpse of bright flashing lights through a gap in the trees. Turning to Gavin, he let out a little squeal of anticipation.

Gavin grinned back at him. "This is going to be SOOO much fun," he said, clapping his hands excitedly.

It was a big funfair, the biggest that Peter had ever seen, and it was already heaving.

A large placard had been wonkily hammered into the ground, informing customers that the ride attendants were only allowed to accept tickets, not cash. These were being sold from a little red kiosk, so they tagged onto the line of people stretching away from it.

The queue moved surprisingly quickly and, before they knew it, they were at the front, being served. Peter's mother had given him five pounds to spend at the fair, and he dutifully offered this to Margo, but she refused to take it.

"Don't be silly, this is our treat," she insisted.

In order to reach the rides, they first had to navigate their way through a selection of food and gaming stalls. Tom quipped that it was just like being funnelled through the duty-free shops after clearing airport security. The comment made no sense to Peter, but Margo found it highly amusing.

From behind their stalls, a motley collection of fairground workers competed for their attention, making energetic come-hither gestures and shouting words of encouragement to entice the gullible punters into parting with their hard-earned cash.

A small group of excited children raced past Peter, squealing with demented laughter as they waved sparklers in the air, ignoring the cautionary calls from the accompanying adults to wait for them.

The delicious smell of salt and vinegar competed with the rich aroma of hot dogs and hamburgers, and Peter found himself becoming hungry again, even though they had only recently eaten.

In addition to the inevitable burgers, fries and hotdogs, there were also concession stalls selling candyfloss and popcorn. Peter spotted two boys from his class over by the toffee apple stand, chomping away at their candy-coated treats with great gusto. He waved a casual greeting in their direction, but they were too busy stuffing their faces to respond.

The fairground's frenetic energy created an incredible atmosphere. The flashing and flickering lights produced an endless kaleidoscope of pretty colours, and the noise levels were off the scale.

Loud music blared from speakers, sirens and bells continuously warned of rides starting up, and the cheerful shouting, laughing and screaming of exhilarated customers filled the night air.

Peter found himself caught in a surging wave of people being swept towards a Big Wheel that towered above the other rides. Thankfully, Tom grabbed his arm and dragged him free of the crowd. With a gentle smile, he redirected Peter towards Gavin and

Margo, who were weaving their way towards a sizeable clearing that contained the Spinning Teacups, Waltzer and Dodgem cars.

A series of muffled screams and eerie howling noises, accompanied by the sort of spooky music he associated with Scooby-Doo cartoons, drifted in from his right, where an elaborately fronted Ghost Train stood in isolation from the other rides.

Peter grinned broadly.

He would *definitely* be going on that!

Gavin and Margo paused when they reached the Spinning Teacups.

"Fancy coming on this one?" Gavin asked, as soon Peter joined them.

"No way," Peter replied, with a grimace.

"I'll come on with you," Tom volunteered; he was game for pretty much anything, Peter thought, enviously. His own dad was a miserable git who never joined in with any fun or games.

"You two go on," Margo said, placing a gloved hand on Peter's shoulder. "We'll wait here for you, won't we Pete?"

# 3

## Remus and McQueen

Aaron Remus wandered aimlessly through the busy fairground. He was on the prowl for potential chickens, the coded term those in the know used for children who – willingly or unwillingly – engaged in homosexual activity with paedophiles.

He took a huge bite out of the greasy hotdog he'd just purchased. It was drowning in a sea of mustard and tomato sauce, and topped with an extra layer of onions. Wiping a smear of red and yellow from his lips, he scanned the face of every male child he passed, surreptitiously running hungry eyes over any who caught his interest. It was an action as instinctive to him as breathing, and not something he made a conscious effort to do.

Like many paedophiles, Remus had been sexually abused as a child. His mother had passed away from a heroin overdose when he was only eight, leaving him in the care of his maternal grandparents. It hadn't been a good fit; he resented their overbearing strictness, and they found him an extremely difficult child who seemed determined to make their otherwise orderly lives a living hell. In the end, unable to tame his disruptive nature, they had reluctantly asked Social Services to intervene and find him a suitable foster family.

When that didn't work out either, the dysfunctional child had been placed in a local authority care home on a full-time basis. Unfortunately, the home had been infiltrated by a well-organised paedophile ring, who preyed on their troubled charges with complete impunity, even renting them out to other paedophiles in the area, one of whom just happened to be the local Superintendent of police.

Whenever visiting paedophiles arrived for a night of pleasure, the children were assembled in the main hall and forced to stand to attention until a selection was made. There were plenty of boys who were much prettier than Remus, and more often than not, he was overlooked in favour of them.

The merciless exploitation he was subjected to during his sexually formative years was so prolific and disturbing that Remus eventually came to associate suffering with erotica, and this had led him to develop a deeply skewed understanding of what sexual gratification should involve.

During his time at the home, Remus formed a close friendship with another resident called Joey McQueen. The two boys were the same age, had arrived within weeks of each other, and had come from similar backgrounds. Like Remus, McQueen was subjected to systemic abuse by the paedophiles running the home. At night, in their dormitory, while the boys around them sobbed themselves to sleep, Remus and McQueen often talked about running away together. One day, when they could take the abuse no longer, they did exactly that.

Having fled the sleepy backwater town in Kent with nothing but the clothes on their backs and a small amount of petty cash they had stolen from the office, the two wayward boys headed for the glitz and glamour of London, where they dreamed of carving out a better life for themselves. When they stepped off the coach at Victoria coach station, they were friendless, homeless and virtually penniless. Desperate for food and money, and without any other means of securing it, they resorted to selling their bodies to older men.

"We're no better off than we were back at the poxy home," McQueen had complained, one bitterly cold evening, as they sat in the window seat of a café off Charing Cross Road, where they could be seen by passing punters.

"Yes, we are," Remus had insisted, treating his friend to a pragmatic half-smile, "because, at least now, we're getting paid for being abused."

Benny Mars had approached them soon after their arrival. Then in his fifties, Benny was a well-connected paedophile with his own stable of rent boys and a seedy little shop in Kings Cross, from where he sold porn magazines and hardcore Swedish and German sex films.

Taking them under his wing, Benny provided food and money in exchange for sexual favours. When the novelty of screwing them wore off, and he no longer wanted them exclusively for himself, he began pimping Remus and McQueen out.

The boys had worked the notorious 'meat rack' at Piccadilly Circus for four gruelling years, loitering around the public toilets, wandering in and out every time a potential punter caught their eye. This inevitably drew the attention of the local plod, and both boys had been arrested several times for soliciting.

To be fair to Benny, in comparison to some of the other pimps working the area, he had treated both boys reasonably well, never overworking them and only beating them when they deserved it. Unfortunately, all chickens have a limited lifespan. Eventually – inevitably – Remus and McQueen lost their childish appeal, and the punters began overlooking them in favour of the younger models on offer.

Thankfully, Benny threw them a lifeline, offering them the job of recruiting new talent from the legions of lost boys who regularly passed through Victoria.

While McQueen didn't have much personality or charm, it turned out that Remus was a natural at seducing the waifs and strays who frequented the cafes and amusement arcades around the coach station.

One of the benefits of running Benny's rent boys was that it enabled Remus to satisfy his own carnal needs for gratis. Since moving to London, he had developed an insatiable appetite for rough sex, and he excelled at manipulating the weak and vulnerable boys he recruited into satisfying his perverse cravings. The younger chickens were often mesmerised by his charm when they first encountered him, although that quickly changed once they got to know him a little better.

Of course, by then, it was too late.

Remus emulated Benny by treating the chickens with emotional indifference; to him, they were trophies or possessions, not people. When he was high, he would engage in marathon sex sessions with them, insisting on doing it four or five times; not caring when they complained of pain or exhaustion, or even when they bled from their back passages, as had happened on several occasions. He had a vile temper on him, and the young chickens quickly learned it was unwise to refuse him when the urge was upon him.

Sometimes, while lying in bed at night, Remus pondered the cruel irony of his situation. He still felt intense anger and resentment at the abuse he had suffered as a child, yet he had evolved into a selfish predatory paedophile, no different from the monsters who had ruined his own life. Now in his mid-twenties, Remus had evolved into a sadist for whom sexual pleasure and rage were forever entwined. He saw nothing wrong with that; as far as he was concerned, it was perfectly normal. Sex and violence had gone hand in glove for as long as he could remember; the only difference was that, nowadays, he was the abuser, not the abused.

It was much better that way.

---

Joey McQueen cupped his hands together to light a cigarette as he watched the exhausted passengers alighting in single file from the coach that had just pulled into Victoria.

According to the electronic arrivals board, it had come in from Bristol.

As usual, he was on the lookout for the fresh-faced chickens who turned up with boring regularity, stupidly thinking that a better life awaited them in the nation's capital.

McQueen had been doing this for so long now that he could spot the vulnerable waifs a mile off. They all had the same haggard faces; most were malnourished; they carried very little luggage, if any at all.

There was a high attrition rate amongst the chickens; some died from drug overdoses, others were jailed for committing petty crimes. A handful became so despondent that they returned to their dysfunctional families to try again.

Rent boys without pimps to look after them were quickly absorbed into London's growing army of homeless. In between turning tricks, they attempted to supplement their income by selling copies of *The Big Issue* to anyone who made the mistake of looking at them as they walked past.

The rent boys who were controlled by pimps like Benny fared no better; they were shipped around London and the home counties like cattle. McQueen had escorted a few himself, handing them over to hard-faced men in exchange for frightened ragamuffins who would then travel in the other direction.

A skinny boy of fourteen or fifteen, with lank brown hair and furtive eyes, had just stepped off the coach. He paused to take in his surroundings, oblivious to the fact that he was now holding up the remaining passengers. After a couple of seconds, the man behind him gave him an impatient shove and told him to get out of his way. Muttering an apology, the boy quickly moved aside, before stopping again to stretch limbs that had all but seized up after so many hours of being confined in a cramped space.

His dishevelled clothing was way too big for him, and McQueen wondered if he was wearing an older brother's hand-me-downs. Shouldering a battered blue duffle bag, the boy pulled his collar up and set off towards the nearest exit.

McQueen took a long drag from his cigarette, then lazily

stamped it out underfoot. Blowing a cloud of smoke from the corner of his mouth, he eased himself away from the wall he had been leaning against and ambled after the boy, whom his well-honed instincts told him was a fruit ripe for the plucking.

---

On his way past the spinning teacups, Remus noticed a small boy and brunette woman huddled together against the cold. As the cups whirled by in a blur of motion, the woman suddenly smiled, then pointed at one containing a stocky man and a boy; both occupants were laughing and screaming. The boy standing beside the woman waved excitedly, treating the riders to the most enchanting smile that Remus had ever seen.

Mesmerised by his beauty, Remus wandered over to the spinning teacups to get a better look at him, his eyes greedily drinking in the boy's smile.

When the ride came to an end, the stocky man and his son joined them. After an animated greeting, the four of them set off towards the dodgems, one big happy family.

Letting his hot dog wrapper fall to the floor, Remus gave them a moment, and then casually followed behind, being sure to maintain a discreet distance.

---

After exiting Victoria coach station, the newly arrived chicken spent the next twenty minutes wandering aimlessly. McQueen followed, wanting to give the boy enough time to get himself properly lost before making his approach.

McQueen had often wondered if someone like him, a former rent boy turned recruiter, had spotted him and Remus when they arrived at Victoria all those years ago; if he had stalked them the same way that he was now following the unsuspecting chicken a few yards ahead of him. Back then, McQueen had naively thought himself streetwise, but the truth was he had been every bit as green behind the ears as the lost boy he was now tracking. Maybe, he thought with a wry smile, if the chicken lived long enough, he might eventually end up following in McQueen's footsteps, by becoming a recruiter himself.

Pausing at the kerb for a gap in the traffic, the chicken wrapped a pair of scrawny arms around his slender body and hugged himself tight. He was shivering. That was hardly surprising; his flimsy denim jacket would offer little protection against the bitter cold, and the lightweight jumper beneath it looked threadbare. His feet were probably frozen solid in the lightweight trainers he wore, and without a hat or gloves, he would be losing heat faster than he could generate it.

McQueen, who was toasty warm in a parka made from the finest Canada Goose down and thick soled walking boots, smiled. It was almost time to introduce himself, and offer the boy a perceived lifeline that, if accepted, would trap him in a world of despair and hopelessness.

---

A heavily tattooed attendant pointed to a sign outlining the ride requirements, then grumpily shooed Peter and Gavin away, telling them they were too small to ride the dodgems unaccompanied.

As the dejected boys sloped off, a woman with two young children of her own pointed towards the far end of the funfair. "There are some child friendly rides over there," she announced with a warm smile. "Including a junior version of the bumper cars."

"Can we go on those, please mum?" Gavin pleaded.

"I don't see why not," Margo said, smiling her thanks at the helpful stranger.

Tom jerked a thumb over his shoulder. "But I *really* wanted to go on the adult dodgems."

"We're here for the children, darling, not you," Margo pointed out.

Tom wasn't ready to throw in the towel. "Why don't you boys

take it in turns to ride with me?" he cajoled, doing his best to make the offer sound more appealing than it really was.

"That's a lame idea, dad," Gavin objected. "If you're *that* desperate, why don't you and mum just stay here. It's not like me and Pete need you to come with us."

Clearly tempted, Tom stared longingly at his wife, who shrugged uncertainly.

"I don't know, Gav," she said, looking all around her. "It's very busy. What if you get lost and we can't find you?"

"I've got my mobile phone with me," Peter spoke up, trying to be helpful.

Pulling off a mitten with his teeth, he dragged the mobile from his pocket and showed it to them. The number was written on a little sticker his mother had plastered across the back.

"It's not a bad idea," Tom conceded, glancing longingly at the dodgems, which had just started up again. "We could agree to meet over by the kids' dodgems in say, forty-five minutes, and if the boys are late, we'll just ring them."

---

Sean Murphy was a walking crime wave; at least that was how the CPS prosecuting lawyer had described the nineteen year old when he appeared before Waltham Forest Youth Court the previous week. He liked the title; it made him feel special, and he hadn't stopped boasting about it since.

Murphy also liked cars, especially the fast, flashy ones, and he had made a bit of name for himself by nicking them and then baiting the local constabulary into chasing him.

When he wasn't stealing cars, Murphy was stealing from them. His fence paid good money for upmarket sound systems, and he had come to the funfair that evening with the intention of earning himself some spending money for the coming week.

Rather than walk all the way around the fair's perimeter, Murphy decided to take a shortcut back to the car park by forging a path through the trees and thick shrubbery beyond the kiddie rides.

Cursing as low hanging branches brushed against his face, constantly threatening to whip his precious Red Sox cap off, he stumbled through the dense foliage until he emerged into the horseshoe shaped clearing that doubled as a car park.

There were upwards of thirty cars parked there, including a couple of nice BMWs and a brand spanking new Range Rover. Confident that there were good pickings to be had here, he rubbed his hands together in anticipation.

When it came to thievery, caution had always been Murphy's byword, so he remained hidden amongst the trees for a few seconds, letting his eyes acclimatise to the darkness and listening carefully for the sounds of movement within the car park. The last thing he wanted, as he broke into a car, was to find himself being watched by a courting couple who were having it off in the next vehicle along.

When he was satisfied that he was alone, he flitted from car to car, looking for any valuables that had been left on display. Five cars in, he spotted a newish looking Toshiba laptop on the back seat. Murphy didn't know much about computers, but they always fetched a decent price from his fence, so he decided to steal it.

Bending down, he picked up a medium-sized stone and weighed it in the palm of his hand. Satisfied that it would do the job, he took several steps back and then threw it like he was trying to skim it across water.

The glass shattered with a loud crack.

After a quick glance around, to make sure that no one was coming to investigate the noise, he elbowed the remaining glass out, and reached inside to snatch the computer off the seat.

It had taken Murphy less than thirty seconds to commit the theft. Tucking his plunder under his hoodie, he scampered back to the trees. If anyone showed up in the next few seconds, he would slip back through the foliage and return to the funfair. Otherwise, he would see what else he could steal.

Having left the adults behind, the two boys zigzagged their way through the crowds, setting a course for the kiddie's rides on the far side of the funfair.

Burping loudly – the hot dog he'd eaten was already giving him chronic heartburn – Remus followed, keeping them in sight without making it obvious.

By a stroke of good fortune, the clearing his van was parked in was only a stone's throw away from the junior dodgems, hidden behind a thick cluster of trees. If he could just lure the chicken he had taken a shine to in there, snatching him should be simple.

First though, he needed to separate the two boys.

A klaxon sounded, and the miniature dodgems began zooming around in little circles. He could see the two boys laughing uproariously as they repeatedly crashed into each other and anyone else who got in their way. It was clear from their sweet, innocent faces that they were having the time of their young lives.

Remus smiled to himself.

With a bit of luck, that was all about to change.

# 4

## The missing puppy

Having finally run out of tickets, Peter and Gavin reluctantly vacated their dodgem cars, which were instantly commandeered by two more smiling children.

"Aw," Gavin moaned, screwing his face up in regret. "I can't believe we've already used up all those tickets mum gave us."

Peter tugged the crisp five pound note his mum had given him from his coat pocket. With a little flick of his wrist, he dangled the crumpled note in front of Gavin's face. "Look what I've got," he said, grinning broadly.

Gavin's eyes widened. "Where did you get that?"

"My mum gave it to me," Peter said.

Gavin made a playful grab for the note. "We can buy loads more tickets with that."

Laughing, Peter took a swift step back. "That's what I was thinking," he agreed, carefully tucking the money back into his pocket for safekeeping.

"I'll race you to the kiosk," Gavin said, eagerly. "Last one there is—"

"Excuse me!" a flustered looking man in his mid-twenties asked, waving a pink dog's collar at them as he approached.

The man's fingertips were stained yellow. He was skinny, unshaven, with tangled, shoulder length brown hair, and he wore a thick British Army style camouflaged smock. It looked old and tatty, like it was on its last legs. Beneath this, he was clad in green army fatigues and black combat boots.

Peter wondered if he was a soldier.

"I was just walking my puppy, but she's slipped her lead. I don't suppose either of you have seen her wandering around the fair, have you?"

The man sounded very concerned, Peter thought, immediately feeling sorry for him. He had always wanted a dog of his own, and he knew his mum would have gotten him one, but his dad had stopped her, complaining that they were too much effort to look after.

"What kind of dog is it?" Gavin asked, frowning at the tiny lead and collar dangling from the stranger's hand.

An expression of great sadness spread across the soldier man's unshaven face. "She's a lovely little Spaniel called Sadie, and she's only ten weeks old." He pointed behind them, towards the forest. "I think the noise of the fair must have scared her, because she ran into those woods a few minutes ago, and I haven't seen her since."

Peter shook his head. "Sorry, mister, we haven't seen her."

"We've only just come off the dodgems," Gavin added.

"Okay," the man said, his narrow shoulders slumping in disappointment. "I'd better get back to looking for her." He started to turn away, then hesitated, as though a thought had just occurred to him. "I don't suppose there's any chance that you boys could spare a few minutes to help me look for her, could you?" he asked, staring at them pleadingly. "I'll give you a fiver for your time if we find her."

Peter frowned. Remembering the endless lectures his mother had given him about not going off with strangers, he shook his head. "I don't think my mum would be very—"

"Is that a fiver each?" Gavin cut in.

The man's smile was calculating. "If you like."

The boys exchanged glances, and Peter could almost hear the cogs turning inside his friend's head as Gavin tried to work out how many extra rides ten pounds would buy them.

"Okay," Gavin said, "but we can't be long, or my parents will tell us off."

"Gav—"

"It'll be fine," Gavin insisted, glowering at Peter to keep quiet.

"I'll tell you what," the soldier man said, smiling affably at Gavin, "why don't you wait here, just in case Sadie returns, while we—" his finger was flicking between himself and Peter like a metronome "—go and check out the car park beyond those trees."

Gavin seemed to be considering this, but Peter shook his head.

"No," he said, firing a disapproving look in his friend's direction. "We promised your mum and dad that we'd stay together."

"That's true," Gavin conceded.

The man wasn't best pleased to hear this. "Surely, it won't hurt, just for a couple of minutes?" he insisted.

Peter crossed his arms, resolutely. "We can't; we promised."

"Fine," the soldier man said after a moment's hesitation, but Peter could tell from his petulant tone that it really wasn't. "In that case, you can both come and help me look for her in the car park."

He set off towards the trees, glancing back over his shoulder every few seconds to make sure they were still following. As soon as they stepped into the foliage, he moved between them and draped an arm around their shoulders.

"It's really kind of you to help me," he said, pulling them into his body and smiling down at each of them in turn.

His breath smelled of stale cigarettes and fried onions, and Peter turned his head way to avoid inhaling it.

"I don't have particularly good eyesight," the soldier man was saying, "so it's a lot harder for me to see Sadie at night."

It was certainly dark inside the trees, and a bit spooky too, Peter thought. He was surprised how quickly the sounds from the fair became muffled. He could feel twigs snapping underfoot. Beside him, the soldier man's stomach suddenly gurgled loudly, making him jump.

The soldier man groaned, and began rubbing his tummy.

"Poxy hot dog," he mumbled under his breath.

"I don't like it in here," Peter said, slowing down.

The soldier man placed a hand between his shoulder blades and gently pushed him forward. "Don't worry, I'll protect you," he promised. "Besides, we're nearly at the car park now."

---

Murphy was on a roll, and he had just broken into his fourth car when he heard the muted sounds of people approaching through the treeline, following a similar route to the one he had taken to get there.

"Shit!" he cursed, hurriedly yanking the expensive stereo system from the brackets securing it to the dashboard. As he jumped out of the car, he snagged the underside of his hand against a piece of jagged glass protruding from the broken passenger window. Yelping at the sudden pain, he glanced down to see a trickle of blood running down his wrist.

There was no time to worry about that, so he bolted for cover, dropping to his knees the moment he was concealed behind the lee of the trees.

---

When they reached the edge of the car park, the soldier man paused, indicating for the boys to do likewise. "I just want to listen for a second," he whispered, clutching his abdomen, which was still making weird noises. "You know, just in case we hear Sadie moving about."

"Why don't we just go in and search for her?" Peter asked. "Surely, she'll come straight over to you if you call her name?"

"Be quiet," the soldier man hissed, raising a finger to his lips.

Peter wasn't sure, but he thought he detected a note of irritation in his voice.

"Okay, follow me," the soldier man said, a few seconds later.

Emerging into the unlit car park, which was basically a bumpy dirt track with a bowl-shaped area at the end, he herded them towards an old Citroen Berlingo panel van that was parked facing into the treeline. It was either dark blue or red; Peter couldn't be sure in the darkness.

"This is my van," the soldier man said, opening the creaky rear doors. "I think I've got a torch in here somewhere."

He leaned inside, rummaged around for a bit, then straightened up, looking frustrated. "It's no use," he sighed. "I can't see anything in this darkness. Can either of you see it?"

He moved aside to let the boys peer into the back of the van.

"I can't see anything," Peter said, squinting into the interior. There were some sacks and old blankets, some frayed lengths of rope and a thick roll of gaffer tape, but no sign of a torch.

"I think it might be right up the front, wedged behind one of the panels," the man said. "Do me a favour, jump in and have a look, will you?"

Peter hesitated for a moment, not wanting to get into the grubby van, but the man had asked so nicely that he thought it would be rude to refuse. "Okay," he said, scrabbling into the rear with the agility of a little monkey.

"You'd better help him," the man said, gesturing for Gavin to join him.

---

Alison Musgrove glanced down at her watch. There was still ten minutes to go before she was due to collect Peter. Although she really hoped he was having fun with his friend, she missed him terribly and couldn't wait to see him again. She knew it was unhealthy for her to be so clingy, but she hated it when they were separated, even for the shortest of times.

"Oh, for goodness' sake, give it a rest," Ciaron said, moodily rolling his eyes at her.

They were sitting on the couch, watching a chat show on TV, but her mind was elsewhere so the programme was just background noise to her.

"What do you mean?" she asked, twisting away from him.

"You know exactly what I mean," he snapped. "You've looked at that bloody watch so often since we sat down that I'm surprised you haven't developed a crick in your neck."

Alison stiffened at the snarky comment. The dig was so unnecessary, yet so typical of her husband. "It's not affecting you, is it?" she said, staring back defiantly. "I just don't want to be late collecting Peter."

She so desperately wished that Ciaron would be more understanding. He knew how much she fretted when Peter was out, and he knew why.

Ciaron responded with a derisive snort. "You need to get a bloody grip on this," he told her. "It's not healthy, the way you obsess about that boy."

She bristled but said nothing. She damn well *knew* it wasn't healthy, but she had no control over it.

"Maybe, you should think about booking some more sessions with a therapist?" he suggested.

Tears pricked at her eyes. She wanted to tell him there was no point, that they didn't help. Nothing did, not the sessions with a grief counsellor, not all the self-help books she'd devoured, not even the Citalopram tablets her doctor still routinely prescribed her. She had already lost two children, and she was terrified that she would lose Peter, too. Didn't they say that bad things happened in threes?

A solitary tear ran down her cheek, and she angrily rubbed it away. When her bottom lip started to tremble, she bit down hard on it to stop herself from crying.

Ciaron's face softened when he saw this, his initial irritation swept away by a wave of guilt.

"Oh, please don't cry, love," he said, softly. Leaning over, he extended his arms, inviting her to come in for a cuddle.

She bullishly pushed him away, stung by his inability to see things from her perspective.

"Get off me," she said, harshly.

He hesitated, then moved closer, pulling her into him.

Alison resisted at first, but then allowed him to wrap her in an embrace.

He kissed the top of her head, then ran his fingers through her long mousy hair, knowing she found this soothing.

"I'm sorry for having a go at you," he said, as she sobbed into his shoulder. "I know I can be a bit of a prat at times, but I don't mean to be."

"I–I can't help worrying about him," she cried, almost choking on the words. "Not after Andrew's miscarriage, not after losing Luke."

The raw anguish in her voice was palpable, and Ciaron screwed his eyes shut as the pain he worked so hard to keep buried resurfaced.

"I know," he soothed, trying to keep his voice steady. "I should be more patient, more considerate, and I promise I'll try to be in future, but you really need to stop worrying about Peter all the time. He's perfectly safe with Gavin and his parents. I'll bet you that, right now, he's whizzing around on a fair ride, laughing his little head off."

It was a bet he would have lost.

---

Remus was pleased that he'd been able to cajole both boys into the back of his van without having to resort to violence. Casting a last furtive glance around the car park to make sure they were alone, he whipped out a kitchen knife from within the folds of his coat. Holding a nicotine-stained finger to his lips, he brandished it with menace. The bigger one instantly started snivelling, but Remus silenced him with a harsh shushing noise.

They hesitated when he ordered them to lay face down on the floor of the van, but when he told them that he knew where they lived, and that he would go there and brutally murder everyone they loved if they called out for help, they soon became compliant.

Jumping into the back, Remus moved quickly to secure them. First, he covered their mouths with thick bands of gaffer tape. Then he draped rough hessian sacks over their heads to prevent them from being able to see. He bound their arms and legs with rope, before wrapping a couple of old blankets over them to conceal their presence.

Closing the rear doors behind him, Remus jumped behind the wheel and started the diesel engine. Turning the headlights on, he steered the Berlingo out of the car park and into Rangers Road. As he accelerated, his eyes repeatedly ping-ponged between the road ahead and the two side mirrors, making sure that no one was paying any attention to the departing van.

If Remus really strained his ears, he could just about make out their muffled crying, but he doubted the pathetic mewling noises would be audible to anyone outside the van.

"Quiet," he shouted, "or I'll make you watch while I kill both your mummies."

Almost immediately, the whimpering stopped.

"That's better," he said, nodding approvingly.

Keeping to the speed limit, Remus guided the van along the winding forest road. Its headlights forged a path ahead, piercing the surrounding darkness like twin laser beams.

He regretted not having been able to separate the boys. He had absolutely no interest in the bigger one, but that wasn't a problem. He would just sell him on. There was a strong market for prepubescent boys. Of course, he would need Benny's help to facilitate a sale, and the greedy old git would demand the lion's share of the profit, but such was life.

The wolfpack had two properties in East London. The first was a two-bedroom flat in Hackney, which was primarily used as a staging post for all the new rent boys that he and McQueen recruited. It was also used to host the occasional parties that Benny threw for his biggest spending clients. These were basically wild orgies in which Benny laid on a few rent boys, lots of recreational drugs, and as much alcohol as they could drink – all free of charge – as a reward for their continued patronage.

The second property, the one he was heading to now, was a terraced house in Leytonstone, and it served an altogether more sinister purpose. The house had a soundproofed holding cell down in the basement. It was where the wolfpack kept the chickens they abducted to order until the clients were ready to take delivery of their purchases.

Remus was going to have to make a quick stop on the way back, firstly to switch the numberplates on the van, and secondly to sedate the chickens. Inside the glovebox, there was a paper bag containing a ground up combination of Temazepam and Diazepam tablets. It would only take a few seconds to mix the powder with the bottle of lemonade lying on the front passenger seat, and then he would force the boys to drink it.

The chickens were only small, and the drugs were powerful; a few mouthfuls each, and by the time they reached the safe house, both would be completely comatose, making it easy for him to carry them in one at time without attracting attention.

# 5

Benny Mars

Amusement arcades were like magnets to the chickens, so McQueen wasn't surprised when the boy he was following entered a particularly busy one near Piccadilly Circus.

Leaning against a wall, McQueen watched as the boy spunked away his money on the slot machines. When he'd run out, McQueen struck up a conversation with him, then gave the chicken a couple of quid's worth of change to fritter away. The boy had accepted it gratefully, not realising he was trading his soul in exchange for a few pieces of silver. When the money ran out, McQueen offered to take him for a cup of coffee.

"I'm just going to ring a friend and have him meet us at the café," he said, ushering the boy out of the door. "His name is Benny, and I'm sure you'll like him."

Benny Mars was a small, snakelike man in his late-sixties, with a pronounced stoop and an aquiline nose. Beneath the grubby trilby that adorned his head, his thinning hair was swept back, and thickly gelled with Brylcreem. The shoulders of the charcoal Crombie overcoat he wore over his light grey suit were covered in dandruff, and the fabric was ingrained with the stench of cigarette smoke.

His detractors, of which there were many, often commented that you could smell Benny Mars coming long before you saw him. It was a barbed reference to an unpleasant BO problem that stemmed from his aversion to washing. Benny didn't much care what others said; he regarded personal hygiene as an unnecessary inconvenience and was always keen to point out that his lack of cleanliness had never prevented him from getting any of the things he wanted out of life.

Benny also suffered from terrible halitosis, which he insisted was an unfortunate side effect of acid reflux and had nothing to do with his having abstained from practicing any form of oral hygiene since his mid-teens.

Benny had been born in London's East End during the summer of 1934. When his parents and two elder sisters were killed during a Luftwaffe air raid seven years later, he was placed in foster care. The family who took him in were strict Catholics who regularly beat him for his many perceived sins. In addition to poor hygiene standards, these included habitual lying, general tardiness, and bed wetting.

By the age of eight, Benny had already started to develop sexual feelings. At primary school, he would peek up girls' skirts and repeat the rude things he had overheard his foster father saying to his wife while they were having sex.

Over the next two years, a growing number of complaints were received about his increasingly inappropriate conduct towards other children, which included him squeezing breasts and pinching bottoms. Appalled by his abhorrent behaviour, his deeply religious foster parents disavowed themselves of Benny, believing him to be possessed by a demon.

Benny ended up in a local care home. It was a highly regimented institution, where corporal punishment was routinely handed out for the slightest misdemeanour.

Soon after his arrival, one of the staff had been dismissed for sexually abusing a little boy in his care. Instead of repelling Benny, as he knew it should, he found the idea of making someone perform sexual acts against their will highly erotic.

Benny had been placed in an all-boys dormitory, and it was there that he first discovered he was more attracted to other boys than he was to girls. At around the same time, he began to develop an unhealthy obsession for human orifices. One morning, when he was twelve, he found himself alone in the communal showers with a six year old. On a whim, Benny forced the smaller boy to suck his finger while he pleasured himself. Afterwards, ignoring the boy's tearful pleading to stop, Benny roughly inserted the same finger into the child's anus. He had frightened the boy into remaining silent by saying that *he* would be the one who got into trouble for letting Benny do this if anyone ever found out, and that it would ruin his chances of ever being adopted.

Later that year, Benny forced a nine year old boy to perform oral sex on him, holding a piece of broken glass against his neck and threatening to kill him if he told anyone.

Emboldened by his successes, he anally raped an eight year old boy a month later.

Although poorly educated, Benny possessed a feral cunning, and he chose his victims carefully, preying on the weakest and most vulnerable because they were the easiest to manipulate or frighten into compliance.

When he was fifteen, afraid that he had finally gone too far with his latest victim, and that the boy would require urgent medical attention after being left with a bleeding rectum, Benny fled the care home to join a travelling funfair that was passing through the area.

Travelling around the country with the funfair, Benny left a trail of young victims in his wake. Some were digitally penetrated; others were forced to perform oral sex on him. A few were brutally raped. For Benny, the ultimate thrill came from luring his unsuspecting victims to deserted locations, usually bombed-out buildings or secluded riverbanks, and then strangling them until they passed out, at which point he set about raping them. On one occasion in late 1954, not long after reaching his twentieth birthday, Benny went too far, and the child died.

The fair had left town the following day, and Benny had gone with it, determined to be more careful in future.

As he hurried along Charing Cross Road, on his way to the little café that McQueen had taken the newly arrived chicken to, Benny ran a grubby finger along the discoloured collar of his ill-fitting shirt to let the heat out.

Panting a little from the exertion of walking quickly, he raised a Benson & Hedges King Size to his thin lips and greedily sucked in a lungful of smoke. The tip glowed brightly in the darkness, like an angry firefly. Grumbling under his breath about how busy it was, Benny weaved his way through the pedestrian traffic clogging up the pavements around him.

"Out of the way, useless bloody tourists," he snapped at a middle-aged American couple who had stopped to admire the grandeur of *The Palace Theatre*, whose red brick facade dominated the west side of Cambridge Circus.

A couple of minutes later, he pushed open the door to the café in Romilly Street and stepped into the warmth. The café was brightly lit and had a contemporary vibe to it. Soft jazz music filled the air, covering the muted conversations of the few patrons dotted around the place. He spotted McQueen at once. Tucked into a small corner booth at the rear of the premises, he was sitting opposite an underdressed and, from the look of it, underfed boy with big blue eyes and collar length, mousy hair.

Benny paused at the counter to order himself a large mug of tea, then slid into the bench seat beside the startled boy.

"Alright, Joey?" Benny grinned, leaning his elbows on the Formica table and steepling his grimy fingers together.

McQueen acknowledged him with a respectful nod. "I'm good, thanks, Benny."

Benny turned his eyes on the boy, who seemed unsettled by his sudden appearance. "Well, well, well," he purred, leaning in to get a better look at the chicken's pale face. "Who have we got here, then?"

The boy's nose wrinkled as he caught a whiff of Benny's rancid breath, and he shuffled sideways to put some distance between them.

Benny responded by sliding his bony bottom across the bench seat until his thigh was pressing against the young chicken's.

The boy was clearly uncomfortable with the unwanted physical contact, but he said nothing.

"What's your name then, young lad?" Benny enquired, pouring sugar into tea the colour of Creosote.

Over the years, he had perfected his technique for handling new chickens. He would gain their confidence with flattery, acts of kindness and the provision of food, drink, clothing and a place to stay. If the boys went along with his demands, as some of them willingly did, all was good, but if they refused, they quickly saw another much darker side to him. He wondered how it would go with this one, and his initial assessment was that the boy was too strait laced to willingly go on the game.

The boy's eyes shot towards McQueen, seeking reassurance.

"Don't be rude," McQueen chided. "You can trust Benny, so answer his questions."

The boy still seemed unsure. He scooped up his mug of coffee and took a quick sip to buy himself time to think.

Benny sat in silence, watching him like a hawk. They were so predictable, these stupid little chickens.

"My name's Gabe," the boy finally said, not meeting the old man's eye. His voice still had a childish quality to it, and he spoke with a distinctive West Country twang.

Benny wondered if Gabe was his real name, or one he had made up on the spur of the moment. It didn't really matter to him either way.

"Is that short for Gabriel?" he enquired.

The boy nodded. "It is, but only my parents call me that. I prefer Gabe."

Benny gave him a warm smile and extended a grubby hand for the boy to shake. "Pleased to meet you, Gabe."

When the boy accepted the proffered hand, Benny held on for a little longer than was necessary, caressing the boy's soft palm with his thumb. "So, what brings you to London?" he asked, arching an eyebrow.

"I'm looking for a job," Gabe said, pulling his hand free and stuffing it under the table, out of reach.

The old paedophile smiled, encouragingly. "A job, you say. Aren't you a bit young to be looking for employment? What are you, thirteen? Fourteen?"

Gabe's face reddened. He looked troubled, and Benny could tell that he was weighing up whether to lie about his age.

"I'm fourteen and three quarters," Gabe finally said, jutting his jaw out defiantly, "but I'm strong for my age, and I'm not afraid of hard work."

Benny exchanged a look with McQueen. The boy had potential.

"Are you hungry?" Benny asked, thinking that the chicken looked like he was wasting away and probably hadn't eaten a good meal in days.

Gabe nodded, slowly. "Starving," he admitted, sheepishly.

"Tell you what," Benny said, raising a hand to get the attention of the server, who was leaning on the counter, talking to a bald man on the other side who was dressed in chef's whites. "Why don't we get you some food, and you can tell us your story while you eat."

---

There was no reply at Gavin's house, which was in complete darkness. Alison peered through the letterbox, then checked her watch again. It was exactly ten o'clock, the time she had specified she would be picking Peter up at.

Were they still at the funfair?

Was it possible that they were all having such a hoot together that they had lost track of time? She experienced a little pang of jealousy, resenting the fact that the Grants had shared an experience with Peter that she had been excluded from.

Alison looked down the road, gazing wistfully in the direction that they would be coming from when they returned from the fair.

The quiet suburban street was completely deserted.

Feeling the warmth haemorrhaging from her body, Alison suppressed a shiver as she tugged the fur collar of her coat tight against her neck. It was cold enough to freeze the knackers off a polar bear, and she was regretting her earlier decision to sacrifice the insulation of her thick winter boots in favour of a pair of Denim topped plimsolls, just so that she could get out of the house a few seconds quicker.

Pulling off a glove, she reached into her coat pocket and withdrew her Siemens mobile phone. She pressed the speed dial for Peter's number, then placed the cold plastic against her ear. It took a moment for the connection to be made, then she heard the reassuring sound of a ring tone.

"Come on," she whispered, her teeth chattering in the cold. "Pick up, pick up."

It rang exactly five times, then the voicemail service automatically cut in. She hung up, gave it thirty seconds and tried again, only to get the same result.

Alison killed the call, telling herself that he probably hadn't heard it ringing, what with all the noise at the fairground.

Alison stood by the garden gate, wondering what to do. Then, unable to stand the biting cold any longer, she pocketed the phone and set off towards Rangers Road, head bowed against the driving wind.

---

Remus was so startled when the harsh ringtone erupted from the back of the van that he swerved to the left and almost mounted the kerb. It hadn't occurred to him that kids as young as the two chickens he had just snatched might have mobile phones on them.

After a few seconds, the ringing stopped, and he breathed a sigh of relief.

Then it started all over again.

Letting out a string of expletives, he berated himself for not having searched them. Thankfully, they were securely bound, and wouldn't be able to answer the bloody thing.

He wanted to pull over and confiscate the phone, but he didn't dare risk doing so on such a busy, well-lit road.

"Fuck it," he snarled, banging the steering wheel with his fist. It would just have to wait until he got to Hollow Ponds.

---

Alison spotted two figures hurrying towards her in the darkness. From their shapes, she could tell she was looking at a stocky man and a petite woman. There was something vaguely familiar about the way they moved, and they were clearly in a rush. Something about their agitated body language made her feel uneasy.

As the couple entered the circular yellow glow of a streetlamp, Alison instantly recognised them as Tom and Margo Grant, Gavin's parents. Even from a distance, she registered the tautness of their faces.

Her heart missed a beat.

Where were the children?

Where was her precious Peter?

Margo raised a hand in greeting when she spotted her. "Alison," she called out. "Is that you?" The distress in her voice was unmistakeable.

"Where are the children?" Alison demanded, breaking into a run. "Where's Peter?"

"We don't know," Tom said, breathlessly. "We couldn't find them at the fair, so we were heading home, to see if they had had gone back without us."

A ball of ice formed in the pit Alison's stomach. This was her worst nightmare come true. "I've just come from yours," she told them, her voice sharp. "There was no sign of the kids there."

"But, if they're not at the fair, and they're not at home, where could they be?" Margo asked. She seemed more confused than worried, which angered Alison beyond words.

"They must have gotten themselves lost," Tom said, glancing over his shoulder in the direction they had just come from.

It was as if all the air was sucked from Alison's lungs, and she felt the world around her begin to spin. She instinctively reached out, grabbing onto Tom's arm to steady herself.

He took her elbow in his hand. "Are you okay?" he asked, staring at her with genuine concern.

Alison was far from okay. Her world had just turned upside down. She didn't know what to think; she didn't know what to do.

*Please God, let my baby boy be safe...*

Taking a deep breath, she tried to hold off the panic that threatened to overwhelm her. She needed to think rationally, not descend into hysteria.

"We need to go back to the fair," she said, shrugging Tom's hand off. "They must still be there."

"But we looked," Margo assured her. "If they were there, we would have seen—"

"Maybe you missed them because they were on one of the rides?" Alison shouted over her.

She was struggling to keep her sense of perspective and not let her imagination run riot, though deep down, she already knew that something terrible had happened. She had been waiting for this dreadful moment to occur since the day that Peter had been born.

Margo opened her mouth to argue the point, but Tom raised a hand to silence her.

"Maybe," he allowed, although he didn't sound overly convinced. Turning to his wife, he said, "Margo, why don't you head back to the house, just in case they turn up there, while me and Alison take another look around the fairground?"

"What?" Margo stiffened, clearly not enamoured by the idea. "Why me?"

Wrapping an arm around her shoulders, Tom drew her in close

and kissed her forehead tenderly. "Please, babe. Someone's got to do it, and we can't expect Alison to, can we?"

Margo glanced sideways at Alison, her face full of resentment, then she nodded, reluctantly accepting the wisdom of his words. "Okay," she said, prising herself from his embrace, "but call me the minute you find them."

She set off at a brisk pace, not quite running, but not dawdling either.

Alison tried Peter's mobile number again, but all it did was ring until the voicemail kicked in.

"Shit!" she snapped, ending the call and redialling.

"Who are you ringing?" Tom asked, peering over her shoulder.

"Peter's mobile," Alison replied, not bothering to look at him. "I keep trying to call him, but it just diverts to voicemail."

"We tried ringing him too," Tom admitted, as they set off towards the fair. "When he didn't answer, we just figured that there was too much background noise for him to have heard it."

"I hope you're right," Alison said, tucking the phone into her pocket as they crossed Rangers Road.

Once inside the fairground, they made their way straight over to the junior dodgems.

Now it was much later in the evening, the customer demographic had noticeably changed. The family groups who had dominated the crowd earlier had been largely replaced by clusters of boisterous teenagers and rowdy adults.

"This is where they promised they would be," Tom explained, anxiously scanning the rides.

"What do you mean by that?" Alison demanded.

Tom shrugged, guiltily. When their eyes met, he found himself wilting under her accusatory stare. "The boys weren't allowed on the adult dodgems on their own, and they didn't want to come on with me, so they came over here instead."

"What the hell were you thinking?" Alison exploded. "How could you let my son wander around a place like this at night, without adult supervision?"

Tom flinched. "But, Ali, he wasn't alone," he protested,

adopting an injured tone. "Gavin was with him, and you know I wouldn't—"

"SHUT UP!" she screamed. Spinning in frantic circles, her eyes raked the fairground for Peter. "He has to be here somewhere," she said, more to herself than him.

Her breath came in short, sharp gasps as she became increasingly agitated. A part of her brain registered that she was on the verge of hyperventilating, but she couldn't control it.

If anything happened to Peter, she would just die.

Tom placed a firm hand on each of her shoulders and forced her to stand still. "Ali, you really need to calm—"

"Get off me," she snapped, slapping his hands away.

Heads turned in their direction.

Tom's face reddened. "Ali, I—"

"I said, get off me!" she yelled, louder this time.

A tall, heavyset man in his fifties, his long grey hair falling well below his wide shoulders, strode down the metal steps of the mini-dodgems and approached them. He was an imposing figure, with a nose that had obviously been broken several times, and cauliflower ears. "Everything alright?" he asked her in a deep voice. His accent suggested he came from East Europe. "This man, he is giving you trouble?"

"No, of course I'm not giving her trouble," Tom said, spreading his arms to placate the brute, who clearly thought they were having a domestic. "Our two young boys have gone missing, and she's having a panic attack. I'm just trying to calm her down."

The man's expression changed from one of controlled aggression to genuine concern. "Is true?" he asked Alison.

She nodded, feeling tears prickle her eyes. "They were on the mini dodgems, but now they've disappeared."

"Just now?" the man asked, his eyes instinctively darting left and right, as if he might be able to spot them, even though he had no idea who he was looking for.

Tom shook his head. "No, about fifteen minutes ago."

The man shrugged. "Maybe they go home?" he suggested.

"We've checked; they haven't," Alison said, flatly.

The big man placed his hands on his hips. "What they look like?"

Speaking over each other, Alison and Tom each began describing their child.

"Shush, please," the big man said, silencing them. Then, with a slight nod towards Alison, he said, "You go first."

"My son's name is Peter and he's nine, but he's small for his age." She held up a hand to demonstrate his approximate height. "He's slim, with blonde hair, and he was wearing a green parka, a woolly hat and mittens."

"My son's the same age but taller," Tom said, holding his hand several inches above Alison's. "He's a bit stockier too, and he was wearing a blue parka with patches on both arms, gloves, and a dark blue beanie hat."

The ride attendant was frowning. "I think I remember these two," he said, stroking his chin thoughtfully. "They ride dodgems several times, have much fun. When they leave, they talk to skinny man holding dog leash. They follow him over there," he said, pointing to a thick cluster of trees a few yards behind the last of the children's rides.

"What's over there, beyond those trees?" Tom asked, squinting in the direction the man had pointed.

The ride attendant merely shrugged.

"Why would they do that?" Alison asked, appalled. "Peter would never go off with a stranger. He knows better than that."

"Did the man force them to go with them?" Tom asked, sounding equally horrified.

The big man pondered this for a moment, then shook his head, emphatically. "No. Man walk off alone, boys follow a few moments later."

"What did this man look like?" Tom demanded, starting to lose his earlier composure.

"Dressed like soldier, but not soldier. Too scruffy; too dirty. More like drug user," the attendant said, turning his nose up in disapproval. "You know type: skinny, grubby, with thin face." He pointed at his cheeks, then sucked them in to demonstrate. "Long, greasy hair and not shaved," he added. "Not nice man."

Tom started walking towards the treeline, then glanced back over his shoulder at Alison. "Call the police," he instructed as he broke into a run. "Tell them we think the kids have been abducted."

## 6

## SUNDAY 4TH NOVEMBER 2001

Alone in the dark

Peter's eyes slowly flickered open. They were sticky with sleep, and he clumsily wiped at them with the backs of his hands. Letting out a long yawn, he groggily raised his head from the lumpy pillow it had been resting on and looked around, confused and disorientated by the unfamiliar surroundings.

The room was as cold as his mum's freezer, and it stank of dampness and mould. Other than a thin sliver of weak yellow light leaking in from underneath the door opposite him, it was in total darkness.

Instead of being wrapped in his lovely snugly quilt, which always smelled of mum's favourite fabric softener, he was covered by a musty smelling blanket and a tissue thin sheet.

He rubbed at the dull, throbbing ache in the back of his head, wondering if he was coming down with a cold. He was desperately thirsty, and his lips felt bone dry as he gingerly ran the tip of his tongue over them.

His bladder was full to bursting point; he needed the loo badly, but he didn't know where it was, and he didn't want to go wandering around in the dark by himself.

Peter's memory was so hazy that he didn't even recall going to bed. Had he stayed over at Gavin's? Was that why the room was so dark, and why the uncomfortable bed was so unfamiliar? Running a hand down his body, he was surprised to find that he was still wearing his clothes. That was most odd. He had never been allowed to sleep in them before.

And he had been having the weirdest dream…

Unbidden, a series of blurred, strobe-like images flashed through his young mind, and with them came a growing sense of dread.

He sat up, suddenly scared. "Mum," he called, his voice little more than a croak.

Peter waited, alone in the darkness, listening for the reassuring sound of her approaching footsteps, expecting to see the door fly open at any moment, and for her to be silhouetted against the light spilling in from the hallway.

Nothing.

It suddenly dawned on him that the room had no windows.

"MUM!" He tried again, a full on shout this time to convey the urgency.

There was a rustling noise a few feet over to his right.

"Who's there?" Peter demanded, pulling the bedclothes all the way up to his neck, as if that would protect him from whatever was lurking in the darkness.

"Is… is that you, Pete?" It was Gavin's voice, weak and slurry, like he had just woken up.

Feeling his body relax, Peter released his breath. "Yes, Gav. It's me. I'm just over here." He waved in the direction that Gavin's voice had come from, stopping abruptly when he realised how futile the gesture was in the darkness.

"Where are we?" Gavin's disembodied voice enquired from a few feet away. He sounded on the verge of tears.

This confused Peter. "Aren't we at your place?"

Gavin gulped loudly, just like they did in cartoons, and Peter imagined his Adam's apple bobbing up and down comically. Under different circumstances, that might have made him laugh, but there was nothing remotely funny about their current situation.

"I don't know where we are, Pete," Gavin said after a slight pause, "but it definitely isn't my place."

"But… if we're not at yours, then where are we?"

Gavin sniffed loudly, then there was a little sob.

Peter realised that Gavin was crying. "Are you okay, Gav?"

"I'm scared." Gavin's voice was a frightened whisper.

"Me too," Peter admitted, glumly.

They sat there in silence for a few seconds, Gavin whimpering, Peter trying to make sense of their predicament.

"The soldier man!" Gavin blurted out, making Peter jump. "The one who lost his dog. He must have brought us here."

*The soldier man?*

The words triggered another snippet of memory for Peter; it was patchy and fragmented, like the dream he had been having. He concentrated hard, trying to organise the confusing images into a sequence that made sense, but he had no idea what order they went in.

Gavin was becoming increasingly distressed. "I want my mummy," he sobbed, pitifully.

Peter felt like crying too, but he forced some swagger into his voice, for Gavin's sake.

"I'll get you back to her," he promised.

"I want my mummy… I want my mummy…" Gavin was saying the words over and over, like a mantra.

Although Gavin was twice Peter's size, he was a big softie at heart. Of the two of them, Peter was the adventurous one. He was the one who caused ripples by questioning a teacher's decision when he didn't agree with it; he was the one who always accepted the dare, even when it was dangerous; and he was the one who always stood up to class bullies like Tommy Evans.

Gavin always relied on Peter to sort things out whenever they got themselves into scrapes, and he knew it would be no different this time around.

"We're going to find a way out of this place," Peter told his friend, injecting a steely determination he didn't feel into the words.

"But... but, how?" Gavin asked, between giant, hiccupping sobs.

Peter shrugged, then remembered that his friend couldn't see the movement. "I don't know... yet. But we'll find a way, Gav. I promise you, we will."

He hoped it was a promise he would be able to keep.

---

Two floors above the soundproofed basement, Aaron Remus lay flat on his back in the smallest of the three bedrooms, feeling close to death. The projectile vomiting had started soon after he'd deposited the drugged children in their temporary prison, and he had never known a bout of sickness like it. It was the hot dog's fault; the vile thing had given him a severe bout of food poisoning. The dry heaving had continued long after his body had expelled its last morsel, and at one point, the convulsions had become so excruciatingly painful that he feared his stomach lining would rupture.

Brushing aside the damp, matted hair that was plastered across his clammy forehead, he swivelled to glance at the radio alarm clock on the bedside table.

*07:00*

He groaned, despairingly. It was time to go down and give them another draught of sedative, but he wasn't sure he had the energy to get out of bed, let alone trudge all the way down to the basement and deal with his captives. Hopefully, they would still be too groggy from the first dose to put up any meaningful resistance.

Resenting the effort it required, Remus cast aside the blankets and forced himself to sit up. The sheets were soaked with sweat, as were his pyjamas, which clung uncomfortably to his wiry frame. Leaning forward, he rested bony elbows on even bonier knees, then cradled his head in his hands. He glanced down at the grey plastic washing up bowl by the side of the bed as another wave of nausea swept over him. The bowl had been a life saver during the night, when he had been unable to make it to the toilet in time, but he hoped he would have no further need of it today.

A minute passed before Remus was able to stand, and when he did, he immediately sagged against the wall; one hand supporting himself, the other clutching his gut. When he finally felt strong enough, he set off for the bathroom.

He splashed cold water over his unshaven face, then scooped a handful into his mouth, swished it around for a couple of seconds to get rid of the vile, acrid taste of the bile, then spat it out. He was desperately thirsty, and knew he needed to rehydrate himself, but he was too afraid to drink anything, in case it came straight back up.

---

The rough concrete floor beneath Peter's socked feet was icily cold, and he wondered why the room didn't have a carpet. Was the soldier man too poor to afford one?

He took a tentative step towards the light spilling in from below the door, then another. On his third, he tripped over something blocking his path and nearly fell. Bending down to probe the mysterious obstacle, Peter was surprised to find his coat and boots lying in a little pile.

Hurriedly pulling his boots on, he set off towards the door, moving with more confidence now that his feet were protected.

The door was made of metal and very solid, not like the cheap, hollow things they had at home. He had accidentally dented one of those a few weeks back, and his dad had flown into a rage over the damage. Afterwards, when he'd calmed down, he had sat Peter on his knee and explained that they hadn't been designed to withstand young boys crashing into them with their toys.

Peter tapped the door with his knuckles, and it responded with a faint metallic clang. This one wouldn't dent if he hit it with a hammer, let alone one of his toys. He groped his way along the door to where it met the frame, sweeping his hands up and down until he found the thick brass handle. He was about to turn it when a worrying thought occurred to him.

What if someone was standing right outside?

Placing an ear against the cold metal, he held his breath and listened. Hearing nothing, he gave the handle a gentle downwards turn.

His heart sank when it didn't budge.

He tugged at it again, this time yanking downwards with all his strength.

It remained immobile.

"It's locked," he told Gavin, who had remained on his bed.

"W–what are we going to do if w–we can't get out?" Gavin fretted, in between sobs.

"We'll find a way," Peter said, firmly. "I–"

"What was that?" Gavin squeaked.

Peter strained his ears. After a moment, he heard it too, the muffled sound of approaching footsteps, followed by the distinctive sound of a clunky key being inserted into the lock.

"Someone's coming," he gasped, releasing the handle and taking a frightened step backwards.

Was it the soldier man?

Was he coming for them?

The key began turning.

"I'm scared," Gavin mewled in the darkness.

"Shhh! Be quiet," Peter whispered.

With his arms outstretched, he ran across the darkened room, stopping only when his right shin slammed into the metal base of his bed. Gritting his teeth, Peter ignored the sharp pain that ran down his leg and made his toes tingle. Kicking his boots off, he jumped onto the mattress and pulled the threadbare blanket over him.

"Pretend you're still asleep," he ordered Gavin.

A dull, blood-red light came on above them, illuminating the room with its eerie glow.

Then the door opened.

The lock to the cell door had always been temperamental, and Remus had to wriggle the oversized key several times – cursing under his breath with every agitated twist of his wrist – before he felt the teeth engage. Every time they used the holding facility, he vowed to oil the door's mechanism, but never did.

Before opening the door, he flicked a switch on the wall, activating the night light inside. Most of the chickens they kept there were afraid of the dark, and the paedophiles mercilessly exploited this, rewarding obedient children with illumination and punishing those who were less compliant with darkness.

He pushed the heavy, double skinned door wide open and peered into the unventilated space. It had a leaf thickness of 64 mm and was attached to the frame by two solid galvanised bolts on the hinged side. He doubted a rhino could break it down, let alone a young child.

The windowless room was approximately ten feet square, with a low ceiling that required anyone over six feet tall to stoop when entering. Two child sized metal cots had been bolted to the concrete floor, one on either side of the door. The interior was illuminated by a single low wattage bulb that dangled from the ceiling by a short wire. The soft red glow it gave off barely reached the four corners. Benny had purposefully chosen the colour in order to give the bleak room the appearance of hell.

Each cot was occupied by one of the chickens he had abducted the previous evening. To his immense relief, they both appeared to be sound asleep.

That was good; it would make his task much easier.

He glanced at the slops bucket in the corner of the room. He'd left it there in case they needed to relieve themselves during the night, and was inordinately pleased that it was still empty; that was one less thing he would have to attend to.

Leaving the door open, he returned to the corridor outside, retrieving a tray from the cardboard box he had balanced it on. It contained two bowls of steaming hot porridge, and two mugs of strong tea, each of which was laced with enough sedative to knock the chickens out for the rest of the morning.

"Wake up," he bellowed as he re-entered the room.

His voice bounced off the thick concrete walls, creating a faint echo.

Neither boy responded, which tried his patience. He really didn't feel well, and he wanted to go back to bed as quickly as possible, not be stuck down there attending to them.

"I said, wake up!" he shouted, angrily.

The boy in the cot to the left shifted under his blanket, but the other one remained as still as a corpse.

With a huff, Remus bent down and placed the tray on the floor, being careful not to spill the cups of drugged tea in the process.

The boy to his left was wriggling about beneath his blanket. Remus whipped it back, exposing the terrified chicken beneath.

Fear burned brightly in the boy's saucer wide eyes.

"Do you need the toilet?" Remus asked, with unnecessary harshness.

The boy nodded. "Y–yes, please," he stammered.

"Come on, then," Remus barked, impatiently waving him up.

Instantly compliant, the boy jumped to his feet. "The floor's very cold," he whinged, hopping from one foot to the other. "Can I put my boots on, please?"

That angered Remus. "No. You bloody well can't," he snapped, pointing a bony finger towards the door. "The bog's out there. If you want to use it, hurry up."

As he ushered the chicken into the corridor, he glanced back at the unmoving form on the other cot. The pretty blonde was much smaller than the lardy wimp he was escorting to the loo, so it stood to reason that the sedative would have a stronger effect on him, which would explain why he hadn't woken up yet.

"Where do I go now?" the bigger chicken asked, looking around gormlessly.

"To your right," Remus said, irritated by the boy's stupidity.

Leaving the cell door open, he shoved the boy along the cluttered corridor until they came to a wooden door at the end.

"In there," he instructed, pushing it open to reveal a cramped cubicle containing an ancient toilet with an overhead cistern. "I'll be waiting for you right here," he said as the boy entered. "Don't take too long."

---

Peeking out through a small gap between the blanket and the bed, Peter watched the soldier man usher Gavin into the corridor. His heart almost stopped when their captor paused in the doorway and looked back at him, brow creased in thought.

*Keep still*, Peter told himself. *Breathe deeply and pretend to be asleep.*

With a surly grunt, the soldier man disappeared.

Listening to their footsteps recede, Peter found himself paralysed by indecision.

How far away was the toilet?

How long would they be gone?

Should he get up and follow them into the corridor, or was it best to remain where he was and continue faking sleep?

Deciding that he might not get another chance, Peter slid out from beneath the blanket, scooped up his boots and coat, and tiptoed over to the door. He really didn't like the idea of abandoning Gavin, but if he could find a way out of the building while the horrid man was distracted, he would be able to find a policeman and bring him back to rescue his friend.

He poked his head into the corridor, sneaking a quick look to his right. The soldier man was standing with his back to Peter, facing a wooden door at the end of the corridor. This, presumably, led into the toilet that Gavin was using.

The corridor's exposed brickwork had large gaps in it from where the mortar had crumbled. It was stacked full of cardboard boxes. A few were open, and these contained glossy, colour magazines with semi-naked women on their covers. Peter had seen magazines like these before, on the top shelf at their local newsagents. His mother called them nudy-mags. He had once overheard his and Gavin's mum speaking about them in hushed whispers, the way adults often did when they were spreading gossip, after one of the other school mums had discovered her husband's secret stash in the garden shed.

Some of the open boxes contained VHS tapes with similarly themed covers.

Peter glanced to his left, and was surprised to see a narrow staircase leading upwards from the other end of the corridor. There were several battered filing cabinets and a load more boxes between him and the stairs. The top drawer of one of the filing cabinets was wide open, making the corridor impossibly narrow at that point.

Peter's stomach did little flips as he stood there, trying to work up the courage to make a run for it. He would have to be quick, but his feet were rooted to the floor.

Would the soldier man punish Gavin if he ran away?

Maybe, but he would punish them both if Peter stayed.

Despite the cold, Peter felt a trickle of sweat run down his temple.

"How long does it take to have a piss?" the soldier man suddenly barked, banging on the toilet door with his fist to hurry Gavin along.

Peter flinched at the outburst, and it was all he could do to stop himself from crying. Taking a deep breath, he stole one last glance in the man's direction, then dashed along the corridor towards the stairs.

# 7

## Hiding in plain sight

Instead of enjoying the restful slumber that a man of his age was entitled to, Gareth Madeley, a highly respected Queen's Counsel and part time Crown Court judge, had spent the previous two nights tossing and turning in his super king-size bed, fantasising about the delights he would soon be experiencing.

He had known Benny Mars for the best part of twenty years, having first met when Benny enlisted his services to represent an uncouth associate called Angus Clifford. A fringe member of Benny's little wolfpack, Clifford had managed to get himself arrested for indecently assaulting a child at the fairground where he worked.

As a paedophile himself, Madeley had instantly recognised a kindred spirit in Benny, who had gone on to become his regular supplier of child porn. The barrister had always secretly envied the way that Benny lived life on the edge; if he wanted something, he took it, and to hell with the consequences. Madeley was far too timid to ever take risks like that. Even making his infrequent visits to Benny's shop to stock up on new material stressed him out.

Benny had invited him to join the inner circle of his wolfpack many times over the years, and although Madeley had been sorely tempted, he had always declined, for fear that it would jeopardise his career. On Friday afternoon, completely out of the blue, the subject had cropped up again, and this time, instead of instantly dismissing the offer, Madeley had found himself gratefully accepting it.

After a quick trip to the toilet, the fourth one he had made that night, Madeley laid down again, padding his pillow to make it comfy. Closing his eyes, he wondered what the first boy Benny procured for him would look like. Blonde, he hoped. He had a soft spot for blondes. A dreamy smile spread across Madeley's face as dozed off.

---

Every fibre in Peter's body screamed at him to run, but he couldn't risk doing that in case it alerted the soldier man. Instead, he crept along the corridor, carefully weaving his way through the boxes.

Behind him, he heard the muffled sound of a toilet being flushed.

"About bloody time, too," the soldier man grumbled.

Peter risked a quick backwards glance, and was relieved to see that their captor was still looking the other–

Crash!

Peter's right shoulder collided with the filing cabinet's protruding drawer, and the unexpected impact spun him full circle. Dropping his boots and coat, he cannoned into a cardboard box that was crammed full of VHS tapes. The box split under his weight, noisily spilling its contents all over the floor. Peter staggered to his feet, massaging his throbbing shoulder. For a moment, all he could do was stand there, staring in wide-eyed fear at the startled man at the other end of the corridor.

*Run!* A frightened voice inside his head urged.

Mouthing obscenities, the soldier man was quick to recover from his initial shock. Arms extended, he sprinted towards Peter.

*RUN!*

Peter spun on his heels, ducked under the protruding drawer, and made a dash for the stairs.

"Come back here, you little bastard!" his angry pursuer yelled, sounding dangerously close.

Peter slipped on one of the many cassettes that now littered the floor, momentarily losing traction. He stumbled sideways, reached out to steady himself against a wall, then carried on running.

He was ten steps away from the stairs... nine steps... eight steps...

Behind him, there was a bestial roar of frustration as the soldier man reached the filing cabinet, tried to slam the drawer closed, but couldn't. Cursing loudly, he ducked under the protruding drawer, slipped on the cassettes that had so nearly proved to be Peter's undoing, and crashed to the floor.

Peter was six steps away from the stairs now... five steps... four...

He could see daylight shining down from above.

Behind him, the soldier man had regained his feet. "I'll kill you for this, you little shit!" he bellowed.

Peter reached the staircase. It was narrow and steep. With a final glance over his shoulder, he grabbed the bannister and began to climb.

The wooden stairs creaked as he clambered up them, his footsteps echoing off the walls.

Before he was even halfway up, they were joined by a far heavier footfall.

Peter's stomach flipped; the soldier man had reached the stairs.

He knew he would be severely punished if he was recaptured, and the fear spurred him on. Peter thrust his head through the open doorway at the top of the stairs to find himself in the hall of a house. He hesitated for a moment, trying to get his bearings. To his left was a kitchen; to his right was the street door.

Beyond that, lay safety.

He could do this; he could get—

Peter felt a sudden pressure on his ankles as an iron grip tightened around them. He tried to pull free, but he wasn't strong enough. For an instant, nothing happened, then he was yanked backwards, crashing face first against the hard wooden floor.

Peter opened his mouth to scream, but before he could even draw breath, he disappeared though the door. His head thudded into several steps in quick succession, stunning him.

As Peter lost consciousness, a terrible realisation struck him: the soldier man had caught him.

He had failed Gavin.

# 8

A request for assistance

Although headquartered within New Scotland Yard, the Homicide Command had three satellite bases scattered around London. One was located in the east, another in the west, and the third in the south. Each satellite was home to nine Murder Investigation Teams, commonly known as MITs.

Each MIT spent every ninth week on call, performing the role of Homicide Assessment Team and fielding a fast response – colloquially known as the HAT car – to all the murders and other suspicious deaths that occurred during that period.

The HAT car was crewed by a DS and two DCs. They reported directly to the on-call DI who, in turn, was answerable to the on-call Senior Investigating Officer.

Performing the role of early shift on-call DI for the east HAT car on this cold November morning, Susie Sergeant sat at her desk in the pokey office she shared with Detective Inspector Tony Dillon on the second floor of Hertford House.

Chin resting in the palm of her hand, Susie stared at the computer screen with an air of bored resignation, attempting to muddle her way through a lengthy forensic psychology evaluation without falling asleep. She paused at the end of a particularly tedious chapter dealing with the thorny issue of mental capacity. "God, give me strength," she muttered, feeling her eyelids growing heavier by the second.

Glancing down at her watch, Susie was disappointed to see that it was only half past nine. With a groan of despondency, she sagged into her chair, resigning herself to the fact that it was going to be one of those long, boring days where nothing interesting happened, and time just dragged.

Susie's eyes wandered longingly to the empty coffee cup beside her keyboard. As tempted as she was to grab a refill, she decided to put it off until she'd read at least one more chapter.

Out in the main office, DS Charlie White was sitting at his desk, putting together the closing report for a trial that had concluded at court a couple of months back. He had spent the past fifteen minutes complaining about the technical difficulties he was experiencing as he attempted to merge data from various documents into a single Excel sheet for inclusion in the report's appendix. White had never been one to suffer in silence, and his bad-tempered outbursts were getting progressively louder as his burgeoning frustration got the better of him.

Susie had done her best to ignore him, but when he stood up and started jabbing at the buttons on his keyboard as though he was trying to gouge them out one at a time, she looked up from her computer screen and shook her head in despair.

"Reg, please sort Charlie's technical issues out for him, before he does my head in," she shouted across the room to where DC Reg Parker, the team's resident telephones and computer expert, was watching White's tantrum in amusement.

"It's no' my fault," White bit back, sounding ultra-defensive. His Glaswegian accent always grew noticeably thicker when he was stressed or angry, like now. "This stupid file thingy keeps corrupting every time I try to add a graph or insert a wee photo onto it."

Susie's eyes narrowed to slits. "Instead of throwing your teddy out of the pram, why don't you make yourself useful and put the kettle on, while Reggie sorts the file out for you?" she suggested with a tight smile.

Before White could formulate a suitably sarcastic reply, the HAT phone chirped into life.

---

DCI Jack Tyler was snuggled up in bed, making the most of a rare lie in with his fiancée, Kelly Flowers. With Susie supervising the early shift, he had decided to devote his entire morning to pampering Kelly. They had recently discovered that she was pregnant, which was great news, but it also meant they were going to have to bring their wedding plans forward by the best part of a year.

Tyler was terribly old fashioned about such things, and he really didn't want their child being born out of wedlock. For her part, Kelly didn't want her bump being too obvious on the big day, in case people jumped to the wrong conclusion and assumed they were only getting married because she had fallen pregnant. To keep both of them happy, the wedding would need to take place within the next three months, which was why they had agreed to sit down straight after breakfast to try and firm up a date.

A sharp, unwelcome trill shattered the blissful silence they were enjoying.

"Oh no," he groaned, knowing that the call was bound to herald bad news.

Beside him, Kelly stiffened, then swore under her breath.

"Bloody typical," she complained as he peeled his arm from around her shoulders and reached for the phone. "You promised you were going to make me breakfast in bed today, and that we were going to finalise a new date for the wedding. Doesn't look like either's going to happen now." As she spoke, she dragged herself into a sitting position, then grumpily kicked off the quilt and threw her legs over the side of the bed.

"It's not like I'm doing it on purpose," Tyler said, sounding hurt. He glanced at the caller ID and grimaced. "It's Susie."

With a weighty sigh, Kelly stood up. "No doubt, she'll be calling because we've taken a job," she predicted, miserably.

Tyler managed a half-hearted shrug. "Not necessarily. She might just need some advice."

"Yeah, in your dreams," Kelly scoffed on her way to the en suite.

Leaving the phone to ring, Tyler watched her go, unashamedly admiring the curves of her naked bottom. "Have I ever told you that you have the most perfectly shaped—"

"Yes, frequently," she said, closing the door behind her.

Tyler pressed the green button to accept the call. "What can I do for you, Susie?"

"*Jack, we've just had an unusual request for assistance from JC,*" she informed him in her soft Irish lilt. JC was the phonetic code for Chingford division, which covered the London Borough of Waltham Forest. "*They had two young boys called Peter Musgrove and Gavin Grant go missing late last night, and they think they might have been abducted.*"

From past experience, Tyler knew that most people who were reported missing reappeared of their own accord within a day or two, none the worse for the experience. "What makes them think the boys have been abducted, as opposed to just running off?"

"*They're only nine years old, and they both come from good families,*" Susie explained.

"Are either of them known to us?" Tyler asked, the inference being that, just because they came from good families didn't necessarily mean that *they* were good.

"*No,*" she said, emphatically. "*Neither kid is known to us or Social Services. From what I've been told, they're not remotely streetwise, and this is completely out of character for them.*"

Tyler sat up a little straighter. "When and where were they last seen, and what's the circumstances of their disappearance?"

"*Gavin's parents took the boys to a funfair in North Chingford last night. They got there at about 8.45 p.m. After going on a couple of rides together, they let the boys wander off on their own, having arranged to meet them forty-five minutes later. Unfortunately, the boys never showed up. When the parents started* asking around, one of the fairground workers remembered seeing two boys talking to a scruffy looking white bloke who was dressed in army fatigues. He said they chatted to him for a couple of minutes, then followed him into the trees."

That didn't sound good, Tyler had to admit, scrabbling for the notepad and pen he always kept by the bed. "If they were snatched last night, why am I only hearing about it now?"

He heard the toilet in the en suite flush, and a moment later Kelly appeared in the doorway. He beckoned for her to rejoin him on the bed, but she shook her head.

"Coffee?" she mouthed, throwing on a dressing gown.

Smiling appreciatively, he gave her a thumbs up.

"*That's the first thing I asked when the call came in,*" Susie admitted. "*The fact that a fairground worker had seen them following a stranger into the trees should have rung alarm bells, but for some reason, the Duty Officer – a chap called Inspector Fellows – only graded their disappearance as medium risk.*"

Tyler winced. "What the hell was he thinking?"

"*Apparently, his rationale was based on the fact that pre-pubescent children don't generally go missing in pairs, so he decided it was far more likely that they had gone off to meet someone than been abducted.*"

Tyler shook his head in dismay. "The man's obviously a fool."

"*I totally agree,*" Susie said, "*and I wouldn't want to be in his shoes if this goes pear shaped.*"

"For the sake of those two boys, let's hope it doesn't come to that," Tyler said, mentally crossing his fingers.

Three potential scenarios came to mind, each of which presented a distinctly different set of challenges. Tyler's gut told him to discount the first one, which was that an estranged parent was responsible. Surely, if that were the case, they would only have taken their own child, not both of them? "I take it that both sets of parents are still together, and that neither boy is adopted or subject to an ongoing custody battle?" he asked, just to make sure.

"*If you're wondering whether a former partner could be responsible, the answer is a resounding no,*" she confirmed, as if reading his mind.

Acknowledging this with a tetchy grunt, Tyler turned his thoughts to the second scenario, which was that the children had been taken to be ransomed, or with a view to blackmailing their parents into doing something against their will?

"Are either of the family's particularly wealthy?"

"*Not that I know of. Why?*"

Instead of answering, Tyler posed another question. "Do any of the parents hold sensitive posts – ones that require a security clearance, for instance – or do they wield any political or economic influence?"

"*According to the MisPer reports, the men have fairly mundane jobs: Grant's a deputy head teacher at a primary school, while Musgrove works as a manager in a local supermarket. Both women are stay at home mums. They're just normal working-class people like you and me.*"

That was a pity, because it only left the third scenario.

"Susie, as I see it, if the boys weren't grabbed by an estranged parent, and this isn't the work of an organised criminal network looking to blackmail the family, that only leaves sexual gratification as a motive."

"*That's my take on it, too,*" she admitted, glumly.

"Ask Chingford's Borough Intelligence Unit to check if there are any reports on the system relating to vagabond types who habitually dress in army fatigues."

"*I've already done that, Jack. There's nothing.*"

"Pity. What enquires have the locals made so far?"

"*There was a street search of the immediate area last night, but that drew a blank. Close family and friends have all been contacted, but they haven't heard from the kids. Local hospitals have been checked, but no-one matching either boy's description was admitted. The control room have reviewed the overnight call logs, but the only incidents reported at the fairground was a series of motor vehicle break-ins.*"

"Is there any possibility that the thefts were down to our missing boys?" Tyler asked. The inference being that they had deliberately made themselves scarce because they thought they were in trouble.

"*Sorry, Jack. I can see where you're coming from, but it just doesn't fit with the profile we're building of them.*"

"I had a feeling you would say that," he admitted, ruefully. "What about CCTV?"

"There's no CCTV coverage of the fairground, but the locals have requested all the footage from Station Road in North Chingford, which is the most likely direction the boys would have taken if they decamped on foot."

"Unless they followed a pervy nutter who thinks he's Rambo into the forest," Tyler pointed out, acerbically. "I don't suppose this Inspector Fellows character had the helicopter fly over the forest using its thermal imaging to search for them, did he?"

"*He did fuck all,*" Susie said, angrily.

"Do either of the kids have mobiles?"

"*Peter Musgrove's got one. The TIU sent his call data through to us a little while ago.*"

The Telephone Intelligence Unit was based at new Scotland Yard, and it acted as liaison between the Met and the various service providers.

"Give me a quick overview," Tyler instructed, pen poised.

"*Okay, so the first thing to tell you is that Peter's mobile is currently switched off. The TIU are monitoring it in live time and will notify us immediately if there's any activity. There were six incoming calls to it last night, the first two were from Gavin's dad and the last four were from Peter's mother. All went unanswered, but Mr Grant says it was extremely loud at the fairground, so he just assumed that Peter hadn't heard it ringing, which is entirely possible.*"

"I suppose," Tyler allowed. "What were the exact times of the calls?"

There was more page flicking as Susie checked her notes. "*The two from Gavin's dad were made at 21:45 and 21:48 respectively. Alison Musgrove's calls are timed at 22:03, 22:04, 22:15 and 22:18. During the first five calls, Peter's phone was cell sited by the mast covering the funfair. However, for the last one, it had moved to the adjacent mast. I've asked Reg about this, and he reckons the change of mast probably indicates that Peter's handset was on the move when it received the last call, but until he gets the full breakdown from the TIU, he can't rule out that the change occurred because the first mast was at full capacity, or had reduced signal strength, which automatically resulted in the call being bounced to the next nearest mast.*"

When a mobile device makes or receives a call, it completes an electronic handshake with a mast. This interaction identifies the general area the handset is in, but it doesn't give you its precise location. To complicate matters, while masts erected in densely populated areas handle lots of traffic, they generally have a relatively short radius. Conversely, masts erected in remote or rural areas generally handle significantly less traffic but cover wider geographical areas.

All masts are split into three distinct sectors, with each having its own antenna. These are erected at 120-degree intervals to ensure the best all-round coverage. Each 120-degree arc is called an azimuth. By plotting the azimuths on a call-by-call basis, it is sometimes possible to work out if the phone is moving, and if so, in what direction it is heading.

"Jack, I'm really worried about those kids," Susie confessed. "*Even if they weren't snatched, and I pray to God that they weren't, last night was bitterly cold, with temperatures falling well below zero, so they could easily have frozen to death if they didn't find shelter.*"

Tyler made a decision. "Susie, call the entire team in. Get them straight over to Chingford for a briefing. I'll be making my way there as soon as I've called George Holland to let him know there's a potential shit storm brewing."

Detective Chief Superintendent George Holland was Tyler's boss, the man in overall charge of the Homicide Command.

"*Is there anything I can be cracking on with while you're on your way in?*" she asked.

"Yes, there is. Get someone straight over to the local authority CCTV control room. If there are any cameras along Rangers Road, or Epping New Road between Rangers Road and Buckhurst Hill, I want the footage downloaded for a two hour period either side of the boys' last confirmed sighting."

He could hear her frantically scribbling away at the other end of the line as she wrote down his instructions.

"*What about allocating a FLO?*" Susie suggested. "*The locals have provided a temporary one, but do you want to appoint someone from the team now, or hang on and see what happens?*"

A good Family Liaison Officer was worth their weight in gold, and if Tyler was going to take control of the investigation, it made absolute sense to get his own people involved as quickly as possible.

"Yes, let's pull the trigger on that now. As there are two families, it should be a double deployment. We'll use Debbie and Kelly; they work well together. If you can inform Debs, I'll brief Kelly on the way in."

"*Anything else?*" Susie asked.

"I'm afraid so," Tyler apologised. "You'll need to ring the Chief Inspector at Information Room and organise the additional troops needed to conduct a fast time search of the forestland surrounding the fairground."

"*Don't you want to wait until Reg has double checked the cell site data, to confirm that the phone really was moving before instigating a search?*" Susie queried.

"No, definitely not," Tyler said, firmly. "Even if the handset was moving, it doesn't necessarily mean that the boys were moving with it. For all we know, Peter dropped it during the abduction, and someone found it on the floor as they were leaving the fairground."

"*I hadn't considered that,*" Susie admitted, sounding a little embarrassed.

"Regardless of what the cell site data shows, those poor kids could be lying in a ditch a few hundred yards from where they were last seen, so we need to start searching the area around the fairground as quickly as possible. We'll also need a couple of dog units and the helicopter, if it's available. If you encounter any resistance, throw George Holland's name into the mix. Say the request comes directly from him, that the matter is top priority, and that any lack of cooperation will be referred straight to the Assistant Commissioner. That should oil the wheels."

"*Are you sure the boss and the AC will be happy with me using their names like that?*" Susie asked, sounding highly dubious.

Tyler allowed himself a Machiavellian laugh. "I suspect they'll both be bloody ecstatic! Can you also speak to the Epping Forest Rangers. Their local knowledge could prove invaluable. Oh, and make sure to ask if they know of anyone dressed in camo gear who's been living rough in the forest."

"*Please tell me that's all,*" Susie pleaded.

"Just one last thing," Tyler said, guiltily. "Make sure Chingford's

Missing Persons Unit knows it's their responsibility to contact Interpol regarding the issuance of a statutory yellow notice, not ours."

The notice related to minors being taken out of the country without parental consent. Once a yellow notice was in force, their names would automatically be flagged at the border crossings in other countries, assuming they were travelling under their real identities.

Tyler didn't, for one moment, think the person who had taken the boys planned to transport them any great distance; just far enough to carry out whatever evil they intended before killing them.

The thought made him feel physically sick.

He finished the conversation by asking Susie if there was anything she wanted to add.

"*Yes*," she said, wearily. "*I wish that Tony Dillon was covering the early HAT shifts this week, not me.*"

# 9

A primal howl of anguish

Standing by the French doors in the kitchen, Alison Musgrove stared listlessly into the back garden while she waited for the kettle to boil. Through a gap in the patchy fog, she caught a brief glimpse of the greenhouse at the bottom, but then it was gone, swallowed up by the rolling mist.

She wasn't even remotely thirsty, but making a cup of tea had at least given her something to do while she waited for the Family Liaison Officer from Chingford police station to stop by and give them an update.

Moving on autopilot, Alison crossed to the counter and finished making the tea, then carried one of the mugs into the lounge, where Ciaron was watching Sky News. He had been glued to the TV set all morning, surfing the news channels in case a story suddenly broke regarding the discovery of two dead children.

She wordlessly handed him the mug and turned to go.

"Thank you," he said, with the faintest flicker of a sad smile.

Acknowledging him with a small nod, Alison left the room.

Closing the door behind her, she stood in the hall for a few moments with her back pressed firmly against the lounge door.

Her eyes drifted to the telephone on the sideboard. The bloody thing had barely stopped ringing all morning, with each new call cruelly raising her hopes before dashing them a few moments later when it transpired that, instead of bringing the joyous news that Peter had been found alive and well, it was just a concerned friend or relative, enquiring whether the boys had turned up yet.

The house, normally so full of life and happiness, seemed unbearably empty without Peter's infectious laughter resonating off the walls.

Looking up at the first-floor landing, Alison was reminded of the countless times she had scolded Peter for running up the stairs in his mucky shoes as soon as he arrived home from school. His failure to remove them had been a constant source of irritation to her, but it now seemed like such a trivial thing. If they ever got Peter back – *when* they got Peter back, she angrily corrected herself – she would give him her blessing to stomp up and down the blasted stairs in his muddy shoes all day long, if that made him happy.

She wiped away a tear, surprised that she had any left after the rivers she had cried over the past few hours.

Peter's disappearance had created a huge vacuum, sucking all the happiness from her life and replacing it with a cold void that could never be filled. She knew that Ciaron was suffering too, but he seemed to be coping with the situation far better than she was. She felt an irrational twinge of jealousy; how could he carry on so stoically when she was barely able to function?

Everywhere that Alison looked, there was something to remind her of her precious son; a favourite toy, a family photograph on the wall, the stack of *Harry Potter* books they were working their way through together, with her reading him a chapter or two every night at bedtime. Her eyes strayed to the muddy football boots still lying on the hall floor. Peter should have taken them out to the conservatory after Thursday night's football practice, but he hadn't; he had just left them there like he always did in the expectation that someone else would sort them out for him.

Alison was still wearing yesterday's clothing, only now they were all creased and crumpled from where she had slept in them. Not that she had done much actual sleeping. Fully clothed, she had lain on top of the bed, dozing on and off in a tortuous cycle that continued until seven a.m., when she had finally given up trying.

Everything that had happened since she'd dialled 999 the previous night seemed so absurdly surreal that it could have been a nightmarish dream.

Only it wasn't.

She relived the key moments in her mind…

Two police cars, their blue lights strobing brightly, arrived at the funfair within minutes of her making the call. A middle-aged officer with a kind face, his name was PC Mead, tried to calm her down while his three colleagues set about searching the funfair. Afterwards, PC Mead and a younger colleague drove them back to Tom's house in order for a formal missing persons' report to be taken.

Alison had called Ciaron from the back of Mead's patrol car, arranged for him to meet her there. He was agitated when he arrived, bombarding Alison with questions, then interrupting her every time she tried to answer. With Margo's help, she eventually calmed him down, but as soon as he walked into the kitchen and saw the two officers sitting across the table from Tom, nursing cups of tea and calmly taking notes, he kicked off again.

"Shouldn't you be out looking for our boys instead of making yourselves comfortable here?" he demanded, clenching his fists belligerently.

"Mr Musgrove," PC Mead responded in a measured tone. "I've already circulated the boys' descriptions, and I can promise you that, while we're sitting here getting the paperwork side of things sorted out, there are plenty of other officers scouring the area for Peter and Gavin."

Alison had found Mead's professionalism, and the way he effortlessly diffused Ciaron's anger, very reassuring.

After the police had taken their leave, Alison and Ciaron

decided to remain with Tom and Margo for a while. Unable to settle, the four of them spent a tense couple of hours pacing up and down, waiting for news that did not come. Finally, Tom rung the station to demand an update. It took the switchboard operator ages to track the Duty Officer down, but eventually Tom was put through to Inspector Fellows, who assured him that everything possible was being done to locate their boys. Fellows suggested that they try and get some rest, before ending the call with a solemn promise that someone would ring them straight away, regardless of how late it was, if there were any developments.

Maybe it was just her way of handling the shock, but Margo seemed to have completely detached herself from the grim reality of the situation, and she kept wandering around the kitchen telling them, "I'm sure they'll turn up soon."

Alison didn't share her optimism.

In the end, not knowing what else to do, Ciaron drove them home.

"We need to be here," he insisted as they stepped across the threshold. "In case Peter turns up during the night and can't get in."

They went to bed, but within an hour, Alison found herself standing in the doorway of Peter's room, staring at her son's belongings. All she could think about was the fact that her son was out there somewhere, all alone and utterly terrified. Sitting on his bed, she buried her head in her hands and cried until she could cry no more. Then, in an effort to distract herself, she began tidying the room up, putting everything away in its rightful place.

As was par for the course, Peter's room looked as though it had just been ransacked by messy burglars. The wardrobe doors had been left wide open; various items of clothing – some clean, some dirty – were strewn across the floor; his prized collection of Marvel comics, which she had spent ages sorting into neat little groups only the other day, was now scatted haphazardly across the little desk that stood beneath the window, so that copies of *The Incredible Hulk* were mixed in with issues of *The Amazing Spider-Man, The Avengers* and *The Fantastic Four.*

She found a pair of dirty football socks in the corner, scrunched into a ball.

God alone knew how long they had been there!

Any other time, seeing the state of his room would have instantly put her in a bad mood, but right then, she would have given anything to have him back home, making the house untidy.

Eventually, having run out of things to tidy up, she returned to bed.

Alison was up again at seven, feeling utterly exhausted. While going through the motions of cleaning her teeth, she heard scuttling noises coming from Peter's bedroom. Dropping her toothbrush into the sink, she sprinted across the landing like a woman possessed, manically calling out his name, thinking he had returned during the night.

Standing in the open doorway, a primal howl of anguish erupted from the deepest depths of her soul when she realised the noises had been caused by Peter's hamster running in its wheel.

Alerted by her hysterical shouting, Ciaron burst from their bedroom in a confused state of panic, only to find her in tatters.

Dropping to his knees, he cradled her in his arms.

Offering no resistance, Alison rested her head against his chest and allowed the tears to fall. "I t–thought I h–heard him," she stammered, her mouth foaming with toothpaste, her entire body wracked by gigantic sobs. "I was so s–sure it was h–him, but it wasn't."

There was nothing Ciaron could say, so he simply pulled her in tighter and begun gently rocking her, running his fingers through her long hair, the way she sometimes liked him to do when she was going to sleep.

"We'll get him back," he promised her, his voice choked with emotion.

She prayed that he was right…

The melodic sound of the chiming doorbell shook Alison from her painful reverie, dragging her back to the here and now.

Peering through the frosted glass at the diffused shape on the other side of the double glazing, Alison decided that the caller was female. That would be the Family Liaison Officer they were expecting, calling to give them an update.

Subconsciously crossing herself, she prayed that it would be good news.

Opening the door, Alison was surprised to find that the woman standing there wasn't a police officer at all. It was her mother, who was supposed to be enjoying some winter sun in Spain. Alison had rung her the previous night, needing to hear her voice, but they hadn't discussed the possibility of Marjorie flying back to the UK.

"Mum!" Alison exclaimed, wondering if the immense shock she felt was reflected on her face.

"Hello, darling," Marjorie said, softly. "I managed to get a seat on the first flight over from Murcia. Has Peter turned up yet?"

Alison shook her head. "Not yet," she said, the words catching in her throat.

For a moment, they stood there, just looking at each other, and then Alison's bottom lip started to quiver.

"Oh, Alison," Marjorie said, rushing forward to embrace her daughter.

Alison flung her arms around her mother's neck and clung on tightly as the floodgates opened again.

# 10

Spineless and Troublemaker

As Gabe's eyes blinked open, the tiny bedroom gradually came into focus. He studied the unfamiliar layout with a growing sense of unease. He was confused at first, but then he remembered where he was and, perhaps more importantly, how he had ended up there.

He was lying on a single bed in a little box room. There was a cheap pine wardrobe and matching chest of drawers on which an old Grundig fourteen inch portable TV sat, its screen covered in a thick layer of dust. The aerial had been snapped off, and someone had replaced it with a metal coat hanger.

The only other item of furniture was a free-standing dress mirror in the far corner, by the bottom of the bed. Its cracked glass surface was even dustier than the TV screen.

The mattress he had slept on was wafer thin. As Gabe shifted his weight, he felt the jagged springs digging painfully into his flesh. With a grimace, he shuffled backwards on his elbows, pushing himself into a sitting position.

"What a dump," he said, taking in the dated decor.

The peeling floral wallpaper was a woeful combination of pinks, greens and purples that looked as though it had been hung during the 1960s. The quilted bedspread was an earthy mixture of oranges, browns and avocado greens, and it clashed violently with the vibrant, if threadbare, paisley carpet.

If nothing else, the bedroom was warm, and accepting McQueen's offer to stay there for a few days had been infinitely preferable to dossing down in a shop doorway and freezing his knackers off, or trying to find a hostel that was willing to take in a homeless teenager without asking difficult questions.

After leaving the café in Soho, they had caught a number 38 bus from Shaftesbury Avenue to a place called Hackney in East London. McQueen had led him through darkened streets that oozed danger until they reached a nearby council estate. Going up to the second floor, the flat they had ended up at had thick iron grills fitted over its door and windows, and when Gabe crossed the threshold, he felt more like he was entering a prison than a refuge.

Gabe hadn't warmed to Joey McQueen; the man was cold and detached, with about as much charisma as a slug. He hadn't liked Benny either; the smelly old man had been far too friendly for his liking, and there was something seedy about him that had made Gabe's skin crawl. Gabe might be young, but he certainly wasn't stupid, and he knew his so-called benefactor had an ulterior motive for buying him a hot meal and offering him a place to lay his head down for a few nights.

The overly familiar way that Benny had pressed his leg into Gabe's the previous night had convinced him the old man was gay. No doubt, he was hoping to receive sexual favours in exchange for his kindness. That was never going to happen, but Gabe figured it was in his interest to string the old creep along, drip-feeding him false hope for as long as the freebies continued.

Gabe yawned, scratched his head vigorously, then repeated the exercise with his balls. Standing up, he arched his back and stretched his hands high over his head, interlinking his fingers and thrusting his hands backwards until the vertebrae between his shoulder blades clicked.

As he performed the movement, he caught a whiff of body odour. He hadn't showered for the best part of a week, and while the pong from his armpits wasn't terrible, he certainly didn't smell like a bed of roses.

Gabe winced when he caught sight of his reflection in the dirty mirror. He hadn't been eating well since he'd run away from home, but even so, he was shocked to see just how much weight he had lost. He ran a finger down his ribs, which protruded like the wooden bars of a xylophone. No wonder his clothes felt so baggy these days.

Still clad in the stained Y-Fronts and T-shirt he'd slept in, Gabe shuffled lethargically into the hallway. Pausing in the open doorway, he glanced up and down the corridor to get his bearings. The street door stood at one end, while the lounge and kitchen were located at the other. In between, there were three bedrooms – the single that he had been given, another single that was unoccupied, and a double that Joey had taken – along with a bathroom and a separate WC.

He could hear the muted sounds of a TV coming from behind the closed lounge door. The noise told him that McQueen was already up.

As he trudged towards the bathroom, the volume suddenly increased.

"You're up, then?" a voice enquired from behind.

Gabe turned to find McQueen leaning against the lounge door-frame, arms folded, a lopsided grin on his face. "After all the weed we smoked when we got here last night, I thought you might end up sleeping in till midday."

Gabe acknowledged him with a shy nod, feeling self-conscious standing there in nothing but his underwear. "Just going to take a shower, if that's alright?"

"Course it is," McQueen said. He pointed towards a door to the left of the bathroom. "You'll find some towels in the airing cupboard."

Gabe glanced at the door. "Thanks," he said, resisting the urge to cover his privates with his hands.

"Tell you what, get yourself showered and dressed, then I'll take you out for breakfast," McQueen offered. "Afterwards, I'll take you to meet a friend."

Gabe opened the cupboard door and removed a frayed blue towel that was only marginally fluffier than a sheet of cardboard. Holding it strategically across his body to conceal his genitals, he nodded his thanks and quickly disappeared into the bathroom, locking the door behind him.

---

Peter awoke with a start. His muscles tensed and his heart rate increased as adrenaline surged through his veins. As his vision cleared, he became aware of an ominous shape looming over him, its head surrounded by an eerie red halo.

It was him!

It was the soldier man.

With a cry of alarm, he shrank back, raising his arms to protect himself.

"It's okay, Pete," a familiar voice soothed. "It's just me."

"Gavin…?"

"Yes, mate. It's me."

Peter's eyes fearfully scanned the room. "Where's the soldier man?"

"He's gone," Gavin assured him. "There's just you and me in here." As he spoke, he reached out and took hold of Peter's wrists, gently pulling his arms down. "Oh, Pete! I'm so glad you're finally awake. When he threw you onto the bed, you weren't moving, and I really thought he'd killed you."

Peter forced himself to breathe slower, and as his heart rate came down, he found that he could think again. "How long have I been lying here?" he asked, wincing at a sharp pain in his jaw. On impulse, he gingerly probed his teeth with his tongue, and was relieved to find they were all still there.

"Not long," Gavin said. "A few minutes, I suppose."

Peter touched the side of his face, winced in pain. "It feels really swollen. I think I must have bashed it against the stairs."

"You do look a bit like a hamster," Gavin confirmed, with a goofy grin.

"I remember trying to escape," Peter began, then paused to marshal his thoughts. "I got as far as the top of the stairs, but then he caught me."

"I saw him chasing you as I came out of the toilet, and I prayed you'd get away," Gavin said. "I thought you had at first, but then he reappeared, dragging you by your ankles." His eyes misted over. "He was *so* rough with you. I begged him not to hurt you, but he just screamed at me to shut up. I wanted to help you Pete, honest I did, but he said he'd hit me if I interfered." The admission triggered tears of shame. "I know I should have been braver, but I was too scared… I'm so sorry, Pete, I let you down."

Peter squeezed his friend's arm. "It's okay," he said, trying to speak without moving his mouth too much. "You did your best."

Gavin shook his head. "No. I let you down. I should've—"

There was a loud clunking noise as the key turned in the lock, then the heavy door opened inward to reveal their captor standing there.

---

Tony Dillon glanced sideways at the beautiful woman sitting beside him. Returning her radiant smile, he decided that he was a very lucky man to have won the heart of a stunner like Imogen Askew. She had that rare mix of beauty, brains and personality, and they had clicked the moment they met.

They had only officially been an item for a couple of weeks, but things were going surprisingly well. Truth be told, their romance was moving much faster than he had anticipated, to the point where she had all but moved in with him.

Imogen was currently employed as a senior researcher for a well-known TV production company, a post she assured Dillon that was merely a stepping stone to greater things. She was ruthlessly ambitious, and had set herself a target of hosting her own TV show within two years. There was no doubt in Dillon's mind that she would make it happen, and he would be surprised if it took her that long.

Accompanied by a gentle, but extremely hairy giant of a cameraman she affectionately called Bear – Dillon was yet to discover his real name – Imogen had spent the past few months shadowing the various teams at Hertford House while filming a fly on the wall TV documentary series about the work of the Homicide Command.

Because he fancied her, Dillon had jumped at the chance to chaperone the pair when his team was called down to Regent's Canal a few weeks back, in order to investigate a dismembered torso that had been found floating in the water. It had been while working on that case that their romance had blossomed, and the intensity of his feelings for her had caught him completely off guard.

Even Tyler, who habitually distrusted anyone connected to the media, had started to warm to her, not that he would admit it. He was far too stubborn for that, but Kelly Flowers had told him so on the quiet.

"I'm surprised you wanted to come along today, what with it being a Sunday," he said as the car rocketed along the M11 towards London. "Especially as it's a missing person's enquiry, not a murder."

Imogen beamed at him, exposing a set of teeth that were so perfect they could have been used to advertise dental hygiene products. "It's a good opportunity to see another strand of the work you guys do," she said, enthusiastically. "Besides, people love a tearjerker story about missing kids." The smile vanished abruptly as she added, "Well, they do as long as it has a happy ending."

"What about Bear?" Dillon asked. "Is he coming, too?"

Imogen nodded. "I rang him just before we left. He was at Hertford House, filming some exterior shots of the building while it's quiet. He's going to cadge a lift over to Chingford from one of the team."

Dillon glanced sideways in surprise. "Why is he working on a Sunday, and not at home with his family?"

Imogen's face took on a wistful look. "Bear isn't married, doesn't have a partner, and doesn't have much of a social life, either. I think he still lives with his elderly parents down by the coast when we're not filming. When we're away on assignments, he tends to throw himself completely into his work."

Dillon's face softened. "Poor sod, He must lead a very lonely existence. If I'd known, I would have invited him to come out with the team for a drink."

She leaned over and patted his arm. "That's very sweet, but I doubt he would have accepted. Between you and me, he's not very comfortable around other people."

Dillon frowned. "He must have hobbies or interests to keep him occupied. Surely, he doesn't just sit in his room on his own and watch TV?"

Imogen thought about that for a moment. "His big love is genealogy. He's always researching his family tree. He sometimes does it for other people too, for a small fee."

"Sounds interesting," Dillon said, although in truth, he thought it was anything but.

They continued in silence for a while, with Imogen applying her makeup and him thinking about the callout. It would either turn out be a storm in a teacup, in which case it would resolve itself pretty quickly, or would evolve into a horror story.

He really hoped it would be the former.

Imogen had become very good at reading his moods. "You're unusually quiet," she observed as they left the motorway and merged onto the A406 towards Barking.

"Am I?" He flashed her a guilty smile. "Sorry. I was just mulling over what Susie told me when she called."

Imogen was studying him intently. "You think they've been abducted, don't you?"

Had he just detected a note of excitement in her voice as the reporter in her caught its first scent of a story? Dillon hesitated a moment, then nodded. "I do. I don't know why, but I don't think we're going to find these kids alive."

---

Remus glowered at the terrified chickens huddled on the cot to the right of the door. The little shit who had tried to do a runner was awake again, which was a big relief. With the benefit of hindsight, he regretted having been so heavy handed with the boy. Under the weak red glow, Remus could see that one side of his face was now a swollen mass of purple bruising; he looked more like Quasimodo than the picturesque angel Remus had snatched.

"Get back to your own bed," he ordered the bigger boy, who instantly complied, looking down at the floor to avoid eye contact. Unlike his spineless friend, the trouble maker stared at Remus with a curious mixture of defiance and hatred. "What are you gawking at?" Remus demanded.

Meeting his gaze, Troublemaker raised a hand to his injured face. "I'm staring at you, you big, mean bully," he had the audacity to say.

Feeling an irrational need to assert his dominance, Remus stepped forward, raising a hand to lash out at him. "You need to learn some manners," he snarled.

"Leave him alone," Spineless shouted, his voice tremulous with fear.

Remus whirled on him. "Maybe I'll beat some respect into you while I'm at it."

Crabbing backwards on all fours, Spineless collided with the cell wall. As he sat there whimpering in fear, a dark stain appeared in the crotch of his trousers.

That was all Remus needed.

With a savage curse, he aimed a wild kick at the disgusting boy's stomach, but Spineless scuttled sideways, avoiding it.

Remus drew his leg back for a second attempt, but before he could let fly, Troublemaker launched himself at him, pulling him back by his belt.

"Get off me," Remus yelled, reaching behind to dislodge the brat.

"Leave my friend alone!" Troublemaker yelled, tugging furiously at his belt.

Remus spun around, using the momentum to send the feisty chicken sprawling onto his cot.

"Stay there," Remus shouted, pointing a warning finger at him. Then he turned to Spineless. "You. Come with me to the toilet. You need to take those piss covered trousers off and clean yourself up."

This time, Remus locked Troublemaker in his cell.

It took ten minutes to clean Spineless up and find him something else to wear.

After returning the first boy to the cell, Remus frogmarched Troublemaker to the loo, so that he could relieve himself. While they were there, Remus examined his facial injuries under the light, checking that the boy's pupil dilation was even, and that there were no broken bones. Thankfully, apart from the motley collection of bruises, the little shit appeared to be in fine fettle.

Afterwards, Remus gave them each a fresh bowl of porridge and a cup of hot, sweet tea. They wolfed the food and drink down without question.

Remus watched on, smiling encouragingly.

The drugs would kick in soon, and they would sleep for hours, allowing him to go back to bed and rest for a while.

"I'll be back with some more food in a few hours," he said as he closed the door on the way out.

"I want to go home," Spineless whined. "Please let me go home."

Remus paused in the doorway. "Maybe later," he said, then locked the door behind him and turned off the light.

# 11

We are keeping an open mind

Melanie Howarth, the duty DI at Chingford, was a well-organised woman in her early thirties. She had an oval face surrounded by a bob of brown hair that fell halfway between her jawline and shoulders. The two-piece charcoal business suit she wore accentuated her athletic build, and as she led Tyler back to her office, he thought she moved with the style and grace of a dancer.

"With it being a Sunday, we're running on minimum strength, but I cobbled together all the spare uniforms I could find and supplemented them with a few officers from early turn CID," she informed him. "They've been ground assigned since nine o'clock this morning, with one half searching the stretch of forest abutting the fairground, and the other half making door-to-door enquiries in nearby streets. I've got an experienced skipper in charge of each group, but, so far, their combined efforts have yielded diddly squat."

Tyler caught sight of Susie Sergeant striding purposefully

towards them. He excused himself from Howarth and moved forward to intercept her.

As was her custom when she was working, Susie wore her strawberry blonde hair – woe betide anyone who dared to suggest it was ginger – in a plaited ponytail. Like Howarth, she was dressed in a business suit, navy blue in her case, and a plain white blouse. Susie had recently separated from her husband, and she had been hitting the gym hard ever since. Her figure, shapely to begin with, was now leaner and harder than ever, and she drew admiring glances from several of the male officers she passed. If she was aware of their interest, she gave no indication of it.

Susie acknowledged Tyler with a taut smile, and he could tell that she had important news to impart.

"I've taken the liberty of calling out an E-fit artist," she said by way of greeting. "He's going to sit down with the fairground worker who saw the boys talking to the suspect later today."

Tyler nodded his approval. It was a smart move.

"And I've just received an update from Reg regarding the telephone data analysis," she continued. "He's convinced that Peter's handset was moving along Epping New Road during the last call it received."

"Apart from us, who else is here so far?" Tyler asked.

"I've sent Dick Jarvis out to seize any CCTV footage he can find. That leaves Steve Bull, Gurjit Singh, Debbie Brown and Charlie White. I've tasked Steve with finding a room that's big enough to brief everyone, and I've told the others to grab a coffee in the canteen and await further instructions."

"That's where I've sent Kelly," Tyler said, thinking that great minds thought alike. "What about the aid order I asked you to sort out?"

Susie expelled a laboured breath from the side of her mouth. "I bullied the Chief Inspector at IR into sending out an aid request to all surrounding stations, and I've drafted in a very experienced PolSA called Jim Breslow to coordinate the search."

A PolSA was a police search advisor, normally an officer of

inspector rank, who had undergone specialist training at the Police National Search Centre.

"In addition, we've got two dog units running to us from their base in Claygate, and the Air Support Unit is going to make one of the helicopters available from midday onwards, which will just about give me enough time to brief everyone."

Tyler was impressed. "What about maps?" The search was going to be a Herculean task, and he didn't want it being impeded because officers on the ground didn't have all the information they needed.

"I've taken care of that," Susie assured him. "We've got ordnance survey maps covering a one-mile radius around the fairground. These include all the little windy roads running through that particular section of forest, along with the various parking areas, cycle paths and bridleways."

"Excellent," Tyler said, impressed by how much she had achieved in such a short time.

Susie flashed him a harried smile. "I've also managed to blag some help from my new found buddies at the Rangers station." She glanced down at her wristwatch. "They should be arriving within the next half hour."

Tyler motioned for Howarth to come over and join them. "Susie, I take it you've already met DI Mel Howarth?"

Susie acknowledged Howarth with a warm smile. "Mel's been very helpful since I arrived."

"Actually, we were on the same inspector's promotion course a few weeks ago, weren't we, Susie?" Howarth added as an aside.

"We were," Susie confirmed. "Poor girl had to put up with me whinging about my ex-husband for three whole weeks."

"Okay, down to business," Tyler said, when they were all sitting comfortably in Howarth's cramped office. "If Reg is happy that Peter Musgrove's phone was moving during the last call it received, that gives us a pretty good idea of when the kids were snatched. If it turned right when it reached the Epping New Road, I'm going to work on the assumption it was heading for the Waterworks roundabout in Walthamstow."

"Why?" Susie asked.

"Because, from there, the suspect would have had easy access to the M11, M25, the A406 and Lea Bridge Road, which would have taken him through Hackney into Central London."

"That's assuming he didn't turn off or stop beforehand," Howarth cautioned.

"For argument's sake, let's assume that he didn't," Tyler said, brusquely. "Susie, ask the Intel Cell to check if there are ANPR cameras between Rangers Road and The Waterworks. If there are, I'll want the details of every London bound vehicle – excluding motorbikes, black cabs and buses – that drove past them during the two hours following the abduction. I'll also want Dick to grab the CCTV from any cameras along the route, same time parameters."

Howarth winced. "Sir, that's going to involve an awful lot of work."

"It is," Tyler agreed, "but don't you think the lives of two children are worth the effort?"

Howarth's face coloured. "Yes, sir. Of course," she said, clearly flustered by the rebuke. "I just meant that it—"

"Let's crack on," Tyler said, cutting her off. "Susie, can I rely on you to make sure the PolSA inspector has all the resources he'll need to manage the search effectively?"

She nodded.

"Good. When Dill arrives, I'll get him to coordinate all the witness and suspect enquiries. I'll also need someone to contact the Public Protection Unit and compile a comprehensive list of every registered sex offender residing in the borough. They'll all need to be visited, so we can establish their whereabouts and movements for last night. Any suggestions?"

"Sounds like a job for Charlie White," she told him.

"Yes, it does," he agreed, making a quick note to that effect in his daybook. "Mel, did the borough FLO manage to get hold of any recent photographs of the two boys, ones that both families are happy to be used for publicity purposes?"

Howarth hurriedly reached into the manila folder resting on her lap, removed two six by four colour photos, and slid them across the desk towards Tyler. "These were taken in September, at the start of the new school year, so the likenesses are excellent. I've had copies made for inclusion in the briefing packs, and for release to the media, should that become necessary."

Tyler grimaced. "Trust me, if those boys aren't found within the next couple of hours, we'll have the media descending on North Chingford in all its glory."

The telephone on Howarth's desk chirped into life. Murmuring an apology, she leaned across Susie and picked up the receiver. "I'd better take this in case it's connected to the case," she said, covering the mouthpiece.

Leaving her to field the call, Tyler, studied each of the photographs carefully, committing the two young faces to memory. The boys were wearing freshly pressed school uniforms; each one sitting on the same hard backed chair in front of the same bland backdrop; each one smiling dutifully into the lens for the photographer.

Peter was small, slim, fragile looking, with mischievous blue eyes, a mop of blonde hair, and a cheeky grin that suggested he was a bit of a prankster. Gavin, on the other hand, was much bigger, perhaps a little on the chubby side, with dark hair and a studious face. There was an air of insecurity about him that made Tyler wonder if the boy suffered from confidence issues.

He hoped they were okay. His mood darkened as he reluctantly acknowledged the grim reality that they were probably both already dead. With an effort, he forced himself to stop thinking about the unspeakable terrors they might have been subjected to.

"Sir...?"

Realising that someone had just spoken to him, Tyler dragged his thoughts back to the present. "Sorry," he said, with a sheepish grin. "I was miles away. Did someone say something?"

"That was the Station Officer," Howarth said, her face grim. "There's a reporter from *The London Echo* at the front desk, and he wants to speak to the officer in charge of the search for the missing boys."

Tyler squeezed the bridge of his nose, feeling a headache

coming on. "Well, until we've formally completed the handover, Mel, I'm afraid that's you."

---

They had eaten breakfast in a nearby café. It was a small out of the way place run by a fat, middle-aged Sicilian with a swarthy face and a surly disposition. The place wasn't flashy; far from it, but it was obviously popular, and surprisingly busy for a Sunday morning.

Leaning back in his chair, Gabe massaged his stomach, which was full to bursting after a full English and two cups of velvety smooth coffee.

"Do you want anything else?" McQueen asked, eyeing him speculatively. Unlike Gabe, he had only picked at his food, and half of it still lay untouched on his plate.

Gabe belched contentedly, then shook his head. "Nah, I'm stuffed. Aren't you going to finish that?" he enquired, nodding at the food now going cold in front of McQueen.

McQueen pushed the plate away. "I never have much of an appetite before lunchtime."

After the toasty warmth of the cafe, the cold air came as an unpleasant shock as they stepped outside, and Gabe pulled his collar around his neck to fend off the biting wind.

"If you're going to be staying with us for a while, I suppose we should sort you out a proper coat," McQueen said, zipping up his parka.

Gabe nodded, noncommittally. He didn't plan to stay with them for a second longer than was absolutely necessary. "What's the plan for today, then?" he asked, eager to change the subject. "You said you were going to introduce me to someone, but I was hoping we could go to the West End again. There's more to do and see up there."

He didn't like Hackney; it was full of dodgy looking characters who skulked around on street corners, watching passers-by with dead eyes, weighing up whether to mug them or sell them drugs.

"There's not much to see around here," McQueen admitted.

"We'll get a bus back up West in a while. We can visit the arcades again if you want. First though, I want to take you to see a photographer friend of ours. He's always on the lookout for new talent, and you're not a bad looking boy so he might be able to use you. Ever fancied being a model? There's good money to be made from it."

Gabe threw back his head and laughed. "Me? A model! You've got to be kidding!"

"I'm serious," McQueen insisted. "If I had your looks, I'd be well up for it."

Gabe studied him as they continued along Mare Street. "What exactly would I have to do?" he asked, intrigued by the proposition.

McQueen gave him a non-committal shrug. "Not a lot," he said. "All you'd have to do is prance around the studio modelling swimwear for the catalogues." He demonstrated his idea of what a modelling routine should look like by striking several exaggerated poses in quick succession, flashing Gabe a series of increasingly cheesy smiles that exposed badly neglected teeth.

Gabe laughed. "Stop it you wanker, people are looking at you."

McQueen glanced around self-consciously, and was relieved to find that Gabe was only pulling his leg. "Very funny," he said, suffering a sense of humour failure.

Although Gabe was dubious about McQueen's modelling suggestion, the idea of earning a few quid for doing very little was very appealing. If he could generate an income of his own, even a small one, it would make him less dependent on Benny Mars and Joey McQueen, and that had to be a good thing.

"And you reckon there's easy money to be made in this modelling malarky, do you?" he enquired, guardedly.

McQueen responded with a truculent shrug. "There is, but there's no point in getting ahead of ourselves. We'll have to see if your face fits first."

Greeting the reporter with a polite smile, Mel Howarth gestured for him to precede her into a small waiting room adjacent to the front office.

He was much older than she had expected, early fifties at a guess, and grizzled with it. A brown Fedora was perched at a jaunty angle atop his large head, and an unruly mess of salt and pepper hair was protruding from the sides. His bloodshot eyes had waxy deposits, and the venous nose and ruddy complexion suggested he was a heavy drinker. As he pushed open the door, she saw that his stubby fingers were nicotine stained, and the nails were bitten down to the quick.

Howarth, who ate healthily and exercised often, thought he looked like a heart attack waiting to happen.

"Good morning," she said, offering her hand. I'm DI Howarth."

The reporter took it, gave it a perfunctory shake and released it. "Ambrose Wilson," he said, gruffly. "Crime correspondent for *The London Echo*."

He sounded like a South London boy, and she pegged him as a working-class lad who had clawed his way up from humble beginnings in the print room.

A wooden table, its top defaced by etchings and graffiti, was bolted to the wall, and there were two hard backed plastic chairs on either side of it.

"How can I help you?" she enquired, indicating for him to take a seat.

Wilson was impatient to get on with the interview. "I'll stand, if it's all the same to you."

Howarth responded with a shrug of indifference.

Taking out a dog-eared notebook and pen, Wilson whipped his tongue over his lips in anticipation. "What can you tell me about the two missing boys?"

"Not a lot I can tell you right now," she said, keeping her tone matter of fact. "Last night, two nine year old boys went missing from a fairground in North Chingford. Because of their age, and the freezing cold temperatures currently prevailing, we are treating this as a high-risk missing persons enquiry."

Wilson affected a bored look. "Yes, yes, I get all that, but what's really going on? Do you suspect foul play?"

Howarth was momentarily taken aback by his pushy demeanour. "As I'm sure you can appreciate, this is a fluid, fast moving situation, and it wouldn't be appropriate for me to say anything more until things becomes clearer."

"Come on," he cajoled, trying to charm a morsel or two out of her. "Surely, you can give me *something* to keep my editor at bay?"

Howarth kept her tone neutral. "I'm not going to be drawn into speculating over why they went missing at this stage."

"So, you're not dismissing the possibility that they were abducted?" Wilson pushed, trying to back her into a corner.

Howarth took a deep breath, buying a couple of seconds to compose herself before replying. "We have no specific information to suggest that is the case—" apart from the worrying account from the fairground worker who had seen them following a stranger into the woods "—but we are keeping an open mind, considering all possible scenarios, and vigorously pursuing a number of lines of enquiry."

Wilson sneered at her over the top of his notebook. "Is it right that a massive search operation is about to get underway?"

Howarth was sorely tempted to ask him how he knew about this, but she knew there was no point; he would never reveal his sources, and she didn't want to give him the satisfaction of appearing rattled.

"That's correct," she confirmed, primly. "Our main priority is to locate the missing children as quickly as possible and ensure that they are reunited with their families."

"So, you think they're still alive, then?" Wilson's sceptical tone implied that he didn't.

"Do you have reason to believe otherwise?"

"No, of course not," Wilson said quickly, "but I'm sure you'll agree it's extremely unusual for two young children to go missing at the same time. As I understand it, neither boy was particularly streetwise, so it's highly unlikely that they've run away, in which case abduction seems like the most logical explanation, don't you think?"

Howard did think so, but she was damned if she was going to admit that to him.

"If there's nothing else," she said, glancing at her watch to make the point that she was pressed for time.

"One last question," Wilson said as she turned to leave. "I noticed officers were carrying out door to door enquiries in the road where Gavin Grant's family reside this morning, but not in the street where Peter Musgrove lives. Does this mean you think one of Gavin's neighbours could be responsible?"

Howarth paused by the door, angered by the man's temerity. "No," she said, not bothering to hide her distaste. "It means nothing of the sort."

# 12

Smile into the camera

The buzzer sounded, and the latch popped open a moment later.

"After you," McQueen said, gesturing for Gabe to go on ahead of him.

Ascending the photographic studio's dimly lit stairway, they found Maurice Hinkleman waiting for them at the top. Shoulders stooped, Adam's apple protruding from a scrawny neck, he could have been a vulture sitting on a branch, patiently waiting for a wounded animal below to die.

The photographer was in his late-sixties, with a horseshoe of straggly grey hair surrounding a bald, liver spotted pate. Despite his advanced years, the watery green eyes on either side of his big beaklike nose were cold and calculating, and there was a horrible looking skin tag on his lower left eyelid that bobbed up and down every time he blinked.

When McQueen introduced them, he welcomed Gabe with a smile that was as false as the dentures it revealed.

The formalities over, Hinkleman invited them into his office for a friendly chat. He was a chain smoker, and the ashtray on his desk was overflowing with the detritus of fag butts and ash deposits.

Wheeling the upholstered swivel chair out from behind his large rectangular desk, Hinkleman gingerly lowered himself into it, wincing as both knee joints cracked loudly, one after the other. Leaning forward, he placed the padded elbows of his thick woollen cardigan on the walnut veneered top and brought his steepled fingers together with exaggerated slowness. Resting his narrow chin on them, the ageing photographer sat there in silence, studying Gabe through dark protuberant eyes.

For his part, Gabe stared back with complete indifference, thinking that the old man looked like a poor man's version of *Mr Burns* from *The Simpsons*.

Apart from the desk, the only other items of furniture were a couple of dusty filing cabinets in a small recess, and three moulded plastic chairs by the back wall. Gabe glanced longingly at them, wondering if Hinkleman was going to invite them to sit.

The lacquered wood panelling was lined with photo frames, each containing the smiling face of a young boy. Gabe assumed these were publicity shots showcasing Hinkleman's best performing clients. He ran his eyes over them, hoping to spot someone he recognised from the telly, but none of the glossy faces were remotely familiar.

"Have you got any modelling experience?" Hinkleman asked. He spoke with a North London Jewish accent that was best described as working-class Cockney with strong Yiddish influences.

Gabe shook his head, gave the man an insouciant shrug. "No, but how hard can it be? All you've got to do is smile into the camera and say, cheese!"

There was a twinkle of amusement in the old man's eyes as he glanced sideways at McQueen, who had taken up station beside him. "He's not short of confidence, I'll give him that," he observed, begrudgingly.

"The kid could probably do a half-decent job if he applied

himself," McQueen opined, sounding as if he didn't really care one way or the other.

Hinkleman studied Gabe with professional curiosity. "You have nice hair and good bone structure," he allowed, stroking his stubbly chin thoughtfully. "Smile for me."

"Do what?" Gabe asked, wondering if he had misheard.

"Smile," Hinkleman barked, snapping his fingers impatiently.

Gabe forced a saccharine grin onto his face.

Hinkleman shook his head. "No, no, no! That won't do at all. Make it look natural, not like you're having trouble taking a shit."

Gabe laughed at the vulgarity.

"That's better," Hinkleman said, nodding approvingly. "Yes, a very nice smile. Good teeth, too. White and even, not like some of the applicants I see. You could do with putting on a few pounds, though. You're a little too thin for my liking. Tell Benny he needs to feed him up." The last was addressed to McQueen, who nodded dutifully.

"Tell you what," Hinkleman said, standing up. "Why don't I show you around the studio, and then we can take a few sample shots to see if the camera likes you."

---

The canteen at Chingford police station had been requisitioned for the briefing, seeing as it was the only place big enough to accommodate all the officers who had been drafted in at such short notice. Those who hadn't been fortunate enough to grab seats were either perched on the edges of tables or slouching against the walls.

Tyler carried out a quick head count. There were fourteen sergeants and eighty-four constables, plus two dog handlers and three Epping Forest Rangers.

According to the Met Office, sunset was due to occur at 16:27 hours, so it was imperative they get everyone briefed and ground assigned as quickly as possible. With this in mind, Tyler clapped his hands and called for quiet.

The deafening buzz of fifty separate conversations quickly died out. There was an air of tense expectation; two young children were missing, and everyone was keen to do their bit to help find them.

Much to Tyler's annoyance, Imogen Askew was sitting front and centre, notebook ready, pen poised. Her hairy cameraman was standing off to one side, peering through the viewfinder of his video camera. The red light was on, which meant that he was already filming.

"Thank you all for coming at such short notice," Tyler began, letting his eyes sweep the packed room. The late comers were spilling into the corridor outside.

"Can you hear me at the back?" he yelled, cupping his hands to his mouth.

"Strength R5, sir," someone shouted, using the standard radio operator's response to denote that they were receiving a clear, strong signal.

Tyler gave the man a thumbs up.

"As you will all have heard by now, two nine year old boys went missing from the funfair in Rangers Road last night. Their names are Peter Musgrove and Gavin Grant. They were last seen following a white male dressed in army fatigues towards one of the car parks. That was at about nine-forty p.m." He paused a moment for effect, then added, "They haven't been seen or heard from since."

He held his hands up to silence the sporadic rumbles of concern that were breaking out. "We're working on the hypothesis that they've been abducted, but even if that's not the case, temperatures dropped well below freezing last night. If the boys wandered off and got lost in the forest, they could be holed up right now, suffering from hypothermia or frostbite and in desperate need of medical attention."

The sombre faces staring back at him mirrored his own concerns.

"The briefing packs your supervisors have been given contain recent photographs of both boys, along with a detailed description of the clothing they were wearing at the time of their disappearance. There's also a description of the IC1 male in army camouflage gear. An E-Fit is being prepared of him, and this will be distributed as soon as it becomes available. DI Sergeant and Inspector Breslow—" he gestured for them to stand up and make themselves known "—will be coordinating the search, and any enquiries you have during the deployment should be directed straight to them. You'll find their contact numbers in your briefing packs."

Realising the two inspectors were still standing, he waved for them to sit down again.

"Now, I know this isn't going to be an easy task. You're going to be searching uneven terrain and dense woodland, and you're going to be out there in the biting cold for a long time, so make sure you wrap up warm."

He looked out of the window and was disheartened to see that it was still pretty foggy. That would hamper the searchers, but hopefully, the mist would be lighter inside the forest.

A hand in the front row went up, catching his eye.

"Yes?" Tyler asked the young constable it belonged to.

"Sir, we haven't got many hours of daylight ahead of us, and I'm guessing there's no way we'll be finished by then. What's the plan for when it gets dark?"

"We're trying to source as many Dragon Lights as we can possibly get our hands on, and these will be distributed as and when they arrive," Tyler assured him. "In the meantime, you'll have to make do with your standard issue torches. Once it gets dark, India 98 will be using its thermal imaging equipment, and the crew will direct ground units to any heat sources they detect. In addition, if you need a particular area lit up, get straight on the radio to them, and they'll assist you with their Nightsun."

The Nightsun is a 1600-watt Xenon Arc Lamp high intensity search light attached to the underside of the helicopter, and it is powerful enough to light up a football pitch.

"We have three Epping Forest Rangers working with us today," Tyler continued, beckoning for them to stand up. "Please make full use of their knowledge and expertise, and don't be afraid to pick their brains."

"Do they know any good tea stops?" a voice called out from the centre of the room, sparking a ripple of laughter.

"One or two," the oldest of the three rangers replied with a wry grin, "but we won't be sharing them with you lot."

"Best we call out Teapot One, then," someone else chipped in.

That was the unofficial name for the Met's mobile catering unit.

Tyler held a finger to his lips to discourage any further banter.

"Before I hand over to DI Sergeant and Inspector Breslow to talk you through the search parameters, I want to make an impassioned plea. Those two children and their distraught families are relying on *you* to reunite them, so please don't allow yourselves to become disillusioned when your teeth start chattering from the cold and you find yourself desperate for a pee; please don't lose focus or allow your minds to wander when you start to get tired, as you inevitably will; please don't let your enthusiasm drop when your feet start aching and your hands and faces get scratched. Time is our enemy; the longer Peter and Gavin remain missing, the less likely they are to turn up alive. Remember, those two defenceless boys are depending on *you* to bring them home. Don't let them down."

Stepping aside to let Susie take centre stage, he was conscious that the energy inside the room had changed subtly, become more charged, as the enormous responsibility he had just placed on their collective shoulders sunk in.

---

Gabe emerged from the changing room wearing nothing but a tight-fitting pair of swimming trunks. They were uncomfortably tight and kept riding up into the crack of his backside.

"I feel like a right prat in these budgie smugglers," he complained to McQueen, reaching into the trunks to rearrange his dangly bits.

"Nonsense," Hinkleman said from the other side of the studio, where he was busy waving a light meter around, taking readings. "They are very becoming."

"You wear them, then," Gabe retorted, sulkily.

That earned him a withering look from the old man, but he didn't care. He was uncomfortable, and he felt stupid.

The high ceilinged studio was approximately thirty feet long by ten feet wide. There were two portable electric heaters on the go, and between them and the heat being generated by the lights, the photographic studio felt like a sweat box.

As Hinkleman arranged the lighting, he boasted about the equipment he had at his disposal. There were backlights, split lights, broad lights, and flat lights.

"You won't find a better set up anywhere," he enthused.

From a selection of roll down backdrops, Hinkleman chose one that depicted a sunny day at the beach. Walking over to a large wooden prop box in the corner, he pulled out a brightly coloured beach ball, a fluffy white towel, and a bucket and spade. "Take these," he told Gabe, holding them out one after the other.

Wondering what he had allowed himself to be talked into, Gabe did as he was told.

"Now, stand here," Hinkleman ordered, pointing to a spot on the floor. "I'm going to be taking portrait shots of you to start with, so I want there to be more space in front of you than behind."

Once he had Gabe standing exactly where he wanted him, he started waving the light meter around again, sticking it right under the boy's nose, then holding it above his head. Tutting to himself, he rushed back and forth between his bewildered model and the lighting rigs, adjusting them slightly each time and then returning to take another reading. When he was finally satisfied, he retreated to his tripod mounted camera, which he told Gabe was a Hasselblad, emphasising the brand name as though it should impress the boy.

"How long is this going to take?" Gabe demanded, petulantly. McQueen had promised to take him back to the arcades in Piccadilly as soon as they were finished, and he was eager to get going. "I'm cooking under these lights, and I'm getting thirsty."

Gabe had already decided that modelling wasn't for him; it was a lot harder than McQueen had led him to believe, and he would have to be willing to make himself look like a right prat every time he posed before the camera.

Hinkleman looked up from the viewfinder, frowned disapprovingly at the interruption, then sighed. "Joey, can you be a dear and fetch us all some squash? And maybe it would help everyone to relax a little if you rolled us a joint. You know where I keep my stash. It's on top of the cash box in the bottom drawer of my desk."

Ten minutes later, the studio was full of thick Marijuana smoke, and all three were giggling. Gabe no longer felt awkward or uncomfortable in his budgie smugglers, and he was sitting on a stool Hinkleman had provided, legs akimbo, drinking his second glass of blackcurrant juice laced with vodka.

"I would never have pegged you as someone who liked a bit of puff," he told Hinkleman, before taking a long toke on the reefer and passing it sideways to McQueen.

"You'd be surprised what I like," Hinkleman replied, treating the boy to a cryptic smile.

Snorting with laughter, McQueen blew little smoke trails out of his nostrils.

"You look like a baby dragon when you do that," Gabe sniggered.

Hinkleman handed Gabe a bottle of baby oil. "Here, rub some of this into your skin. It will make you look better."

Gabe accepted the bottle and tipped some of the clear liquid into his hand. "Really? How will it do that?" Despite his scepticism, he began rubbing it into his chest and shoulders.

"All the best models do this," Hinkleman assured him. "It gives their skin a healthy sheen."

"If you say so," Gabe said, rubbing away.

"Right, let's get back to business," Hinkleman said, returning to the camera.

Gabe took a final drag of the reefer, then walked over to the backdrop, rearranging his swimming trunks as he went.

Hinkleman directed him to pose holding the beachball in front of him, then came over for a final light meter reading. "You've missed a few spots with the oil," he tutted, putting the light meter into his pocket.

"Where?" Gabe asked, looking down at his torso in surprise.

"Stay still," Hinkleman ordered. "Now that you're in position, I don't want you moving unnecessarily. I'll attend to it for you."

Before Gabe could protest, he started rubbing the boy's shoulders with both hands.

"This won't do at all, it's all uneven," Hinkleman complained. With another tut, he reached for the baby oil and poured a liberal portion into his palm. "Stay still," he snapped when Gabe stiffened.

He began running his hands up and down Gabe's back and sides, then let them wander around to his chest and stomach. While he did this, McQueen walked over and slipped the cannabis joint into Gabe's mouth, holding it there for him while the boy took a long drag.

Mellowed by the effects of the cannabis, Gabe began to giggle. "Hey, that tickles," he slurred, as Hinkleman started rubbing away at his legs.

Hinkleman smiled up at him. "The things we have to do for our art," he said with a leer.

---

An hour later, when the shoot was over and Gabe was taking a quick shower to rinse the baby oil off, Hinkleman and McQueen adjourned to the photographer's office.

"Where did you find this one?" Hinkleman asked, closing the door behind him.

"He came into Victoria last night," McQueen informed him. "I followed him off to the arcades and picked him up there."

Hinkleman grunted. "I don't think he's gay," he said, sitting down behind his desk and opening the bottom drawer, from which he removed a bottle of brandy and two small glasses.

McQueen responded with a surly shrug of indifference. "Doesn't matter," he said. "We've recruited plenty of straight boys over the years. Once we've got a hold over them, they'll suck cock as well as any homo."

It was true. While many rent boys were gay, plenty of straight chickens turned to prostitution in order to fund their drug habits, pay off massive debts, or to avoid the scandal that would follow if Hinkleman sent explicit photographs to their families and loved ones, illustrating the sordid sex acts their beloved sons had performed with older men while out of their minds on drugs. Once they had been corrupted, it was almost impossible for the chickens to escape their pimps and return to a normal life, free from exploitation and abuse.

Hinkleman sipped his brandy and leaned back in his chair, swirling the amber liquid around the glass and smiling contentedly. "Okay, so how are you planning to make him amenable to working for us?"

Hinkleman was the fourth and final member of Benny's inner circle, and the closest thing he had to a friend and confidant. The pair, who had known each other since the mid-seventies, were the founding members of their little clique, which had expanded and contracted over the years as new members came and went.

When Hinkleman had set up his photographic studio ten years earlier, he had invited Benny to come in as a silent partner. The deal was that Benny would provide half the funding in exchange for regular access to pornographic material that he could sell on.

Over the years, Hinkleman's clients had provided a rich and diverse pool of talent from which the two elderly predators selected the weakest and most vulnerable, preying on them for their own sordid gratification. Of course, the gullible parents who brought their ugly, talentless children to Hinkleman in their droves had no idea what went on behind their backs.

Some of the kids were covertly filmed as they undressed in the changing room, or while rubbing baby oil into their nubile young bodies prior to the shoot. They were the lucky ones; the less fortunate were methodically groomed and physically violated.

It was Hinkleman who had come up with the idea of installing hidden cameras in the master bedrooms at the flat in Hackney and the safe house in Leytonstone. The orgies that Benny hosted at the flat were routinely filmed; it was an open secret, and the videos featured his clients having consensual sex with the rent boys that Benny had laid on. The filming at the house in Leytonstone occurred with much less frequency and far greater secrecy, and it never involved consensual sex. The films that were shot there catered for a very specialised market, whose target audience consisted solely of sadistic paedophiles with a penchant for watching young children being defiled. Benny and the other three members of his inner circle were the regular cast members, and were always hooded to avoid being identified, but there had been a few occasions where big spending clients, who were willing to fork out exorbitant amounts of money for the privilege of raping comatose children, were invited to participate.

The tapes from both venues sold like hotcakes on the black market, and each one they released raked in a small fortune for Benny Mars and Maurice Hinkleman.

"Benny doesn't think he'll put himself on the game willingly," McQueen said, his tone conversational.

"What about getting him into substance abuse?" Hinkleman suggested. He was, of course, referring to one of the opioids, like crack-cocaine or heroin.

McQueen shook his head. "As you've seen for yourself, he's partial to a bit of blow, but I don't think he's interested in trying anything stronger."

The photographer grunted his disappointment. "Pity, really. That would have made it much easier to get him working for us."

"Short of locking him in a room and forcibly injecting him until he becomes an addict, I don't see that happening," McQueen said. Some of the Oriental pimps used this method on the girls they trafficked into the country, but it was messy and drawn out, and regularly ended with fatalities.

"What about blackmail?" Hinkleman enquired. "What do we know about his parents? We could slip him a Mickey Finn, and film one of us having fun with him while he's out for the count. Would the threat of having us sending a copy sent to his mum and dad bring him around to our way of thinking?"

McQueen considered this. "It might work. When I asked him why he'd come to London, he was proper evasive. I figure it was either trouble with his parents or the law – it usually is – but I don't know for sure."

An idea came to Hinkleman. "Doesn't Benny have one of his special parties scheduled for Tuesday evening?"

McQueen nodded. "Yeah, so?"

"Perhaps we should invite young Gabe along? Who knows what he might be up for once he's had a good drink and snorted a few lines of coke?"

McQueen chuckled, realising that Hinkleman had taken a bit of shine to Gabe. "Yeah, why not? If you play your cards right, and turn on the old charm, maybe he'll even let you take his cherry?" he joked, holding his glass out to toast the photographer.

Hinkleman liked the sound of that. Raising his glass, he clinked it against McQueen's. "You know what," he said, licking his lips lasciviously, "maybe, he will."

# 13

An organised wolfpack

It was getting on for five o'clock. The sun had gone down a half hour earlier, and the searchers were now working in the dark, relying on the artificial light their torches provided.

It was becoming an increasingly tense situation for all involved, and hopes of finding the two boys alive were diminishing with every passing minute.

Tyler had returned to his office in Hertford House straight after the briefing, leaving Susie to coordinate the search. For him, the day had passed in a frenzy of activity as he made the opening entries in his Decision Log, organised the resources he would need for the coming days, and drafted a plethora of actions for his Office Manager to allocate.

He had spent far more time on the phone than he would have liked, and was currently fielding an irate call from Kelly Flowers, who was uncharacteristically angry.

"I know it's insensitive of them," he soothed. "Go out and

politely tell them to fuck off. In the meantime, I'll try and arrange for a uniform patrol to come over and keep them away from the house."

Although Ambrose Wilson, the crime reporter for *The London Echo*, had been the first to get wind of the situation, it hadn't taken long for word to reach his fellow newsies, and during the afternoon they had flocked to Chingford in their droves, besieging the station in search of a story. Some of them, it seemed, had also plotted up outside the Grant family's home in Crescent Road, and when Kelly and Debbie Brown arrived there a few minutes earlier, to provide Gavin's parents with an update on how the search was progressing, they had been horrified to find several news vans parked outside the house and a small posse of reporters banging on the front door in search of an interview.

"*I've done that,*" Kelly snapped. "*I even threatened to nick one gobshite who was pushing his luck for causing harassment, alarm and distress. They've backed off, at least for now, but the experience has left the family in pieces, Jack. It's immoral for those selfish bastards to hound them like that, just to get a few words for a by-line.*"

"I know," Tyler placated her, wondering if her pregnancy was starting to affect her hormones and make her more emotional than usual. Was that even a thing? He thought he remembered reading something to that effect, but he was too afraid to ask in case she bit his head off. "Like I said, I'll see what I can do about getting someone posted outside to keep them at bay."

Kelly let out a long sigh. "*Thank you, and I'm sorry for taking my frustrations out on you.*"

Tyler was staring out of his office window, watching the rush hour traffic speed along the A406 towards the flyover. Even in the darkness, the towering gas works beyond the dual carriageway was an ugly blight on the Barking skyline.

"I take it you didn't encounter any reporters at Peter Musgrove's place?" he asked, knowing the boy's family lived in Woodedge Close, which was only a couple of streets away.

"*No, thank goodness,*" Kelly said. "*But it probably won't be long until they start showing up.*"

She was probably right, and he made a mental note to get uniform to fly the flag there as well.

"How are the two families holding up?"

"*Much as you would expect,*" she said, lowering her voice.

"Pass on my regards, and assure them we're doing everything humanly possible to find their kids."

"*I will do,*" Kelly promised. "*Speaking of which, has there been any activity on Peter's phone?*"

"No," Tyler said, with a heavy heart. "The TIU are still monitoring it, but it's as dead as a Dodo."

Hopefully, the boys hadn't suffered a similar fate.

"*What about CCTV? Has that thrown up any new leads?*"

"It's still being viewed."

There was a brisk knock on his office door.

Tyler turned to find George Holland standing in the doorway. In his late fifties, with thinning fair hair, Holland had what was best described as a lived in face. He was dressed in a single-breasted charcoal suit, immaculate white shirt and red tie.

Tyler wasn't a gambling man, but he would have bet a month's wages that, beneath his tailored jacket, Holland wore his trademark red braces.

Seeing that Tyler was in the middle of a telephone conversation, Holland acknowledged him with a curt nod.

Tyler beckoned him in and pointed towards the empty seat opposite his desk. As Holland sat down, Tyler held up a finger, indicating that he would only be a minute.

"Kelly, I'm sorry but I've got to go into a meeting with the boss now. I'll give you a call if there are any developments."

Hanging up, Tyler sat down at his desk and hurriedly opened his daybook. "Thanks for coming in, boss. I really don't like how this one is panning out."

"Neither do I," Holland admitted, unbuttoning his jacket and crossing his legs.

Tyler caught the briefest flash of red braces behind Holland's jacket, and mentally punched the air. He had often wondered why the boss only ever wore red ones. One day he would work up the courage to ask.

"Do you remember the Sidney Cooke case from the mid-eighties?" Holland asked, interrupting his musings.

"Vaguely," Tyler replied, trying to recall the details. "Wasn't he involved in the murder of Jason Swift?"

Swift was a fourteen year old rent boy who had been gang raped and murdered by Cooke and his cronies back in 1985.

Holland nodded, grim faced. "That's right. Cooke ran a gang of predatory paedophiles known as The Dirty Dozen. They were also convicted of abducting and murdering a six year old boy called Barry Lewis, and a seven year old boy called Mark Tildesley, who I seem to recall disappeared from a fairground in Berkshire during the summer of 1984."

Tyler felt his stomach tighten. "From a fairground? Do you think Cooke's gang could be responsible for this?"

Holland shook his head. "I seriously doubt it, Jack. To the best of my knowledge, they're all still safely banged up inside one of Her Majesty's less salubrious establishments."

"Then, why bring it up?" Tyler asked, wondering if he were missing something.

Holland tented his fingers. "Because those bastards weren't the only active paedophile gang plaguing London. There were others who were equally deplorable. There was a big purge after The Dirty Dozen case, and the Met succeeded in taking some of the worst ones out of circulation, but mark my words, more will have cropped up since then, and they'll be spreading their insidious evil like the malignant cancer it is."

"You think this could be the work of a gang then, not an individual?" Tyler asked, not liking the sound of that.

Holland allowed himself a moment's reflection, then nodded sombrely. "I do, Jack. It's risky abducting one child, let alone two, and it strikes me that whoever did it must have known they would be opening a huge can of worms, but they still went ahead. That makes me think we're dealing with an organised wolfpack, not an individual."

"A wolfpack?" Tyler was confused by the unfamiliar turn of phrase.

"That's what these vile bastards call themselves: wolfpacks," Holland explained, spitting the word out with contempt. "They don't think the way we do, so don't waste your time trying to understand what makes them tick."

Tyler's eyes narrowed, and he regarded his boss with open suspicion. "That's not your way of suggesting we should involve the NPIA in this, is it?"

The acronym stood for National Policing Improvement Agency, but they were laughably referred to by many officers who had used their services with unsatisfying results as the 'no point in asking' police.

"We can discuss that later," Holland said, evasively. "Right now, we need to focus on what we're going to say during tonight's press conference."

Tyler stiffened. "What press conference? I haven't sanctioned a bloody press conference!"

"No, but I have."

Tyler opened his mouth to protest, but Holland held up a hand to silence him.

"Look, Jack, the media interest is already spiralling out of control, so for the sake of damage limitation I've agreed to hold a press conference this evening. I know it will be painful for the families, but it will really help our cause if they say a few words into the camera."

Tyler groaned, imagining Kelly's reaction to being told that. He didn't know how the Musgroves would feel about it, but after having the newsies banging on their door and pestering them so aggressively, he seriously doubted the Grant family would be keen to participate.

Holland was studying his reaction with a thoughtful frown. "Have you got the hump because I didn't consult you beforehand?"

Tyler put his pen down, leaned back in his chair and began massaging his temples. "Yes, a little, but it's not just that. Tom and Margo Grant have been getting grief from some media types who've set up a basecamp outside their house. I've just had Kelly on the phone, ranting at me about it."

Holland's face softened. "Ah, I see," he said, softly. "Well, tell Kelly she's going to have to talk them into it. If the boys have been abducted, it's vitally important that we try and make their captors think of them as people, not just objects, and there's no better way of doing that then by letting them see how much pain and suffering they're causing the parents."

Tyler sighed, feeling the fight drain out of him. As usual, Holland was right.

A press conference would also raise public awareness and encourage potential witnesses to come forward. The challenge would be in weeding out the wheat from the chaff, because as soon as the story went live on national TV, the incident room and Crimestoppers help lines would be inundated with calls, most of them from time wasters.

"How much information do you propose we disclose?" Tyler asked, gradually coming around to the idea.

There was always a delicate balance to be struck when involving the media. Releasing too much information at an early stage often did more harm than good, but if they didn't share enough to keep them satisfied, the journos might start digging around themselves, and that could cause all sorts of problems.

Holland considered this. "Nothing too specific, just enough to whet their appetite. I've told Press Bureau we're willing to provide the media with regular updates, as long as they don't start running riot with speculation or causing the boys' parents any undue distress."

Tyler didn't trust the media. "Do you honestly think they'll play by those rules?"

"I believe so," Holland said after a moment's reflection. "After all, we want the boys returned safely, and they want a major story, so it's in everyone's interest to cooperate."

Benny Mars was nursing his second G&T of the afternoon when Madeley arrived at the quiet pub in Soho he had chosen for their secret rendezvous.

"Sorry I'm a tad late," the barrister said, sinking into the seat opposite. After removing his hat and jacket, he cast a nervous glance around the room, fearful that someone might recognise him. He needn't have worried; the only other patrons in the bar were a small group of elderly tourists, Americans or Canadians from the sound of them.

"Not a problem," Benny said, graciously.

Madeley leaned back in his seat. "I still don't see why we couldn't have had this discussion over the phone and saved ourselves a trip."

"I told you. I don't discuss supplying chickens over the phone." Benny took a sip of his drink, savoured the flavour before continuing. "So, am I to take it you want me to go hunting for you?" he asked with a coy smile.

Madeley glanced around the room again. When he was satisfied that no one was looking at them, he leaned forward and spoke conspiratorially. "Yes, I want you go hunting for me. I'm in the market for a boy under ten, with blonde hair, blue eyes, and a pretty face. Can you find me someone like that?"

Benny's eyes were cold and calculating. "For the right money, I can find you anything or anyone you want."

Madeley swallowed hard as he considered the endless possibilities. "And you can arrange a neutral location for me to… to enjoy the chicken in?"

"I have a safe house that's fully equipped for such encounters," Benny confirmed. "It's for the exclusive use of the wolfpack's inner circle, of which you are now one."

Producing an initialised silk handkerchief from his pocket, Madeley dabbed at the little beads of sweat breaking out on his forehead. "And afterwards… You know, when I'm finished… You're sure there won't be any evidence to link me to the chicken?"

"I'll get rid of all the evidence."

"And what about the boy? How can I be sure he won't say anything?"

"Like I said, I'll get rid of *all* the evidence." Benny's face was expressionless, his voice emotionless, but the implication was clear.

Madeley's eyes widened. For a moment, Benny thought he was going to change his mind, but then he nodded, slowly, resignedly, as if accepting it was the only way.

"And how long..." Madeley swallowed hard. "How long would it take you to find me a suitable chicken?"

Benny laughed. It was a cruel, mocking sound. "I don't know. A week; a month. It'll take as long as it takes."

"The sooner, the better," Madeley pleaded, sounding pathetically desperate. "I don't mean to rush you, but I've waited a very long time to do this, and I'm really rather keen to get on with it."

Benny spat into his palm, then extended the hand to seal the agreement. It was a trait he had picked up while working as a rigger with travelling funfairs. "So, we're agreed? You want me to proceed?"

Madeley hesitated for a moment, then accepted the grubby hand.

All that remained was to agree the price, but from the dreamy look in Madeley's eyes, Benny knew that the newest member of his inner circle would stump up whatever fee he demanded.

# 14

It's time to face the press

The wind chafed at Benny's exposed skin as he emerged from Leytonstone station, sapping the heat from his ageing body faster than a vampire could drain its victim's blood. Pulling his Trilby down to prevent it from being blown off his head, he set off for the safe house at a brisk pace.

Arriving a few minutes later, he was surprised to see lights on upstairs. Apart from him, the only people with keys were Hinkleman, Remus and McQueen, but they knew better than to go there without first clearing it with him.

Had there been a break in?

There were no obvious signs of a forced entry at the front, but it was possible that thieves had broken in through the rear door, having accessed the garden via the railway line running along the back of the property.

Benny hesitated by the door, unsure how to proceed. He didn't dare call the police; apart from all the illegal kiddie porn that was stored in the basement, the discovery of which would result in him being arrested on the spot, the filing cabinets contained confidential client information and detailed records of all his transactions. Plus, how would he explain away the soundproofed cell and the master bedroom with its covert cameras?

With a shaking hand, Benny inserted the key into the lock. Turning the handle slowly, he eased the door open and peered in, ready to turn and run if confronted by burglars. The hallway was empty, so he stepped inside, holding the door ajar in case he needed to make a quick exit. Almost immediately, he heard footsteps coming from the floor above. They were clunky, not the sort of quiet padding he would expect from a house breaker.

Benny considered calling out, but couldn't quite summon the courage. He froze when a dirty pair of combat booted feet appeared at the top of the landing.

To his horror, they started to descend the stairs.

Benny was halfway out of the door by the time he recognised Remus.

"What the fuck are you doing here?" he demanded, quickly regaining his usual bluster.

Remus was equally shocked to see him. "I come and stay here sometimes, just for a day or two, when I need a break from being with Joey."

"Since when?" Benny bristled. "You know I don't like anyone coming here without my permission."

"Sorry, Benny," Remus mumbled, guiltily. He was unable to meet the older man's eyes. "I should have told you."

"Yes, you bloody well should have," Benny snapped, slamming the door behind him.

"I won't do it again," Remus promised.

Benny searched his face for signs of insincerity, but found none. "You look pale. Are you okay?" Pale was an understatement; Remus' skin was the colour of alabaster.

"I've had a bad case of food poisoning."

Benny draped his coat over the bannister, then plonked the Trilby down on top of it. "Are you sure it's just food poisoning?" he demanded, running spindly fingers through Brylcreemed hair. "I'll be severely pissed off if I end up catching a nasty stomach bug from you."

Remus nodded. "I ate a dodgy hotdog at the fair, last night. Been paying the price ever since."

"Come on then," Benny said, placing a hand on his shoulder. "Let's go through to the kitchen. I'll make you a nice cup of tea."

It was only when Remus tensed that Benny noticed how jittery he was.

"Why don't you go in there and warm up," Remus suggested, pointing into the living room, where the electric fire was on. "I don't mind making the tea."

An alarm bell went off inside Benny's head. Remus was a lazy bastard; always had been, always would be. There was no way he would volunteer to make anyone a brew, especially if he was feeling unwell. "Is there something in the kitchen you don't want me seeing, Aaron?" Benny's voice was harsh, accusatory.

Remus forced a strangled laugh. "No! Of course not. I was just trying to be a good host, that's all."

Pushing him aside, Benny stomped off towards the kitchen.

"Benny, wait!" Remus called after him.

There was no mistaking the panic in his voice.

Benny burst into the kitchen, his eyes angrily raking the room. At first, nothing seemed amiss, and he began to wonder if he had let his overly suspicious nature get the better of him, but then he noticed the tray on the sideboard, with two bowls of porridge and two cups of tea on it.

Porridge and tea; the staple diet for captive chickens.

Benny span to face the younger man, who was watching him with growing unease.

"What the fuck's going on?" Benny snarled, pointing towards the tray and its giveaway contents.

Remus seemed to wilt under his gaze. "Benny, I can explain…" he began, but then realised he couldn't.

"This had better not mean what I think it does," Benny warned.

Pushing past Remus, he returned to the hallway and opened the door leading down to the cellar.

Remus followed behind, becoming increasingly fretful. "Benny, please let me explain!"

His pleas fell on deaf ears as Benny descended the stairs to the basement. "How many times do I have to tell you to tidy this mess up?" he snarled as he weaved his way through the filing cabinets and haphazardly stacked boxes.

Stopping by the cell door, Benny fumbled in his trouser pockets for his keyring. "Where the fuck is it?" he mumbled, growing increasingly agitated.

"Benny, please don't be angry with me," Remus pleaded, wringing his hands together in contrition. "I really can–"

With two quick steps, Benny closed the distance between them and slapped Remus hard across the face. "Be quiet," he ordered. Finally fishing the keyring from his pocket, he marched back to the security door. "God help you if you've got any chickens in there."

As he yanked open the heavy door, Remus rushed forward, barring his way. His hands were raised in subjugation. "Benny, I can–"

"Shut the fuck up!" Benny snapped. "I'm sick of listening to your pathetic whining."

Remus opened his mouth to speak again, but then thought better of it.

"Turn the light on," Benny ordered.

Stepping aside, Remus dutifully toggled the switch.

When the dull red light flickered into life, Benny found himself staring at two terrified chickens, both of whom were looking up at him from their cots.

"What the fuck is going on?" he demanded, his eyes alternating between the captive boys and Remus.

Kelly ushered both sets of parents into the briefing room at New Scotland Yard. They moved sluggishly, like lambs being led to the slaughter, and she could feel their anxiety radiating off them.

It resembled a small theatre with a raised podium, beyond which row upon row of tiered seating extended backwards in a wide semi-circle. A rectangular table, draped in the MPS flag, had been set up at the front of the podium. There were six stiff backed seats behind it, each with a slender black microphone and nameplate in front of it.

A massive MPS crest dominated the wall behind the table, and beneath this the service motto proudly declared that the Met was '*Working for a safer London.*'

The Grants were struggling to take it all in. Tom wrapped Margo in his arms and whispered assurances that they would get through the press conference together. "We have to be strong for Gavin's sake," he said, kissing the top of her head gently.

Behind them, Alison and Ciaron Musgrove were surveying the room in strained silence, their faces pale and gaunt, their eyes red rimmed.

To Kelly, they seemed completely bereft of hope, and she couldn't begin to imagine how she would feel in their place. For a moment, knowing how much darkness existed in the world, she found herself questioning whether she and Jack were doing the right thing by having a baby.

Pushing Tom away, Margo turned to face Debbie, her tear streaked face a mask of pain. "I'm sorry, but I just don't think I can go through with this," she said in a wobbly voice.

"You *can* do it,' Debbie assured her. "I know you feel like running a mile in the opposite direction, but those boys are relying on you, and the best way you can help them is by going on TV and making a heartfelt appeal for anyone who knows anything to come forward."

"But... but what if I freeze, or burst into tears?" Margo protested, working herself up even more.

Debbie's face softened. "Margo, no one's going to be judging you, so it really doesn't matter if you break down."

It might even help, Kelly thought. "Debbie's right," she said. "Surely, you can see that an impassioned plea from the two of you will have a much bigger impact than anything the DCI might say?"

Margo nodded, reluctantly at first, but then with increasing acceptance. "Yes, I do, but… I don't know if I have the strength."

"You won't be facing the cameras alone," Debbie assured her. "Tom's going to be right beside you, and Alison and Ciaron will be just the other side of Mr Tyler and Mr Holland. It doesn't matter if you cry; it doesn't matter if you fall apart. All that matters is that you ask the public for information regarding the boys' whereabouts."

Tom took Margo's hand in his and squeezed it. "You can do this," he encouraged her.

"You have to," Debbie said, making it clear that she really didn't have a choice.

Margo gratefully accepted the Kleenex that Kelly offered her, and began dabbing her eyes. "Yes, you're right," she sniffed. "I'm sorry for getting so stressed."

---

"WHAT THE FUCK IS WRONG WITH YOU?" Benny screamed, spraying Remus' face with spittle.

They had come up to the lounge, where they could talk freely.

Remus swallowed, hard. "Benny, I–"

"Shut up!" Benny snarled. His face was incandescent with rage. "You know the rules. Unless we're snatching them to order, we don't prey on kids who are likely to be missed."

Remus hung his head in shame, but that just made Benny all the madder. "What the fuck possessed you to do it?" he demanded, throwing his arms in the air and shaking his head incredulously.

"Benny I–"

Benny grabbed the collar of Remus' green NATO jumper and pulled him down to eye level. "Did you snatch those boys to order? Are you trying to steal my clients by undercutting me?"

"No, of course not!" Remus said, shaking his head in fierce

denial. "I–I took them for myself, not for anyone else. I would *never* betray you, Benny. I promise."

Releasing his grip, Benny stepped back, puzzled. "Why would you be stupid enough to risk snatching two chickens, if not for money?"

Remus was struggling for words. His mouth was opening and closing, but no sounds were coming out.

"Spit it out," Benny barked, clapping his hands impatiently to chivvy him along.

Remus flinched at the repetitive noise of the clapping. "I only wanted the blonde one, but I ended up having to grab them both."

"Un–fucking–believable," Benny muttered, palming his forehead.

Remus seemed to deflate before his eyes. "I just couldn't help myself," he confessed, sounding like an alcoholic trying to justify falling off the wagon. "The blonde was the most beautiful chicken I'd ever seen, and I just *had* to have him. The other one was… well, just there."

"But what possessed you to do it? You've got free rein over all the boys in my stable. You can shag yourself silly if you want, and from what I've heard, you frequently do."

Remus acknowledged the dig with a guilty nod. "I know, but he was perfection itself, and all I could think about was how incredible it would be to break him in." He paused long enough to pull off a bolshy shrug. "It's alright for you and Mo; over the years you've both broken plenty of chickens in, but on the rare occasions we get to share a really young boy, all I ever get is other people's sloppy seconds."

Benny's face had turned the colour of puce. "If you've endangered my operation, just to fulfil a pathetic fantasy, I'll castrate you," the old man fumed. "I mean it, Aaron. If you've put me or my business in jeopardy, I'll cut your bollocks off."

Tears were running down the younger man's face. "Benny, I'm sorry. I didn't–"

He reeled under the impact of a backhanded slap he hadn't seen coming. Staggering backwards, he fell onto the sofa, clutching his cheek. When he withdrew his hand a moment later, the left side of his face had a bright red imprint on it.

Benny was pacing the room, struggling to get his temper under control.

"Benny, I—"

"Quiet! I need to think." Pulling out a packet of cigarettes, Benny lit one and began puffing furiously. "Where did you snatch them from?" he demanded.

Remus nervously cleared his throat. "From a funfair in Chingford."

"Were you working alone, or did Joey help you?"

Remus shook his head. "Joey doesn't know anything about this."

Benny grunted. Joey had always been the brighter of the two boys; he had far too much sense to pull a stupid stunt like that. "Did anyone see you snatch them?"

"Of course not!" Remus replied, indignantly. "I've been doing this long enough not to make mistakes."

"You damn fool," Benny snapped, bunching his fists. "Everyone makes mistakes, especially cocky little morons who've become overly complacent."

Remus flinched at the rebuke. "I wasn't being cocky," he assured his mentor. "I just meant that I was very, *very* careful."

For all of their sakes, Benny hoped he had been. "How did you get them here?" he asked, taking a seat and gesturing for Remus to do likewise.

"In the back of my van."

With a laboured sigh, Benny began massaging his temples. "You'd better tell me everything," he said, wearily. "Start from the beginning, and don't leave anything out."

---

There was a brisk knock on the door. A moment later, Kelly Flowers poked her head around. "It's time," she announced, smiling encouragingly.

After being shown the briefing room, Alison and the others had been ushered into a small anteroom to prepare themselves for the upcoming appeal. A harried looking press officer, whose name Alison had already forgotten, had breezed in to introduce himself and explain the process, before hurriedly taking his leave to organise the arriving media. Since then, Debbie had been coaching them on what they should and shouldn't say.

Kelly had organised some refreshments, but these still sat on the side, completely untouched.

Alison had been dreading this moment. As she stood up, her legs began to shake, and for a moment, she wasn't sure they would take her weight.

As if reading her mind, Debbie appeared by her side and gave her arm a little squeeze. "You'll be fine," she whispered, reassuringly.

Unable to speak, Alison merely nodded. Feeling totally numb inside, she moved towards the door on autopilot.

"Remember everything we've gone through," Debbie was saying as she flitted around the room, chivvying the others to their feet. "The DCI will open the press briefing. He'll do most of the talking, and then he'll hand over to you to make an appeal."

It had been decided that Alison would speak on behalf of Peter, and that Tom would do likewise for Gavin.

"Keep your answers short and sweet, and try not to panic," Kelly added as they lined up in single file behind Debbie. "If someone from the media asks you a difficult question, either Mr Tyler or Mr Holland will intercede to take the pressure off you."

"It sounds very busy out there," Ciaron said. "How many reporters are we expecting?"

"A lot," Kelly admitted.

Alison felt a ball of ice form in her stomach.

"In addition to all the reporters, there will be TV cameras and a lot of photographers," Kelly forewarned them. "I know it's easy for me to say, but try to blot everyone else out, and just concentrate on the people asking the questions."

She was right, Alison thought bitterly; it *was* easy for her to say.

"I feel sick," Margo blurted out, and Alison saw that her complexion was indeed tinged with green.

"You'll be fine," Tom insisted, wrapping an arm around her.

"Do any of you need to visit the loo?" Kelly asked, her eyes lingering on Margo a shade longer than any of the others. "If you do, now is the time to say so."

They all shook their heads, even Margo.

"Right," Kelly said, taking a deep breath and opening the door. "In that case, it's time to face the press."

# 15

An unprincipled narcissist

Gareth Madeley settled down in front of the TV to watch the evening news. He was nursing a large scotch and feeling very pleased with himself; the meeting with Benny Mars had gone remarkably well, and by greenlighting the child snatcher to proceed, Madeley felt as though a great burden had finally been lifted from his shoulders.

As a younger man, he had constantly fought against the paedophilic urges that dominated his every waking moment, pretending it was just a silly phase he was going through, one that he would soon grow out of. That had been incredibly stupid of him. Living his life in denial, he now realised, had been akin to holding his breath underwater: he could manage it for a few seconds, but, eventually, he had to come up for air.

Madeley had recently celebrated a milestone birthday, and it was the stark realisation that he now had considerably less time ahead of him than behind that had persuaded him to accept Benny's offer this time around. He had stipulated that the chicken had to be over five – he wasn't a monster, after all – but under ten, with blonde hair and a pretty face. Closing his eyes, he sculpted a mental image of the prize he was to receive.

Not so much a prize as a reward, he corrected himself.

*"... despite the onset of darkness, and the bitter temperatures prevailing outside, the search of Epping Forest continues for the two missing children as authorities become increasingly concerned for their safety."*

The concern in the female reporter's voice was so palpable that it dragged Madeley away from his happy place. Opening his eyes, he caught a brief glimpse of a shivering woman, her breath bellowing around her head like ghostly ectoplasm, before the image switched to a smartly dressed anchor man back in the studio.

Unlike his windswept colleague, not a single lacquered hair was out if place. *"Thank you, Lydia,"* he said, sombrely shuffling papers. *"Well, we can now go live to New Scotland Yard, where the police have been joined by the missing children's parents, and they are just about to make an urgent appeal for information."*

Turning the volume up, Madeley watched with interest as the scene changed to a briefing room in which six people were seated behind a long table, facing the camera. The two suited men in the middle were clearly senior detectives, while the dishevelled figures on either side of them could only be the two sets of parents.

Photographers were snapping away, recording every moment of their misery and distress for tomorrow's papers. The non-stop strobing of flashguns was accompanied by the jarring sound of expensive motor drives whirring.

After a moment, the detective on the right, the younger of the two by a good twenty years, held up his hand and signalled for quiet. He was a good looking man of around thirty, with short brown hair, blue eyes, and a strong jaw. Introducing himself as DCI Tyler, he surveyed the assembled media with a steely-eyed gaze that signalled he wouldn't tolerate any showboating from ambitious reporters looking to make a name for themselves.

"*As you all know,*" Tyler began, addressing his audience in a clear, articulate voice, "*Peter and Gavin went missing from the fairground in Rangers Road just before ten p.m. yesterday evening. This is totally out of character for these boys, neither of whom is particularly streetwise. They haven't been seen or heard from since then, and we are deeply concerned for their safety. An intensive search of Epping Forest commenced this morning, supported by dog units and the police helicopter. It will continue late into the night and, if we still haven't found the children by then, it will recommence in even greater numbers at first light tomorrow.*" He paused for breath before continuing. "*We are appealing for anyone with information about Peter and Gavin's whereabouts to come forward as a matter of great urgency, so that we can safely reunite them with their families.*"

Madeley was impressed. Tyler had a sincerity about him that seemed to captivate his audience. The detective paused a moment for dramatic effect, then looked straight into the camera lens.

"*At this point, I would like to invite Peter's mother, Alison, to say a few words.*"

The camera immediately panned left, coming to rest on the woman sitting furthest away from Tyler.

Madeley dispassionately took in the red rimmed eyes and dark circles beneath them. If he was reading her body language correctly, she no longer harboured any hope of seeing her cherished son alive again.

"*Peter,*" the woman began, her voice weak and tremulous, her bottom lip quivering from the effort of not breaking down in tears. "*My darling boy, if you're watching this appeal, please dial 999 and give the operator your location. I promise you; no one's angry with you or Gavin. Neither of you is in any trouble. All we want is to have you back home with us, and to know that you're both safe and well…*"

She broke off, screwing her eyes shut as she tried to steady her breathing.

Madeley saw big fat tears trickle down her cheeks.

"*Mr Grant,*" Tyler said, stepping in quickly when he realised that she was unable to continue. "*Would you like to say anything to Gavin?*"

Grant was a big man, but he seemed to visibly shrivel as he cleared his throat and looked into the lens.

"I–I just want to say… we love you, Gav. Please let us know where you are so we can…" Breaking off, he covered his face in an outburst of grief.

It was a real tearjerker moment that made for great TV, and Madeley was spellbound by the unfolding drama. As he watched, Margo Grant reached out a trembling hand and placed it on her crying husband's shoulder.

"*Gavin,*" she said, somehow finding the strength to take over from him. "*Please come home. We are so worried about you, and it's killing us, not knowing where you are. Please…*" She choked on the word, shaking her head to indicate she couldn't go on.

The briefing room was shrouded in a miasma of despair in which no one dared to speak.

The camera slowly zoomed in on Gavin's heartbroken parents. Oblivious to everyone around them, they huddled together, trying to comfort each other.

And then, a callous voice shattered the respectful silence that had descended upon the room.

"*Ambrose Wilson. The London Echo,*" a reporter sitting in the front row called out. "*Tell me, DCI Tyler, do you suspect foul play?*"

"*We're keeping an open mind to all possibilities, but we will not be drawn into speculation,*" Tyler replied coldly, eyeing the reporter as if the man was something unpleasant that he had walked into the building on the bottom of his shoe.

"*What are the chances of finding the boys alive after all this time?*" Wilson persisted, unperturbed by the filthy looks he was attracting, or by the anguished howl his question had elicited from Margo Grant.

"*We remain hopeful of finding both boys alive,*" Tyler said through gritted teeth.

In the comfort of his living room, Madeley threw his head back and chuckled throatily, thinking that, beneath his professional exterior, the detective probably wanted to punch the irritating reporter. And who could blame him? *The London Echo* correspondent was obviously an unprincipled narcissist intent on milking the situation for his own gain.

Wilson opened his mouth to say something else, but the detective got in first.

"*Let me reiterate, if anyone has any information that might assist us to find Peter and Gavin, please contact us at once, either by ringing the incident room helpline direct or by calling Crimestoppers.*"

As he spoke, two telephone numbers were superimposed across the bottom of the screen.

"*Last night, temperatures fell below freezing point,*" DCS Holland said, speaking for the first time. "*And they are expected to do the same again tonight. If the boys are sleeping rough, they risk frostbite and hypothermia, so it is imperative that we find them as quickly as possible.*"

Side-by-side photographs of the missing boys, both looking resplendent in freshly pressed school uniforms, filled the screen.

Madeley leaned forward in his seat to get a better look at them.

Gavin Grant was a pleasant enough looking lad. Slightly overweight, he bore an uncanny resemblance to his tearful father. Peter Musgrove, on the other hand, was so pretty that he took Madeley's breath away. If only Benny could find him a boy like that! The very thought made the ageing paedophile's heart race.

The news anchor moved onto the next story, something about the coroner for Blackpool and Fylde launching an investigation after four deaths had occurred at the hands of a surgeon at Blackpool's Victoria Hospital, but Madeley wasn't interested.

He muted the TV and sat there in silence.

It seemed obvious that the boys had been abducted. How else could their disappearance be explained? He knew he should feel awful for the children and their families, but he didn't. All he felt was jealousy for the people who had abducted them, knowing they were going to enjoy the forbidden fruits he so desperately craved.

"Lucky bastards," he muttered under his breath.

---

When Remus returned from feeding the chickens their evening gruel, he found Benny watching the evening news. Casting a nervous sideways glance at his leader, he sat down quietly, wishing the old man would hurry up and take his leave.

When the story about the two missing children came on, Remus felt his chest tighten. He was unable to breathe. For one terrible moment, he actually thought he was going into cardiac arrest, but then he realised it was just a panic attack. Dragging his knees up to his chest, he snatched up a cushion and hid behind it. Peering over the top a moment later, he began anxiously muttering, "Oh, shit! Oh, shit! Oh, shit!"

Benny sat through the entire press conference in stony silence, not looking in the younger man's direction once. When it ended, he calmly picked up the remote control, switched the TV off, then spun around and viciously launched the device at Remus' head.

Remus held the cushion in front of his face like a gladiator's shield. With a soft plop, the remote sunk into it before dropping harmlessly into his lap.

In an instant, Benny was on his feet. "I ought to gut you like a fish and throw your body into the canal," he snarled. The veins protruded from his thin neck like cables.

"I'm sorry, Benny," Remus said, peeking out from behind the cushion. "I would never have snatched the little fuckers if I'd realised it was going to cause this big a stink."

Benny was regarding him as though he wasn't the full ticket. "Are you for real?" he shouted, turning even redder. "What did you think would happen?"

Remus manufactured a hapless shrug. "I don't know," he admitted after a moment's hesitation. "I guess I just assumed that everyone would think the kids had run away together, like me and Joey did from the care home."

Benny squeezed the bridge of his nose. He wanted to scream at Remus, to throw more things at him, to beat him to within an inch of his worthless life… but what would that achieve?

"Listen to me," Benny said, looking him straight in the eye. "You fucked up big style by grabbing both of those chickens, but if you do as I say – exactly as I fucking say – we can still turn this situation to our advantage."

"I'll do whatever you tell me to do. I'll–"

"Quiet!" Benny bellowed. "I'm trying to think."

Biting his bottom lip, Remus hugged the cushion, too afraid to say anything else.

For the best part of a minute, Benny paced up and down the room, staring at the floor and muttering angrily under his breath. When he finally turned to face Remus, there was a glint of purpose in his eyes. "Okay, this is what we're going to do. You'll keep the chickens locked in the basement, drugged up to the eyeballs so that they don't make any fuss, while I find us a buyer for them."

Remus shook his head. "I don't mind selling the bigger one, but I want to keep the blonde for myself."

Benny swatted the protest aside. "I don't give a flying fuck what you want, you worthless little shit. I'm selling them both."

"But I snatched them, so they're *my* property," Remus objected, feebly.

Benny's laugh was cruel, abrasive. "And you're my property, so you'll do exactly what I say, or do you think you're a big enough man to go challenge me for the wolfpack's leadership?"

Remus looked away, shaking his head submissively. "Just tell me what you want me to do," he said in a flat voice.

"What I want you to do is guard these chickens with your life; you don't fuck them, and you don't tell anyone else about them. I mean it," Benny added, raising his voice authoritatively as Remus opened his mouth to speak. "Not even Joey or Mo. For now, the less people who know about this, the better. Can you do that for me?"

Remus nodded, reluctantly. He knew better than to challenge Benny's authority. "Sure, Benny," he said with a lacklustre smile. "Whatever you say."

Benny stared at him, unsure whether the compliance was real of affected. "I mean it, Aaron. If we handle this right, we can turn a tidy profit. If there's time, after the client's finished with him, you can have your way with the blonde before we dispose of him."

"Why can't I break him in before you sell him?" Remus pleaded, sounding like a truculent schoolboy.

"Because he's worth far more to us as a virgin."

"But—"

"If you damage the goods, I'll damage you," Benny snapped, looking around for something else to throw at the young fool.

---

Tyler hadn't had a proper opportunity to speak to the boys' parents before the press conference. There had just about been time for a quick hello before he was whisked away to prepare. Now that the pressure was off, he wanted to introduce himself properly and thank them for their participation.

He found all four sitting around a small coffee table in the anteroom they had been allocated. Kelly and Debbie were standing over by the rear window, giving them some space.

The shellshocked parents looked up as he entered the room, and both fathers made to stand, but he waved them back to their seats.

"I just wanted to say that you all did incredibly well in there tonight."

They looked completely washed out, especially Tom Grant, who moved like an old man as he lowered himself back into his seat.

"I made a complete fool of myself," Tom said, clearly embarrassed by his emotional outburst.

"Nonsense, I thought you showed incredible bravery," Tyler assured him. "You all did. Your emotions were heartfelt and understandable, and I would have thought less of you if you hadn't been so upset." The truth was that the outpouring of such raw emotion was exactly what Tyler had been hoping for. Not only would it get the public on board, and encourage them to come forward with information, it might – just might – make whoever had taken the boys think of them as people, and not just as objects for their sexual gratification. "Honestly, I can't overemphasise how important your contribution was."

"So, what do we do now?" Ciaron Musgrove asked. "We can't just sit here all night, drinking tea and patting ourselves on the back for performing well on TV."

There was something about the man that made Tyler instinctively dislike him. It wasn't necessarily anything the supermarket manager had said or done; it was just his aura. It was abrasive, confrontational. Perhaps that was just his way, and he meant nothing by it, but it grated. In light of what the poor man was going through, Tyler really wanted to like him, and he felt slightly guilty for not doing so.

"Kelly and Debbie will run you home shortly and—"

"No," Ciaron said, his voice quivering with anger. "That's not good enough."

Alison placed a hand over his to silence him, but he pulled it away from her. The poor woman flinched but said nothing.

"I've sat at home all day," Ciaron continued. "I've had enough of it, and I want to get out there and help with the search."

Tom Grant was nodding, supportively. "I do, too. I feel so powerless doing nothing."

Tyler exchanged glances with the two FLOs, hoping they would step in and work their magic, but they merely shrugged.

*Thanks, girls...*

He took a moment to compose his thoughts, knowing he had to word this in a way that didn't cause offence. "Realistically, I don't know how much longer it will be feasible for the searchers to carry on for tonight, and to be brutally honest, because of the difficult conditions they're operating in, your presence would be more of a hindrance than a help."

Ciaron bristled, but Tyler held up a placating hand. "I'll make you a deal: if we still haven't found the boys by the morning, you can both join the search party. If you're serious about doing that, I'll have one of the girls pick you up at first light. In the meantime, go home, try and get some rest so that you don't collapse on us tomorrow, because it could be another very long day."

Ciaron looked like he wanted to argue, but after a moment's reflection, he nodded, accepting that Tyler's words made sense.

"Okay," he said, reluctantly. "But I'll be there tomorrow, and nothing you or anyone else says will stop me from getting involved."

"Do you think we'll find them alive?" The question came from Alison Musgrove.

The poor woman was a tortured soul, with sunken eyes and a look of sheer desperation.

Tyler hesitated, then cleared his throat, aware that he was pussyfooting around the question. "I don't know, Alison," he replied, candidly. "All I can tell you is that we will do absolutely everything within our power to bring them back to you."

But would that would be enough?

## 16

# MONDAY 5TH NOVEMBER 2001

Turn that poisonous filth off!

The sun rose at 07:17 hours, drifting slowly over the horizon, but never getting high enough to burn off the thick frost that had set in during the night.

It promised to be another bitterly cold day, and as Tyler pulled into the clearing the RVP had been set up in, he pitied the searchers for the daunting task that lay ahead of them.

The number of officers involved had swollen to 200, and as they hadn't all been able to fit into the canteen at the same time, the briefing had been carried out in two instalments. As this was now an ongoing operation, catering services had been called out, and everyone had been fed a hearty breakfast before being deployed. It would probably be the only hot meal they got all day.

In addition to all the extra officers, over a hundred concerned members of the public had turned up at the RVP, all eager to offer their help. They were currently being sorted into groups by a gnarly old sergeant who was dividing them according to age, fitness and the amount of time they were willing to volunteer.

Tom Grant and Ciaron Musgrove were there too, standing a little distance apart from the rest of the searchers. They looked pale and tired, like they hadn't slept much. Tyler nodded at them as he drove past, but neither man seemed to recognise him.

Tyler spotted Bear, video camera hanging by his side, chatting to a couple of uniforms by the open door to the large blue van that housed the mobile command unit for the search. He rather liked Bear. The videographer was a gentle giant of a man; quiet and very unassuming, unlike Imogen Askew, who Tyler could confidently say was neither quiet nor unassuming. Whatever her faults, Bear was obviously very fond of her, and Tyler found the way that he always looked out for her, protecting her like she was his little sister, rather endearing.

Tyler pulled up beyond the command vehicle, on a side of the clearing that bordered a large working stable. The two were separated by a barbed wire fence that shimmered with frost, looking for all the world like a scene on a Christmas card.

Killing the engine, he sat there for a few moments, studying the large crowd of civilians huddled together in the middle of the car park and wondering if the individual responsible for Peter and Gavin's abduction was hidden amongst them. None of the men he could see matched the suspect's description, but people could easily change their appearance.

Tyler's breath misted as soon as he left the warmth of the car, and the air was so crisp that it chilled his lungs. "Cold, cold, cold!" he complained, pulling his winter coat on. Drawing the collar tight, he set off towards the forest, wishing he'd thought to bring gloves and a scarf.

The early morning mist drifted eerily across the uneven ground, obscuring his feet and ankles, and absorbing the sound of his footsteps. Passing through a set of wooden stiles, Tyler followed the rutted public footpath to where Susie Sergeant stood shoulder to shoulder with Jim Breslow. They were both staring intently at an ordinance survey map Breslow was holding up.

"Morning," Tyler called out as he approached from behind.

Susie waved a mittened hand at him. "Morning, Jack," she said, her breath billowing around her head before slowly dissipating in the breeze.

He waved back, thinking that she looked like a Michelin Man in her thick, knee length puffer jacket. "Have you seen today's headlines yet?" He enquired.

The duty Press Liaison Officer at NSY had rung him while he was driving to the RVP, and she had read a small selection out to him. To be fair, most newspapers were reporting responsibly, but *The London Echo* and a couple of other redtops were using inflammatory headlines to boost their sales:

*'Will the mystery child snatchers strike again?'*

*'Parents afraid to let their children out alone with evil child snatchers still on the loose!'*

*'Peter and Gavin's disappearance; is this the work of a paedophile gang?'*

Susie's face took on a guarded expression. "Why, is there something in them I should know about?"

Tyler shook his head, made a dismissive gesture with his hand. "The usual culprits are doing a bit of scare mongering, but it's nothing more than we would expect from them."

Susie's mouth twisted downwards in a cynical sneer. "So much for the press playing nicely," she observed, drily.

"We're just discussing today's plan of action," Breslow

announced in his West Country drawl, at the same time holding his map out for Tyler's perusal.

The PolSA inspector was a slightly eccentric man in his mid-fifties with bushy Dickensian sideburns stretching all the way down to his chin. "We've divided the forest into a number of manageable grids, and I'm ticking them off as we search them."

Tyler winced when he saw how many unticked boxes remained. "Is there any way we can realistically speed up the process?" he asked, slapping his arms to generate some heat.

Breslow gave him a brittle smile. "I assume you do want us to do this properly?"

Tyler did want them to do this properly; they *had* to do this properly.

"Yes, of course."

"Then you'll just have to accept that it's going to be a painfully slow process," Breslow told him, bluntly. "There are no shortcuts. First, we send in the dogs, then we put a line of people abreast of each other and methodically work our way through the terrain that's in front of us, combing it inch by blooming inch."

Tyler pointed towards several large pools of stagnant water in the distance, some of which looked as thick as sludge. "Will searching those pools be very time consuming?"

Breslow followed his gaze, then snorted. "Massively, but we've got twice the number of people we had yesterday, three times as many if you count all the civvies. Plus, in addition to the two GP dogs, we've got two cadaver trained mutts with us today, and we'll deploy them into the worst areas."

Cadaver dogs were especially trained to pick up the scent of decomposing flesh and other human remains, unlike general purpose dogs, who were predominantly used to track the scent left by living people.

Tyler sighed, resigning himself to the fact that the search was going to take days, if not weeks, to complete. "It looks like you've got your work cut out, so I'd better leave you in peace to get on with it."

As he turned to go, Susie called out to him. "Jack, will you do me a huge favour and ring the sketch artist at NSY on my behalf? He promised to e-mail me the E-fit of our suspect this morning, but as I'm going to be stuck out here till at least lunchtime, it might be better if he sends it to you instead."

"Of course. I'll chase him up as soon as I get back to the office," he promised, giving Susie's arm a gentle squeeze.

---

Frank Stebbins rapped on Craddock's door and entered without waiting to be called in. "Hot off the press, I've just heard back from the method index people," he said, excitedly waving his hastily scrawled notes at his boss.

Craddock looked up from his Decision Log, peering over the top of his reading glasses in annoyance. "Bloody hell, Frank! Can't I even get five minutes of peace without some inconsiderate bugger disturbing me?" he complained, grumpily. "Can't you come back later, when I've finished writing up this blooming log?"

Stebbins floundered, unsure whether to push on or retreat. "But you'll want to hear this right away," he insisted, with uncharacteristic boldness.

Craddock sighed theatrically, as he was prone to do, then tossed his pen onto the desk and removed his reading glasses. "Oh, very well then," he conceded. "Come in and sit down. You're making the place look untidy."

Stebbins sat to attention, keeping his back ramrod straight and his knees pressed tightly together, like a schoolboy hauled up before the headmaster. He cleared his throat before speaking. "You won't believe this, but it turns out there are two almost identical unsolved murders on record. One was committed in a rural part of Wales at the beginning of the year, the other in Northumberland three months ago."

Craddock was all ears now, his Decision Log brushed aside to make room for his folded arms. "Well don't just leave me hanging in suspense, young Frank. Tell me everything!"

Stebbins was smiling now, like he always did when the boss called him that.

"That's all I know, so far. I've got the case reference numbers and the names and contact details for the two SIOs. I didn't know if you'd want me to call them on your behalf, or if you'd prefer to do it yourself."

Craddock held out his hand, beckoned impatiently. "Give me those details," he said, gruffly. "I'll phone the SIOs. Meanwhile, you speak to the HOLMES administrators, see if we can be granted temporary 'read only' access to the other two accounts. It'll be interesting to see if we can make any connections."

HOLMES was an acronym for Home Office Large Major Enquiry System, and was a homage to Baker Street's most famous sleuth. The system was basically an electronic filing cabinet into which all the information gathered during a major investigation was entered, allowing data to be searched and cross referenced with comparative ease.

Every HOLMES investigation was given its own unique reference number, and the beauty of the system was that it was national, so forces from different parts of the country could be granted access to each other's accounts when cross border offending occurred.

HOLMES had been developed in response to the Byford Report, which had been commissioned to examine the many failings of the Yorkshire Ripper investigation after Peter Sutcliffe's eventual arrest in Sheffield in January 1981. It ranked as one of the largest criminal investigations in British history, with over 250,000 people being interviewed. Sutcliffe himself had been interviewed nine times, and all the information needed to link him to the killing spree had been in the system long before his arrest, but the connection had never been made because the data was seen and evaluated by different people, stored in different locations, and never cross referenced.

Stebbins stood up, his weary limbs protesting at the effort it took. "I'll get straight onto it," he promised, heading for the door.

"You do that," Craddock said, reaching for the telephone. "I'll start making calls. Keep your fingers crossed, Frank. This might give us the break we need."

"I hope so, boss," Stebbins said on his way out the door.

"So do I," Craddock muttered quietly under his breath.

As SIO, he had to project confidence and positivity, but privately, he admitted to himself that they were running out of ideas.

---

Alison inhaled the smoke greedily, and the nicotine hit instantly made her feel lightheaded. A moment later, she was coughing her lungs up. With a grimace, she tossed the cigarette to the floor and stamped on it, wishing she had never lit up. "Now I remember why I gave up smoking," she said, wiping her mouth with the back of her hand.

"Why don't we go back inside and have some tea," her mother encouraged.

The kitchen was at the rear of the house, so it was safe from the prying eyes of the media, who seemed to have set up a permanent basecamp outside. After catching one nosy photographer spying on her through their telephoto lens, Alison had taken to keeping the living room curtains permanently drawn. She felt trapped inside her house, and she was struggling to cope with the terrible sense of intrusion.

To her amazement, the story was attracting world-wide media coverage. That morning, while popping down to the local Co-Op to grab some milk, she had been accosted by a very polite Japanese reporter who was doing a human-interest article for a Tokyo newspaper. It was beyond crazy; in the space of two days, her family had gone from being boringly average, living out their humdrum lives in complete obscurity, to household names.

"You really need to eat something," Marjorie berated her daughter. "I can see the weight dropping off you, and you'll be no good to Peter if you're too weak to look after him when he comes back."

Alison walked back into the kitchen without replying. She knew her mother was right, but in times of stress, her appetite always suffered.

Extinguishing her own cigarette, Marjorie dutifully followed her. "Let me make you some breakfast," she offered.

"I'm not hungry." Alison's voice was flat, lifeless.

"But you need to—"

"I said, I'm not hungry." The stress was making Alison snappy, and she immediately regretted the outburst. "I'm sorry, mum. I know you mean well, but I don't need food; I need Peter."

---

Kevin Murray was in a bleak mood as he pulled the clanking diesel pool car up outside a mid-terraced house in Upper Walthamstow. Beside him, Charlie White checked the address against the one in his daybook and nodded.

"Aye, this is the one."

Killing the engine, Murray unbuckled his seatbelt with a disgruntled sigh. "I've decided I don't like this job, Whitey."

The Scotsman raised an uncaring eyebrow. "You should resign then," he suggested. "Maybe become a road sweeper or something like that."

Murray shot him a filthy sideways glance. "Very funny. I'm just making the point that I don't like this new job we've taken."

"Och, you poor wee thing!" White replied in a voice reeking of sarcasm. "Why don't you let the DCI know how you feel? I'm sure he'll swap it for another one, if that would make you happier."

Giving him the finger, Murray angrily pushed open the Astra's creaky door, which resisted him all the way. Slamming the door much harder than necessary, he stomped over to the front gate.

This was the second day on the trot that they had been lumbered visiting sex offenders who resided in the Waltham Forest area, and it was proving to be very unpleasant work. On more than one occasion, the detectives had left thinking that the man they had just spoken to had something sinister to hide.

"What's this horrible cretin's name?" he asked White.

"His name's Lionel Eberhard, and he's got one previous conviction for possessing indecent images of children."

The thought of someone pleasuring themselves while they watched children being abused made Murray's skin crawl. "C'mon then, let's get it over with." Muttering obscenities under his breath, he opened the garden gate and followed the winding path up to the brown pebbledashed house. "Mind that big dollop of cat shit," he called out, hurriedly sidestepping the turd he'd just spotted.

Murray tried ringing the doorbell but the battery was dead, so he hammered on the door with his fist. They waited a few seconds but no one came. "Perhaps he's out?" he conjectured.

White crossed to the bay window. Cupping his hands against the glass, he peered in. "No, someone's definitely in there."

Murray banged again, louder this time. "Police! Open up!"

After a few seconds of relentless pounding, the door opened inwards and a man in his mid-fifties cautiously poked his head through the gap. "Yes?" he enquired, glancing nervously from one stern-faced detective to the other. His face was flushed, and he was breathing heavily.

Murray caught a faint whiff of sweat, and something else... fear perhaps?

White produced his warrant card for inspection. "Are you Lionel Eberhard?" he asked, keeping his face neutral, his voice business like.

The man hesitated, then nodded.

"What do you want?" Eberhard asked, running a hand through an unruly mop of greying hair. The movement pulled his thin blue dressing gown wide open, revealing a grubby string vest beneath, from which little tufts of hair poked through the gaps.

"Why are you so out of breath?" White asked, answering the question with one of his own.

Eberhard hadn't been expecting that, and it put him on the back foot. "I–I was upstairs getting dressed, so I had to run down to answer the door."

Murray frowned. "If you were upstairs, who did I just see watching TV in the living room?"

"No one," Eberhard said, a little too quickly. "The TV's not on."

Murray noticed the bulge in Eberhard's grimy dressing gown. "Have you got a boner, Mr Eberhard?" he asked, staring pointedly at the man's groin.

With a sharp intake of breath, Eberhard turned away, making hurried adjustments to his dressing gown. "You can't go around saying things like that!" he spluttered, his face crimson with embarrassment.

"I just did," Murray smirked, enjoying the man's discomfort.

"Well, you shouldn't have," Eberhard huffed. "And don't think you're going to get away with it. I'm going to complain to your superiors."

Murray responded with a blasé shrug. "Go for it."

On seeing the policeman's total indifference, Eberhard's bluster seemed to desert him. "What do you want?" he demanded, petulantly. "I'm a very busy man, and I don't need you lot harassing me."

"It's cold out here," Murray said, pushing the door open and barging past Eberhard. "Why don't you invite us in, so we can talk in the warmth?"

Eberhard's eyes widened in alarm. "But I don't want you in my—"

"Very kind of you to ask us in," White said, brushing the paedophile aside and following Murray into the hall.

The sounds of a TV were coming from an open door halfway along the hall.

"I thought you said the TV wasnae on?" White asked, taking a step in that direction.

"Stop!" Eberhard called, abruptly. "What do you think you're doing? You can't come into my house without a warrant."

"You invited us in, remember?" Murray pointed out. "And we're only here to speak to you, not search the house, so we don't need a warrant."

Eberhard was becoming increasingly flustered.

"Are you okay?" Murray enquired, feigning concern. "You look a bit pale. Perhaps we should adjourn to the lounge, so you can sit down while we talk?"

The remaining colour drained from Eberhard's face, and he shook his head, vehemently. "No. I don't want to—"

"Excellent," Murray said, taking hold of his arm and frog-marching him towards the lounge. "This way, is it?"

---

Sean Murphy's moral dilemma was doing his poor head in. After watching the news on TV, he now realised that he had witnessed those poor kids being abducted on Saturday night, and he really wanted to let the police know what he'd seen. The trouble was, he couldn't, not without implicating himself for breaking into all those cars.

"What's the matter with you?" Jenny Cartwright demanded. She was staring at him from across the table at McDonald's in Walthamstow Central, where he had taken her for lunch. "You've hardly said a word all morning. Honestly, I might as well be sitting here on my own."

Murphy took a huge bite out of his Big Mac. "Just got something on my mind, babes," he said, chewing as he spoke.

Jenny was a pretty girl, with a decent figure and kind heart, but she was also a terrible gossip, which meant that a secret shared with her didn't remain a secret for very long.

"Did you see that appeal on TV last night?" he asked, casually. "The one about the two boys who went missing from Chingford on Saturday."

Jenny's face adopted a sad expression. "It's terrible. I was almost in tears when I saw their poor parents hugging each other." She lowered her voice, as if sharing secret information. "I reckon they've been grabbed by a pervy child molester."

Murphy looked away, feeling sick.

"In fact, they're probably long dead by now," Jenny added, her voice matter of fact.

Murphy nearly choked on his burger. "Jesus!" he spluttered, spraying food from his mouth. "Don't say things like that!"

She gave him a strange look. "What's got into you? You're not normally so squeamish."

"I'm not being squeamish!" he protested, taking the comment as a slight on his masculinity. "It's just that they're only kids, and no one wants to see a kid hurt." He took another bite, chewed it with lacklustre for several seconds. "Who knows? Maybe, someone who saw something will come forward."

Jenny gave the side of her dainty nose a knowing tap. "You mark my words, Sean Murphy, those poor boys are already six feet under."

Murphy's appetite had deserted him. Tossing the uneaten half of his burger onto the tray, he stood up. "Come on," he said, irritably. "I've got things to do, so I can't sit here chatting shit to you all day."

"Don't you want the rest of your chips?" Jenny asked, scooping a handful up as he dragged her out of the restaurant.

---

The film playing on Eberhard's TV showed a young boy, aged eight to ten years old. Apart from the canvas hood over his head, he was completely naked, and from the limp state of his body and limbs, it was clear that he was unconscious, almost certainly drugged.

As soon as he saw it, Murray's blood began to boil. Balling his fists, he took a menacing step towards Eberhard. "You evil bastard," he hissed, grabbing the man by his dressing gown lapels and driving him backwards, slamming him into the nearest wall.

The air was expelled from Eberhard's lungs with a satisfying "Oomph!"

Murray was hoping the paedophile would make a fight of it, but he didn't. His shoulders just slumped in resignation, and he offered no resistance.

Spinning Eberhard around to face the wall, Murray removed a pair of handcuffs from his belt and applied them to his prisoner's wrists, tightening them way beyond what was needed to secure him.

Eberhard yelped out in pain, but Murray ignored him.

"Lionel Eberhard, I'm arresting you for possessing indecent images of children," he said through gritted teeth. His voice was like cold steel as he recited the caution.

"I'm sorry," Eberhard said, sounding like the pathetic excuse for a human being that he was. "It's an illness, I can't help it."

Out of the corner of his eye, Murray could still see the TV screen, and his stomach curdled as three white men, late middle-aged from the look of their flabby naked bodies, gathered around their victim. Apart from the demonic face masks they wore to conceal their identities, they were naked and in a state of arousal.

"Turn that poisonous filth off!" Murray barked at White, who was staring at the screen in shock, looking like he was going to be sick.

# 17

I want my lawyer

Benny had been trying to reach Madeley all morning, but annoyingly, the barrister's mobile phone constantly deferred to voicemail. He hadn't left any messages; only fools made amateurish mistakes like that.

He had spent the morning reaching out to his wealthiest clients, inviting expressions of interest from them over the two chickens. He had already received five bids for the pretty blonde and three for his chubby companion. The offers had been respectable, but Benny had bounced them all back, instructing the bidders that they would have to do much better.

Madeley was the last person on his list of prospective buyers, and as the blonde was a perfect match for the physical requirements he had given Benny, he was confident that the barrister's bid would be the highest.

At 1.15.p.m. Madeley finally answered his phone. "I've been

trying to reach you all morning," Benny said, unable to hide his irritation.

"*I've been in court,*" Madeley replied, as if it should have been glaringly obvious.

Given what the man did for a living, Benny conceded that it probably should have.

"I've found the perfect specimen for you."

"*Really? This is incredible news!*" Madeley sounded surprised and a little nervous. "*Can you tell me a little more about—*"

"Not over the phone," Benny cut him off. "Can we meet later this afternoon, or early this evening?"

"*Regrettably, I can't,*" Madeley apologised. "*I'll be at court until five, and then I've got to rush back to chambers for a very important meeting that's likely to drag on for hours. I'll be tied up at The Bailey again all day tomorrow, but we could meet afterwards, perhaps find a nearby café?*"

"I think it would be much better if you stopped by the shop," Benny countered. "That'll be a bit more discreet, don't you think?"

Madeley sighed his displeasure, but didn't argue the point. "*What time do you close?*"

"Five-thirty."

"*Very well,*" Madeley conceded. "*I'll come to you.*"

"Good, but don't enter the shop until I put the closed sign up."

Hanging up, Benny poured a generous tumbler of scotch. His clients had until midnight the following day to make their final bids. The winners would be informed first thing on Wednesday morning, and the handover would occur the following day.

Feeling inordinately pleased with himself, Benny raised his glass into the air. "Here's to you, old son, for turning what could have been a total disaster into a very profitable situation," he toasted himself.

The chickens would be delivered to the winning bidders on Thursday afternoon and returned to the safe house for disposal that same night. By Friday morning, they would be lying in an unmarked grave in the middle of nowhere.

Having just concluded a long telephone conversation with an American forensic psychologist called Dr Kate Cassidy, Tyler felt a desperate urge to stretch his legs, so he printed off three copies of the E-fit that had been sent through to him earlier in the day, attached a covering note, then set off for the Major Investigation Room.

DS Chris Deakin, his Office Manager, nodded to him as he walked in. Tyler was of the opinion that, if he was the ship's captain and his office was the bridge, then Deakin was his chief engineer and the MIR was the engine room. He handed the three copies of the E-fit to Deakin for indexing.

"This is the man we think abducted the kids."

"He certainly looks like a wrong-un," Deakin concluded after a couple of moments of intense scrutiny.

Pulling over a chair, Tyler flopped down next to the MIR skipper. "I've just had a lengthy conversation with an NPIA recommended expert on sex offenders," he said, stifling a yawn.

Deakin grimaced. "Blimey! Are things so bad that we've had to involve the no point in asking police?"

"Believe it or not, they might actually prove helpful in this instance," Tyler begrudgingly admitted, thinking that there had to be a first time for everything. "According to the good doctor, most of the men who join these wolfpacks aren't paedophiles in the sense that we understand it. Apparently, it's more appropriate to think of them as sadistic sexual killers who get immense pleasure from the abuse and torture of the young and the vulnerable. Quite a few who target rent boys are practicing homosexuals who also have consensual sexual relations with each other. They simply use the children they snatch as objects to fulfil their warped sexual fantasies."

"I thought paedos only liked having sex with children," Deakin said, frowning.

"Some do," Tyler confirmed, passing on his new found knowledge. "But some are equally attracted to adult men if they're homosexual, or adult females if they're straight. That's why a lot of them are married, with children of their own."

Deakin scratched his head. "Well, that's as clear as mud, then."

Tyler chuckled. "That's exactly what I said."

Gurjit Singh was sitting in an alcove opposite them, manning the Incident Room hotline, which Tyler noticed wasn't particularly hot at that precise moment.

The Asian detective was dunking a chocolate biscuit into his cup of tea. "The way I see it, boss," Singh began, before pausing to suck the melting chocolate off his soggy biscuit, "is that regardless of whichever box the experts want to put these sick bastards in, we hunt them down in exactly the same way as we do every other criminal."

"Yes, of course," Tyler allowed. "But if we could work out what makes these people tick, we might be able to get into their heads and anticipate their next move."

Having successfully sucked all the chocolate off, Gurjit was now delicately nibbling at the digestive base, dropping crumbs all over his chest. "No offence, but I don't think I want to get into the heads of these creeps. I reckon they contain the stuff that nightmares are made of." Suppressing a shiver, he reached across the desk and removed another digestive from the packet.

"That's why the boss gets paid the big bucks," Deakin said with a rueful grin. "Because, unlike you and me, he doesn't get a choice."

---

When they marched Eberhard into Chingford police station, Murray was miffed to find there were two prisoners ahead of them in the queue.

"I don't care if you're Murder Squad, mate. You'll just have to wait your turn like everyone else," the gaoler snapped when he asked how long it would take.

They were still waiting an hour later, when DI Howarth came down to the custody office to see how they were getting on. "Don't tell me he hasn't been booked in yet?" she asked, staring incredulously at White.

White just sighed, which was answer enough.

"Which one's Eberhard?" Howarth enquired, looking around the packed custody office.

White pointed to an insignificant looking man in a stripy dressing gown, string vest and odd socks, who was sitting alone on a wooden bench. "That's the wee perv, over there."

Unaware that he was being talked about, Eberhard had a vacant expression on his face as he massaged the deep welts on his wrists, which had been caused by the handcuffs digging into his flesh.

"Do you think he could be connected to Peter and Gavin's disappearance?" she asked.

White shook his head. "Sorry, as much as I wish it were otherwise, there's nothing to suggest yon paedo's involved."

"Pity," Howarth said, sounding disappointed.

Murray wandered over, carrying two polystyrene cups full of steaming liquid. "You asked for tea with two sugars," he said, handing one to White.

The Scots man accepted it gratefully, then took a sip. "Gah," he said, with a grimace. "There's no sugar in it."

Murray grinned. "I know, they didn't have any."

"What made you suspect Eberhard?" Howarth asked, looking from one to the other.

"We were acting on professional instinct, ma'am," White said, and left it at that.

"Yes, very commendable, but what exactly tipped you off that he was committing an offence?" Howarth persisted.

"Well," Murray said, after a moment's contemplation. "The dirty old git opened the door with a flushed face and a hard on, and then had the cheek to claim his TV was switched off, even though we could hear it playing."

Howarth stared at him blankly, none the wiser.

"It's like this," Murray said, spelling it out for her. "When I saw his boner and flushed face, I realised that we'd interrupted him while he was knocking one out, and let's face it, men like him don't watch normal porn, do they?"

White snorted. "Aye, Kev's an expert on watching porn, and on knocking one out, so he knows the signs to look out for."

It was clear from Howarth's reaction that she didn't know whether to laugh or be offended. In the end, she just turned and walked away, instructing the custody sergeant to ring her when Eberhard was finally booked in, so that she could send down a couple of divisional DCs to interview him.

"Did you have to make me sound like a sex mad deviant?" Murray complained as they walked Eberhard down to his cell.

"Just telling it as it is," White said, struggling to keep a straight face.

"I want my lawyer," Eberhard whined as they ushered him into the cell.

"Shut up, you horrible little nonce," Murray snapped, slamming the cell door in his face.

"Charming," Eberhard said, peering through the open wicket.

Murray slammed that closed, too.

---

Tyler wasn't sure how it had happened, but somehow, Gurjit had talked him into covering the hotline while he popped to the loo.

"Don't worry," Gurjit assured him on his way out of the door. "It hasn't rung once in the past hour, and I'll only be gone five minutes."

Predictably, the moment Gurjit vanished, the bloody thing started ringing.

Tyler groaned. Reaching for a pen and pad, he picked up the receiver, fully expecting to find himself talking to someone who wanted to report having seen the boys hiking in Scotland a week before they disappeared, or wanting to put forward their next-door neighbour as a potential suspect because his eyes were too close together.

"Incident room, how can I help you?"

At the other end of the line, over the background noise of a busy road, Tyler was sure he could hear breathing, but the caller didn't speak.

"You've come through to the police incident room," he

repeated, wondering if the caller had misdialled, and was now dithering over whether to apologise or just hang up.

"I...I've got some information about those two boys who were snatched from the funfair in Chingford..."

The voice belonged to a nervous male with an East London accent. He sounded young, awkward, unsure how to proceed.

"Thank you for calling," Tyler said, injecting a note of friendliness into his voice. "Before we start, I just need take some details from you. What's your name, please?"

A sharp intake of breath. "*No names,*" the voice insisted. "*I can't get involved.*"

"Okay," Tyler soothed. "Perhaps you should just tell me what you know, and we'll go from there."

"*Well, it's like this... I was in the car park on Saturday night when this bloke turns up with two kids in tow.*" There was an awkward pause. A siren blared in the background, then faded away. "*I know it was them because I saw the TV appeal last night and recognised them straight away from that.*"

"Go on," Tyler encouraged.

"*Well, they went over to a Citroen Berlingo panel van. The bloke opened the back and looked in, then he told the boys to hop in.*"

"You're telling me they went willingly?"

Another pause, longer this time. "*Well, sort of. They got into the back willingly enough, but then he pulled out this big knife and started waving it at them. From where I was hiding, I thought I could hear them crying, but I couldn't be sure. Anyway, he got in after them... I couldn't see what he was doing after that, but he looked proper out of breath when he jumped out a couple of minutes later.*"

"You said you were hiding. Why was that?"

"*Don't want to say,*" the boy said quickly, defensively.

"Fair enough." It wasn't, but the caller was incredibly jittery, and Tyler didn't want to press him too hard, in case he rung off. "How far away from the van were you hiding?"

"*Err... Not far. I was in some bushes a few yards away.*"

"Was anyone else in the bushes with you?" Tyler asked, wondering if the caller had been canoodling with a girl.

"No... I was alone."

"And had you been to the funfair that night?"

"Well, yeah...but what's that got to do with anything?"

"I'm just trying to get things straight in my head, and I wondered if you were returning to your car when you saw the man with the boys."

"Look mate," the caller said, getting narky. "*Do you want to know what I saw or not? Because, if you're going to start interrogating me, I'll hang up now.*"

"Please don't do that," Tyler implored. "What you saw could be very important."

"*Important? Yeah, that's what I thought,*" the caller said, sounding slightly mollified.

"Can you describe the man you saw for me?"

"*He was a white geezer, about six feet tall and very skinny. He was unshaven, not a beard, just a few days' stubble. He was dirty looking, and his hair was long, shoulder length I would say.*"

Tyler was making detailed notes. "Okay, that's very helpful," he encouraged. "Can you remember what he was wearing?"

"*He was dressed like a soldier,*" the caller said without hesitation. "*You know, camouflage jacket and green trousers. Oh, and he had army style boots on as well.*"

That gelled with the description the fairground worker had given.

"Do you think you would recognise this man if you saw him again?"

There was a moment's hesitation before the boy answered. "*Well, it was dark, and there were no streetlights, but I guess I got a fairly good look at his ugly mug, so probably. Why?*"

"Because, if there's a chance you would recognise him, we might need you to attend an identity parade at some point in the future, to see if you could pick him out of a line-up."

"*No fucking way!*" The caller sounded horrified. "*I told you, I'm happy to tell you what I saw, but I ain't willing to get involved.*"

Tyler recalled that a half dozen cars had been broken into that night. Could the jittery caller be the person responsible for the mini crime spree? It would certainly explain his reticence to get involved. "Let's revisit the van you mentioned," he said, quickly. "What colour was it?"

"*Dark. Either red or blue.*"

"And you're sure it was a Citroen Berlingo?"

The caller snorted, as if insulted by the question. "*I'm sure.*"

"I don't suppose you made a note of the registration number, did you?" Tyler asked. It was a long shot, and he wasn't hopeful, but it was worth a try.

"*Well, I do remember part of it,*" the caller said.

# 18

The two wankerchiefs on the coffee table

Susie met up with Mel Howarth at a roadside café near High Beach. It was a typical greasy spoon affair. Apart from them, there was a smattering of lorry drivers, a couple of leather clad bikers and a group of unshaven men in the high-vis jackets of road workers. It wasn't the kind of establishment she would have normally chosen to eat in, but there was nothing else for miles around, and she didn't want to risk driving all the way back to Chingford in case the searchers made a significant find while she was away. Plus, it was toasty warm inside, and she really needed to thaw out for a little while after spending so many hours out in the cold.

They chose a wobbly Formica table at the rear, where they could talk without fear of being overheard. Sitting down, Susie stared at the chipped mug of strong builders' tea in her hand.

"I'm frightened to give it a stir in case the spoon dissolves," she told Howarth, who had wisely opted for a can of diet soda.

Two burly men were seated at the table opposite. One had his back to them, exposing the crack of his hairy arse for all to see. Susie grimaced at the sight and quickly averted her eyes. "Well, if that's not enough to put me off my bacon sandwich, I don't know what is," she said with a shudder.

"Luckily, I'm a vegetarian," Howarth replied with a grin.

Susie reached into her shoulder bag and groped for the blister pack of paracetamol she kept in there. "I've got the headache from hell,' she confessed, popping two into her mouth and washing them down with the foul brown liquid. "Gah," she shuddered, wishing she had followed Howarth's example and chosen a can, instead.

"The DCI asked me to drop off a copy of the E-Fit," Howarth said, handing her over an A4 sheet of paper. "I believe you were expecting it."

Susie accepted the document with a smile of thanks. Leaning back in her plastic seat, she studied the grainy image in silence.

"Have you heard about the bloke who rang in, earlier today?" Howarth enquired.

Still looking at the E-Fit, Susie nodded. "Jack rang me with the news a little while ago. Now that we know the make of van the suspect used, and have a partial index for it, I'm hoping the officers viewing the CCTV will be able to find it. In the meantime, our Intel Cell is working with the PNC Bureau to prepare a detailed list of every Berlingo that's registered within the Greater London area. Worst case scenario, we'll visit every van until we find the right one."

Howarth flashed Susie a sorrowful smile. "But that could take ages, and the odds of those poor boys still being alive by then are almost non-existent."

Susie looked up from the image. "True," she acknowledged. "But unless we can work out the rest of the van's registration number from the CCTV footage, we won't have a choice."

---

Tyler had just concluded a lengthy telephone conversation with George Holland, in which they had discussed the delicate issue of whether the resource intensive search of Epping Forest should be scaled down, or even called off altogether, in light of the information provided by the anonymous caller earlier in the day.

Not only was the search costing the Met a small fortune, but the officers involved were operating in harsh conditions and working exhaustingly long shifts, and neither detective wanted this punishing ordeal to continue for a moment longer than was absolutely necessary.

If the caller was to be believed, Peter Musgrove and Gavin Grant had been ushered into the rear of a Citroen Berlingo on Saturday night, before being driven away from the funfair by a scruffy white male dressed in army fatigues. The description he had provided of the suspect matched the one given by the fairground worker on the night of the abduction, which made him seem credible, but the fact that he had refused to provide his name or make a written statement rang very loud alarm bells and called into question his reliability and motivation as a witness. If the caller was a genuine witness, and not a crank or a hoaxer, it made no sense whatsoever for him to conceal his identity.

Tyler had theorised that the caller was potentially the same man who had broken into all the vehicles in the fairground car park, and was withholding his personal details for fear of being linked to those crimes and arrested if identified. That might be so, Holland had accepted, but there was no way that they could accept the word of an anonymous caller at face value.

"Can you imagine the flack we'd come under if we called off the search without corroborating the caller's identity and credibility, and the boys' bodies were subsequently discovered in the forest?" Holland had said with a shudder. "Heads would roll, and rightly so."

He had a point; for all they knew, the caller was the man who had abducted the children, ringing in to provide misinformation that would throw them off the scent and frustrate the enquiry. It wouldn't be the first time that something like that had happened.

In the end, they had decided that they had no option but to let the search continue for the time being.

With a world weary sigh, Tyler opened his decision Log. The fact that they had considered all of this, along with the conclusion they had reached and their rationale behind it, needed to be thoroughly documented, because if the boys weren't found in Epping Forest, some sanctimonious penny pinching twat of a senior officer at The Yard would want to know why the search wasn't called off as soon as the anonymous witness had provided the information about the boys being driven away in a van.

---

Debbie Brown was waiting outside Eberhard's house when White and Murray returned.

"Been here long?" White asked, keying them into the address.

"Only a few minutes," she said, rubbing her arms to generate some heat.

"We really appreciate the help," White said, closing the door behind them. "The quicker we finish here, the quicker we can hand this pile of poo over to the locals."

Debbie gave him a sad smile. "To be honest, I was glad of an excuse to escape my FLO responsibilities for a couple of hours. Don't get me wrong; the boys' parents are lovely people, and they've gone out of their way to make us feel welcome, but their world has just come crumbling down around them, and being in their orbit for too long can be really draining."

White nodded his understanding. "Aye, I know exactly how you feel. Being stuck in his orbit for long periods can be really draining, too," he said, nodding at Murray.

Ignoring the jibe, Murray led them into the lounge and dumped his exhibits bag onto the floor. "Let's start in here, shall we?" he said, handing each of them a pair of Nitrile gloves.

Debbie ran her eyes over the gloomy room. "What exactly are we looking for?"

White gestured towards the large TV. "The nonce we arrested was watching a videotape of a poor wee bairn being gang raped by three men, so I would suggest we're looking for more films."

"Dear God!" Debbie gasped, appalled.

"Aye, I know," White agreed, shaking his head in disgust. "It was horrible. I cannae get the images out of my head."

Murray was making his first entry in the search log. "I think I'll start by seizing the two wankerchiefs on the coffee table," he said, nodding at a couple of soiled tissues that had been deposited in an ashtray.

Following his gaze, Debbie dry heaved. "What a sicko," she said, recoiling at the sight.

"Are you referring to Kevin or the suspect?" White sniggered.

"Ha–bloody–ha!" Murray responded with a sneer. "Debs, why don't you start going through that big pile of videos?" he suggested, picking the first of the tissues up with two fingers and holding it as far away from his body as he possibly could to avoid catching an unwanted whiff of the suspect's semen.

Debbie removed a handful of VHS tapes from a rack beside the TV stand and began flipping through them, reading their labels one by one. "These are just bog-standard thrillers and comedies," she said, putting them down again.

Murray was halfway through bagging the second tissue. "You can't go by the covers," he warned. "You'll need to physically watch each film."

"You're joking?"

Murray shook his head. "Rewind them to the beginning and play them all the way through on fast forward," he instructed.

Debbie remained dubious. "That seems a bit pointless to me."

"Trust me, it's not," White assured her. "I didnae realise this until today, but paedophiles often hide their child abuse recordings in the middle of innocent material. The first and last hour of the VHS tape we confiscated earlier had a PG rated feature film on it. The kiddy porn had been cleverly inserted in the middle. You would never know it contained illegal footage without playing it all the way through."

"Bloody hell!" Debbie said, looking at the video in her hand as though it were an alien artefact. "They really are devious little buggers, aren't they."

"Devious little buggerers, you mean," Murray corrected her with an evil chuckle.

Debbie gave him an acerbic look, then shook her head in disgust.

There were fifteen videos in all, and none of them appeared to be counterfeits. The boxes had professional looking sleeves in them; the cassettes had what appeared to be genuine studio labels with holographic symbols affixed to them. There was absolutely nothing about any of them that would have aroused suspicion.

It took an hour and a half to speed through all the tapes on fast forward. The first twelve were perfectly innocent, but the thirteenth contained hidden material that was every bit as vile as the tape Eberhard had been watching prior to his arrest.

Murray averted his eyes the moment he realised what he was looking at. "Hanging's too good for these people," he seethed.

Debbie forced herself to look for a few seconds, but her face quickly drained of colour. "I can't watch anymore," she said, when she could bear it no longer. Ejecting the tape, she handed it to Murray to be bagged and logged.

The fourteenth tape was porn free, but the last one contained deeply disturbing footage of children being abused. A small, dog-eared calling card was tucked behind the cassette's plastic sleeve. It was grubby with age. A man's first name, mobile telephone number and address had been handwritten on it. "Do you think this could be relevant?" Murray asked, showing it to White.

The Scotsman turned it over in his hand. "Aye, we'd better bag it, just in case."

They gave the rest of the house a cursory search, but there were no more video tapes. Beneath Eberhard's mattress, Murray found a stash of ten by eight colour photographs featuring various young boys in skimpy swimwear. Their skin glistened as if covered in oil. All were smiling, but a few of the models seemed uneasy, as if they felt uncomfortable posing.

A couple of shots were stuck together and tacky to the touch. "I dread to think why that is," Murray said, bagging them.

"These photos look like they've been taken in a professional studio," White said, peering over his shoulder.

"Yes, they do," Debbie agreed. "I might be wrong, but I get the impression some of these boys are posing reluctantly." A note of anxiety crept into her voice. "I hope they didn't end up being subjected to the same kind of treatment we saw in those vile films."

Thirty minutes later, the search concluded.

"I'm just going to pop to the little boy's room before we take our leave," Murray announced, detouring into the bathroom

Debbie glanced down at his nether region, then raised an eyebrow. "Never has a saying been more apt," she decreed.

White found that hilarious, and held out his hand for her to high five him.

# 19

## Mad not bad

The sun had set for another day, yet they were still no closer to finding the missing boys. Susie was determined to keep the search going for as long as possible, but at some point, she would have to stand the searchers down to get some rest.

There had been some unwanted excitement earlier in the day, when one of the cadaver dogs found what appeared to be a shallow grave. A Crime Scene Manager had been hurriedly called down to the scene. Under his careful supervision, the earth had been slowly removed until the rotting corpse of an old dog was exhumed.

When it was announced that the remains were those of an animal, not a child, the relief felt by the searchers was indescribable, but the euphoria was short lived.

Inevitably, as the day progressed, more and more people began expressing concerns that it was now only a matter of time until they found a similar shallow grave containing the boys' bodies. Susie did her best to keep spirits high, but secretly, she agreed with them.

Tyler jogged up the stairs to the first floor of Hertford House. He had just come from the Command Corridor on the ground floor, where he spent fifteen minutes pitching an idea to George Holland. The DCS had given a cautious seal of approval, on the strict proviso that Tyler sought further advice from a forensic psychologist before proceeding any further, and he hadn't been remotely amused when Tyler jokingly enquired if he was earning a big fat commission for every NPIA referral he made.

Filled with a new sense of purpose, Tyler breezed into his office. Closing the door behind him, he threw himself into the chair behind his desk and put in a call to the NPIA contact desk, asking to be put back in touch with Dr Cassidy, the psychologist he had spoken to previously.

"*I'm sorry, sir,*" he was told, brusquely. "*Kate's on her way to the airport to catch a plane to Zurich. She'll be attending a conference for the rest of the week and won't be available to deal with any calls.*"

Tyler groaned. "But this is incredibly important," he said, and proceeded to give the woman a brief overview of the case. Under duress, she promised to find him a suitable replacement, but when he hung up, he wasn't overly hopeful.

He was just about to update his Decision Log when the phone rang, making him jump.

"Bloody hell," he gasped, impressed that they were calling him back so quickly. "DCI Tyler speaking."

"*Boss, it's Dick. I've found some footage of the suspect's van. Any chance you can pop down to the CCTV viewing room?*"

Three minutes later, he was leaning over Jarvis' shoulder, staring down at the monitor. "Come on then," he said, sounding like a big kid. "Show me."

Jarvis grinned. "I've identified six cameras between Rangers Road and the Waterworks Roundabout that recorded footage of the van. As you'll see in the compilation I've cobbled together, it's much clearer in some than in others. Ignore the times shown in the top right of the screen. They're all out by several minutes."

"It's great news that you've found all this footage of the van."

"It is," Jarvis allowed, "but there's also some bad news."

"Which is…?"

"That I still can't make out the missing digits from the van's index plate."

Tyler swore. That *was* bad news.

"We're not beaten yet," Jarvis assured him. "There's an ANPR camera on the approach to the Waterworks Roundabout, and I think the van drove straight past it. I've given Dean the camera's location, and he's going to have it checked. He reckons we should have the results back by mid-morning tomorrow."

"That's an outstanding piece of work," Tyler enthused, giving him a hearty slap him on the back.

Blushing from the praise, Jarvis pressed the play button. "There's the first sighting of the van," he said a moment later, when it appeared on screen. "It's driving along the stretch of dual carriageway opposite Bancroft's School in Woodford Green."

The pole mounted CCTV camera was angled downwards to face oncoming traffic. The picture quality was reasonable, but the headlights of approaching vehicles were so dazzling that it was impossible to read the number plates.

Tyler studied the van. It was being driven perfectly normally, neither going too fast nor too slow. There was nothing to make it stand out from the vehicles around it.

"Looks like there's only one occupant."

Jarvis nodded. "That's right, and the next camera along gives us a slightly better view of him."

That camera was located by a set of traffic lights at the junction with Whitehall Road.

"We get lucky here," Jarvis said. "The Berlingo stops at red traffic lights, and we get a brief glimpse at the driver's face."

As he spoke, the Berlingo stopped beneath the camera, affording them a clear view into its cab. The driver had long scraggy hair and was wearing an army style camouflage jacket. For a single moment, he stared up at the camera, then turned away.

"I've been trying to pause it at the right spot for ages, so I can grab a screen shot of his face," Jarvis told him. "But it's proving impossible."

Pulling over a chair with squeaky casters, Tyler plonked himself down next to Jarvis. "Here, let me try."

"Are you sure you remember how to operate the controls, gov?" Jarvis asked. "I mean, no disrespect, but it's a long time since you were a lowly DC doing grunt work."

"It's muscle memory, like riding a bike," Tyler assured him.

Jarvis grinned. "In that case, be my guest."

Tyler rewound the tape a couple of seconds, then pressed play. "It's all in the timing," he said, flexing his fingers.

As soon as the driver started to look up, he jabbed the pause button, hoping to freeze frame the image in such a way that he could get a clear, unobstructed view of the man's face.

Bands of static flickered across the screen, from top to bottom, distorting the picture.

"If anything, that's just made it worse," Tyler admitted.

He pressed rewind again, conscious that Jarvis was smirking at his efforts.

"Based on that performance, I wouldn't recommend you take up cycling again anytime soon," Jarvis observed.

"I'm just getting warmed up," Tyler insisted, rewinding the tape and pressing play. "I'm sure I'll have better luck this time."

A moment later, he hit the pause button. The blizzard of static was even worse than before. Tyler rolled his eyes in annoyance.

"Oh, for goodness's sake!"

"Bad luck, sir," Jarvis commiserated.

Tyler tried three more times before conceding defeat. Sliding his chair away, he gestured towards the monitor. "All yours, Dick."

"Are you sure?"

A sheepish grin spread across Tyler's face. "I think my inadequacies as a CCTV operator have been painfully exposed, don't you?"

"Don't feel bad about it," Jarvis consoled him. "Our reflexes get slower as we grow older, and you're practically a pensioner now."

"Cheeky git," Tyler said, but he was smiling.

Kelly sat Alison and Ciaron down in the lounge. She had called ahead to say she was coming over with an update, and from the ashen colour of their faces, she knew they were expecting it to be bad news.

"There's been a development," she began. "We received an anonymous call to the Incident Room hotline this afternoon. It came from a male who claims to have witnessed the boys being herded into the back of a small van in the fairground car park on Saturday night."

A tortured gasp escaped Alison's lips, and Ciaron immediately wrapped his arm around her shoulders and pulled her to him.

"The description the caller gave matches the one the fairground worker supplied on the night they went missing," Kelly explained. "We believe the call was genuine, and if it is, it confirms that the boys were abducted. We still don't know why."

Alison was sobbing uncontrollably.

Holding her tightly in his arms, Ciaron was visibly trembling, and Kelly could see that he was really struggling to keep his emotions in check.

"Did he... did he hurt them?" he managed to ask, the words catching in his throat.

Kelly shook her head. "No. From what we understand, the boys got into the van willingly."

"That's bullshit!" Ciaron yelled, making Kelly jump. "There's no way that Peter would have willingly gone off with a stranger. He knows better than that. He *must* have been taken against his will."

Kelly gave him a couple of seconds to calm down before replying. "Ciaron," she said, speaking with heartfelt compassion. "The people who commit crimes like this are very cunning, and very persuasive. They'll have had a plausible story to trick the boys into accompanying them, and by the time Peter and Gavin realised that something was wrong, it would have been too late."

Alison's head twisted away from her husband's chest, where it had been buried. Her bloodshot eyes fixed on the detective, and they were filled with more pain than anyone should ever have to bear.

"Is he dead?" Alison demanded, clearly on the verge of hysteria. "Is that why you're here, to tell me that my baby boy is dead?"

Kelly raised both hands in a calming gesture. "There's no evidence to suggest that's the case, and we're proceeding very much on the basis that they are still alive."

Alison latched onto Kelly's words. "You really think they could still be alive?"

"I do," Kelly said, with far more confidence than she felt.

"That's good to know," Alison said, wiping the tears from her eyes.

Kelly took a deep breath. She wasn't looking forward to the next part of their conversation. "Okay, so the main reason I'm here is that the DCI wants to make a second televised appeal later tonight." She paused, bracing herself for another outburst from Ciaron. "And he wants the two of you, along with Gavin's parents, to be there beside him."

Surprisingly, it was Alison, not Ciaron, who kicked off.

"No! I can't face another one. I just can't…" Breaking free of Ciaron's embrace, she shakily pushed herself to her feet and rushed out of the room.

Ciaron half rose, calling after her.

"Leave me alone," Alison yelled, slamming the door shut behind her.

Ciaron spun to face Kelly. "How can you be so cruel that you'd even consider putting her through another poxy appeal?" he snapped. "Can't you see, she's hanging on to her sanity by a thread? Christ, woman! She's already lost two children. If Peter dies, it will destroy her."

His words stung, and Kelly felt a warm flush creep up her face. "I wouldn't ask if there were any other way," she told him, aware that her hands were shaking. She could feel Ciaron's anger coming off him in waves, but she understood it was a defence mechanism to mask the fear he felt inside, and that it wasn't really directed at her at all.

As Ciaron went off in search of his wife, Kelly wondered whether Alison was the only one hanging on by a thread.

---

Tyler had been joined in his office by Dillon and Bull. The three of them were sitting around the small coffee table, eating kebabs. Tyler hadn't wanted to take a break, but he hadn't eaten anything since breakfast and he was absolutely famished, so when Dillon turned up with a food parcel, he grudgingly accepted it.

As he ate, he told the others about his plan.

"What will you do if the NPIA doesn't call you back?" Dillon asked.

Tyler took a large bite out of his chicken kebab, munched happily for a few seconds. "If I don't hear anything by five o'clock, I'll crack on without their input. To tell you the truth, Dill, I only put the call in to keep George happy."

Dillon took a sip of his Diet Coke. "Won't George be a tad annoyed if you don't wait for the expert to call you back?"

Tyler bristled at that. "Look, Dill, I'm the SIO. This is my call to make. If it all goes tits up, I'll be the one who's held to account, not George."

"Granted," the big man said, before shovelling a bundle of chips into his mouth. "But there's no point in putting George's nose out of joint."

Tyler vented his frustration by taking a massive bite from his kebab and chomping away angrily. "I've made up my mind," he declared, when his mouth was finally free of food. "I'll give the shrink until five o'clock to get back to me, but not a minute longer."

Dillon and Bull both glanced up at the clock on the wall, which revealed there was only ten minutes left until the deadline Tyler had just set arrived, then locked eyes with each other.

As if on cue, the landline on Tyler's desk started ringing.

"That could be the NPIA now," Dillon suggested.

Giving his half-eaten kebab a wistful look, Tyler placed it on the coffee table. "If it is, their timing sucks," he complained, hurriedly wiping his fingers with a napkin as he scurried over to his desk.

"DCI Tyler speaking."

"*Ah, yes. Good afternoon.*" A man's voice. Educated, articulate, accentuating the vowels like someone from a 1940s news reel. "*My name is Dr Crawford. I'm a forensic psychologist, and I've been asked to give you a call by the National Policing Improvement Agency. Is this a good time to speak....?*"

Tyler glanced longingly across the office to the remnants of his kebab, which Dillon was now eyeing up. "Thank you for getting back to me," he said, brusquely. "I'm investigating the abduction of two young boys who were snatched from a fairground in Chingford on Saturday night and–"

"*Is that the case that's been all over the news, by any chance?*" Crawford interrupted.

"It is," Tyler confirmed. "We've got another televised appeal scheduled for later tonight, and during the broadcast I want to speak directly to the suspect."

"*Interesting,*" Crawford said, in the way that academics often do when pondering a hypothetical question.

"One of the boys had a mobile phone with him, and we think there's a good chance the suspect hung onto it," Tyler continued. "On the assumption that he has, I'm going to leave a voicemail message on it for him. During the TV appeal, I'm going to ask the suspect to listen to it. What I want from you is some constructive input on how I go about convincing him to do that."

"*Why leave a message in the first place?*" Crawford asked, sounding baffled. "*Couldn't you just speak directly to him while you're on TV?*"

"I could," Tyler agreed, dragging the last word out. "But the purpose of the exercise is to get the suspect to turn the phone on and listen to the voicemail."

That way, the TIU would be able to ping the phone, which would show them what area it was in. The plan was to have a couple of detector vans on standby, ready to deploy in the hope of triangulating the signal and narrowing its location down to a specific street. Tyler explained all of this to the psychologist.

"*Ah, I see,*" Crawford said. He seemed genuinely impressed. "*Very clever of you; very devious, too.*"

---

Locking herself in the downstairs toilet, Alison grabbed a handful of hair and tugged it hard, wanting to hurt herself. She felt she deserved to suffer for letting Peter down so badly. Her instinct had been to accompany him to the funfair, but he had rebelled against her, arguing that he was old enough to go alone. Instead of siding with her when she'd asked him to back her up, Ciaron had agreed with Peter. Afterwards, when they were alone, he had scolded her for making such a fuss, warning her that if she didn't stop mollycoddling him, Peter would grow up to be a wimp.

Now he might not grow up at all.

She knew that Ciaron felt terrible for having reacted that way, and that he probably felt as guilty as she did for Peter's disappearance, but he wasn't good at expressing himself in words or showing his feelings, which meant that he just came across as angry and argumentative.

Every time that Alison thought about Peter, and what he might be going through, a coldness engulfed her soul, causing it to shrivel a little more. Soon there would be nothing left.

There was loud a bang on the door.

"Are you all right in there, Ali?" It was the worried voice of her mum.

"Just give me a minute," Alison shouted, wishing they would all go away and leave her in peace.

She splashed some cold water over her face and hurriedly tidied her dishevelled hair. As she straightened up, another wave of panic engulfed her, making her feel dizzy and breathless. As the room began to spin, Alison reached out a trembling hand to steady herself.

"Ali, darling?" her mother called from the other side of the door. "Please let me in."

"Mum…" Alison called out. As she unlocked the door, her knees buckled beneath her. She was vaguely aware of the tiled floor rushing up to meet her, but then everything went black.

---

*"The mind of a sadistic predatory paedophile is a complex web of emotions and compulsions,"* Dr Crawford explained. *"Try thinking of it as a corrupted computer program that misinterprets all the data that's been inputted and therefore yields incorrect results."*

"In other words, they're broken?" Tyler said, wondering where he was going with this. All he wanted to know was how he could make his appeal irresistible to the child snatcher.

*"Yes, exactly!"*

"So, mad not bad?"

*"That's how I see it,"* the psychologist admitted.

Tyler didn't agree, and he was tempted to tell Crawford that, if that was how he really saw things, he should consider paying his optician a visit to replace the rose-tinted spectacles he was wearing with a pair that enabled him to see the ugly truth about these people.

He had put the call on loudspeaker to enable Dillon and Bull to follow the conversation.

*"It's all about dominance,"* Crawford espoused. *"Their condition compels them to exercise complete power over their victims, and it's much easier to do that with a frightened child than it is with an adult."*

"Why are they so obsessed with having power over others?" Tyler asked. He was struggling to comprehend how a terrified child's fear could possibly serve as an aphrodisiac.

*"It usually happens because an overbearing parent denied them any control over their own lives while growing up. Quite often, they will have been the victim of sexual abuse themselves, and this will have distorted their perception of what is and isn't an acceptable sexual behaviour. To them, might is right; as long as they are the ones in control, they make the rules."*

Tyler had reached the end of his patience. The discussion had descended into an intellectual debate, and it was taking them nowhere.

As if that wasn't bad enough, Dillon had finished the rest of his kebab.

"Dr Crawford, I don't want to seem rude, but time is of the essence, so I'm going to cut to the chase. What I need from you is a few insights on what I should say to the suspect to persuade the sick fucker to turn the boy's phone on. Can you help me with that, or not?"

## 20

Marmite on toast

When Alison came around, she was lying on the sofa with everyone clustered around her. Her mother and the detective were standing over her, and Ciaron was sitting next to her, perched precariously on the edge of a cushion, holding her hand.

She had no idea how much time had elapsed, or how she had got there. The last thing she remembered was opening the toilet door.

"W–what happened?" she asked, groggily.

Ciaron gave her hand a little squeeze. "You fainted," he said, "but you're okay now."

She tried to push herself into a sitting position, but the movement instantly made her feel giddy. With a groan, she laid back down and closed her eyes.

"You need to eat something," her mother said, fretfully. "It's no wonder you passed out, starving yourself like this."

"I'm not hungry," Alison muttered, weakly.

"Marjorie's right," Ciaron said, softly. "Let her make you some Marmite on toast. That's your favourite. You'll feel much better once you get some food inside you."

Alison sighed. "Fine." She didn't have the energy to argue. Besides, she knew they were right. She couldn't even remember the last time she had eaten.

Giving her a strained smile, Marjorie slipped away the make the toast. "I'll put the kettle on while I'm in the kitchen," she said, trying to sound upbeat. "I'm sure we could all do with a nice cup of tea."

---

Descending the stairs to the basement, Remus crossed the corridor to the holding cell. The narrow space was looking much tidier now that he had dragged the broken filing cabinet to one side, and neatly stacked the countless boxes of porn mags and VHS tapes. He had even oiled the lock on the cell door and, for the first time in months, the key turned freely when he inserted it.

Flicking the light switch, Remus unlocked the cell door and went in.

Both boys were sound asleep, which was good. After seeing their faces plastered across his TV screen day in, day out, he now knew that their given names were Peter and Gavin, but to him, they would always be Troublemaker and Spineless.

After making sure they were both still breathing, he spent a few seconds inspecting Troublemaker's bruises, which were healing nicely. Standing up, he kicked the slops bucket, and was pleased to find it empty.

Satisfied that all was as it should be, he closed and relocked the door, then turned off the light. He would return at ten p.m., when it was time for their last feed of the day. He would even let them use the toilet while he was there. He was generous like that.

The press conference commenced at eight-thirty. Unlike the last one, which had been broadcast live, tonight's appeal was being pre-recorded, and would be aired during the late evening news in half an hour's time. The seating arrangements had been kept to the same format as before, with Holland and Tyler flanked by both sets of parents.

They didn't seem quite as overawed this time around. Not that they looked comfortable; far from it.

When the press liaison officer gave him the nod, Tyler cleared his throat and stared into the cameras.

"I want to share an important development with you," he announced solemnly, then paused for dramatic effect.

The atmosphere inside the packed room was electric; the media knew there had been developments, but they had no idea what these were.

"We now have reason to believe that Peter and Gavin were abducted from the fairground in Chingford on Saturday night, and that they are being kept against their will by the man who took them."

There were gasps and muted mumblings. Some of the reporters were furiously scribbling away at their notepads, while others were holding up miniature recording devices, extending their arms as far forward as they could so that the inbuilt microphones would catch every word. All looked tense. He could see it in their eyes; this was big news, and it would sell a lot of papers.

"Two witnesses have come forward," Tyler revealed. "One saw a man leading the boys into the treeline, while the other saw him ushering them into the back of a small van." He purposefully refrained from describing the vehicle. "An E-Fit has been prepared of this individual, who witnesses describe as a white male of slim build and about six-foot tall. He is thought to be in his mid-twenties, with matted shoulder length hair. On the night in question, he was wearing an army style camouflage jacket. We are appealing for anyone who recognises the individual depicted in the E-Fit to contact the police immediately, either by calling the Incident Room direct or via the Crimestoppers helpline. All calls will be treated in the strictest of confidence."

Hands started going up as impatient journalists vied to have their questions answered. When Tyler gestured that he wasn't finished, there was a moment's hesitation, then the hands reluctantly came down one by one.

Staring straight into the camera, Tyler's expression was deadly serious. "I now wish to make an important personal appeal to the man who took Peter and Gavin from the fairground." Praying that he wouldn't fluff his lines, he took a deep breath before continuing. "We know that Peter had a mobile phone with him when he was taken, and in the hope that you still have this in your possession, I have left you a private, personal message. It's for your ears only. I hope that you will listen to it as soon as you can and give serious consideration to the contents."

The message had deliberately been short and sweet, enough to arouse interest, no more. If the psychologist was right, the brevity of it, along with the choice of words – "*...a private, personal message. It's for your ears only...*" – would stroke the child snatcher's ego, making him feel powerful and important.

Tyler nodded to indicate that he had finished speaking, and the room immediately erupted into a riot of noise, with reporters shouting over each other in their quest for answers, each determined to be the first voice recognised.

"DCI Tyler, what's in the message you left the kidnapper?"

"Are you going to offer him a deal to release the kids?"

"Why is your message to the child snatcher so secret?"

"Do you have any more details on the van the boys were put in?"

"Do you think the boys are going to be sold as sex slaves?"

The mothers of both boys were crying, as was Tom Grant, but Ciaron Musgrove just sat there, his face a mask of angry impotence.

Tyler raised his hands and motioned for quiet. Only when an orderly silence returned did he consent to field questions. Predictably, the first was from Ambrose Wilson.

"DCI Tyler," the reporter began. "Why have you left a personal message for the man who abducted the children?"

"I'm afraid I cannot comment further on that," Tyler said, forcefully. "The contents are strictly between me and the man who took Peter and Gavin."

Again, he was following the psychologist's advice by implying that no one else was privy to the information contained within the message, not even his fellow detectives.

"Are you telling us that not even the boys' parents know what's in the message?" Wilson persisted, even though Tyler had just indicated for another reporter to speak.

Tyler took a deep breath, hoping to give the impression that he really didn't want to discuss the matter further. Secretly, he was rather pleased that the irritating man was persisting with this line of questioning; if the suspect was watching the broadcast, that would surely stimulate his curiosity, making it even more likely that he would power up the phone and listen to the message. He fixed Wilson with an acid smile. "I'm sorry Ambrose, but I really cannot elaborate any further."

Tyler answered a further half dozen questions from other reporters, only two of which touched on the mysterious message, before calling the proceedings to a halt.

The cameras stopped rolling, and the lights were switched off. Kelly escorted the parents to a side exit that led to the same anteroom they had used previously, thereby avoiding the reporters who were hoping to get a quote or two from them on their way out.

"Jack," a woman's voice called out as Tyler stood up to follow them. He turned to see Imogen Askew hurrying towards him. Dressed in an elegant, figure-hugging two-piece blazer and skirt, with matching blue shoes, she looked every inch the successful businesswoman. Her hair was immaculate, like something out of a shampoo advert. As always, a legal pad and a biro seemed to be welded into her hand.

"I wondered if I might have a quiet word?" she said, a little breathlessly.

Tyler looked around, half expecting to see her shaggy haired cameraman tagging along behind, but there was no sign of him. "Of course."

She gave him an apologetic smile. "This is a bit delicate," she began, which immediately made him suspicious. "I've had Terri on the phone, pressuring me to use my relationship with Tony to wheedle her an exclusive interview with the boys' parents."

It was only when Tyler's jaw started aching that he realised he was grinding his teeth. "How bloody typical of her," he retorted, angrily.

Terri Miller was Imogen's boss at the TV production company. Tyler had first met her a couple of years back, when she was still a struggling reporter for *The London Echo*, performing the job that Ambrose Wilson had since taken over. At the time, Tyler had been investigating a serial killer who was running amok in Whitechapel, and Miller's underhand shenanigans at a crime scene had almost led to the contamination of important evidence. Miller had since moved into TV journalism, becoming a household name, and she was going to narrate the fly on the wall documentary that Imogen and Bear were currently filming about the Homicide Command.

Tyler affected a weary sigh. "You know, I really thought she had matured beyond pulling cheap stunts like that, but I guess it's true what they say about leopards never changing their spots." His eyes hardened. "I can't say I'm surprised by her stooping so low, but you…" he let the sentence trail off.

Imogen had the decency to blush. "I promise, I'm only asking under pain of death. I think it's underhand and unprofessional of her, and I really hope you refuse."

Tyler was surprised. "You do?"

"Of course," she assured him. "I really care about Tony, and I wouldn't take advantage of our relationship to progress my own career, let alone hers."

A wry smile appeared on Tyler's face. "Well, I guess there's hope for you yet. Tell Terri from me—"

"Oh, don't worry," Imogen cut him off. "I'll tell her that I made a real pest of myself, and that I tried every trick in the trade to persuade you, but you refused anyway."

"Naturally, I'll confirm that, should anyone ask," Tyler promised, treating her to a conspiratorial wink.

---

Bottle of beer in one hand, remote control in the other, Remus made sure he was seated in front of the TV in time for the nine o'clock news. He would have been surprised if the broadcast hadn't featured a segment on the missing boys, but he had expected a regurgitated version of the same boring claptrap they had been showing all day: a short clip of the searchers beating their way through the overgrown forest, followed by a few seconds of the tearful parents at the previous evening's press conference. When the boys' faces appeared on his screen the moment the opening credits faded, he instinctively knew there had been a major development. The revelation that two witnesses had come forward hit him like a punch.

How was this possible?

He had been beyond careful.

The situation went from bad to worse when the detective leading the enquiry announced that an E-Fit had been prepared of the suspect. There was something about his demeanour that made Remus feel extremely nervous; the man looked as hard as nails, a little cynical, and very determined; not the sort of person to give up easily.

When a disturbingly good likeness of his unshaven face filled the screen, Remus felt his bowels turn to water.

And then the detective started speaking directly to him, announcing that he had left Remus a personal voice message on Troublemaker's mobile phone, and asking him to listen to it.

Why would they have left *him* a message?

Was that normal practice?

Remus didn't think so.

The mobile phone was in the bottom of his rucksack, where he had thrown it after relieving the boy of it during the brief stop at Hollow Ponds. He had planned to destroy the damn thing as soon as he got back to the safe house, but after being taken ill, he had forgotten all about it.

A horrible thought struck Remus, one he found even more terrifying than the prospect of someone recognising him and calling the police.

What would Benny say when he saw the news?

How would he react?

Not well, that was for sure.

Remus forced himself to calm down and think the situation through. If someone put his name forward after seeing the E-fit, the police would go looking for him at the bedsit he shared with McQueen in Holborn. He hadn't been there for days, and there was nothing there to link him to the safe house in Leytonstone. As long as he held his nerve until the boys were dead and buried, everything would be fine. Sure, the police might drag him in for questioning at some point in the distant future, but so what if they did? He would simply deny any involvement, and without physical evidence to tie him to the missing chickens, the fact that he resembled the man in their stupid E-Fit was irrelevant.

As soon as the news finished, Remus rushed up to his bedroom. His rucksack was on the floor by the side of the bed, where he had dumped it on Saturday night. He hurriedly poured the contents onto the mattress and rummaged through them until he found the boy's phone. His finger hovered over the power button for several seconds, but as much as he wanted to, he couldn't bring himself to switch it on.

What if the message contained something he didn't want to hear?

That was silly, he told himself. It probably contained a grovelling plea for him to return the boys unharmed. Maybe one of them had a medical condition, and the cops wanted him to be aware of it, like he gave a damn.

Feeling conflicted, Remus threw the phone back onto the bed. He was curious about the message, but a nagging voice in the back of his head told him it would probably be better if he didn't listen to it.

Leaning back in his chair, Bartholomew Craddock rubbed his bleary eyes and allowed himself a very long yawn. After consulting his watch, he pushed back his chair and rose wearily to his feet. Wandering out to the main office, he called for everyone's attention.

"Right, you lot, it's almost ten, so bugger off home and get some much needed rest. We've got a long way to go yet, and you're no good to me half dead."

There were a few mutters of thanks as his team of weary detectives began closing down their computer terminals, locking half read files away, and generally tidying up their unfinished work before grabbing their coats. He remained in the doorway, watching them as they shuffled towards the exit in dribs and drabs.

Within five minutes the office was empty.

Apart from Frank Stebbins, who was sitting at a HOLMES terminal in the small alcove at the rear of the room, ensconced in a report he was reading.

"Frank, are you deaf as well as stupid?" Craddock boomed. "Go home, have a drink, get some sleep. Tomorrow's a new day."

"In a minute," Stebbins called back, absently.

Massaging his lower back, which was stiff from where he had spent all afternoon sitting at his desk, Craddock bimbled over to chivvy him along. "Now, look here, young Frank. You're no good to—"

"I think I've found a link between our victim, and the first two," Stebbins cut him off, excitedly.

Craddock grabbed a chair from a nearby desk, wheeled it over, and flopped down like a giant walrus coming to rest. "Would you care to share this exciting development with your Uncle Barty?" he enquired, casually. "Or are you planning to leave me in limbo until I work it out for myself?"

Stebbins grinned, knowing Craddock's bear with a sore head routine was just an act. "All three men are of a similar age, and all three are paedophiles."

Craddock groaned, then performed an overly theatrical eye roll that would have done a West End performer proud. "Is *that* it?" he asked, distinctly underwhelmed by the revelation. "If it is, you're more in need of rest than I first thought."

"No, that's not it," Stebbins replied, crabbily. "All three have worked as ride attendants and riggers in travelling fairs at some point, and all three have, at one time or another, been questioned by the police in relation to young boys who went missing, having last been seen at the fair."

That was interesting. Craddock considered the connotations. "Can we show that they ever worked together at the same fairground, or that they knew each other in any way?"

"That's what I'm trying to do now," Stebbins said. "I've been reading through their research dockets to see if there's a connection."

Craddock grimaced, then squirmed uncomfortably in his chair. "Do they deliberately manufacture these blasted things to cause discomfort?' he complained.

"Out of interest, did anything come out of your recent conversations with the other SIOs?" Stebbins asked, swivelling to face his boss.

Craddock pulled a face like he had just been sucking lemons. "It was a complete waste of time," he griped, fidgeting in his seat again. "Like Clifford, the two previous victims lived alone in remote areas, which means there's no CCTV to go on, and no witnesses to speak to. The killer is obviously very forensically aware. Once he gets inside their homes, he takes his time and leaves no clues behind. Like us, the Welsh and Northumberland constabularies conducted financial investigations, but these led nowhere. Unlike our victim, the first two had mobile phones." He allowed himself a smug smile. "Not that having the victims' call and cell site data has helped my counterparts to advance their respective investigations."

"I take it that everyone accepts there's a cross border serial killer on the loose; one who's actively targeting ageing paedophiles?"

Craddock snorted. "Well, the junior minister for policing at the Home Office wasn't too pleased when I informed her earlier today, but the evidence is irrefutable, so she could hardly dispute it. There's talk about establishing a Joint Task Force to oversee the combined investigations, with yours truly heading it."

Stebbins was impressed. "That's a high honour, indeed," he said, staring at his boss admiringly.

Craddock wasn't so sure. "Or a poison chalice, depending on which way the enquiry goes."

---

"Here's an interesting little statistic for you," Dillon said, kicking his shoes off and swinging his feet up on the coffee table in his lounge. They had just arrived home, and he was absolutely exhausted. "According to the expert Jack spoke to today, most people who are sexually abused don't become abusers themselves, but most sexual abusers were subjected to sexual abuse during the formative part of their life." He accepted the cold beer Imogen offered him with a grateful smile and raised it in a toast. "Here's to catching the evil bastard who snatched Peter and Gavin," he said before taking a long swig.

It was almost midnight, and he had to be back in the office for eight the following morning, so the beer was probably a very bad idea, but after the day he had had, he needed a little something to help him unwind.

Imogen flopped down beside him and rested her head on his broad shoulder. "I spoke to Jack after this evening's press conference at The Yard."

"Did you? What about?"

Imogen recanted her earlier conversation with Tyler, outlining the request she had reluctantly passed on from Miller.

When she'd finished, Dillon barked out a mirthless laugh. "I bet he took that well!" he said, shaking his head at Miller's temerity.

Imogen grinned. "He wasn't too impressed with her, but he was absolutely fine with me." She went silent for a few moments, then said, "If I'm being completely honest, I'm a little worried about him. He looked utterly exhausted, and he seemed to be under a great deal of pressure."

Dillon shrugged. "That's only to be expected. After all, there's an awful lot riding on this case."

Imogen nodded her understanding. "Yes, I suppose there is. I mean, with all the publicity, it's the sort of case that can make or break a career."

"That's not it at all," Dillon corrected her. "Jack doesn't give a toss about his career. All he cares about is finding those poor kids and reuniting them with their parents. You don't know him like I do. If they turn up dead, he'll never forgive himself for failing them."

Imogen's brow furrowed. "But that's ridiculous!" she said, pouring scorn over the suggestion. "He's doing everything he possibly can."

"You know that, and I know that," Dillon explained, with a twinge of sadness. "But in Jack's eyes, that won't be enough."

She thought about this for a moment. "I thought homicide cops were meant to be hard-nosed bastards?" she eventually said, wrapping an arm around his waist.

Dillon smiled. "We are when we're dealing with ruthless villains, but our hearts can be broken just as easily as the next person's when we see children suffering."

## 21

## TUESDAY 6TH NOVEMBER 2001

*A displacement of his own guilt*

Phillip Diggle's eyes sprung open the moment his alarm went off. He had always been a light sleeper, and the discordant sounds instantly aroused him from his slumber. He sat up, aware that his body was caked in sweat. With a shaking hand, he reached for the glass of water on his bedside table, downing its contents in one go. According to the alarm clock, it was five o'clock. If he was going to get to the forest before the search recommenced, he would need to get a wriggle on.

His sleep had been fitful at best these past couple of days. The abduction of the two missing boys had left him badly shaken, ripping the scabs off his own wounds and triggering the unwelcome return of the harrowing nightmares that had plagued him after Robbie's abduction.

The nightmares always began the same way, with his younger self sitting up in his sleeping bag, eyes wide with fear. On seeing the two men crawling through the rip in the tent wall, he opened his mouth to scream, but one of them was upon him in an instant, smothering the noise before it could start. Straddling him, the masked intruder wrapped his gloved hands around Phillip's slender throat and squeezed tightly, cutting off his air supply. The man wore a red ski mask, but his eyes and mouth were visible through the gaps cut in them. The last thing Phillip saw before passing out was the strange circular skin growth on his attacker's lower left eyelid. The way it popped up in front of the pupil had made Phillip think of a gunsight.

Phillip always woke up at that point, gasping for breath, tearing imaginary hands away from his neck, his sweat ridden body violently shaking.

He still remembered that terrible night as clearly as if it had happened yesterday. The two masked men had been long gone by the time he regained consciousness, and they had taken Robbie with them. Phillip's larynx had been so badly bruised that he'd been unable to scream for help. Dazed, confused, terrified, he had stumbled next door to his parents' tent to raise the alarm. The police doctor who examined Phillip later that night had told his distraught parents that he was very lucky to be alive.

Robbie's abduction had triggered a massive police investigation, one that had been on a par with the current search for the two missing boys, but despite all the resources that had been poured into it, and the intense media coverage that continued for weeks afterwards, Robbie had never been found.

To this day, Phillip struggled to understand why the child snatchers had chosen to kill him and snatch Robbie, instead of the other way around.

Dragging his fractured mind back to the present, Phillip threw aside the quilt, stood up and stumbled into the hotel bathroom. After relieving himself, he entered the shower cubicle and scrubbed the sweat from his hirsute body. He spent the next few minutes standing beneath the powerful jet, letting the hot water soothe the crick out of his neck.

While towelling himself dry, Phillip's mind returned to Peter Musgrove and Gavin Grant. Statistically speaking, he knew it was highly unlikely that they were still alive, and he wondered if their bodies would ever be found.

Robbie's never had been.

Phillip understood what the two families were going through in a way that few others could. After Robbie's disappearance, he had watched his parents' previously strong relationship slowly deteriorate. It hadn't happened overnight; it had been gradual, like the erosion of cliffs constantly battered by the sea. He had been powerless to comfort them, and although they had never blamed him for what happened, he had always felt responsible.

In many ways, it would have been better if Robbie's body had been discovered a day or two after his disappearance. At least the family could have given him a proper burial, which would have enabled the grieving process to begin. As it was, Phillip's parents had never truly found closure, and the constant raising and dashing of their hopes, as every false sighting of Robbie was investigated and then debunked, had all but destroyed them.

The first paedophile that Phillip tracked down and killed, wrongly believing that he was one of the men responsible for Robbie's death, had been a repugnant Welshman called Rodney Llewellyn. Tied to a chair, with a knife pressed against his dick, Llewellyn had tearfully confessed to a multitude of sex crimes, but had vehemently denied having any involvement in Robbie's murder. Thinking that it would save his life, he had given up a paedophile whose crimes were even worse than his own, one he suspected might have been involved in Robbie's death. That information had led Phillip to Northumberland, and a man called Gary Newton.

Before his very painful death, Newton had told Phillip all about Angus Clifford, a man he had briefly shared a cell with during the late seventies. According to Newton, Clifford had openly bragged about his involvement in the Norfolk campsite snatch, which remained one of the highest profile child abduction cases in UK history.

It had taken Phillip several months to locate Clifford, who now lived the life of a recluse at a remote cottage in Caister. With a sharp blade pressed against his flaccid member, Clifford had immediately confessed his involvement in Robbie's abduction. The other men involved were called Benny and Mo, but he claimed not to know their last names or where they could be found, insisting that he had lost touch with them soon after snatching Robbie.

"Tell me where the boy was buried," Phillip had demanded of him.

"I swear I don't know," Clifford had sobbed as Phillip's blade bit into his skin. "Benny took care of the kid, like he did with all the chickens we snatched. Why do you care, anyway?"

"I care because the boy you defiled was my twin brother," Phillip had told him, at which point he had cut off Clifford's manhood. Ramming it deep inside Clifford's mouth, Phillip had let him suffer for a while longer before slitting his throat.

That night, knowing that one of the three men responsible for his brother's death had finally been punished, Phillip had slept like a baby. He felt no guilt or remorse; why should he? He wasn't a cold blooded murderer; he was an executioner who was performing a civic service by ridding the world of vermin.

It hadn't taken him too long to identify the man that Clifford had referred to as Mo. Phillip had thoroughly researched his next target; he knew where Mo lived and where he worked. The next step was to interrogate him, and find out where Benny was.

First, though, he had to help the searchers look for the missing children.

---

Having frozen his nuts off yesterday, Ciaron Musgrove was dressed more appropriately today. Layers were the answer, someone had informed him, and he had put on so many that he could barely bend his arms.

Tom Grant stood in gloomy silence beside him. The two men were a little way apart from the rest of the group, who were respectfully giving them plenty of space. Ciaron had caught a few of the searchers casting sympathetic glances in his direction when they thought he wasn't looking, and there had been several occasions in which muted conversations had stopped abruptly as he and Tom approached the speakers.

Although everyone was trying to remain upbeat and positive, it was an open secret that the longer this went on, the less likely it was that they would find the boys alive.

Ciaron was making a concerted effort to pretend otherwise around Alison, but the charade was eating him alive. He so desperately wished that he could speak about his maelstrom of conflicting emotions, but every time he tried to say something, he ended up getting irritable with her. It was so easy for Alison; she had always worn her heart on her sleeve, but he wasn't made like that. He really struggled to share his feelings with others, retreating further into himself the more difficult things became. He had done it when their first baby was stillborn, and again after losing Luke to SIDS. He knew this made him seem harsh and uncaring, but nothing could be further from the truth.

Since Peter's disappearance, Ciaron had found himself constantly snapping at Alison, picking fault over everything she did. Deep down, he knew that his outbursts of anger were a displacement of his own guilt, a deflection mechanism he had constructed to manage the fact that he felt totally inadequate as a father and a husband.

He envied Tom Grant. The man was so open about his emotions, effortlessly communicating his feelings to his wife, and offering her the kind of support that Ciaron could only dream of providing Alison.

"I think we're moving out shortly," Tom said, dragging him away from his maudlin thoughts.

They had been placed in the same search group as yesterday, which was led by a no-nonsense sergeant from Newham called Lizzy Cotton. She was a strong, kind woman, and she had taken good care of them. He especially liked the fact that she didn't give them any special treatment or try to hide anything from them.

The forest covered a massive area, and even with all the resources at their disposal, Lizzy had told him that it could take weeks to search it properly. Secretly, Ciaron couldn't help but wonder how much longer the search would realistically be allowed to continue for at this level of intensity. It had to be costing a fortune, and at some point, someone was going to start making noises about scaling it down.

Casting the worrying thought aside, Ciaron pulled his woollen cap down over his ears. "I'm going to pop to the loo before we set off," he informed Tom. "You coming?"

Tom shook his head. "I'll wait for you here."

"I won't be long," Ciaron promised. "Let's hope today's the day we find them."

*And that they're still alive...*

He thought it best not to voice that thought.

---

Remus sat on the edge of his bed, staring down at the rucksack containing Troublemaker's phone. He was so intrigued by the detective's mystery message that he had lain awake thinking about it for most of the night. He had retrieved the phone from his rucksack a half dozen times, intent on turning it on, but each time he had bottled out.

The knowledge that a senior policeman had gone to all the effort of leaving him a personalised voicemail – and had all but begged him to listen to it on national TV – made Remus feel powerful and in control; it made him feel incredibly important, and he was desperate to hear the pathetic policeman beg him to release the chickens.

Without conscious thought, his hand darted into the bag. It reappeared a moment later, clutching the boy's mobile. Breathing excitedly, his thumb hovered over the power button, but then he lost his nerve again and tossed it back into the bag.

Maybe later...

"How are you bearing up?" Phillip Diggle asked Ciaron, who was standing directly in front of him in the slow moving line to use the Portaloos behind the command vehicle. "If you don't mind me asking," he added quickly.

Ciaron eyed him warily. "What do you expect me to say?" he retorted aggressively. "My son has been abducted. How would you be holding up in my place?"

"I don't have a son," Diggle said, with a sad smile. "But I did have a twin brother. He was abducted back in 1976, when we were nine."

Ciaron's face drained of colour. "I'm so sorry," he said, all anger gone from his voice. "I would never have spoken to you like that if I'd known."

"It's fine," Diggle assured him, and it was. "I completely understand your reaction, and I pray that we'll find your son, along with his." He nodded towards Tom Grant, who was chatting to a female uniformed sergeant in the middle of the clearing.

The door opened and a man emerged from the Portaloo, holding the door open for Ciaron to go inside.

Wishing that he hadn't given into the impulse to speak to Ciaron Musgrove, Diggle waited until the poor man closed the toilet door behind him, then stepped out of the queue and walked away.

---

The ANPR results that Dean Fletcher was waiting for were e-mailed over a few minutes before eleven, and there was a big pile to sort through. With the partial index that Colin Franklin had provided in front of him for comparison purposes, Fletcher began flicking through them.

He had almost reached the bottom of the stack, and was just starting to think it wasn't there, when he found the registration number he was looking for.

"Bingo!" he said, breaking into a huge smile.

He was tempted to take it straight to Tyler, but forced himself to exercise restraint. His fingers glided over the keyboard in a blur as he carried out a PNC check to obtain the registered keeper details. After pressing the print button, he closed the application and began running the van and its keeper through the various Met intelligence databases.

It wasn't until he had fully exhausted his research that he pushed his chair back and set off in search of Tyler.

## 22

Are you looking for business?

Remus was becoming increasingly concerned about the chickens. Following Benny's orders, he had upped the dosage of the sedatives, but the drugs were starting to have a noticeably detrimental effect on their health. He had just been down to the holding cell to feed them their lunch and take them to the loo, but they had been sound asleep when he entered, and he had struggled to wake them. Naturally, he'd forced them to get up and visit the toilet, but they had been groggy and confused, and so wobbly on their feet that, had he not steadied them as they drunkenly stumbled along the corridor, they would have fallen flat on their faces. It wasn't that he cared about their wellbeing or anything like that; they were going to die anyway, so that was irrelevant. It was just that he didn't want to risk damaging the goods before they were sold.

Jim Stone and Paul Evans had been keeping observation on the tiny florist's shop for the best part of two hours. They were parked in the mouth of a side street, with the front of their pool car jutting out into Caledonian Road. From this rather precarious position, they could just about see both the front of the shop and the entrance to the side alley that ran along the back, which was where the Berlingo was currently parked.

There had been a mad scramble to get eyes on the premises while a search warrant was applied for, but the initial excitement had long since turned to boredom. Evans was quite content to listen to talkSPORT on the radio, but Stone was becoming increasingly restless.

"I think I'll carry out a quick recce inside the shop," he suddenly announced.

"I'm not sure the boss would approve," Evans cautioned.

Stone shrugged his concern aside. "Stop worrying. What harm can it do?"

Before Evans could reply, Stone was out of the car and walking briskly towards the little parade of shops.

A bell tinkled as he entered the florists, and a middle-aged white man looked up from where he was putting together a bouquet of flowers. He greeted Stone with a bright smile.

"Good afternoon, sir. I'll be right with you."

"That's okay," the detective responded. "I'm not in a rush."

"Are you after anything in particular?" the florist enquired, dusting his hands.

"Err..." It suddenly occurred to Stone that he wouldn't know a geranium from a chrysanthemum. The only flowers he'd ever purchased were roses for his wedding anniversary and lilies for a funeral. Thankfully, the arrival of a genuine customer saved him from making a fool of himself. "Why don't you see to this nice lady first," he suggested, ushering her in front of him.

As soon as the florist was distracted, he quietly slipped out of the shop.

Returning to the car, he rang the office. "There's only one bloke working in the shop, and he doesn't look anything like the E-fit of our suspect," he told Fletcher, who had answered the phone.

"*I'll let the boss know,*" Fletcher replied.

"Any idea how long that bloody search warrant's going to be?" Stone asked. "We've been waiting here for two hours."

"*Should be with you in a few minutes,*" Fletcher assured him. "*Whitey and Kevin are bringing it over from Highbury Corner Magistrates Court.*"

Stone glanced down at his watch. "Well, you'd better tell them to hurry up. The florist shuts at five-thirty."

---

Euston Road was gridlocked when Madeley emerged from Kings Cross station. He coughed as he breathed in the thick diesel fumes, and dreaded to think what all the toxins were doing to his lungs.

A sallow faced woman with lank hair and blotchy skin was twirling around the pavement like a demented ballet dancer, waving her scrawny arms in the air to the sounds of an imaginary tune. The commuters flocking into the station ignored her crazy antics, and she seemed equally oblivious to them.

"Are you looking for business?" she asked Madeley, dreamily running an admiring finger down the lapel of his expensive overcoat.

Madeley stiffened at the unwanted contact. "Most definitely not," he replied, frostily. Brushing aside the offending hand, he continued on his journey.

Madeley hated Kings Cross; he saw it as a wasteland of sleaze and depravity that had been overrun by the prostitutes and drug dealers who loitered in every doorway and on every street corner. As he crossed Pentonville Road, his attention was drawn to the two unsavoury characters loitering by a telephone box on the other side of the junction. The nearest one was cupping a crack pipe in his grubby hands. It flared brightly as he took a long drag, illuminating his unshaven face and dead eyes in a demonic crimson glow.

Turning left into Caledonian Road, he cast a furtive glance over his shoulder to make sure the addicts weren't following him.

Benny's sex shop was the first in a little parade that also included a second-hand TV sales and repair centre, a florist, an Italian delicatessen and a betting shop. The windows on either side of the unassuming entrance were blacked out, and the only clue to what was sold inside could be found in the two small, faded words that were written above the door in swirling gold calligraphy: ADULTS ONLY.

It was coming up to 5:25 p.m. Recalling Benny's instructions not to enter until he had closed up for the day, Madeley continued walking until he reached the deli. As he had a few minutes to kill, he might as well grab himself a posh coffee.

---

Charlie White found a parking spot outside a shop selling reconditioned televisions, but it wasn't until he had manoeuvred into it that he realised just how close they were to the florist shop they were there to search. "Do you think we're too close to the target address?" he asked. "Because I really can't be arsed to find another spot."

Murray was halfway through dialling Jim Stone's number. "Nah, this'll do fine," he said, not bothering to look up. He pressed the green button and raised the mobile to his hear. "Hello, Jim. We've just arrived…"

"*Have you got the warrant?*"

Murray tutted. "Well, of course we've got the warrant. I wouldn't be calling you otherwise, would I?"

"*What took you so long? Did you get lost?*"

"No, Jim,' Murray replied in a world weary tone. "We didn't get lost…"

"*Then you must've stopped off for lunch, because you've been bloody ages.*"

Murray took a deep breath, released it as a theatrical sigh. "No, Jim. we didn't stop off for lunch either," he replied in a bored monotone.

There was a knock on the driver's window.

Both detectives turned to see a frizzy haired white woman grinning in at them. She was holding up a half empty bottle of Bacardi.

"What a minger," Murray said, as she wiped her mouth on her sleeve.

"*Who are you calling a minger?*" Stone bristled.

"Not you, Jim. We've got a drunken prossie banging on the window."

"*She probably recognised you as one of her regulars,*" Stone laughed. "*You don't owe her money, do you?*"

The sex worker rapped on the window again.

"Sod off," White and Murray said in tandem.

Instead of taking the hint, the woman rested her scrawny rump against the driver's window and took another large swig of Bacardi.

The two detectives exchanged disbelieving looks.

"Cheeky cow,' White said. He gave the horn a quick toot, and waved her away when she looked in his direction.

Unperturbed, she bent down and peered in at them, gesturing for White to unwind his window, which he reluctantly did.

"Jim, I'll call you back," Murray said, and hung up.

A combination of cheap perfume and strong booze instantly wafted in. The sex worker was eyeing them with interest. "I thought I knew all the local plod, but I haven't seen you two around here before."

"We're just passing through," Murray said, wishing she would sod off.

"No seriously, what are you doing?" she demanded.

White gave her a tight smile. "If you must know, we're looking for a one-legged barman who's been stealing from that pub over there." He jutted his chin at the pub across the road.

The sex worker imbued another shot of Bacardi, swished it around like mouthwash before swallowing. "Really?"

"Oh, aye," White said, with mock sincerity. "He made off with all the hops."

It took a moment for the pun to sink in, then she threw back her head and cackled loudly. "You saucy bugger! You almost had me going with that one," she said, leaning in to playfully punch his arm.

"He's a real comedian," Murray said, drolly.

"I'll say," she agreed, enthusiastically. "You know, it makes a nice change to meet a copper with a sense of humour. Most of you lot are as miserable as sin."

The detectives looked at each other, and White mouthed "Get rid of her!"

Murray cleared his throat. "Well, it's been nice to meet you, but I'm sure you've got somewhere more important to be." As he spoke, he shooed her away.

"Oh, I'm in no rush," she insisted, leaning on the roof of the car and giving them a bird's eye view of her sagging cleavage. "So, come on then, what are you really doing around here?"

Averting his eyes from her breasts, White affected a sigh. "If you must know, we've just stopped so that my mate can pop into that deli and buy us both a cup of coffee."

"Why don't you buy me a coffee for a change?" Murray protested.

"Privilege of rank," White said. "I like mine white with two sugars," he added, before Murray could object. "Go on, off you go, and take *her* with you."

Cursing under his breath, Murray joined the drunk on the pavement. "You'd better be on your way," he told her.

"You can buy me a coffee too, if you like," she offered, smiling up at him with rheumy eyes.

"I don't think so."

As he set off towards the deli, she attempted to link her arm through his, but he shrugged her off. "Oi, behave yourself," he chastised, but not unkindly. A part of him admired the woman's nerve, not that it was going to get her anywhere.

"I like you," she said. "I'd give you a very good discount if you were interested in doing a bit of business."

Murray stopped, turned to face her. "Don't take this the wrong way," he said, pointing in the direction that she had been travelling in before stopping to pester them, "but sod off!"

Jim Stone watched in amusement as the tipsy sex worker looped her arm through Murray's. He leaned across and nudged his colleague's elbow. "Paul, look!" he said, grinning. "I think that ropey looking bird's propositioning Kevin."

A smile spread across Evans' face. "Here, what's the difference between a hooker and a drug dealer?" Without waiting for a reply, he declared, "A hooker can wash her crack and use it again."

The two men looked at each other and burst out laughing.

"My turn," Stone said, wiping a tear from his eye. "Did you hear the one about—"

Evans glanced over to the alley, and his eyes went wide in alarm. "Shit!" he gasped, fumbling for the ignition.

Following his partner's gaze, Stone saw that the Berlingo was about to drive off.

Evans pulled out of the parking spot, then slammed his brakes on. Checking over his shoulder, he rammed the gear lever into reverse and floored the gas pedal. The Astra lurched backwards, screeching to a halt in front of the alley. The Berlingo had just started to edge out, and its startled driver had to brake hard to avoid T-boning the pool car.

He slammed his palm down on the horn, venting his anger in a long, sustained blast.

Both detectives were out of their car in a flash. Leaving their doors wide open, they sprinted over to the Berlingo. Stone yanked open the driver's door and reached in, taking control of the key and switching the ignition off. The man behind the wheel, whom Stone recognised as the shop's proprietor, emitted a little yelp of fear, no doubt thinking he was about to be carjacked.

"Don't hurt me! I haven't got any money!" he screamed, raising his hands to protect his face.

"Relax," Stone said. "No one's going to hurt you."

Evans appeared beside Stone, holding up his warrant card for inspection. "Calm down, mate. We're police officers."

"Is this your van?" Stone asked him.

The driver nodded meekly, his mouth opening and closing as he tried to make sense of what was happening to him. "Y–yes, it's mine," he shakily confirmed a moment later. "Who else would it belong to?"

Stone patted him on the shoulder. "Sorry mate," he said. "Didn't mean to give you a fright, but we had to make sure you didn't do a runner."

The driver's eyes widened in confusion. "A runner?" he repeated, sounding utterly dumbfounded. "Why would I do that?" He took another look at Evans' warrant card, then unclipped his seatbelt and eased himself out of the van. "What the hell is this all about?"

"It's about the two missing boys on the news," Stone told him. "They were abducted by someone using this van."

The driver's jaw dropped. "Is this someone's idea of a bloody wind up?" he demanded, looking from one detective to the other.

## 23

You have my word on that

As soon as Benny switched the sign dangling from the shop door from the 'open' to 'closed' position, Gareth Madeley rapped on the glass pane.

Benny opened the door and stuck his head out, quickly looking left and right before turning his attention to the barrister. "Come in, come in," he said, ushering his visitor inside.

Locking the door behind them, Benny led his guest through to a small parlour at the rear of the premises. It contained a couple of worn leather armchairs, a scuffed wooden coffee table, and a large Panasonic television. A cheap VHS video player lay on the floor beside it.

"Take a load off," he said, gesturing towards the two burgundy armchairs.

Madeley did as he was bidden, choosing the seat nearest to a three-bar electric wall heater. "I haven't been back here before," he said, flicking an imaginary fleck of dust from one of the knees of his finely tailored trousers.

"Not many people have," Benny confessed, sitting down opposite him.

Removing his gloves, Madeley held his hands out towards the heater to warm them up.

Benny retrieved a bottle of Ledaig single malt scotch whisky from the coffee table and broke the seal. There were two tumblers next to it, and he poured a liberal measure into each, before handing one to Madeley.

"As this is such a special occasion, I thought I'd splash out on a bottle of the good stuff," he said, flashing Madeley an indulgent grin.

The barrister twirled the amber liquid around several times before raising the glass to his nose to savour the delicious peaty aroma within. "A decent choice," he acknowledged, taking a sip. "Now, let's get down to business. When last we spoke, you implied that you had found me a suitable chicken, and as you can imagine, I'm rather keen to hear more about him."

"Oh, I've found you a chicken alright," Benny confirmed, with a sly grin. "But he's not just any old chicken. No, no, no. This one is *special* in every sense of the word."

The whisky glass halted halfway to Madeley's lips. "Special? In what way?" he asked, unable to mask his excitement. "Tell me everything."

Benny spread his arms, a salesman about to launch into his pitch. "Make no mistake about it, what I'm about to offer you is a once in a lifetime opportunity. If you decide to proceed, I can guarantee you the most exquisite experience of your life." He paused for dramatic effect. "The chicken I'm offering you is nine years old. He has shiny blonde hair, and what can only be described as the face of an angel."

Madeley was sitting up straighter now, hanging onto every word.

"Not only is this chicken a real looker," Benny continued, "but right now, he's one of the two most famous children in the whole country."

Madeley's brow creased into a deep furrow as he considered this. "What do you mean, the two most famous…" The words trailed off as his mind made the connection. "Surely you're not talking about the missing children who've been all over the TV, are you?"

Benny's smile was answer enough.

Madeley was shocked. "You abducted those kids?"

Benny swatted the accusation aside with a flamboyant wave. "Me? Good heavens, no. I had nothing to do with that. I just so happen to know the bloke who did, and I thought the blonde was a perfect match for the order you'd placed with me, so I reached out to my associate to enquire if he was still available. It turns out he is, but as you can imagine, there's a big market for talent like that within our community, so the asking price is quite considerable. Luckily for you, I'm owed a big favour by the man who snatched him, so I was able to negotiate a very good price for you, if you're interested."

Madeley said nothing, but Benny could almost hear the cogs turning in the barrister's head.

"They say a picture paints a thousand words," Benny said, as he crossed to the video player. Bending down, he inserted a VHS tape and pressed the play button. A moment later, a recording of a BBC news bulletin filled the screen. When the images of the boys came on, he pressed the pause button. "Look at him," he urged, seductively. "Imagine that smiling face lying on your pillow, waiting for you to claim it."

Madeley was transfixed. "He's beautiful," he said, dreamily. "But the risk would be—"

"I've told you before," Benny interrupted, speaking firmly but kindly. "There won't be any risks involved for you, just a wonderful afternoon of untold pleasure."

Drinking in the boy's image, Madeley swallowed hard. "I'm not sure… I need time to think."

Benny could see that Madeley was almost there; all he needed was a little push in the right direction. He crossed to the barrister's side, running a hand across his shoulders.

"There is no time. A number of lucrative bids have already been submitted by other interested parties. If you want him, you'll have to make a commitment right now, or it will be too late."

"How much would he cost me?"

Returning to his seat, Benny took another sip of his drink, then smacked his lips together in appreciation before reaching into his jacket pocket and withdrawing a folded scrap of paper. A figure was written on it. It was ten per cent higher than the highest bid he had received from his other clients. He placed the paper on the coffee table and slid it over.

Madeley scooped up the paper. His eyes widened when he unfolded it. "That's a phenomenal amount of money."

"Trust me," Benny said. "This chicken is worth every penny, and more besides."

Madeley glanced at the boy's frozen image on the screen. "He is divine," he admitted.

At that point, Benny knew he had the man. "You might think this is an awful lot of money, but you're getting mates' rates because I'm owed a big favour by the seller. Anyone else bidding for him will have to pay considerably more."

"Is the boy still a virgin?"

Benny smiled. "Naturally."

"And you can assure me that he will remain that way? I don't want him if he's already been sullied."

"You have my word on that," Benny pledged, placing a gnarled hand over the spot his heart would have occupied, if he'd had one.

Madeley gulped down the remaining whisky and held his glass out for a refill. "Very well," he said, once Benny had poured it. "I confess, I am rather enamoured by the boy, and although the price is high, I'm willing to pay it, as long as you can assure me there will be no risk involved."

"You have my word on that too," Benny promised him.

Tyler sat behind his desk. He felt unbelievably tired, and his head was pounding. Taking a sip of lukewarm coffee, he popped the two paracetamols that Imogen Askew had just handed him into his mouth and swallowed them with a grimace. He had reluctantly allowed her to sit in on the strategy meeting he was holding with Dillon and Bull, but that had been interrupted a few minutes earlier by a telephone call from Charlie White, who was still down at the florist shop in Caledonian Road.

"*We've just finished searching the premises,*" White was saying. "*There's sod all here but flowers and plants, so the question is, do you want Mr Lithgow arrested, or can he be allowed to lock up and go home?*"

Tyler sighed. "Is he on the register?" he asked, meaning the Sex Offenders Register.

"*No,*" White said immediately. "*He hasnae got any form, and there isnae any intelligence to suggest he's a scallywag. Plus, he doesnae fit the description of the suspect.*"

"That doesn't mean he isn't involved," Tyler pointed out.

"*True,*" White allowed, "*but he seems like quite a nice chap, and after spending two whole days speaking to nonces, I'm no' picking up that vibe from him.*"

That didn't mean anything; these people were good at disguising themselves so that they could blend in. "What arrangements have you made regarding the van?" Tyler asked, still undecided.

"*Kevin's arranged for a full lift. When the transporter arrives, we'll get the Berlingo shipped off to Charlton car pound for a full forensic examination, but my gut tells me we'll be wasting our time.*"

"Why do you say that?" Tyler demanded.

"*Two reasons,*" White told him. "*Firstly, Dean's confirmed Lithgow's claim that his numberplates were stolen while the van was parked up overnight at the back of the shop a couple of weeks ago. There's a crime report on the system to that effect.*"

"And the second reason?" Tyler asked, making a hurried note of what he'd just been told in his daybook.

"*I rang Colin a few minutes ago and asked him to describe the van in the footage we've got from Saturday night's abduction. The two vans are very different.*"

"In what way?"

"*Well, for starters, the suspect's van had a GB badge on its rear offside door, whereas this one doesnae. But the main difference is that Mr Lithgow's van is covered with professional sign writing, advertising his shop. The suspect van had nothing on it like that.*"

Leaning back into his chair, Tyler expelled his breath in a loud, frustrated gust. "Bollocks! That's not what I wanted to hear. How did Lithgow react when you told him you were seizing his van?"

At the other end of the line, White snorted. "*He had a proper hissy fit at first, but he's a reasonable chap, and he's calmed down now.*"

"Charlie, give the duty CSM a call, run what you've told me by him. Unless he has any objections from a forensic point of view, don't bother seizing the van. Call out a SOCO and have it photographed, checked for fibres and swabbed at the scene. Then it can be returned to Lithgow." Covering the receiver, he looked at Dillon and Bull in turn. "Can either of you see a problem with that?"

They both shook their heads.

"What about arresting him?" Tyler asked. "In light of what Charlie's just told us, I'm minded not to."

"I honestly can't see any point," Bull said, looking to Dillon for support.

Tyler followed his gaze. "Dill?"

"I think Stevie's right, Jack, but it's your call."

"Charlie, don't arrest him, but see if he's willing to let us borrow his phone for a few hours, just to eliminate him as a suspect."

He waited while White put the request to Lithgow. There were raised voices at the other end of the line, but they were too muffled to decipher what was being said.

A full minute later, White was back.

"*Boss, Mr Lithgow wasnae very happy at first, but when I explained that the child snatcher appears to have used his stolen numberplates, and that it was important we clear his good name to prevent his reputation from being tarnished by the media, he practically fell over himsel' in his eagerness to cooperate.*"

Tyler couldn't help but smile. White had probably overegged the pudding by saying that, but if it got them what they wanted, the exaggeration was fine by him.

"Good man, Charlie. Grab his phone, tell him we'll get it downloaded and returned to him ASAP, then let him go about his business." After White had gone, Tyler smiled wearily at the others. "Where were we, before Charlie interrupted?"

"We were discussing the message you left for the suspect," Imogen said.

Tyler bit his tongue. He knew Imogen was trying to be helpful, but he had been addressing his fellow detectives; she was there purely as an observer, not a contributor.

"I spoke to the TIU before we sat down," Bull said. "The phone is still switched off, and there hasn't been any activity on it since you made the media appeal."

Tyler nodded, feeling strangely deflated. He had been utterly convinced that the suspect would listen to the message, and it had come as a real body blow to find out that he hadn't.

"There's still time," Dillon said, optimistically.

"I know," Tyler said, but the words felt hollow.

"How's the search going down at the forest?" Bull asked.

Tyler grimaced. "Too slowly for my liking. It's an impossible task, a bit like looking for a needle in a haystack, without even knowing where the haystack is. Everyone's working tremendously hard, and we're covering a lot of ground, but it's not getting us anywhere."

He stood up and walked around his desk to the door. "I need a break. Let's reconvene in ten minutes. In the meantime, I'm going to make us all a fresh brew."

---

With the rush hour coming to an end, Kings Cross station was a lot quieter than when Madeley had arrived an hour ago, but Euston Road was still just as congested. If anything, traffic had intensified, degrading the air quality even more.

To his surprise, the sex worker ballerina was still twirling around the pavement outside the station entrance. When she saw him, she smiled in recognition and shouted, "You sure you don't want to do some business?"

Ignoring her, he entered the station and descended the escalator to the platforms, where he waited for the Circle line train that would take him to Moorgate.

Although outwardly calm, Madeley was in a state of near euphoria. All he could think about was the blonde chicken's beatific smile. The price he was going to pay for enjoying his nubile body was extortionate, but he didn't care. Benny had said it would take a couple of days to put all the necessary safeguards in place, but hopefully, by Thursday afternoon the boy would be his.

---

After showing Madeley out, Benny treated himself to another glass of malt whisky to celebrate the absurdly profitable deal he had just negotiated. With the blonde chicken now sold, all that remained was to secure a buyer for the boy Remus called Spineless.

He was a plain looking child, and slightly chubby with it, so he was never going to command as much as his prettier friend, but his fame guaranteed he would still merit an eye watering sum. Benny had already received two very decent bids for Spineless, but he was waiting for the third client who had expressed an interest to come back with his final offer. That particular client had a penchant for oversized boys, and Benny was expecting his bid to be higher than the others, which was why he was willing to give the man a little extra time if needed.

By the time Benny locked up, it was getting on for seven o'clock. He noticed a man in a white paper suit examining the florist's van as he drove out of the alley, and assumed it had been broken into. He wasn't surprised. The alley was dark, unoverlooked and had no CCTV coverage, and the idiot who owned it was always leaving his personal belongings in clear view on the front passenger seat, practically begging someone to steal them.

The journey to Hackney would take no more than forty

minutes, which meant that he would be there in plenty of time to get ready for the orgy. Driving his Daimler along Caledonian Road, he called Joey to make sure the preparations were all in hand.

"Have you stocked up on booze?"

McQueen laughed. "*I've got enough alcohol here to float a small ship.*"

"What about drugs?" They always laid on a nice selection of recreational drugs to fuel their client's desires and help them shed their inhibitions.

"*I've got blow, Charlie, amphetamines and E-tabs for the clients, and the usual combo of sedatives for any chickens who need a little persuading.*"

Benny grinned. "Good lad. How many chickens have you ordered?"

The clients didn't attend Benny's little shindigs for the alcohol or drugs; they came for the free rent boys that Benny provided.

"*Three from our stable, plus the youngster you told me to invite.*"

For the past few weeks, Benny had been having fun with a fresh-faced chicken called Adam, a twelve-year old who had arrived in London the previous month. So far, Benny had kept the boy exclusively to himself, but he had decided it was time for him to start working for his keep. This would be his first time being rented out to others, and Benny didn't think he was going to like it.

"Keep an eye on him once the fun starts," he told McQueen. "He knows what's expected of him, but I think he's going to be problematic until he's properly broken in."

"*What about Gabe?*" McQueen asked.

"Bring him along," Benny said. "I want to see how he reacts. Perhaps, if we get him high enough, he might even be tempted to join in the fun."

McQueen sniggered. "*Mo's got his heart set on breaking him in,*" he confided. "*He's hoping to slip the boy a Mickey Finn before the night's over and claim his cherry.*"

Benny bristled at that. "Mo can hope all he bloody wants. He knows the rules. I'm the leader of this wolfpack; I get to break the new chickens in, not Mo."

Remus was sitting on his bed, holding Troublemaker's phone. He felt like a prisoner, trapped in the house with the two chickens while everyone else was running around getting ready for the orgy. He hated the thought of missing out on all the free alcohol and drugs, and to add insult to injury, Benny was going to be passing around a new rent boy, which meant he would miss out on that too.

Feeling an irrational surge of anger, he hit the power button. After a few seconds the screen burst into life, and a ping announced that there was a new voicemail message. Remus' thumb hovered uncertainly over the green button as he internalised over what to do.

Maybe, listening to the voicemail would cheer him up, maybe it wouldn't.

"Sod it," he said, and pressed the button. After all, what harm could it possibly do?

Almost immediately, the detective's voice began to play in his ear.

# 24

The orgy

Gabe looked around the packed living room, studying the faces of the men gathered there. They varied in age from mid-thirties to late-sixties, and if their fleshy jowls, expensive designer clothes and ostentatious bling were any kind of indication, none of them was short of a bob or two.

There were twenty guests in total, none of whom Gabe recognised, although Joey had confided in him that a couple of well-known public figures were present.

As host, Benny was actively encouraging his clients to make the most of the free alcohol and drugs on offer, and although the party had been in full swing for less than an hour, most people were already pissed out of their heads or as high as a kite.

While McQueen remained in the kitchen, dispensing the booze and drugs, Benny and Mo circulated amongst the guests, making small talk. Gabe didn't like the way the old photographer kept shooting him furtive glances, smiling lustfully whenever their eyes met.

The guests all seemed to know each other, and they were standing in little cliques, laughing and talking amongst themselves as he passed amongst them, politely enquiring whether they needed a refill.

The lights had been dimmed, and the air was thick with acrid smoke from all the cigars, cigarettes and cannabis joints. Music was playing, and the atmosphere was one of charged expectation.

A folding wooden table, the sort of thing decorators used for pasting wallpaper, had been erected beneath the room's solitary window. A Christmas themed tablecloth had been draped over it, even though it was only early November, and this was covered with an assortment of nibbles, crisps and sandwiches.

Gabe had initially wondered why there were no female guests present, but the recent arrival of four rent boys, one of whom looked even younger than him, had solved that mystery.

McQueen ushered the four boys into the bedroom that Gabe had been using since his arrival, telling them to hurry up and get themselves ready for the evening's entertainment.

When Gabe popped in to offer them a drink a few minutes later, he heard one of the boys complaining that it was going to be a brutal session. Dressed entirely in black, he was about sixteen, skinny, with spiky black hair, dark eyeliner and black nail varnish, all of which gave him a Goth like appearance.

By contrast, the boy standing next to him had dyed his hair peroxide blonde. Dressed in garishly bright clothes, his movements had a distinctly feminine quality to them, and Gabe saw he was wearing mascara, blusher and red lipstick. He responded to the Goth's observation by laughing in weary resignation. "Well, if it's anywhere near as bad as the last one I attended, none of us will be able to sit down for the rest of the week without wincing." Raising a hand to his mouth in slapstick fashion, he adopted a pained expression.

The Goth laughed.

A third rent boy, tall and rangy, with shoulder length mousy hair, was studying his face in the tall mirror. "Take my word for it," he said, as he squeezed at an angry looking zit on his chin, "the only way to get through nights like this is to get off your rocker on all the free cocaine that Joey's handing out."

"Trust me," the Goth told him. "I plan to be totally spaced out before the first cock is unzipped."

Gabe noticed that the youngest boy was just sitting on the edge of the bed, his face ashen, his eyes fearful.

"Are you okay, mate?" he asked, after taking the drink orders from the other three. "Can I get you something to drink?"

The boy shook his head. "No, thank you," he said, staring miserably at his feet.

"What's your name?" Gabe asked, wondering if he was okay. He certainly didn't seem it.

"Adam," the boy replied, listlessly.

Adam's face was very pale, and his cheeks were slightly sunken, as though he had recently lost weight. His clothing was loose, rumpled and dirty, and he looked like he needed a good wash and a hot meal. Having been homeless himself, Gabe recognised the signs of someone who had been living rough, not eating properly and not getting enough sleep. "What about some food?" he encouraged. "I could bring you some nibbles and crisps if you want?"

Adam shook his head again, and the movement seemed to drain him.

Gabe noticed that his eyes were moist, as if he were fighting back tears.

"Can you show me where the toilet is?" Adam asked, meekly.

"Yeah, sure," Gabe said, giving him a friendly smile.

Gabe escorted him to the loo. He was about to walk off, but then he decided it might be better to wait and show Adam back to the bedroom.

During the brief interlude between Sinéad O'Connor finishing *Nothing Compares 2 U* and The Pet Shop Boys beginning *It's a Sin*, Gabe thought he heard muffled sobs coming from within the toilet.

Placing his ear against the door, he listened intently, but with the music playing again, it was impossible to hear anything more.

Gabe rapped on the door. "Adam, are you okay in there?"

There was no response.

Gabe knocked again, harder this time. "Adam?"

"What's going on?"

Gabe spun to find Benny standing there, hands on hips, staring at him accusingly. He instinctively took a backwards step, to avoid inhaling the old man's rancid breath.

"It's one of the boys Joey organised for the... er, evening's entertainment. He's in the loo, and I don't think he's feeling very well."

"Which one?" Benny demanded.

"Adam."

"Oh, it would be him," Benny said, shaking his head in irritation. Pushing Gabe aside, he hammered on the door. "Open up," he yelled, angrily. "And be quick about it."

For a moment nothing happened, but then the door opened inward to reveal a teary-eyed Adam. Benny reached in and grabbed him firmly by the collar. "What's your problem?" he demanded, dragging the boy out.

Tears were streaming down Adam's face. "Please, Benny," he begged, ineffectually trying to prise the old man's hand open. "I don't want to do this... please don't make me."

Wrapping an arm around the boy's neck, Benny affected a strained smile. "Don't be daft," he said, ruffling Adam's hair with his free hand. "You'll enjoy it once you get going."

Adam's eyes widened, and he attempted to pull free, but the old man tightened his grip until the boy yelped.

"Come with me," Benny snarled, angrily frogmarching him along the corridor to the single bedroom next to Gabe's. Opening the door with his free hand, he shoved Adam inside, then turned to Gabe. "Tell Joey I need a glass of his special lemonade for one of the chick– for one of the boys."

Gabe just stood there, staring open mouthed at him, appalled by the callous way the old man was treating the distressed boy.

"Well, don't just stand there," Benny snapped. "Get me that

bloody drink, and make sure you tell Joey it has to be a one of his special lemonades. Got it?"

Gabe nodded, too shocked to speak. Then, wilting under Benny's fierce scowl, he spun on his heels and set off towards the kitchen.

---

Reg Parker barged into Tyler's office without knocking. His face was flushed, and he was breathing heavily from having just sprinted across the office. "Boss! The TIU just rung me with news that Peter's mobile's been online."

Tyler was out of his chair in an instant, fuelled by adrenalin. "Where was it pinged?" Grabbing his daybook, he followed Parker into the main office.

"It shook hands with a mast in Leytonstone," Parker informed him. "The bloke from the TIU reckons the phone was live for approximately two minutes, which is about the time it would have taken to listen to your voicemail twice."

"Is it still active?" Tyler asked, excitedly.

Parker shook his head. "No. It was switched off again straight afterwards."

Dillon, Bull, and Imogen, who had all been sitting in with Tyler, were following at a more sedate pace.

"Can the TIU tell us which azimuth the phone's in?" Dillon asked.

Parker made a show of crossing his fingers. "They're trying to do that as we speak."

Fletcher hurried over, carrying three A3 sized maps he had just printed out.

"There you go," he said, placing one copy in front of Parker and handing a second to Tyler. Dillon held out a hand for the third one, but Fletcher kept that for himself. "I'll print out some more in a minute," he said, when Dillon looked at him expectantly.

Picking up a marker pen, Parker consulted the image on his computer screen, then drew a large X on the corresponding spot on the paper copy. "This is the mast that carried out the electronic handshake with Peter's phone," he informed Tyler.

"Mark mine up, too," Tyler requested, handing his copy over.

Parker obliged, then as an afterthought, he drew crude circles on both maps before handing one back to Tyler. "That circle represents the approximate radius of the mast. I'll print a more accurate version out as soon as the TIU e-mails it over."

Dillon and Bull sidled up on either side of Tyler to get a better look.

"Well, this is cosy," Tyler observed, feeling hemmed in.

"We'll have to share, seeing as I didn't merit my own copy," Dillon sulked, shooting Fletcher an injured look.

"How far away is this mast from the site of the abduction?" Bull asked, tapping the X on Tyler's map.

Parker examined his own map. "I dunno. Probably two or three miles at a guess."

"Stevie, give the MIR a ring and have them raise a High Priority action for Colin to seize all the local authority CCTV within the mast's radius," Tyler instructed.

"It'll probably be quicker if I pop in there and speak to Chris directly," Bull said, heading for the door. "Then I'll nip downstairs to the CCTV viewing room, to let Colin know it's coming his way."

Tyler's eyes were alive with the thrill of the hunt as he turned to his partner. "Dill, I need you to arrange for a couple of cars to carry out an urgent street search of all the roads within the cell's radius. If we can locate that van, we might still be in time to save those kids."

"But we don't even know its registration number," Dillon objected. "It was on false plates when the suspect abducted the kids."

"True," Tyler acknowledged, "but we know one of its rear doors has a GB sticker on it, so we trawl the area for a Berlingo van displaying one of those. Surely, there can't be too many of those knocking about, can there?"

Dillon blew out his breath. "It's a big ask, Jack. And we don't have any spare capacity to play with, so unless you want me to rob

Peter to pay Paul, I'm going to have to try and find staff from elsewhere."

Tyler's forehead scrunched into a thoughtful frown as he pondered this. Dillon was right; everyone on the team was tied up. Under normal circumstances, he would have rung the local duty officer and asked them to supply a couple of patrol cars to carry out the street search during night duty, but every station for miles around had been stripped down to the bare bones to provide the massive aid commitment needed to search Epping Forest. "You're right, Dill," he conceded. "Grab your coat. We'll have to do it ourselves."

---

Gabe watched as McQueen poured a small glass of lemonade, wondering what he was going to add to it to make it so special? He naively assumed that the secret ingredient would be alcohol, but instead of adding booze, McQueen produced a paper bag from his pocket, then proceeded to tip its powdery contents into the fizzy drink before giving it a vigorous stir with a teaspoon.

"What's that?" Gabe asked, trying to make the question sound casual.

"Just something to help the boy relax."

Something about the way McQueen said this disturbed Gabe. He wasn't sure why; perhaps it was just the casualness of his delivery that made the words sound so sinister?

On their way to the bedroom, McQueen signalled for Mo to join them.

"They're in there," Gabe said when they reached the bedroom that Benny was holding Adam in.

Mo turned to him. "We'll take it from here. You can sling your hook."

"But—"

"Mo's right," McQueen cut him off. "Why don't you go and see if anyone needs a refill?" Without waiting for a reply, he rapped on the door.

Gabe hesitated. He knew it was unwise to question their orders. "I just want to make sure Adam's okay, first."

McQueen's face darkened, and Gabe realised that he had seriously overstepped the mark. Thankfully, before McQueen could say anything, the door opened wide and Benny beckoned them all inside.

Adam was lying on the bed, partially undressed. He was on his right side, with his back towards the door. The soft heaving of his body betrayed the fact that he was crying.

"Sit up and drink this," Benny barked, holding his hand out for the drink McQueen was carrying.

Moving as if in a trance, Adam slowly complied. After taking the first sip, he grimaced and tried to hand the drink back. "I don't want it. It tastes funny."

Exchanging complicit looks, Mo and McQueen moved swiftly, taking up positions on either side of Adam. Pinning his arms down, they restrained him while Benny forced him to drink the laced soda. All three men ignored his frightened pleas to stop, and the gurgling noises he made as he almost choked on the liquid being poured down his throat.

Gabe didn't know what to do. He wanted to shout at them to stop, but he seemed to have lost the power of speech.

When the glass was empty, McQueen and Mo released Adam, who sagged down onto the bed, coughing and spluttering. As the fast-acting sedative began to take effect, McQueen and Mo finished undressing the boy while Benny watched on, smiling lasciviously.

"Why don't you boys go outside and have a fag?" Benny suggested, unbuckling his belt with a leer. "You can have a go on him yourself, after I've finished."

"Oh, I plan to," Mo assured him, rubbing his hands together in excitement.

Gabe was utterly revolted. These men had drugged Adam, and now they planned to take turns having sex with him against his will. Feeling sick to his stomach, he wondered what kind of people he had got himself involved with.

Gabe knew that lots of runaways ended up becoming rent boys

or prostitutes to make ends meet, but just because they sold their bodies for money, they shouldn't automatically lose the right to say no when they didn't want to have sex. Adam had made it abundantly clear that he didn't want to participate in the orgy. He had literally begged Benny to allow him to leave. The old man's response had been to pin him down and force a sedative down his throat. Now he was going to be gang raped.

Gabe no longer felt safe around these people. If they were willing to do that to Adam, what was to stop them from doing it to him? In that instant, he knew that he had to get away from them as quickly as possible, but how was he going to manage that without money? One thing was for sure, he would never again eat or drink anything they offered him.

Wrapping an arm around Gabe's shoulders, Mo escorted him back to the living room.

"Be a good lad and fetch me a drink," the photographer said, leaning in close to be heard above the music. "I'll have a large vodka with a splash of tonic water."

Gabe cringed when the old perv patted him smartly on the rump as he was sent on his way.

After fetching Mo his drink, Gabe decided that he needed some fresh air. Weaving his way through the drunken partygoers, he headed back to the hallway.

Take That were belting out *It Only Takes a Minute,* and one of the guests began singing it to him as he walked past, twisting and gyrating and inviting Gabe to join him.

Forcing a smile, Gabe politely shook his head.

McQueen was still standing guard outside the bedroom, making sure no one interrupted Benny. "Where are you going?" he demanded as Gabe approached.

"It's a bit too hot and smoky in there for my liking," Gabe explained. "I need some air."

McQueen shook his head. "It's not safe for you to be wandering around the estate on your own at night. If you're that desperate for fresh air, open a window. Personally, I think it's overrated."

Gabe considered arguing the point, but the semi-suspicious way that McQueen was staring at him made him think twice. He was about to return to the living room when the door behind McQueen flew open to reveal Benny standing there, stark naked, a look of fury plastered across his withered face.

"What's the matter?" McQueen asked, instantly picking up on his dark mood.

"There's been a bit of an accident," Benny told him, lighting up a cigarette and taking a deep drag. "I'll need you to sort it out for me."

Gabe recalled hearing that, if you didn't douche before having anal sex, you would probably end up shitting yourself, and he wondered if this was what had happened to Adam. The thought filled him with anger and disgust; as if being drugged and raped wasn't degrading enough, poor Adam had also suffered the indignity of soiling himself.

Peering into the room as Benny stepped clear of the doorway, he saw that Adam was lying face down on the bed, one arm hanging over the edge of the mattress. The rent boy's eyes were half open, but they had glazed over, and there was no trace of life in them.

Trying not to make it too obvious, Gabe studied Adam's bony ribcage, hoping to see his chest rising and falling.

There was no movement at all.

"Oh, shit!' McQueen said, more out of anger than concern. He rushed into the room and bent over the unmoving boy, feeling his wrist for a pulse. "For fuck's sake, Benny, what have you done?" Releasing the boy's arm, McQueen locked eyes with Gabe. "Go and fetch Mo for me," he snapped. "Do it now! And be discreet."

Gabe nodded dumbly, then ran off, nearly tripping over his own feet in his haste to get away.

He returned a couple of minutes later, with the photographer in tow.

"What's so important that it couldn't wait a few more minutes?" Mo demanded, his bloodshot eyes ping-ponging between Benny, who had now put his trousers on, and McQueen. "Gabe said it was urgent, but he wouldn't say what the problem…" his voice trailed off as he caught sight of the unmoving boy. "What did you do?" he groaned, looking straight at Benny.

Beckoning them into the room, Benny sucked smoke deep into his lungs, then noisily exhaled it through his nostrils. "It was an accident. I must've squeezed a little too hard." A stroppy shrug. "You know how these things happen?"

Gabe could hardly believe his ears. He walked over to the bed in a daze. Sure enough, there were purple bruise marks around Adam's throat. Turning away, he clamped a hand over his mouth and screwed his eyes shut.

"What's wrong with you, Benny?" He heard Mo raging. "Why do you always have to strangle the chickens first? Is that the only way you can get it up these days?"

"Keep it down," McQueen cautioned, hurriedly closing the door.

Gabe opened his eyes in time to see Benny taking a step towards Mo. His bony fists were clenched in anger.

Mo held his ground. "If you get a kick out of strangling the little fuckers, that's your business," he hissed, jabbing a gnarled finger into his friend's chest. "But don't ruin the fun for everyone else. Maybe, next time, you should go last, then it won't matter."

"Fuck off," Benny fumed, slapping the finger away. "I'm the leader of this wolfpack, and it's my prerogative to go first."

McQueen stepped between them. Intent on diffusing the situation, he placed his palms on their respective chests, and pushed them apart. "Instead of bickering amongst ourselves, we need to work out what we're going to do with the body," he said, forcefully.

Benny unclenched his fists. "Yeah, you're right. Good lad." He patted McQueen on the shoulder.

"Do you want me to get rid of the guests, so we can clear this mess up?" McQueen asked.

Benny took another drag from his cigarette. "No. There's no point in ruining their fun. That would be bad for business. We'll leave the chicken in here till everyone's gone, then we can tidy the place up and get rid of the body." Ushering the others out of the room, Benny produced a key from his pocket. "Joey, get the other boys to start circulating. The sooner our wealthy guests get to shoot their loads, the quicker we can get rid of them."

McQueen turned to go, then hesitated. "What should I say to the other chickens, if they ask where their mate is?"

Benny responded with a mirthless laugh. "Tell them I terminated his employment."

## 25

## WEDNESDAY 7TH NOVEMBER 2001

It's a shovel

Tyler was so tired that his eyes kept slipping in and out of focus as he studied the line of parked vehicles along his offside. To his left, Kelly Flowers was busy scrutinising everything parked along the nearside.

Kelly smothered a yawn. "This is madness, Jack," she complained. "We need to get some sleep before we drop."

Tyler knew she was right. The next office meeting was due to start at eight, which was only a few short hours away.

"You didn't have to tag along," he pointed out. "I told you to go home and grab some shut eye, but you wouldn't listen." The last thing he wanted was for her to over-exert herself and risk endangering the baby, but when he had tried to explain this to her, she had dug her heels in. He had considered ordering her to go off duty, but there had been no point; she would have only refused, and then she would have sulked.

Kelly sighed her exasperation. "I've told you; I'll go home when you do."

A few seconds passed in awkward silence, with Tyler feeling increasingly guilty.

"Kelly, I–"

Kelly's phone rang. She checked the caller ID then raised it to her ear. "Hi, Tony," she said, wearily. She listened for a few seconds, then glanced sideways at Tyler. "Uh-huh, I'll tell him."

"Tell me what?" he demanded, suspiciously.

"That Tony says you're an idiot."

Tyler huffed. He hated it when they ganged up on him.

"What's that?" Kelly asked. She listened for a moment, then smiled. "Imogen said she agrees with Tony."

To Tyler's intense annoyance Imogen had insisted on accompanying Dillon, as if she were now a fully-fledged member of the team and had a say in the matter.

"Tell him we'll give it fifteen minutes more, then call it a night," Tyler offered by way of compromise.

Kelly repeated this for Dillon's benefit, then smiled at his response. "I know, I know," she said, nodding her heartfelt agreement. "But he'll be like that anyway." Ending the call, she turned to Tyler. "Tony's worried that you're going to be like a bear with a sore head at the office meeting if you don't get some shut eye."

Suddenly the 'But he'll be like that anyway,' comment made sense.

Tyler was exhausted, but the thought of resting while the missing children were in danger filled him with guilt; if they died while he slept, how would he ever be able to live with himself, knowing that he had been more concerned about grabbing eight hours of shut eye than searching for them?

Beside him, Kelly yawned expansively. He glanced in her direction and was alarmed by how pale and drawn she looked. In that instant, he realised he was being unreasonable; it was one thing for him to work himself into the ground, but he couldn't allow Kelly and the others to do the same out of a misplaced sense of loyalty to him. "Okay, call Dill, tell him we're heading back to the office, and he's to do likewise."

According to the clock on the dash, it was almost three a.m. when McQueen pulled the Daimler into the little clearing and killed the engine. With the trees blocking out the little moonlight there was, it was so dark that he could barely make out his hand in front of his face.

It was spooky being all alone in the dark, and the eerie noises the wind kept making as it whipped through the trees was giving him the heebie-jeebies.

Heavy rain was forecast, and McQueen could already feel the first traces of it in the air. Keen to get the gruesome task over with before the storm broke, McQueen opened the Daimler's boot to reveal a large roll of old carpet and a shovel. Benny had fetched the carpet from the garage that came with the flat as soon as the orgy had finished, and he and Hinkleman had wrapped Adam's corpse in it while McQueen and Gabe tidied up the rest of the flat.

Leaving Adam where he was for the time being, McQueen grabbed the shovel, switched on his torch and set off into the forest.

Twigs crunched underfoot, brambles tugged at his clothing, and low hanging branches swept against his face. He kept to the path for a while, then veered off to traverse a series of small hillocks. He eventually reached a small clearing that was surrounded by a wall of nasty looking thistles. They were hardly impregnable, but the fact that you would probably end up getting pretty badly scratched as you forced your way through them would undoubtedly put most people off from trying.

Prodding a thistle with his fingertip, McQueen instantly recoiled in pain. Sucking a pinprick of blood from the injured digit, he decided that the clearing was as good a spot as any to bury the dead rent boy in.

Leaving the shovel there, McQueen retraced his tracks to the car park.

Benny had wrapped a number of strips of gaffer tape around the carpet to prevent it unrolling, but this had also made it rigid and unwieldy, so it took McQueen an age to manhandle the damn thing out of the boot. Breathing heavily, he hoisted the carpet onto his shoulder. As he adjusted the weight a low moaning noise escaped from within.

It was the most terrifying sound that McQueen had ever heard.

"Be cool, be cool," he told himself. "It's nothing to worry about, just air escaping from the body."

Weighed down by the extra weight of Adam's body, McQueen's progress was painfully slow, and the return trip to the clearing seemed to take twice as long as the first. At one point, he walked straight into a tree. Staggering backwards, the bottom of the carpet became entwined in the surrounding bracken and was almost ripped from his grasp.

McQueen stopped regularly to catch his breath and move his burden from one shoulder to the other. To his horror, Adam's body continued to make its ghostly wailing noises, and by the time he crested the final hillock, McQueen was a jabbering wreck.

Finally arriving at the clearing, McQueen dropped his burden onto the cold, hard earth, then collapsed to his knees, where he greedily sucked in air.

When he got his breath back, he retrieved the shovel and beat a path through the thicket at its thinnest point. Once inside, he scraped away the bed of leaves covering the forest floor. He had expected the soil to be rock hard, given how cold it had been over the past few days, but it proved to be remarkably pliant.

It took forever to dig the hole, and he repeatedly cursed Benny for refusing him permission to bring Gabe along to share the workload. Occasionally, McQueen thought he heard noises coming from the body, but each time he paused to listen, there was only silence.

"It's all in your fucking head," he berated himself, convinced that his overactive imagination was playing tricks on him.

Benny had insisted that the grave be at least six foot deep, but the moany old git wasn't the one having to do all the digging, so the hole McQueen actually dug was considerably shallower than that. When he was finished, he removed a folding penknife and sliced through the strands of gaffer tape, one at a time. Pocketing the knife, he unrolled the carpet until Adam's naked body was lying on its back, its open eyes staring up at him.

He looked down at the dead boy with something akin to pity.

Then a very strange thing happened.

Adam blinked at him, and in a barely audible voice, mumbled, "Please... help... me..."

---

Stumbling out of bed, Tyler groped his way through the darkness toward the en suite, intent on having a shower before getting dressed.

"What are you doing?" a sleepy voice called as he turned the shower on.

Tyler popped his head back into the bedroom. "Sorry, didn't mean to disturb you. I'll give you a shout when I'm out of the shower."

"What?" Grumpily propping herself up on one elbow, Kelly turned the sidelight on, then squinted at the time display on the alarm clock. "Why are you having a shower at three-thirty in the morning?" she demanded, sounding very confused.

"Three-thirty...?" Tyler disappeared into the en suite, then came back after turning the shower off. "I must be losing my marbles," he said, as he returned to bed. "I thought it was time to get ready for work."

"Be quiet," Kelly complained. "You're keeping me awake."

She was snoring within seconds, but sleep eluded Tyler, so he lay there, tossing and turning, thinking about the case.

---

McQueen stared down in horror at the naked figure writhing its way across the uneven ground towards him like something out of a zombie movie.

"Help me," Adam rasped. Extending a claw like hand, he seized McQueen's ankle with surprising strength.

With a high-pitched yelp of fear, McQueen jumped back, pulling his leg free. "You were dead!" he spluttered. "I saw you lying on the bed, not breathing."

"What have you... done to me?" Adam croaked, grabbing for his leg again, but missing.

A skein of lightning flashed across the sky, momentarily transforming night into day. For a split second, the hole that McQueen had just dug, along with the shovel protruding from the earth at a forty-five degree angle, was illuminated.

Adam's eyes widened in fear. "You bastard," he gasped, unsteadily pulling himself up onto his knees. "You were... you were going to bury me alive!"

"What was I meant to do? I thought you were dead!" McQueen protested. He took a step towards Adam, holding out a hand. "Let me get you back to the car. We'll go back to the flat. Benny will know what to do."

At the mention of Benny's name, Adam scuttled backwards on all fours; a frightened dog cowering from its abusive master. "No! I'm not going back there!" he screeched. "If you want to help, call the police."

"I can't call the police, you know that," McQueen said quietly. He couldn't let Adam call them, either.

Adam reached for the shovel, used it to haul himself to his feet. Panting heavily, he looked around the enclosed clearing, confused and afraid. "HELP ME!" he screamed, leaning on the handle to steady himself. "SOMEBODY, ANYBODY, PLEASE HELP ME!"

"Be quiet," McQueen hissed, raising a finger to his lips.

"HELP ME!" Adam yelled at the top of his voice. "HE'S TRYING TO KILL ME!"

In that moment, McQueen realised that Adam wasn't going to play ball. He wasn't going to return to the flat, get himself cleaned up and carry on like nothing had ever happened. He was going to make a big fuss; go to the police and ruin everything.

McQueen couldn't allow that.

"HELP!"

Rushing forward, McQueen kicked the shovel away.

Adam fell to the floor, landing face down. Rolling onto his back, he began kicking out at McQueen's shins and ankles, trying to keep him at bay.

Pushing Adam's feet aside, McQueen jumped astride the naked boy and attempted to clamp a hand across his mouth. "Shut up!" he hissed.

Adam twisted free. "HEEELP!"

McQueen tried to silence him again, but Adam bit into the heel of his hand, drawing blood.

"Aaargh!"

As soon as McQueen withdrew his injured hand, the screaming started all over again.

"SOMEONE HELP ME!"

McQueen wrapped his hands around Adam's scrawny throat and squeezed as hard as he could, grinding his fingers deep into the boy's soft flesh.

Another streak of lightning flashed across the sky. One half of McQueen's face was bathed in harsh light, while the other remained shrouded in darkness.

Thunder followed; loud and concussive.

Adam's hands flew to McQueen's wrists, frantically trying to pull them away, but McQueen was too strong for him. He arched his back and thrashed his legs. He dug his nails into McQueen's flesh, but all to no avail.

Eventually, Adam's writhing stopped and his body went limp. His hands slipped away from McQueen's wrists, coming to rest by his sides.

To make sure he really was dead this time, McQueen continued strangling Adam long after he stopped resisting. Eventually, he released his grip, staring down at his hands, which were frozen into claws. Blood was oozing from the ugly bite mark on his left hand. For all he knew, the little fucker was HIV positive; a lot of the rent boys were. Heart pounding, vision blurred, breath coming in ragged gasps, McQueen checked for a pulse, but found none. Adam's eyes were open, but his life force was spent.

"Shit," McQueen whispered, sliding off of Adam in a state of near exhaustion. For a while, all he could do was sit there and gulp down air. His limbs felt leaden, his hands were shaking, and his head was spinning from a lack of oxygen.

And then the rain began to fall. There were only a few droplets at first, but then the heavens opened with a vengeance. McQueen forced himself to stand up. Moving in a daze, he grabbed Adam's slender wrists and dragged him over to the grave. He shoved the body in with his foot. It landed face down with a dull thud. McQueen began shovelling dirt onto the corpse, covering the head up first to dehumanise it. He cringed as raindrops hammered into him with the force of tiny ball bearings. It seemed to take forever to fill in the grave, and by the time he was finished, he was soaked through.

---

PCs Paxman and Alder had decided to grab a quick cup of coffee to see them through the last couple of hours of the graveyard shift. The rain that had battered the windscreen with such ferocity for the past twenty minutes, was finally starting to ease off.

"Well, this rain's killed off any chances we had of getting a prisoner in." Paxman grumbled.

Alder sighed, pragmatically. "They say that rain's the best policeman there is."

Paxman pulled a face. "Even without the rain, tonight's been as dull as dishwater."

Apart from a couple of domestics and an accident, there had hardly been any calls, and certainly nothing to get the adrenalin flowing.

The rain had now subsided to little more than an annoying drizzle.

A couple of hundred yards ahead of them, a car pulled out of one of the little clearings on their left, heading towards London.

It had no lights on.

Paxman nodded at it. "Let's give that one a pull. You never know, he might be over the limit." While an arrest for drink driving wasn't as exciting as nabbing a burglar or a robber, it was better than nothing.

Alder was less optimistic. "More likely, it's a courting couple who've just stopped for a quick bunk up." Nonetheless, he unclipped his radio, intending to carry out a PNC check as soon as they got close enough to read the registration number.

---

McQueen had cranked the Daimler's heater up to full blast. Turning the radio up, he settled back into the soft leather contours of his seat and gunned the accelerator, eager to return to civilisation. He was soaked through, and shivering from the cold and the shock. The bite on the heel of his hand, which he could no longer see because it was caked in so much mud, was stinging like a bitch.

He needed a stiff drink to calm his nerves. If there was any cannabis left, he might treat himself to a large joint, to dull the memory of what he had just done.

McQueen glanced down at the mobile phone in the centre console, thinking he should probably report in. When he picked it up, he saw there were six missed calls from Benny. With a sigh, he rung him back. It took a few moments for the connection to be made, then Benny's voice was loud in his ear, impatient and full of stress.

"*Well, is it done?*"

"Yes. It's all done," McQueen replied in a flat voice.

"*Any problems?*"

Any problems? Any fucking problems! McQueen almost laughed out loud. How the hell was he supposed to answer that one?

*Yeah, there was one incy-wincy little snag, Benny. The little fucker you strangled wasn't quite dead, so I had to finish the job off for you... Thanks for that!*

"No. No problems," he said, after a moment's hesitation.

"*Good. Get your arse —*" There were three little beeps and then the line went dead.

McQueen checked the signal strength, cursed when he saw

there were no bars. He was about to press redial when flashing blue lights lit up his rear view mirror.

"Could this fucking night get any worse?" he groaned, feeling his heart sink. Tossing the mobile onto the passenger seat, he indicated left and pulled over.

---

To Alder's surprise, it wasn't a courting couple at all; the Daimler contained one male occupant, an unkempt white male in his twenties. He was out of the car almost as soon as it stopped, dripping wet and clearly agitated.

Alder smiled to himself as he emerged from the patrol car. When people reacted like that, it was usually a sign that they didn't want the police looking too closely at what was inside their vehicle.

Maybe they would strike lucky with this stop after all?

"Evening, officers," the driver said, forcing a smile. "Is there a problem?"

"It's morning," Paxman corrected him. "Not evening, and the problem is you were driving without any lights on."

The man glanced edgily over his shoulder, taking in the Daimler's rear lights, or rather the lack of them. He theatrically slapped his forehead with a mud covered hand. "Sorry, officer," he said, rolling his eyes in self-deprecation. "I can be a right plonker, sometimes. Thanks for pointing it out. I'll turn them on straight away." Throwing Paxman an army style salute, he spun on his heel and set off towards the Daimler.

"Not so fast, sunshine!" Alder said, beckoning him back with a crooked finger. "We're not done with you yet."

A pained expression crossed the driver's face. "But I said I was sorry, and I've got a dodgy gut, so I really need to get home as quickly as I can, before I shit myself." He clutched his abdomen to emphasise the point.

Alder was unmoved. "You just pulled out of the car park back there," he said, pointing back along the deserted road in the direction they had come from. "What were you doing in there at this time of the night?"

"Of the morning, you mean?" the driver corrected him.

Paxman exchanged a world-weary glance with his partner. "Looks like we're going to be here for a long time," he said, tipping his flat cap upwards so that it rested on the back of his head.

The driver, realising his smart mouthed comment had backfired on him, let out a little groan. "Sorry, I was just joking," he said, pressing his palms together in a show of contrition.

'What were you doing in the clearing?' Alder asked again, and this time there was an edge to his voice.

The driver shrugged. "I told you. I've got an upset stomach. I was caught short on the way home and had to stop for an emergency dump."

Alder removed his notebook from his tunic pocket, flicked to an empty page. "Name?" he demanded.

"Joseph Stanley McQueen."

"Is this your car?"

McQueen shook his head. "No. It belongs to my uncle, Benny Mars. It's registered to him." Without being asked, he recited the address of the flat in Hackney in a bored monotone, as if he had done this a hundred times before and was starting to find it wearisome.

Alder nodded, satisfied. That matched the PNC details he had been given over the radio before stopping the car. "Do you have the owner's permission to drive it?"

McQueen laughed, relaxing a little. "Yes, of course I do. If you don't believe me, why don't you ring him and check?"

Alder wrote the telephone number down, then radioed the station controller and requested that a call be made to Benny.

"Do you have your driving licence and vehicle insurance certificate with you?" Alder asked, while they waited for a response.

McQueen shook his head. "Sorry, no. But if you give me a producer, I'll be happy to take them both into my local nick tomorrow."

Paxman was studying McQueen's footwear, which was covered

in mud. His trousers and hands were muddy, too. "What have you been doing to get in that state?"

McQueen shifted uncomfortably. "I told you, I had to stop for a dump. It was Sod's law that as soon as I pulled my kacks down, the heavens opened. I had the runs so I couldn't stop, and I ended up getting soaked through." A hapless shrug. "What else could I do? I was shitting through the eye of a needle, so I just had to grin and bear it."

His story evoked a sympathetic half smile from Paxman. "Is there anything in the car that shouldn't be there?"

McQueen shook his head, vigorously. "Nothing. You can take a gander, if you want."

Paxman nodded to Alder, who wandered over to the car and began rummaging around inside. When he finished, he looked up and shook his head, disappointed not to have found anything.

"See, I told you," McQueen said, smiling at them.

"What about in the boot?" Paxman asked.

The smile faltered. "Nothing there, either."

Paxman looked at him for a long moment, his face giving nothing away. "Open it," he said.

"But—"

"Open it."

McQueen sighed. "You're wasting your time," he said, irritably. "And mine."

The boot came up with a loud squeak. "It needs oiling," McQueen pointed out, quite unnecessarily.

Paxman brushed him aside and started searching the boot. A roll of old carpet took up most of the available space. It was wet and covered in mud. "Why is there a carpet in the boot?" he asked, struggling to pull it aside.

"It's been in there for days," McQueen said, dismissively. "We keep meaning to take it to the dump, but we haven't gotten around to it yet."

Paxman grunted, then removed a muddy shovel. "And this?" he asked, holding it out for McQueen to see.

"It's a shovel," McQueen responded, sarcastically.

"I know what it bloody well is," Paxman snapped, "but why is it caked in fresh mud?"

McQueen sighed. "Because I just used it to bury a steaming hot pile of runny shit," he responded, stroppily. "What do you think I've been doing, digging up buried treasure?"

"Run a name check on him," Paxman told his colleague, hoping the cocky little bastard would be wanted on warrant.

"Known, not currently wanted," Alder reported back a couple of minutes later, relaying the result from the control room.

"What's he known for?" Paxman asked.

"Soliciting," Alder said, regarding McQueen with a derisory sneer. "He's a rent boy."

"A former rent boy," McQueen corrected, self-righteously. "These days, I'm strictly legit."

Paxman leaned in, sniffed at his breath. "Have you been drinking?"

McQueen's newly found composure dissolved in an instant. "Just the one," he said, suddenly nervous again. "But that was a good couple of hours ago."

They administered a breath test. Alder crossed his fingers, hoping the Electronic Screening Device would go straight to red, indicating a failure and giving them a reason to arrest him. They waited for a full minute, but although the light went from green to amber almost immediately, it didn't go all the way to red.

"This shows us that you've had a drink but are not over the limit," Alder said, holding the ESD's screen up for him to see.

McQueen flashed them a triumphant smile. "So, I can be on my way?"

Paxman nodded. "Go on, piss off," he said, dismissing him with a wave of his hand. "And make sure you put your lights on this time."

When they were back in the car, the two policemen watched in brooding silence as the Daimler drove off.

McQueen even had the audacity to wind down his window and wave farewell.

"Cheeky fucker," Paxman said as the car's taillights receded.

"There was something very wrong about him," Alder observed.

"I agree," Paxman said, stroking his chin thoughtfully. He started the car, then performed a lazy U-turn. "Tell you what, before we grab that coffee, let's just take a quick peek at the clearing he came out of. I want to see if there are any other cars in there, or anything that might give us a clue as to what the little shit was really up to."

## 26

Bad, bad dog!

The sound of the street door slamming woke Gabe from his fitful slumber. Sitting bolt upright, he was aware of a vein throbbing in his temple, and he could feel his breath coming in short sharp gasps. He had been in the middle of a vivid nightmare about Adam, and the terrible, cloying anxiety he had experienced during the dream had followed him into wakefulness.

There were footsteps out in the hallway, then muffled voices.

"What's the matter with you, getting yourself tugged by the Old Bill?" That was Benny. His voice was tense, angry, argumentative. "The bastards rang me to confirm you were allowed to be using the Daimler."

"It was just a routine stop," McQueen said, surly and defensive. "They gave me a breath test and sent me on my way."

Through bleary eyes, Gabe glanced at the clock on his bedside table.

*04:30*

'They didn't find anything in the car?" Benny again, clearly worried.

"I wouldn't be here if they had, would I?" McQueen retorted, stroppily.

A pause, then a hefty sigh. "I suppose not," Benny allowed. "Did you bury the body properly, like I told you?"

"You know I did." McQueen sounded drained, like he was running on empty. "I rang you straight afterwards, so why are you asking me again?"

"Because I have to be sure," Benny snapped, anger flaring again. There was another dramatic sigh, then the tension seemed to evaporate from the old man's voice and he became conciliatory. "You're a good boy, Joey. Come and have a drink with me. You've earned it."

Their voices faded as they adjourned to the living room.

Slipping out of bed, Gabe crept over to the door and opened it an inch, hoping to hear more of their conversation.

"What about Gabe?" Benny asked, as he ushered McQueen into the living room.

"What about him?" McQueen replied, sounding confused.

"Can he be trusted?"

The door closed, blotting out McQueen's answer.

"Fuck!" Gabe cursed. They were talking about him, and he needed to know what they were saying; what they had planned for him. Biting his bottom lip nervously, he tip-toed along the hall and pressed an ear to the lounge door. If they caught him eavesdropping, he would be in for it, but he had to take that chance, in case they were plotting a similar fate for him as the one that had befallen Adam.

Their voices were muffled, but he could make out the gist of the conversation.

"Can we trust the boy?" Benny wanted to know.

"I don't see why not. He helped us clean up the mess, and that makes him an accessory to what happened. If he rats us out, he'll get done for murder, too."

A ball of ice formed in Gabe's stomach.

Was that true?

"Why not just give him a few quid to keep him sweet, and make sure he understands that he'll go down with the rest of us if he says anything?" McQueen suggested. "He might not approve of what happened, but he's not stupid; I'm telling you, that boy's a born survivor, and he won't do anything to drop himself in the shit."

"I suppose you're right," Benny conceded, but he didn't sound overly sold on the idea.

"Relax," McQueen soothed. "Eventually, we'll get him drunk or stoned, and then Mo can take some photos of him giving one of us a blow job. If he doesn't want us sending the snaps to his family, he'll have to start turning tricks for us, and then we'll own him."

Benny's laughter was a cruel staccato.

"We should at least give the lad a chance," McQueen said. "After all, what's the alternative?"

"The alternative," Benny growled, "is that we get rid of him now, and you get to make another trip to the forest."

"Leave it out," McQueen groaned. "Let me at least try and reason with him first."

"Yeah, alright," Benny said, begrudgingly. "But I'll expect you to keep a close eye on him. I mean it Joey, if he fucks up, I'll hold you responsible."

"I'll make sure he doesn't," McQueen promised, his words more a yawn than a sentence.

"You do that. The sooner that chicken's broken in, and working the meat rack for us, the better."

---

As soon as Kerry Bembridge opened the tailgate of her little hatchback, the Red Setter bounded out, tongue lolling, tail wagging with excitement. His chestnut-coloured fur billowed in the early morning wind as he ran circles around her, barking happily.

"Yes, Barney, I'm excited about our walkies, too," Kerry laughed, gesturing for the energetic mutt to go on ahead of her.

Barney sprinted a few yards into the forest, then skidded to a halt. He did a long wee, then set about sniffing out the right spot to poo in. He was normally very particular about where he did his business, but on this occasion, he was squatting before Kerry had even reached the footpath.

The unpleasant noises coming from his backside warned her that poor old Barney was suffering from yet another upset stomach. That was hardly surprising, though; the daft mutt was forever eating the dead things he found rotting in the woods.

When he'd finished, Kerry took a quick look at the runny mess he'd left behind and grimaced. Barney had found a decaying rabbit's corpse during yesterday afternoon's walk, and the little sod had eaten half of it before she could prise the rest of the carcass from his mouth.

"That'll teach you for eating the little bunny," she scolded, fanning her nose.

Barney gave her a playful bark in return, then disappeared into the dense foliage bordering the footpath. Leaving him to run free, Kerry strolled briskly along the winding path, enjoying the birdsong and the solitude of her early morning walk. Every now and then, Barney reappeared, bursting through the bushes a few yards ahead of her. He stayed long enough to have a quick sniff or another wee, then vanished from sight again.

Kerry inhaled deeply. It had rained heavily overnight, producing the earthy fragrance that she so loved. Barney was in his element too; making the most of all the wonderful scents and smells the rainfall had triggered.

Sticking to the footpath, Kerry listened to her faithful companion as he erratically weaved his way through the surrounding woodland, following his nose wherever it led him.

After a while, Kerry reached a natural dip between two small hillocks. She was about to turn around and head back to the car when Barney caught a new scent. Raising his head high in the air, he stiffened. Then, quivering with excitement, he let out a loud bark and scampered off towards the furthest hillock.

"Barney! Barney, come back," she yelled.

It was too late. Barney had disappeared, and he would be too focused on the scent to listen to her, so there was no point in shouting at him. With a sigh of resignation, Kerry set off after him, pulling his leash from her pocket, ready to clip it on when she finally caught up.

After clearing the second hillock, Barney ran up to a thicket and began barking with increasing gusto as he tried to find a way through.

"That's quite enough, Barney," Kerry admonished, wondering what had gotten into him. Even by his standards, this was a bit much. "Come here at once."

Barney turned to look at her, weighing up whether to obey the command or make a run for it. Then, with a high-pitched bark of frustration, he dropped to his stomach and began scrabbling through a gap beneath the bushes and brambles.

"You little bugger," Kerry growled, lunging forward to grab his hind legs before they completely disappeared. But Barney was too quick for her, and she ended up lying face down in the soggy dirt, clutching at empty air.

Kerry swore profusely. At this rate, she was going to be late for work. She peered under the bushes. On the other side, Barney was churning dirt up with his paws and sending it flying in all directions.

"Barney, you naughty boy! Stop that at once, and come back here!" she shouted, dreading to think what he had found. No doubt it would be another badly decayed animal.

Kerry began circling the thicket, trying to find a way in before the stupid mutt gorged himself silly on its rotting corpse. "Bad dog!" she yelled. "Bad, bad dog!"

She finally stumbled across a narrow section of thicket that looked as though it had recently been beaten down. As she burst into the clearing, Barney looked up from his find, tongue lolling, and he seemed mightily pleased with himself.

---

It was getting on for ten by the time that Gabe wandered into the kitchen to grab some breakfast. McQueen was standing with his back to him, making coffee. He was wearing the same clothes he had worn the previous day. There were huge splodges of dried mud all over them, and they were badly creased, as if he had slept in them.

"Morning," Gabe said, trying to act normally.

McQueen glanced over his shoulder, acknowledging him with a sullen nod. His face was pale and drawn, like a junkie going through withdrawal.

"Want a brew?" McQueen asked, his voice flat.

Gabe shook his head. "No thanks." After what had happened the previous night, he would never again feel safe accepting anything that McQueen offered him, in case it was laced with a sedative.

"Suit yourself," McQueen mumbled. Picking up his coffee, he brushed past Gabe on his way out.

Gabe noticed the bandage wrapped around McQueen's left hand and wrist. It hadn't been there the previous evening. A faint circle of little red spots showed through.

After preparing himself some cereal and a glass of orange juice, Gabe wandered into the living room.

Joey didn't bother looking up from the TV screen, which was showing the latest news update on the search for the two missing children.

"Where's Benny?" Gabe asked, sitting down opposite him.

"He left ages ago."

Gabe spooned some cornflakes into his mouth. He had lain awake for hours trying to decide how best to behave around McQueen after the worrying conversation he had overheard him having with Benny. He no longer felt safe around them and planned to break away as soon as he could.

When Gabe finished his cereal, he put the bowl down on the coffee table. Clearing his throat, he turned to McQueen. "Joey, I know what happened to Adam last night was an accident," he began, hoping the lie sounded genuine, "but, I took a big risk by helping you to clear up afterwards."

"And we're grateful," McQueen said.

"Yeah, but gratitude won't get me anywhere if the police find out."

McQueen was staring at him over the rim of his mug. His eyes were no longer far away; they had narrowed to slits and were full of malicious intent. "Why would they find out, unless you're planning to tell them?" His voice was low and dangerous.

"Don't be daft, I would *never* do that," Gabe said, quickly. "I came to London to escape from the police back home. I'm looking at a long stretch inside if they catch me."

McQueen sneered. "What for, a bit of shoplifting?"

"I wish," Gabe told him, morosely. "I'm wanted for an aggravated burglary. Some people I was hanging out with broke into a rich couple's house. They knocked the old man and his wife about, then tied them up while they ransacked the place. I was their lookout."

"What's the point you're trying to make?" McQueen demanded.

Gabe's heart was racing. "Just that, well… I figure I deserve a reward for helping you to clear up the mess afterwards." If he could wheedle some money out of McQueen, he might be able to pay for a cheap hostel when he got away from them.

A slow, calculating smile spread across McQueen's thin face. The idea that Gabe was motivated by money was something he could easily relate to. "The death was an accident," he insisted. "The only reason we didn't call the police is that we don't want them poking their noses into our business."

"Which is what, exactly?" Gabe asked, although he already had a pretty good idea.

McQueen was silent for a few seconds, and Gabe could tell he was weighing up how much to reveal.

"We're in the adult entertainment business, and we specialise in the procurement of individuals who provide certain… personal services." He was studying Gabe for his reaction.

"You mean you supply rent boys. Like Adam, and the other three lads who were here last night?" Gabe kept his tone light-hearted, so that McQueen wouldn't think he was being judgemental.

McQueen nodded, still studying him carefully. "That's right. Have you got a problem with that?"

Gabe had a massive problem with it, not least because he had come to understand that some of the rent boys – innocent and vulnerable young boys like Adam – were being forced to become male prostitutes against their will.

"No problem at all," he said, breezily, trying his hardest to sound as callous and uncaring as the man he was speaking to. "As long as you understand that I'm not going to do *that* for you. I want to be on the firm, and I don't mind what else you want me to do, but I'm not renting my arse out."

McQueen's face was completely devoid of emotion as he studied Gabe. There was no anger, no amusement; no way of telling what he was thinking.

They continued to hold eye contact, and it became a battle of wills as to who would blink first.

"We'll see," McQueen eventually said, looking away.

---

Tyler was struggling to make any sense of the lengthy call data report he was muddling his way through, so the sudden ringing of his mobile came as a welcome distraction. The caller ID revealed that the incoming call was from DCI Andy Quinlan. With a huff, he discarded the tedious report, scooped up the handset, and pressed the green button.

"Unless it's really important, Andy, I'm a bit squeezed for time, so can I call you—"

Quinlan cut him off. "*Jack, listen. At eight o'clock this morning, a dog walker stumbled across a shallow grave in Epping Forest. It contained the body of a young boy. The HAT car's making its way there as we speak, and I'm about to leave KZ to join them.*" KZ was the phonetic code for Hertford House, where the east contingent for the Homicide Command was based. "*It occurred to me that, given what your team is dealing with, you might want to accompany me to the scene.*"

Tyler couldn't speak. He tried to, but his breath just caught in his throat. He closed his eyes, suddenly overcome by grief.

"*Jack…?*"

Tyler dry washed his face, took a deep breath and told himself to get a grip. He had only managed a couple of hours sleep, so he was tired and emotional.

"Yes, sorry Andy. I'll need to make a few calls first, but if you give me the RVP details, I'll meet you there as soon as I can." Tyler was surprised by how steady his voice sounded. His hand, by contrast, was shaking as he reached for a pen. He had hoped never to receive this particular call, but deep down he had always known it was inevitable.

As Quinlan described the little clearing between the Robin Hood and Wake Arms roundabouts in which the RVP had been set up, Tyler checked his ordinance survey map to see if it lay within the area the search team had already covered, knowing that the Met would have to answer some pretty uncomfortable questions if it was. To his relief, the body had been found a good half mile outside the parameters set by Susie Sergeant and Jim Breslow.

"*If the victim's one of your missing children,*" Quinlan was saying, "*I assume your team will take responsibility for processing the scene?*" He sounded apologetic, as if he was embarrassed to be asking the question.

Tyler felt strangely detached, as if he was having an out of body experience and was observing the conversation from above. "Yes, of course," he heard himself reply. "George Copeland's my lead exhibits officer for this one. I'll get him to meet us there. Have you requested a CSM yet, or do you want me to do it?"

"*Sam Calvin's the duty Crime Scene Manager. I've briefed him, and he's already en route.*"

After speaking to Quinlan, Tyler made four calls.

The first was to George Copeland.

The second was to DCS Holland.

The third call was to Dillon, who was overseeing the street search for Berlingo vans with GB stickers on their rear doors, which had recommenced earlier that morning.

Finally, he made the call he had deliberately put off until last.

"Kelly, are you free to speak?"

"*What's wrong?*" she asked, instantly picking up on the strained tone of his voice.

"It's bad news. A young boy's body has been found in Epping Forest this morning. I need you and Debbie to get over to Peter and Gavin's parents straight away, to apprise them of this before the media get wind of it, and it's plastered all over the news."

## 27

### God's crying

Leaning against the bus stop in Elsdale Street, Phillip Diggle watched the old man emerge from his grubby, ground floor flat, double lock the security grill, then give it a little tug to make sure it held firm. He looked fragile, and moved with a jolty stiffness that made Diggle wonder if he suffered from arthritis.

Maurice Hinkleman looked nothing like the terrifying demon that Diggle remembered so vividly from his childhood. Perhaps that was because his attacker was now an old man?

Hinkleman wore a dark woollen cap, a scruffy overcoat and scuffed shoes. He had the unkempt appearance of a man who no longer bothered to take good care of himself, but perhaps he never had.

Hinkleman passed within twenty feet of Diggle, which was close enough for him to get a good look at the ugly skin tag on the elderly paedophile's lower left eyelid. As soon as he saw it, he knew that he was looking at the man who had tried to kill him all those years ago.

A fire ignited in the pit of Diggle's stomach, fuelled by the hatred he felt for this loathsome creature. It spread outwards at alarming speed, consuming all the oxygen in his lungs. It suddenly became difficult to breathe, and as Diggle gasped for air, his limbs began to tremble violently.

The flashback struck with the force of a thunderbolt, transporting him back through time, into a tent in the Norfolk countryside that his nine year old self was sharing with his twin brother, and a summer heatwave that people still reminisced about twenty-six years later.

Diggle's knees buckled, and he sagged against the bus stop. He wrapped an arm around it as he slid down to the floor. A tiny, pathetic whimper escaped his lips as the strobing images flashed though his mind...

The tent was being ripped open; the two sinister masked men were clambering through the gap; he was sitting up, trying to scream; Hinkleman jumping astride him and strangling him. There were disjointed impressions of the frenetic activity going on all around him as poor Robbie was dragged from his bed. Then there was nothing but blackness as he passed out.

---

When Remus glanced out of the bedroom window and spotted the two uniformed police officers inspecting his van in Hampton Road, a side street almost directly opposite the safe house, he nearly wet himself with fear. One was peering through the driver's window, the other was standing at the rear, talking into her radio.

*Shit!*

Irrationally, because he knew they couldn't see him through the net curtains, he jumped back from the window and pressed his back into the wall. A moment later, realising just how silly he was being, he took another cautious peek. The cop who had been looking through the window was now trying the doors.

"Shit!"

Their interest in the van could only mean one thing; the police now knew that it had been involved in the abduction. Or, to be more precise, they knew that a Berlingo had been used.

But how was this possible…?

There hadn't been any CCTV at the fairground; of that, he was sure. In fact, now that he thought about it, he hadn't seen any cameras until he'd reached Buckhurst Hill.

The only possible explanation was that one of the witnesses who had come forward had seen the van drive off. He silently cursed them, wondering why these interfering people couldn't just mind their own business.

Outside, the two officers had returned to their patrol car. Closing the doors behind them, they drove off.

Closing his eyes, Remus let out a taut sigh, thanking his lucky stars that he'd had the presence of mind to switch the van's plates before and after the abduction.

Benny rented a lock up further along Grove Green Road, which he used to store the Daimler in whenever he went away, but he wouldn't have need of it again until after Christmas, when he made his annual two-month pilgrimage to Bangkok in search of sun, sea and debauchery. There was a spare key for it in the kitchen drawer. Remus decided to wait a few minutes, in case the police came back, then relocate the van to the garage.

It would be safer there.

---

Diggle's eyes opened with a jolt. He was lying flat on his back, having passed out. He looked around in confusion, feeling dazed and disorientated. For a moment, he couldn't understand why he was lying in a cold, drab street in Hackney, watching the ominous storm clouds rolling through the skies above him, and not in a camp site in the picturesque countryside during the height of summer.

Then Diggle's mind rebooted, and he regained the ability to think straight. He dragged himself onto his knees, moving with as much jolty stiffness as the old man he had been watching. Standing up, he leaned against the lamp post and sucked in cold, crisp air.

He had absolutely no idea how long he had been out; it could have been seconds or minutes. Blinking sweat from his eyes, Diggle scanned the street in search of Hinkleman.

He spotted the old man a couple of hundred yards ahead, head bowed against the wind. That told him he had only been unconscious for a few seconds at most. He shook his muddled head to clear it, but his mind was still reeling from the dark memories and the painful emotions the flashback had stirred up.

Hinkleman was on his way to work. When he reached Mare Street, he would turn right and walk the relatively short distance to his studio in The Narrow Way.

Pushing himself away from the lamp post, Diggle set off on wobbly legs, hoping to get ahead of him.

---

The wind rocked the car as Debbie Brown peered through its rain-streaked windscreen. She wished she were back home, curled up on the sofa with one of her cats. "It was pissing down like this when we buried my mum," she said in a subdued voice. "I was only eight, and I'll never forget the vicar saying it was because God was crying. Well, if you ask me, it feels like God's crying again today, over that poor dead boy." As she spoke, she wiped away a tear of her own.

They were parked outside Ciaron and Alison Musgrove's house, composing themselves for the ordeal to come. They had already broken the terrible news to Tom and Margo Grant, and even for a hardened FLO like Debbie, who was used to delivering death messages and dealing with the pain and devastation that came with them, it had proved to be a very traumatic experience.

Margo had initially refused to accept the news. Retreating into herself, she had fervently insisted that she would have known if Gavin were dead, and that the body therefore had to be Peter's. Tom had tried so hard to put on a brave face for his wife's sake, but in the end, he had broken down and she had been the one who ended up comforting him.

Debbie had explained that it was too early to be able to say with any confidence whose body it was. She had promised to update them as soon as she learned more, but cautioned DNA testing might be required to confirm the child's identity, in which case it would take a couple of days for the results to come back.

Dabbing her eyes with a tissue, Debbie glanced sideways at Kelly to see if she was ready for round two. "Are you okay, hon? You've been a bit subdued since we left Margo and Tom's."

Kelly was staring straight ahead, watching the rivulets of rain run down the windscreen. "Not sure, to be honest," she admitted. "These children have found a way through my defences."

Debbie flashed her a sympathetic smile. One of the first thing they were taught on the Family Liaison Officer's course was the importance of never becoming emotionally involved; it was too draining, and it affected your impartiality. "Yeah, I know what you mean."

"There's something else," Kelly confessed, hesitantly. "Please don't say anything, as we don't want it becoming public knowledge yet, but I'm pregnant."

Debbie's face brightened, and a smile of wonderment spread across her face. "That's amazing news," she said, reaching over to squeeze her partner's hand. "You and Jack must be over the moon, and don't worry; I won't say a word to anybody."

Kelly smiled back, but Debbie could tell she felt conflicted.

Kelly's guilty smile all but confirmed this. "I'm so happy to be expecting, but I feel terrible for being so excited when Peter and Gavin's parents are going through sheer hell."

"Oh, Kelly," Debbie said, giving her hand another squeeze, harder this time. "That's a very noble sentiment, but you can't allow yourself to think like that. It's not your fault that these children have been abducted."

"I know," Kelly said, with a rueful smile, "but I can't help it. And it's not just that. Seeing how quickly their lives have been turned upside down, it makes me wonder how I'm going to keep my own baby safe. I mean, you've seen how protective Alison is over Peter, but that didn't stop some evil bastard from snatching him."

Debbie nodded her understanding. "I know what you mean, but

you can't live your life in fear, because that's unhealthy. You could drop dead of a brain aneurism at any moment, or get knocked down crossing the road; any of us could. It's beyond our control, and if you spend too long worrying about all the bad things that could happen, you'll end up going mad. All we can do is live our lives to the best of our ability. The rest, I'm afraid, is down to fate."

Alighting the car, they hurried along the garden path, their coats held above their heads to keep the worst of the rain at bay. Once they were under the canopy, Debbie took a deep breath and rang the doorbell. "Time to put your game face back on," she said, mustering a smile.

---

Kelly noticed that a trestle table had been erected beneath the heavily curtained windows of the Musgrove's lounge since her last visit. A white linen cloth had been draped over it, and upon this rested a half dozen framed photographs of Peter. Alison had arranged a circle of scented candles around them. It was almost as if she had had a premonition that bad news was coming and had hastily erected a shrine. The thought made Kelly shudder.

*Pie Jesu* was coming from a speaker beneath the trestle table, but Ciaron crossed to the stereo system and turned the music off as soon as they entered the room.

There were flowers everywhere, sent in by well-wishers from all over the country.

"There's been an important development," Debbie began once they were all seated. She and Kelly were on one sofa, while Alison and Ciaron sat facing them on the other.

Alison's face immediately closed down, becoming totally unreadable. Beside her, Ciaron's jaw muscles rippled with tension, and he silently reached out to take her hand in his. They were instinctively closing ranks, and it suddenly felt very much like an us and them situation, Kelly reflected, sadly.

Debbie took a deep breath and looked from one to the other. "I'm really sorry to have to tell you this, but the body of a young boy has been found in a shallow grave in Epping Forest this morning."

"No!" Alison whispered, sounding like a wounded animal. She began shaking her head, slowly at first, but then with increasing mania. "NO! NOO! NOOO!"

Ciaron made to wrap an arm around her shoulders, but she shrugged it off. Standing up, she hurriedly crossed to the table-come-shrine. Picking up a ten by eight portrait of Peter's smiling face, Alison gazed at it for a long moment, then clutched it tightly to her chest. "This can't be happening," she sobbed, swaying like she was going to fall.

Kelly rushed over to her, but Alison held out a hand to stay her. "Don't touch me!" she snapped.

Kelly hesitated, then stepped away.

Alison glowered at her for a moment, then leaned back against the wall and let out a little simper. Her knees suddenly buckled, and she slid down until she was resting on her haunches. Cradling her head in her hands, she rocked backwards and forwards. "Is it... is it Peter?" she asked, her voice at breaking point.

Kelly knelt down beside her. "We don't know," she said, speaking softly. "The body was found by a dog walker, who dialled 999. We'll know more in a few hours."

"How come a dog walker found the body, and not one of the search parties?" Ciaron asked, sounding more bemused than angry. "Don't tell me we missed it?"

Kelly shook her head. "The body was found a good half mile beyond the current search radius."

Ciaron dry washed his face. When he looked up, he seemed exhausted. "Tom and I have spent the past couple of days searching for the boys," he told her, mustering a sad smile. "We would have been back out there at first light today, but the girls insisted we accompany them to the church service being held in Chingford at midday, to pray for the boys' safe return." He paused, then barked out a cynical laugh. "Looks like it's a bit late for that now, doesn't it?"

Tyler felt physically sick. He wanted to cry. He had never experienced a moment like this. Staring down at the partially revealed naked body lying face down in the shallow grave, he knew with absolute certainty that the news being delivered by the FLO's would devastate Peter and Gavin's families.

With its owner unable to reach it, the dog had done a pretty good job of digging the body up, unearthing the top of the head, an entire arm, and the bottom half of one leg.

The faces of both missing children were burned into Tyler's memory, but as he could only see the back of the dead boy's head, that was of no help whatsoever.

He mentally ran through their physical descriptions. Peter had blonde hair and was small for his age, appearing much younger than his nine years. Gavin, on the other hand, was a lot bigger and he looked much older. Plus, his hair was much darker. Tyler could clearly see the corpse had dark hair, which suggested that he was looking at Gavin's body.

Leaving Jim Breslow in charge of the search party, Susie had driven over to join him at the crime scene. She now stood silently by his side, as moved by the terrible sight as he was.

George Copeland and Sam Calvin, dressed in full barrier clothing, were supervising the erection of a tent over the grave.

Tyler glanced up at the depressingly dark sky; if anything, the rain was falling harder now than when he arrived, ten minutes earlier. He could feel the relentless pitter patter of each drop through the protective oversuit he wore.

"We need to get that thing up before the running water irreparably damages the scene," Andy Quinlan said, looking on grimly as two crime scene technicians fought against the elements to bang tent pegs into the ground.

"Why couldn't this rain have held off until later?" Tyler asked. The question was rhetorical, of course. Like Quinlan, he was worried that the heavy downfall would wash away the muddy footprints around the grave, and the disturbances in the mud that suggested a struggle, but could just as easily have been caused by the killer dragging his victim across the ground towards the grave.

Behind them, an ungainly blue Tyvek suited figure came trudging along the dip in the land between two hillocks. Sliding sideways in the mud, he carried a heavy metal case in one hand and a large tripod in the other.

"Morning, Mr Tyler, Mr Quinlan," the SO3 photographer called, breathlessly. He stopped when he caught sight of Susie, and his entire face lit up. "Hello, Susie! I wasn't expecting to see you here," he enthused. "Or should I say ma'am, now that you've reached the dizzying heights of DI?"

"Morning, Ned," Susie replied, her tone subdued. "Susie's still fine."

"Make sure you only walk on the metal plates that I've placed along the common approach route, and whatever you do, don't step on the earth around the grave," Sam Calvin shouted out.

"Will do," Ned Saunders replied, jauntily. He was puffing by the time he reached the others at the top of the hillock. "Well, I must say, you could have picked a nicer day to invite me out to the woods," he observed, winking at Susie as he set up his tripod. "How are we supposed to have a picnic in this weather?"

Beneath his Victoria mask, Tyler gritted his teeth. He wanted to snap at Saunders, to tell him to behave with some decorum, but that would be unfair. The photographer knew nothing about the victim, or the job. All he had been told was that he was to attend Epping Forest to take photographs of a dead body. That was something he did on a daily basis, and as anyone who regularly dealt with death would tell you, the only way to remain sane was to inject a little gallows humour into the situation every now and then.

With the tent now in place, Calvin wandered over to join them.

Tyler had always found Calvin a bit one dimensional. He didn't make jokes; he didn't discuss football; he didn't watch TV. Conversation with him tended to be boring, and he suspected that, if the man had any hobbies at all, they would probably involve train spotting or stamp collecting, or something equally mundane. However, it had to be said that, whatever Calvin lacked in personality, he more than made up for in his ability to do the job, and he was undoubtedly one of the best CSMs in the business. With the possible exception of Juliet Kennedy, who was currently sunning herself in Mexico, Tyler couldn't think of anyone he would rather see running this particular crime scene for him.

"What have we got?" Tyler asked, getting straight down to business.

"It's certainly an interesting one," Calvin said, pulling his face mask off. "The body is that of a naked white male, and from the size of the two visible limbs, I'd speculate that he's probably aged between nine and twelve. The rigor mortice and lividity markings suggest that he's been dead for less than twenty-four hours, and if he wasn't killed right here, I'd bet a week's wages that he hasn't been moved very far from where he was. There are no visible wounds, so I can't give you an obvious cause of death at this stage. I estimate the grave to be about three feet deep, which is way too shallow to protect it from the attentions of wild animals or overly overexuberant dogs. I'd say the grave was only dug last night."

Tyler arched an eyebrow. "What makes you think that?"

"During the recent cold spell, the ground would have become rock hard. If the grave had been dug during that period, none of the earth around it would have been disturbed."

"That makes sense," Tyler accepted.

"I'm so glad you think so," Calvin observed, dryly. "Anyway, for the first time in ages, we had heavy rainfall last night, and as the soil around here is clay based, it gets very gooey very quickly. We can thank the inclement weather for the footprints the killer left us." He pointed out the nearest ones as he spoke. "They look like trainer prints to me, probably a size nine or ten. Once they've been photographed, we'll take plaster casts."

"What about the other disturbances," Tyler asked. "Do they indicate a struggle, or were they caused by the killer dragging the body over to the grave?"

Calvin stroked his chin thoughtfully. "Almost certainly the latter," he said after a moment's reflection.

Copeland strode over, looking thoughtful. "Might be something;

might be nothing," he said with a self-deprecating smile. "But I've just noticed a couple of dark smudges on the leaves the killer trod down to get into the clearing. They look like dried blood to me." A shrug. "Could be animal blood, of course, but, under the circumstances, it might be worth getting them photographed and swabbed."

"Definitely," Calvin said.

Tyler patted the Yorkshireman's shoulder. "Good spot, George."

"Blood spot, you mean," Copeland grinned.

## 28

Surprise!

Gabe had resigned himself to having McQueen shadow him everywhere until Benny decided he could be trusted, so he couldn't believe his good luck when McQueen ordered him to hotfoot it over to Maurice Hinkleman's studio in The Narrow Way and collect an important envelope for Benny.

Before setting off, Gabe liberated one of the knives from the wooden rack on the kitchen worktop. If the old perv got fresh with him, Gabe would threaten to cut his shrivelled todger off. That would certainly cool his ardour.

Gabe was on his way out of the door when McQueen called for him to hang on a moment. "Get a bus if you can," he instructed, handing over some loose change. "It'll be quicker than walking."

Gabe frowned. "What's the rush?"

"It's a quarter to twelve, and we've got to get that envelope over to Benny's shop before three, which is when the client's due to collect it."

Turning left out of the estate, Gabe set off towards the main road, keeping his head bowed against the cold and the rain. During his previous visit to the studio, Hinkleman had mentioned that he kept a cash box in the bottom drawer of his desk. Gabe had no idea how much money it contained, but he planned to find out.

He walked past a graffiti covered phone box with all its windows broken. On impulse, he stopped, turned around and went inside. It stank of piss, but he did his best to ignore this. Lifting the receiver, he dialled a number from memory, feeling ridiculously nervous. He had no idea what he would say when she–

"*Hello?*"

Her voice was as familiar to him as his own, and despite all his uncertainty, Gabe smiled when he heard it. "Hello, mum."

A startled gasp, then, "*Gabriel? Is that really you?*"

She sounded shocked, as though she hadn't expected to hear from him again.

Gabe's eyes prickled with tears. The guilt he had suppressed since running away suddenly caught up with him, and he found himself struggling to breathe, let alone talk.

"*Gabriel...?*"

"Yes, mum. It's me." He almost choked on the words.

"*Where are you? Are you okay? I've been so worried.*"

There was a faint trace of anger in her voice, mingled with relief, but he could hardly begrudge her that. "I'm fine, mum," he said, feeling anything but. "I can't tell you where I am, not with the police looking for me."

There was a confused pause. "*But they're not looking for you anymore. Haven't you heard?*"

"You must be mistaken, mum," he said, wishing she wasn't. "They're after me for that break in at the Cooper place."

His mother tutted angrily. "*I assure you, I'm not mistaken, dear,*" she declared, primly. "*The three rogues who broke in told the police that you had nothing to do with what happened, and that you didn't meet up with them until afterwards. If you had bothered to keep in touch, you would have known that.*"

Gabe was stunned. Could this be true? Was he free to return home?

"Mum, who told you this?"

"*The detective heading the case paid us a visit two weeks ago. She would have told you in person, if you had been here, but you had run away by then.*"

"What exactly did she say?" Gabe asked, convinced that his mother must have misunderstood.

"*That you've been eliminated from their enquiries and are no longer a suspect. She gave us a form to that effect, so I know it's official.*"

Gabe closed his eyes as a flood of relief washed over him. He was no longer wanted by the police. His friends had done the decent thing and covered for him, even though he was every bit as guilty as they were. He wanted to laugh; he wanted to cry; but most of all, he wanted to go home.

---

By midday, Hinkleman's brutal hangover was finally starting to ease off. In his youth, he could handle the booze no problem, but these days it took him the best part of a week to recover from going on a bender, which is exactly what he had done after they had gotten rid of Adam's body.

He had an hour long shoot booked for one o'clock, so he decided to set the studio up in advance, then grab some lunch. After setting his precious Hasselblad up on its tripod, he took a step back and sighed contentedly. He loved spending time in his studio with the unsuspecting chickens.

"Don't be shy," he would tell them when they were posing in their skimpy swimming trunks, their nubile bodies glistening with baby oil. "We're all boys here, and you haven't got anything that I haven't." Sometimes he would even expose himself to prove it.

The buzzer sounded down below, signalling that someone was at the studio door.

That would be Gabe, calling for the A4 manila envelope and all the indecent images of young children it contained.

Hinkleman pressed the entry buzzer. Down below, he heard a dull metallic click as the street door's lock sprung open. "I'm up here, in the studio," he shouted down, then turned away without waiting for a reply.

---

Oliver Trowbrush had light blue eyes, sandy hair and big dimples. He was a spirited boy, with a mind of his own and an annoying tendency to answer back.

"I don't want to have my stupid photograph taken," he protested, attempting to prise his small hand from the vice-like grip his mum was holding it in.

"You'll do as you're bloody well told," she scolded, squeezing even tighter. Her name was Liv, which was short for Olivia, and as she never tired of telling Oliver, he had been named after her. "Mr Hinkleman said you were a natural when you tried out for him, and that you could make a decent living from modelling."

Oliver sneered at her, aware that any money he made would find its way into the pockets of David Poynton, the useless waste of space slob his mum was shacked up with. She might be besotted with the bone-idle git, but Oliver couldn't stand him. Neither could his grandmother; she was always badmouthing Poynton, telling anyone who would listen that he was a wrong 'un, a sponger and a layabout, and that he would never be able to hold down a decent job as long as he had a hole in his arse.

"But I don't want to be a model," he objected.

"Course you do," Liv insisted as she dragged him along The Narrow Way. "And you should be grateful that we went to all the trouble of finding a photographer of Mr Hinkleman's calibre to help you get started."

Which Oliver took to mean that his services were either completely free or considerably cheaper than anyone else's.

"I don't care," he said, disrespectfully. "I don't want to be a lousy model; I want to go over Vicky Park and play football with my mates."

"Ungrateful git," Liv hissed, cuffing the insolent ten year old around the back of his head.

On instinct, Oliver ducked, and the glancing blow felt more like a caress than a whack. Straightening up, he gave her a gloating smile, which was a big mistake on his part, because it infuriated her into taking a second swipe at him, and this one hit home with considerable force.

"I don't want any more lip out of you, young man," Liv warned as they arrived at the studio. "Mr Hinkleman's a very nice man, and he's doing us a big favour, so when I get back from having my hair done, I don't want to hear that you've misbehaved. Do you understand?"

Rubbing the back of his skull, Oliver nodded, sullenly. "Yes, mum," he said, through gritted teeth.

Liv jabbed at the buzzer. "It's Liv Trowbrush and Oliver," she said, pressing her mouth against the intercom.

The best part of a minute passed without a response, so Liv pressed the buzzer again, this time holding it in for much longer.

"Hello...? Mr Hinkleman, are you there?"

Beside her, Oliver was picking his nose to relieve the boredom.

Liv slapped his hand away, tutting at his uncouth behaviour. "Disgusting boy," she grumbled under her breath.

When another minute passed, Liv began to fret. They had been a little late for their appointment, thanks to David insisting that she cook him a fry up before leaving. Was it possible that the photographer had assumed they weren't coming and gone out?

"If he ain't there," Oliver said, daring to sound hopeful, "can I go and play footie?"

From inside the premises, they heard someone running down a flight of stairs. Oliver's face crumpled with disappointment, while Liv breathed a little sigh of relief.

She poked her son's chest with a forefinger. "Remember, you little cockroach, keep your big trap shut for once, and do exactly as you're told."

The door opened.

Liv straightened up, affecting a smile. To her astonishment, instead of the elderly photographer, she found herself standing face to face with a panic-stricken teenager who was clutching a metal cash box to his chest. His hands, Liv noticed, were stained red, and the handle of a knife was protruding from the front of his jeans.

For a moment, they both just stood there, transfixed.

Then Liv screamed.

The boy holding the cashbox flinched at the ear-splitting noise, then roughly barged her aside and ran towards Amhurst Road as if he were being pursued by the devil himself.

---

The crew of the Immediate Response Vehicle were startled by a piercing scream that killed their conversation dead. Sitting up straight, both officers tried to pinpoint the source of the noise.

"Where the hell did that come from?" PC Susan Vickers demanded, grabbing the steering wheel a little tighter.

There was a second scream, equally long, equally ear piercing.

"There!" PC Martin Smith said, pointing at a white youth who had just broken into a sprint a hundred and fifty yards ahead of them, and the screeching woman he was fleeing from.

"Could be a robbery," Vickers speculated. "Call it in."

Smith spoke excitedly into the radio. "All units, all units from Golf Delta Two-One, active message! We've got an IC1 male making off on foot from The Narrow Way towards Hackney Central station. He's mid to late teens, with lank brown hair, wearing a blue denim jacket."

"*What's he concerned in?*" the controller asked.

"We think it's a robbery."

"*Golf November Two nearby and assisting,*" the crew of the station van put up.

As Vickers accelerated after the fleeing suspect, the screaming woman ran straight out in front of the patrol car, waving her arms in the air to get their attention.

Vickers slammed on the brakes. "Stupid cow," she growled, angrily motioning the woman and her child aside.

"He's got a knife!" the panicked woman was yelling. She pointed towards an open doorway behind her. "He's just come out of Mr Hinkleman's studio, and his hands are covered in blood."

"What do we do?" Smith asked, deferring to Vickers, who was the senior constable by several years.

What Vickers *wanted* to do was go after the suspect, but if the blubbering woman had spoken the truth, there was a strong chance that the proprietor was badly injured inside his studio.

"Shit!" Vickers cursed, unclipping her seatbelt. "Circulate his description." Alighting her car, she dragged the informant onto the pavement. "Wait there," she said, forcefully. "My colleague will speak to you as soon as he comes off the radio."

"But where are you going?" the woman asked, staring at her gormlessly.

Vickers sighed, thinking that some people really were too stupid to live. "I'm going inside to see if anyone's hurt."

"Wait!" the woman shouted after her. "I've just remembered, the little shit was carrying a grey cash box. I think he must have robbed poor Mr Hinkleman."

Leaving Smith to attend to the witness, Vickers pushed open the door and looked up the stairs. "Hello!" she called out. "It's the police. Is anyone in?"

No answer.

Unsheathing her extendable metal baton, Vickers racked it out to its full length before ascending the narrow stairway. For all she knew, there might be more suspects inside.

She paused at the top, looking around to get her bearings.

"Hello!" she shouted again.

Vickers spotted an office off to her right, and as that was the most likely place for a cashbox to have been stolen from, she decided to start there. Crossing the short hallway, she paused in the open doorway, looking in.

The curtains had been drawn, making the room dark. It stank of stale cigarette smoke. An upholstered leather chair had been wheeled out from behind the large desk and repositioned in the centre of the room to showcase the elderly man sitting in it, staring sightlessly back at her.

This, presumably, was Mr Hinkleman.

In the dim light filtering in from the corridor, she could see Hinkleman's scrawny wrists had been gaffer taped to the arms of the chair, and his trousers and underpants had been pulled down around his ankles. His skinny legs were akimbo, and his lap was a horrible mess of blood and gore. His chest was also stained scarlet, and there was a livid gash across his neck.

The walls were peppered with the photographs of smiling boys, and it seemed to Vickers that, like her, they were all looking directly at the slain photographer's mutilated nether regions.

Her hand groped the wall to the left of the door, eventually finding the light switch. She flicked it up, bathing the room in a weak yellow glow.

"Jesus!" she breathed, unable to take her eyes off the macabre sight. She took a step closer, peering at Hinkleman's open mouth. There was something wedged inside it, a gag perhaps?

Vickers took another step nearer and leaned in, frowning. That was when she realised the gag wasn't a gag at all; it was the victim's severed penis and testicles.

---

The station van hurtled along Amhurst Road towards The Narrow Way. PC Jim Carraway and his partner, PC Jason Nordstrom, had only been in Dalston Lane when the call came out, and it had taken less than a minute for them to get there. The blue lights were on, but Carraway had abstained from using the siren, for fear of alerting the fleeing suspect.

"Come on, come on," he growled in anticipation. "Show yourself."

As if in answer to his wish, a skinny white male came bounding around the corner, clutching a gunmetal grey box to his chest. His hands were covered in blood, and there were ugly red smears of the stuff across the front of his denim jacket.

Carraway let out a triumphant whoop. "Gotcha!"

On seeing the van, the suspect skidded to a halt, spun on his heels and headed straight back the way he had just come.

Carraway accelerated up to The Narrow Way, only to find his onward progress thwarted by a double decker bus that was coming the other way. With a savage curse, he slammed on the brakes, bringing the van to a juddering halt.

"Don't just sit there," he shouted at his much younger operator. "Get after him!"

To his credit, Nordstrom was out and running before his driver had finished yelling.

After waiting an age for the bus to pull away, Carraway drove into The Narrow Way, but by then, there was no sign of Nordstrom or the fleeing suspect.

A crackle of static, and then Nordstrom's excited voice burst from the speaker. *"Suspect's gone right, right, right, into Bohemia Place..."*

Wasn't that the turning that Carraway had just driven past? "Why couldn't you have told me that five seconds earlier, you great dipstick?" he demanded of Nordstrom.

By the time that Carraway reversed back to Bohemia Place, a busy service road that paralleled the railway arches beneath Hackney Central mainline station, Nordstrom was a spec in the distance.

Uttering a string of profanities, Carraway performed a U turn, intending to circle the block and get ahead of the chase.

---

Knowing that the entire relief would be listening to the foot chase, Nordstrom focused on giving a clear commentary over the radio. He was relatively new to the station, and he wanted to make a good impression, not come across as someone who flapped under pressure.

Up ahead, the suspect suddenly launched an object sideways into the air. It was long and slender; a knife, perhaps?

"The suspect just lobbed something..." Nordstrom transmitted, looking over his shoulder to see where it had landed. "It went into one of the two big metal bins outside a green fronted garage that services taxis…"

"*Unit chasing from Golf Delta Two-One, be advised that the suspect has just decamped from the scene of a murder and should be approached with caution.*" The voice belonged to Susan Vickers, and she sounded shaken, which was most unlike her.

This was no longer a simple robbery, and Nordstrom made a conscious effort to dig deep and pick up his pace. No way was he going to suffer the ignominy of allowing a murderer to escape.

Ten yards ahead of him, the suspect was almost at the tunnel that linked Bohemia Place to Nursery Lane on the other side.

Nordstrom's lungs were on fire, and despite his earlier resolve to catch the suspect, he could feel himself fading rapidly.

A very strange thing happened as his quarry entered the tunnel. He suddenly stopped running and dropped to his knees, completely exhausted.

The stolen cashbox fell from his grasp and skidded along the floor.

Behind him, Nordstrom slowed to a walk, smiling at the wondrous sight of Carraway and two other officers waiting for them at the other end of the tunnel.

The station van and an Immediate Response Vehicle were parked sideways across the road, their blue lights strobing brightly as they bounced off the walls.

"Surprise!" Carraway shouted, giving Nordstrom a friendly wave.

Puffing like a steam train, Nordstrom removed his quick cuffs from their pouch. Placing a hand on the suspect's shoulder, he dragged the unresisting boy to his feet.

"You're… nicked… mate," he said, breathlessly.

# 29

He's already been sold

Staring out through the rain smeared windows of his sex shop into the bustling street beyond, Benny was indulging in a spot of people watching. The black privacy film meant that he could see out, but passers-by couldn't see in, so he could ogle them without fear of being noticed. Sometimes, when one of the nosy buggers was cupping their hands against the glass and trying to peer inside, Benny would stand directly in front of them and make obscene gestures.

He was about to go and make himself a fresh cup of coffee, when he spotted a local prostitute trying to waylay one of his customers. He smiled to himself, knowing she would get no joy from him. Sure enough, the man shoved her aside and entered the shop.

"I need to speak to you about the chicken who was up for sale," Lionel Eberhard said, having first checked to see that they were alone. "The one I expressed an interest in."

"You're too late. He's already been sold."

Tutting his annoyance, Eberhard brushed rain from the shoulders of his overcoat. "But I told you I wanted him, and that I would top any other offers you received."

Benny shrugged. "The deadline was midnight last night, and as I didn't hear from you, I assumed that you'd lost interest." He spread his arms, apologetically. "Sorry, Lionel, I've already informed the successful bidder that he's won the auction, and I can't go back on my word. It would be bad for business."

"Now look here, Benny," Eberhard protested. "We've known each other for a very long time, and I'm one of your best clients. Through no fault of my own, I was unavoidably detained last night, so I couldn't get back to you, but we had a provisional agreement, and I expect you to honour it."

Benny was unmoved by the outburst. "You know the rules. You should have rung me and asked for an extension." He idly wondered what could have been important enough to prevent Eberhard from submitting his bid in time.

Eberhard glared at him, shiftily. "I couldn't. I didn't have my phone with me."

Benny spread his arms again. "Not my problem."

Eberhard stamped his foot like a truculent child. "I *want* that boy." Another stamp. "I *must* have that boy." Yet another stamp. "I *will* have that boy." A puddle was forming at his feet from all the rain that was dripping from his waxed overcoat.

"And I told you," Benny said, starting to lose patience. "He's already been sold."

"I'll give you ten grand more than the other bidder offered," Eberhard persisted.

Benny hesitated before answering. He was a greedy man, and he was tempted by the offer, but he knew it would reflect badly on him, perhaps even damage his reputation. "I can't. I've already given my–"

"Twenty grand!" Eberhard interrupted.

Benny could feel his resolve weakening. Was there a way he could do this without alienating the other client? He licked his lips, greedily as he pondered this.

"Twenty-five grand!" Eberhard shouted.

Benny chewed his bottom lip.

Eberhard could certainly afford it. He was a National Lottery winner, not that anyone would ever guess that from the drab way that he dressed. The eccentric millionaire didn't even own a car, and he still lived in the grubby terraced house he had shared with his mother until her death, which ironically had occurred the week after he'd won the lottery. Benny doubted that Eberhard had spent a fraction of his winnings, and he was more than happy to relieve him of some of it.

"I suppose I could say that something happened to the chicken, and that he's no longer for sale," he said, softly, almost to himself.

Eberhard grinned broadly. "Yes, yes," he said, clapping his hands enthusiastically. "That would be splendid."

---

It was getting on for 1 p.m. when Quinlan drove through the gates to Hertford House, having just returned from the crime scene in Epping Forest. He was starving, and the canteen had lasagne on the menu today, which was one of his favourites. Pulling into one of the bays reserved for SIOs, he killed the engine and reached for his briefcase. Before he could open the door, his job mobile started to ring.

The caller was DI Carol Keating, his second in command, informing him that Hackney Borough had requested the HAT car's attendance. He listened carefully, making neat little notes in his daybook.

"*It sounds like an interesting one,*" Keating told him. "*An elderly photographer's been tied to a chair in his studio and tortured. Apparently, the suspect cut his dick and balls off and then crammed them into his mouth before stealing a cashbox containing a couple of grand.*"

Quinlan winced. "Interesting's not the word I would have used."

"*I'm about to head down there,*" Keating informed him. "*Do you want to meet me there?*"

Quinlan groaned. So much for grabbing some lunch. "I've literally just pulled into KZ," he said, wearily. "If you come down to the front entrance, we can drive over there together."

While he waited for her to arrive, he rung Dillon. "Tony, it's Andy Quinlan. We've just taken a job over in Hackney, which means I'll need you to release the extra staff I loaned you this morning to search for that Berlingo van."

"*That's okay,*" Dillon said, understandingly. "*We're all but finished now, anyway. Have we identified the boy that was dumped in the forest, yet?*"

"Not yet," Quinlan said, thinking back to the shallow grave and the lifeless youngster it contained. "Sam Calvin said it could take a few hours to clear all the dirt away, and we won't be able to get a proper look at his face till then."

"*What about Jack? Is he still at the scene?*" There was concern in the big man's voice, and not for the first time, Quinlan was struck by how protective Dillon was of Tyler.

"Yes, but Susie's there with him. I doubt they'll be down there too much longer, though. There's not an awful lot they can do there, other than get in the CSM's way."

Sam Calvin, they both knew, wouldn't appreciate that.

"*So, what's the job you've taken?*" Dillon asked.

Quinlan filled him in. "Luckily for us, someone saw the suspect fleeing the scene, all covered in blood, and flagged down a passing patrol car. The little shit was detained nearby, with the cashbox still in his possession."

"*Sounds like it's a fairly tight case,*" Dillon said, sounding envious.

The matronly figure of Carol Keating emerged from the main entrance, grimaced at the rain, then hurried over to the car, one hand pressed down against her head as though that might protect her from the deluge, the other clamped across her ample bosom. Like everyone else who knew her, Quinlan thought that Carol Keating bore an uncanny resemblance to the late Hattie Jacques of *Carry On* fame.

"Fingers crossed it is," Quinlan said.

The passenger door opened as he was putting his mobile away, and Carol slid in beside him, dripping all over the interior. "It's raining cats and dogs out there," she announced, in case he hadn't noticed.

---

When Gabe still hadn't returned to the flat by 1:30 p.m., McQueen started to fret. He dialled the number for Mo's studio, but there was no answer. He dialled again; got the same result. Cursing, he tried the old man's mobile, but after a few rings, it went to voicemail.

Something was wrong; he could feel it in his waters. Grabbing his coat, he stormed out of the flat.

He flagged down a passing taxi as soon as he reached the main road. "The Narrow Way, please, mate," he said, sliding into the back.

Traffic was light, so the journey only took six minutes. He asked the cabbie to drop him in Lower Clapton Road, at the top end of The Narrow Way. Jumping out, he paid his fare, giving the driver an extra quid as a tip, then cut through the grounds of St. John's church.

When he reached Hinkleman's photographic studio, he was appalled to see two police cars parked outside. There was blue and white cordon tape across the front of the premises and a bored looking constable was standing guard at the door.

McQueen popped into the newsagents a few doors along. "Alright, Mr Patel. Don't suppose you know what's going on at Mo's studio, do you? The place is crawling with Old Bill."

Patel shook his head with great sadness. "It's terrible," he lamented. "Mo was robbed a little while ago, and was killed in the process."

McQueen's eyes widened in shock. "What? You're kidding me!"

Patel flashed him a sympathetic look. "I know Mo was your friend," he said, leaning across the counter to give McQueen's hand a brief squeeze. "I'm so very sorry for your loss."

"Do the police know who did it?" McQueen asked, jerking his hand away.

"It was a scruffy white teenager in a denim jacket. A woman saw him fleeing the scene and alerted the police," Patel informed him. "I heard they arrested him nearby."

*A scruffy white teenager in a denim jacket...*

That had to be Gabe!

McQueen left the shop without uttering another word.

This was a disaster!

Benny would blame him for this, and rightly so. If McQueen had been chaperoning the boy like he'd been told to, Mo would still be alive.

Another thought struck him. If Mo was dead, the police would search the studio, and they would find the envelope containing all the child porn. He groaned, self-pityingly.

Could this fucking day get any worse?

---

The afternoon had passed in a maelstrom of activity.

The exhumation of the body from its shallow grave in Epping Forest had continued with pain staking slowness, carried out with all the planning and care of an archaeological dig. Sam Calvin had called in a forensic geologist, and under her supervision, each layer of soil was carefully sifted through to ensure that no physical or forensic evidence was missed.

Calvin had also arranged for a forensic ecologist to attend the scene and take samples from the soil and various plants and bushes; these would be compared to any trace evidence found on the suspect's clothing or shoes, or in his vehicle when he was finally arrested.

Less than a mile away, despite the inhospitable terrain and inclement weather, the PolSA search had continued under the watchful eye of Inspector Breslow. To their great credit, not one searcher had complained about the terrible conditions they were working in, or their soul-destroying lack of progress.

The news that a boy's body had been found in Epping Forest had sparked a media frenzy, as Tyler had known it would, and he had been forced to implement a patrolled exclusion zone around the crime scene to protect it from nosy reporters.

Most of the main TV channels had drafted in panels of so-called experts to analyse the situation. These invariably consisted of retired detectives who had been taken out of mothballs especially for the occasion, and a bunch of distinctly average academics. Tyler had branded them all glory chasers; people who would say anything the networks wanted in exchange for a few minutes of prime-time exposure.

At seven o'clock that evening, Tyler called a supervisor's meeting in his office. Dillon, Susie, Charlie White and Steve Bull were all there, along with Chris Deakin, who would be taking the notes from which all the ensuing actions would be issued.

"We really need to get a grip on this case," Tyler began as soon as they were all seated. "Because at the moment, all we seem to be doing is going round in ever decreasing circles and getting nowhere fast; at least, that's how it feels to me." He looked around the room, daring anyone to challenge him.

There were reluctant nods of agreement.

"What about the voicemail message you left the suspect?" Bull asked. "Has he listened to it again?"

Tyler shook his head. He had kept the two detector vans from the Technical Support Unit on standby at Wanstead police station all day, ready to deploy and triangulate its position if Peter's phone was switched on again.

"I spoke to Sam Calvin a few minutes ago," Susie said, changing the subject. "The morticians were getting ready to remove the boy's body from the forest. The SPM has been arranged for Friday morning. Apparently, Creepy Claxton's performing it."

Dillon groaned.

Tyler shot him a look of sympathy. The big man was squeamish about being around dead bodies at the best of times, and Tyler was genuinely worried that the sight of a child laid out on a cold metal slab, awaiting a Special Post Mortem, would prove too much for him.

"I've decided that I should probably attend that one," he announced.

Dillon frowned, clearly surprised by the break in protocol. "But—"

Tyler held up a hand to silence him. "I need to be there for this one. You can come along too, if you want, but I can't see the point of us both suffering."

Dillon hesitated, then shook his head in relief. "Nah, if you're going anyway, I think I'll give it a miss."

The telephone on Tyler's desk rang.

He snatched the receiver up, annoyed at the interruption. "DCI Tyler speaking."

His brow furrowed as he listened.

"Are you absolutely sure?" he eventually asked.

Thanking the caller, he hung up and looked at each of his colleagues in turn.

"That was George Copeland. He reckons the victim isn't one of our missing children."

---

Mo's unexpected death had left Benny badly shaken, even more so than the discovery of Adam's body in Epping Forest so soon after it had been buried.

Benny knew he was incapable of making emotional connections in the same way that most people did, but Mo Hinkleman had been the closest thing he had to a friend. In addition to being Benny's confidant, Mo had been his business partner. Over the years, Benny had come to rely heavily on him, and his passing would leave a huge void.

It had been Mo's idea to film the orgies that were held at the flat in Hackney; it had been his idea to video the wolfpack's inner circle raping the drugged children they held captive at the safe house in Leytonstone. Mo had installed and maintained the hidden cameras at both addresses, and he had skilfully edited the footage, adding background music and title sequences to make the productions look sleek and professional. The videos he produced had earned the wolfpack an absolute fortune.

It had also been Mo's idea to sell the risqué photographs he took of the skimpily dressed chickens at his studio; that had been another big money earner for them.

How would any of these lucrative practices continue without Mo to run the technical side of things?

"What the hell were you thinking, letting the boy go to Mo's studio unaccompanied?" he demanded of McQueen, who was sullenly nursing the black eye that Benny had given him for letting Gabe out unsupervised.

They were sitting in the lounge of the Leytonstone safe house. Remus was there, too.

"I–I'm sorry, Benny," McQueen said, averting his eyes. "We had a long talk, and he said all the right things, so I thought I could trust the little cunt..." He shrugged, lamely. "Turns out I was wrong."

"I don't get it," Remus interjected, looking questioningly from one to the other. "Why would one of our rent boys stab Mo?"

McQueen bit his lip pensively before answering. "Gabe isn't a rent boy, at least not yet. He isn't gay either, and he made it clear he wasn't up for any funny business, but you know Mo; he had the hots for him, and he wasn't going to take no for an answer. My guess is, when Gabe arrived to collect the envelope, Mo came on a bit too strong, and Gabe panicked, grabbed a knife and shivved him."

Benny shook his head. "I don't buy it. Mo wasn't the type to get physical when chickens refused him. He just drugged the little shits, and then had his way with them when they were too weak to resist."

"Yeah, but he was totally besotted with Gabe," McQueen insisted. "Maybe he offered Gabe a laced drink, but the kid declined."

Benny considered this. "And what? You expect me to believe that, in his frustration, Mo forced himself on the boy?"

McQueen shrugged. "Maybe not forced himself on him in the sense that he was violent. More likely he cornered the kid and wouldn't take no for an answer."

Benny grunted. It was possible, he supposed.

In the end, it didn't really matter why Gabe had stabbed him; the fact was, Mo was dead and nothing was going to change that. "Apart from the envelope that Gabe was supposed to collect, is there anything incriminating at the studio?"

The question was addressed to McQueen, who had spent more time there than either of the others.

McQueen considered this. "Nothing. Mo kept all the incriminating negatives in the basement filing cabinets here, along with the all master tapes of the videos we've made."

"How sure are you?"

"Pretty sure."

Benny's eyes narrowed to slits. "You were pretty *sure* you'd buried Adam's body in a deep enough hole that it would never be discovered, and look how that turned out!"

McQueen's ears reddened, and he looked away.

"Well?" Benny demanded.

"I'm telling you, Mo never kept anything incriminating at the studio. He wanted the place to be squeaky clean, in case anyone ever complained about him and the police paid him a visit."

"So, where will the negatives be?" Benny asked.

"Mo had another darkroom set up at his flat. He always printed the dodgy stuff up round there. That's where the negatives will be, not at the studio."

"I've got a spare set of keys for Mo's place," Benny said. "You'll have to nip round there, Joey. Spin the place and remove anything incriminating before the police search it."

McQueen's eyes widened in alarm. "What if they're already there?"

"If the police think it was a workplace robbery, searching his home address won't be high on their list of priorities," Benny said, dismissively.

"I'll go, if you like," Remus offered.

"No, you won't," Benny snapped. "You'll stay here and look after the two chickens you lumbered us with."

McQueen's ears pricked up. "Chickens? What chickens?"

"Never you mind," Benny said, glowering at Remus for making

him reveal something that he hadn't wanted McQueen to know about yet. Fishing a keychain from his pocket, he separated the spare keys for Hinkleman's flat, then thrust them into McQueen's hand. "Get yourself straight over to Mo's gaff, and don't come back till you're sure there's nothing there that can link him to us."

---

Gareth Madeley had just arrived home when his mobile chirped into life. To his surprise, Benny's name came up on the screen. "Is there a problem?" he asked, guardedly.

"*Yes, there bloody well is,*" Benny's angry voice grated in his ear. "*One of my employees was arrested for murdering a photographer called Maurice Hinkleman earlier today. From what I can gather, the police are treating it as a robbery gone wrong.*"

By employee, Madeley assumed that he meant a rent boy. "And what, pray tell, has that got to do with me?" he enquired in a frosty tone.

"*The boy in question is privy to certain sensitive information, and I want to make sure he keeps his gob shut when he's interviewed.*"

"Benny, I'm a barrister. If he's charged, then I'll happily represent him at court, but what you need right now is a solicitor."

There was a groan of impatience, followed by a lengthy stream of uncouth cursing. When he finally calmed down, Benny asked, "*Can you find me one? You know, someone who shares our mutual interests.*"

Madeley didn't know anyone like that. He had purposefully steered clear of anyone who might be remotely like that. "Benny, at this stage all you need is someone to advise your employee to make no comment to all questions asked. Any solicitor can—"

"*I want someone I can trust; someone I can relate too, if you get my drift.*"

Madeley sighed. "I'm sorry, Benny," he said, firmly. "I don't have any contacts who fit that bill. As you well know, you're the only similarly minded individual I've ever confided in."

"*Bollocks!*" Benny snarled, then hung up.

# 30

*This place won't search itself*

When the gaoler unlocked the door to detention room number one at Shoreditch police station, Detective Constable Zoe Sanders moved into the doorway and studied the teenager sitting on the blue plastic-coated mattress that ran along the far wall. The boy was cradling his head in his hands, and he didn't look up at first. When he did, his face clouded over with worry.

In her late twenties, Sanders was tall and slim, with long auburn hair tied into a neat ponytail. "Come on, Gabe," she said, gesturing for him to follow her. "It's time to interview you."

Gabe's clothing had been seized for forensic examination upon his arrival at the station many hours earlier. When he stood up, the all-in-one paper suit he had been provided with crinkled loudly. Without a word, he shuffled after her in plimsolls that were too big for his feet.

"Can't we at least find him some footwear that fits?" Sanders asked the gaoler.

He responded with a weary shrug. "Sorry, that was the closest size we had."

Sanders led Gabe over to the custody officer's desk, where she signed him out for interview.

"This is Caroline McPhee," she said, introducing Gabe to a stern faced, frumpy woman in her late forties, with dull clothing and even duller eyes. "Ms McPhee is the duty social worker, and she's going to act as an appropriate adult in the absence of your parents."

Treating Gabe to a cold smile, McPhee turned to the custody sergeant. "Where's our solicitor?"

"Gabe doesn't want one at this time," Sanders answered for him.

McPhee placed her hands on her hips. "Well, I'm not sure that's terribly wise of you, Gabriel," she patronised him. "I would prefer—"

"It's Gabe, not Gabriel," he cut her off. "And I've already said I don't want a solicitor, so let's just get on with it."

Sanders smothered a smile. "This way," she said, pointing towards the corridor that led down to the interview rooms.

Pushing open the heavy, soundproofed door to interview room number two a few seconds later, she indicated for them to precede her in.

Inside, a rectangular table was bolted to the wall, and there were two hard backed chairs protruding from either side of it. The fabric was torn on all the seats, exposing thin foam inside.

A slightly overweight man with a shiny bald head occupied one of the two chairs closest to the door. Dressed in a crumpled brown polyester suit, he half rose as they entered. After a polite nod to McPhee and Gabe, he smiled warmly at Sanders.

"Ah, there you are," he said, cheerfully. "I was beginning to think you'd got lost."

"This is my colleague, DC Niall Fergusson," Sanders said, taking the seat next to him, and indicating for McPhee and Gabe to sit on the two chairs opposite.

Gabe chose the one closest to the wall, and promptly slouched against it.

"Gabe, can you be careful not to lean on the thin magnetic strip running along the side of the wall," Sanders asked with a smile. "Only that's the alarm, and everyone will come running in if you accidentally set it off."

Gabe looked down at the thin strip to his left, then adjusted his position so he was well away from it.

"Thanks," Sanders said, giving him another smile.

The boy looked troubled, fearful, unsure of what to expect.

The interview room was small and oppressive, its grubby magnolia walls in desperate need of a fresh coat of paint. The single fluorescent light above them was flickering slightly, which Sanders found very annoying.

Unwrapping two audio tapes, Fergusson placed them into a black tape deck on top of the table. "Ready?" he asked his colleague.

When she nodded, he pressed the start button.

Sanders went through the formalities, reading the script verbatim from an A4 sized idiot card sellotaped to the table. Once all the legal formalities were over, and the lengthy caution had been given, the interview began in earnest.

"Gabe, you've been arrested on suspicion of murdering an elderly photographer called Maurice Hinkleman at his studio in The Narrow Way earlier today. You were seen decamping from the studio carrying a cashbox that has since been identified as belonging to the victim, and a knife. There was a significant amount of blood on your hands, and over the front of your denim jacket. There was also blood on the knife handle. I'm going to ask you some questions about this incident, but before I do, this is your opportunity to tell me exactly what happened in your own words. Will you do that for me?"

According to the flimsy research docket she had been given, Gabe had no previous cautions or convictions recorded against him, but he had recently been interviewed in relation to an aggravated burglary on the outskirts of Bristol. The victims, a wealthy elderly couple, had been tied to kitchen chairs while their house was ransacked.

Although Gabe had eventually been eliminated as a suspect, Sanders felt that the similarities in Modus Operandi – the fact that the victims were elderly, and that they were tied to chairs while their premises were searched – was strikingly similar.

Slumped in his chair, spine curved, shoulders rounded, head bowed so far forward that his chin almost touched his chest, Gabe gave the impression that his spirit was broken, yet when he spoke, there was a note of defiance in his voice.

"I didn't kill him," he said, softly but firmly.

"Can you speak a little louder," Sanders encouraged.

Gabe met her gaze. "I said, I didn't kill him. Mo was tied to the chair when I arrived. I tried to help him but…." Gabe closed his eyes, grimaced at the memory. "I thought someone had stuffed a red gag into his mouth, but it wasn't a gag, it was…"

His voice faltered, and a violent shudder ran though him.

"Go on," Sanders encouraged.

"It was his knob and balls. Someone had…" Gabe swallowed hard. "… Someone had cut them off and jammed them into his mouth."

As he spoke, the colour drained from his face.

"What did you do?" Sanders asked.

"I went over to feel for a pulse in his neck, like they do on TV, but then I saw that his throat had been cut as well. There was just so much blood. His chest, his lap, his legs, they were all covered. It was *everywhere!*" Gabe shuddered again, even more violently, and wrapped his arms around his body. "The look on Mo's face, it was awful, like he'd died screaming."

"Was Mo your friend?"

Gabe seemed genuinely surprised by the question. "No! Look, I'm not gonna lie. I couldn't stand the dirty old perv, but I wouldn't wish that on him. I wouldn't wish *that* on anyone."

He sounded so sincere that Sanders wondered if he might actually be telling the truth. "Were the curtains open or closed when you arrived?"

Gabe frowned, trying to recall. "Closed, I think. Why?"

"What happened next?" She asked, keeping her voice neutral.

Gabe licked his lips, then glanced sideways at the social worker for guidance.

She shrugged disinterestedly, as if to say you didn't want my advice earlier, so why would you want it now?

Gabe hesitated a moment before answering. "I nicked the cashbox from the bottom drawer of his desk. I knew he kept it there from my last visit, when he took some photographs of me."

"Was that a spur of the moment thing, or did you go there intending to steal the money?" Sanders asked.

"I was sent there to collect an envelope by a bloke called Joey, but… I knew the money was there, and I was hoping I'd get the chance to nick it while I was there."

An A4 manila envelope containing child pornography had been found in the top drawer of Hinkleman's desk. Sanders wondered if this was the envelope Gabe was talking about.

"What did you want the money for?" Sanders asked, half expecting him to say he had planned to use it to purchase drugs.

"I needed the money to get away from London." Looking down at his feet, Gabe performed a lacklustre shrug. "Anyway, I'd just grabbed the cash box when the buzzer sounded. I thought it might be Joey, coming to check up on me, and I panicked."

Sanders raised an enquiring eyebrow. "That's the second time you've mentioned Joey. Who is he?"

Gabe fidgeted in his chair. "I've been staying with Joey at a flat in Hackney for the past few days."

"Where is this flat?"

"It's on an estate near Broadway Market. I don't know what it's called but I could show you it on a map."

"How do you know Joey?"

Taking a deep breath, Gabe told the detectives everything that had happened to him from the moment he stepped off the coach at Victoria station on Saturday evening, all the way up to his arrest. Once he started, he couldn't stop; the words just kept spilling out. He became emotional as he described what had happened at the party. Through his tears, he told them about the drugs and the booze, and the male prostitutes that Benny had laid on. Finally, he told them how a defenceless young rent boy called Adam had been drugged, raped and murdered.

"Adam begged them to let him go," Gabe sobbed. "He didn't want to have sex with Benny, but Joey and Mo pinned him down while Benny poured a strong sedative down his throat. The poor sod almost choked on it."

"How do you know it was a sedative?" Sanders asked.

Gabe hung his head in shame. "Benny sent me into the kitchen with orders to tell Joey to prepare one of his special lemonades. I watched him make it. He tipped a load of powder from a paper bag into the lemonade, then stirred it until it dissolved. Then he called Mo over. I followed them back to the bedroom... I watched them hold Adam down while Benny made him drink the lemonade." Leaning forward, Gabe buried his face in his hands and cried uncontrollably.

McPhee tentatively placed a hand on Gabe's shoulder and rubbed it until the sobbing abated. "Maybe we should take a break?" she suggested. "Give Gabe a couple of minutes to compose himself before continuing."

Sanders nodded. "Gabe, would you like to take a quick break?"

Gabe looked up, shook his head. Tears were streaming down his cheeks, and he angrily wiped them away with the sleeve of his paper suit. "I watched them drug Adam, but there was nothing I could do to help him. Nothing!"

Sanders nodded understandingly, said nothing.

"That's when I decided that I had to get away from them," Gabe continued. "That's why I stole the money from Mo."

Bubbles of snot were coming out of both nostrils, so Sanders handed him another tissue. She was fast running out of them.

"Thank you,' Gabe said, blowing his nose like it was a trumpet.

"Benny sent us all away while he had his wicked way with Adam, but something went wrong. When we returned to the bedroom, Adam was lying on the bed, naked. There was bruising all around his throat." As he spoke, his hand subconsciously rose to his neck, retracing the area he had seen bruising on Adam. "Mo was going mad at Benny, demanding to know why he had to strangle the chickens first, asking if it was the only way he could get it up these days."

"Chickens?" Sanders queried. "What did he mean by that?"

Gabe shrugged. "I dunno. I've heard them refer to boys as chickens several times, but I don't know why."

"And what did Benny say to this?"

"He said that he must've squeezed too hard, and that accidents happened. That really pissed Mo off. He told Benny he should go last next time, so as not to spoil the fun for the others. I thought Benny was going to explode, he was so angry. He shouted that he was the leader of the wolfpack, and it was his right to go first."

"What did he mean by wolfpack?" Sanders asked.

Gabe spread his hands. "Fucked if I know."

Sanders glanced at Fergusson, to see if he was familiar with the term, but he just shrugged and gave her a blank look.

"Just to be clear, Gabe," she said, gently. "When and where are you saying Adam was murdered?"

"Last night, at the flat in Hackney."

"Is the body still there?"

Gabe shook his head. "No. While me and Joey tidied up after the party, Benny and Mo wrapped Adam's body in an old carpet. Then, they carried it downstairs to Benny's car, and Joey took it somewhere to be buried. He wanted me to go with him, you know, to help dig the grave, but Benny wouldn't allow it."

"What time did he leave?" Fergusson asked, speaking for the first time.

Gabe considered this. "I dunno. It was gone two. He got back at four-thirty. I know this because he woke me up, and I looked at the clock on the bedside table."

"And has Joey said anything to you about where he disposed of the body?" That was Fergusson again.

Gabe shook his head. "Joey was in a funny mood this morning." He frowned as something occurred to him. "I don't know if it means anything, but he had a bandage wrapped around his left hand and wrist, and there were little bloodspots showing through."

The detectives exchanged glances.

"What's the matter?" Gabe asked, picking up on the look they had given each other. "Do you think I'm lying?"

"Not at all," Sanders assured him.

Beside her, Fergusson scribbled something on his notepad and slid it sideways.

It read: *We need to take a break so we can pass this information on!*

Running her eyes over the note, Sanders gave him an almost imperceptible nod.

"Gabe, this envelope that Joey sent you to collect, do you know what was in it?"

Gabe shook his head. "I asked, but Joey wouldn't tell me."

"Okay, Gabe," she said, smiling disarmingly at the boy. "In light of what you've just told us, I think we need to take a short break so that we can run this information by our boss."

---

Mo's flat was in complete darkness when McQueen arrived. There were no cops stationed outside; no crime scene tape; no sign of them having paid a recent visit. Nonetheless, he waited for several minutes before approaching the door, just to satisfy himself that the sneaky bastards weren't lying in wait for him.

Using the keys Benny had given him, he unlocked the security grill, then the door itself. With a last glance around, he stepped into the hallway, closing the door behind him as quietly as he could.

As a precaution against leaving fingerprints, he was wearing an old pair of yellow washing up gloves that he'd found in the safe house kitchen. Benny had told him not to bother with them; he had been in the flat so many times that his dabs were bound to be all over the place, but wearing the gloves made McQueen feel safer.

For a moment, he considered switching the lights on, but then thought better of it. Instead, he pulled a pen torch from his pocket. Using its thin beam to guide him, he set about searching the flat for anything that might link Mo to the rest of the wolfpack.

He started in the lounge, scooping up several VHS tapes that he knew contained child porn. These were hurriedly thrown into the rucksack on his back. A quick perusal of the master bedroom, kitchen, toilet and bathroom revealed nothing out of the ordinary. That only left the spare bedroom, and McQueen had deliberately left this till last because that was the room that Mo had converted into a darkroom.

As soon as McQueen opened the door, the pungent metallic-like odour of the chemicals hit him. Mo was forever telling him how much he loved the distinctive smell of a photographic darkroom, but McQueen didn't share his fondness. Shutting the door behind him, he found the light switch. There were two of them; the first one he tried bathed the room in red, so he flicked the other one up and a normal light came on.

There were worktops along the walls. One was set up for printing; the other for developing. He had heard Mo refer to these as the wet and dry sides of the darkroom.

The negatives that McQueen had gone there to find were lying on the worktop beside the enlarger. He thrust them into his pocket and set about searching the drawers beneath the worktop. The top one contained unopened packets of photographic paper. He ignored these. The middle drawer contained a stack of glossy colour prints, all featuring naked or semi naked children. These went straight into his rucksack. The bottom drawer contained rolls and rolls of developed negatives. There was no time to sort through them, so they joined the photographs and videos in the rucksack.

The three large plastic lab trays sitting on the wet side worktop were empty, but the labels affixed to them stated they were to be filled with developer, stopping agent and fixer.

On the shelving below, McQueen found bottles containing hard to pronounce chemicals and a couple of funnels.

Satisfied that he had found everything that mattered, McQueen switched the light off and left the room, eager to get away from the vile smell.

As he crept along the hall towards the street door, he heard voices outside.

"That's funny," one of them said. It was a man's voice, deep and a little gruff. "The security grill isn't locked."

"Well, there's no sign of forced entry so Hinkleman probably just forgot to lock it," another voice said, dismissively. This one was slightly higher in pitch, and it sounded younger, more enthusiastic. "Come on. Open it and let's get on with the search."

The voices belonged to police officers, and they were obviously there to search Mo's flat.

McQueen backed away from the door, feeling trapped. There was no other way out; all the windows had security grills fitted to them, as did the backdoor in the kitchen, which led out to the small rear garden.

"Shit! Shit! Shit!" he hissed, unable to see a way out of his predicament.

A moment later, he heard the unwelcome sound of a key being inserted into the street door lock.

---

"I'm telling you, Jack," Quinlan insisted. "If half of what Zoe just told me on the phone is true, then our cases are connected."

"It certainly sounds that way," Tyler cautiously agreed.

"The injuries that Gabriel Warren described seeing on the rent boy's neck mirror those on the body from Epping Forest. It's too much of a coincidence for them not to be linked," Quinlan continued, hammering home his point.

It was hard to argue that point, Tyler accepted. "Speaking of coincidences, I'd never heard the phrases 'chicken' or 'wolfpack' until I started investigating Peter and Gavin's abduction, yet here they are cropping up in Warren's interview."

"We don't know what the terms mean yet," Quinlan admitted, "but I've instructed my Intel Cell to find out."

"I can save you the trouble," Tyler said, with a wry smile. "A chicken is any child that a paedophile has sex with, and a wolfpack is the grandiose title these predatory paedophile gangs use to describe themselves."

"There you are then," Quinlan said, jubilantly. "Even more evidence that I'm right." His face darkened. "I hate to say it, but I think we've stumbled across one of these wolfpacks." Holding up his hands, he dramatically ticked a finger off. "Firstly, we've got three men drugging a rent boy who later turns up dead." A brief pause to tick off another finger. "Secondly, we've got Warren using terminology we know paedophiles use; terminology he picked up from them." A third finger was ticked off. "Thirdly, we discovered an envelope containing explicit child porn in Hinkleman's desk drawer. If you add all of that together, you're left with the inescapable conclusion that Benny, Joey and Hinkleman are members of an organised paedophile gang."

Tyler tugged at his bottom lip as he considered this. "I take it you think that Warren killed Hinkleman as an act of revenge for helping Benny to rape and murder his friend?"

Quinlan spread his arms as if it were done deal. "Frankly, I don't see how anyone viewing the evidence dispassionately could conclude anything else."

"Okay, I'm convinced," Tyler conceded with a weighty sigh. "It's just a pity we can't connect them to Peter and Gavin's abduction. Then, everything would fit neatly into one big puzzle."

Quinlan stiffened, and his eyes glazed over as if he were having an epiphany. "Jack," he said, a moment later. "That might not be as ridiculous as it sounds."

Tyler shot him a quizzical look. It had been a throwaway comment, nothing more. "What do you mean?"

"I've just remembered something else that Zoe told me," Quinlan said. As he spoke, he removed his glasses and began polishing the lenses. "Joey told Warren that he and Benny offered a procurement service for wealthy clients who had very special tastes in boys. Warren assumed he meant supplying rent boys like Adam, but what if he didn't? What if he was actually referring to snatching young children to order? What if this wolfpack we've stumbled across, Benny, Mo, Joey and whoever else, really are the ones behind Peter and Gavin's abduction?"

Tyler was looking at him in awe. "That's a hell of a leap, but I can't deny it fits."

With a self-deprecating smile, Quinlan held his glasses up to the light, inspected the lenses to make sure they were clean enough before slipping them back on. "If I'm right, we need to throw everything we have into tracking down Benny and Joey."

Tyler glanced down at his wristwatch, grimaced when he saw how late it was. With an air of weary resignation, he lifted the telephone receiver from its cradle. "I'd better give George Holland a call before he goes to bed, and let him know we're going to need more people."

---

DC Andy Coltrane slid the Yale key into the lock and gave it a little twist. The door to Hinkleman's flat opened smoothly, revealing a central hallway with a number of doors leading into various rooms.

"Hello! It's the police. Is anyone there?" he called out.

Beside him, DS Gary Conway, older, more experienced and definitely more cynical, sighed. "Andy, we know Hinkleman lived here alone, and as he's currently lying on a cold mortuary slab, I really don't think we need to announce ourselves like that."

"Sorry," Coltrane replied, sheepishly. "Just force of habit." Stepping across the threshold, he fumbled for the light switch.

Following him in, Conway closed the door behind him. "It's as cold in here as it was out there," he complained, rubbing his hands together briskly.

Coltrane was carrying an exhibits bag, not that they thought they were going to need it. The search was a formality. Hinkleman was the victim, not the suspect, and from what they could tell, his murder was a stranger attack; a robbery gone wrong, so there was no reason to think there would be anything of any evidential value at the flat.

Granted, some very disturbing child pornography had been found at the studio, but the photographs were obviously intended for a client, and had nothing to do with the murder. Still, there were procedures to be followed, boxes to be ticked. "Where shall we start?" he asked his sergeant.

Conway blew out his breath in a laboured sigh as he looked

around. "Looks like the lounge and the kitchen are at the back of the flat, with the bedrooms, bathroom and bog branching off the hall. Let's start at the back and work our way forward. Hopefully, this won't take too long."

Pushing past his junior colleague, Conway strode purposefully towards the kitchen. "Come on, Captain Sluggish," he called over his shoulder. "This place won't search itself."

Pulling a rude face at his sergeant's back, Coltrane dutifully followed along behind. Despite Conway's insistence that the flat was empty, he felt compelled to take a quick peek in each room, just to satisfy himself that they really were all alone.

Opening the first door, Coltrane peered inside. This was obviously the victim's bedroom. Sparsely furnished, it contained a double bed, a pine wardrobe and a matching chest of drawers.

"What are you doing?" Conway barked from the kitchen, where the light had just gone on.

"Just being nosy," Coltrane shouted back.

"Well, don't be," Conway reprimanded him. "Get your arse in here so we can crack on."

Cursing under his breath, Coltrane pulled the door shut and trudged along the hallway. "Keep your hair on, I'm coming."

---

Inside the cramped wardrobe, McQueen breathed a sigh of relief when he heard Mo's bedroom door close again. Unable to find a way out of the flat, and not knowing what else to do, he had hidden in there and prayed he wouldn't be found.

Unfolding himself from the ball he had curled into, McQueen emerged from the confined space and retrieved his rucksack from under the bed, where he had flung it in panic. Trying to control his ragged breathing, he tip-toed to the door and placed an ear against it. He heard muffled voices coming from the direction of the kitchen, one deep and moany, the other lighter and more conciliatory.

The two police officers were noisily opening and closing

cupboards, constantly bickering as they worked. Hoping they would be too distracted to notice him, he gently turned the handle and eased the door open, afraid that the hinges would squeak.

Thankfully, they didn't.

McQueen risked a quick glance to his left, to where the two plain clothed cops were searching the kitchen. One was young, tall and slim, the other middle-aged, short and fat. The tall one was standing on a chair, searching the space above the cupboards, while the shorter one was down on his knees, pulling stuff out from under the kitchen sink.

Neither were looking in his direction.

Keeping his back to the wall, McQueen scuttled along the hallway like a rat.

Behind him, the bickering and cupboard door slamming continued, but the dreaded shout of alarm never came.

On reaching the street door, McQueen carefully turned the latch and eased it open. With a final glance over his shoulder, he slipped through the gap and gently closed the door behind him.

McQueen wasn't a religious man, but as he disappeared into the darkness, he offered up a silent prayer of thanks for the miracle of getting out unnoticed.

## 31

# THURSDAY 8TH NOVEMBER 2001

We just have to be patient

Tyler worked late into the night, continuing until he could no longer focus his eyes or think straight. By then, he was too tired to drive, so he decided to sleep at the office.

Lying down on his hard office floor, he used his folded jacket as a pillow and his overcoat as a blanket. Despite his fatigue, he was unable to make his mind go blank, and he was still thinking about the case when he finally dozed off.

His turbulent thoughts followed him into his dreams, turning them into nightmares and leaving him feeling even more exhausted when he woke up than he had been when he had fallen asleep.

Kelly had been distinctly unimpressed when he'd told her to go home without him, and had been extremely vocal in expressing her fears that he was going to burn himself out if he carried on like this for much longer.

He could tell from her frosty demeanour, when she arrived at work this morning, that she was still annoyed with him for not taking proper care of himself.

Although there was to be a team briefing at eight o'clock, Holland had insisted on meeting up with Tyler, Quinlan and their respective second in commands beforehand, so that he could be brought up to speed before addressing the extra troops he had drafted in to help them. The pre-briefing-briefing was to be held in the small meeting room in the Command Corridor at 7 a.m.

Tyler and Dillon arrived ten minutes early, only to find Susie Sergeant and Carol Keating already there.

"Morning, ladies," Tyler said, flopping down opposite them.

On seeing Keating, Dillon launched into his impression of Sid James's trademark dirty laugh, and she dutifully responded with her well-honed imitation of a Hattie Jacques giggle, then clutched her chest romantically and cooed, "Ooh, Sid!"

"It never grows old," Dillon beamed, delighted by her response.

"Trust me," Tyler grumbled, watching from the sidelines. "It really does." If he had heard them perform their dreary *Carry On* routine once, he had heard it a thousand times.

"What's the matter with you?" Dillon asked, looking hurt.

"You're the matter," Tyler growled, sounding very much like the Grinch who stole Christmas. "Why do you always have to be so full of beans at such an ungodly hour?"

"But the morning's the best time of the day," Dillon insisted, knowing full well that Tyler held a very different view.

Keating and Susie watched the exchange with amusement.

"Tony, leave the poor dear alone," Keating admonished the big man. She flashed Tyler a sympathetic smile. "You know he doesn't function well before nine o'clock."

Like the grown up he was, Tyler responded by poking his tongue out at her.

George Holland strode into the room at seven o'clock on the dot. With a perfunctory greeting, he took his seat at the head of the table.

Uncharacteristically, Andy Quinlan was a couple of minutes late. Apologising profusely, he hurriedly took a seat. Like Tyler, he had worked late and slept in his office. His eyes, magnified by the lenses of his tortoiseshell glasses, were red rimmed and puffy.

"Now that we're all here, let's start with a quick recap of what Andy's suspect said during interview yesterday evening," Holland decreed with a taut smile.

Quinlan cleared his throat. "Gabriel Warren named three men: Benny, Mo and Joey. He doesn't know their surnames. He alleges that, during a drug fuelled homosexual orgy at a flat in Hackney, Mo and Joey held down a rent boy called Adam while Benny poured a powerful sedative down his throat. Benny then raped and murdered Adam, and Joey subsequently disposed of the body. Warren claims to know very little about these men, and nothing at all about any of the other individuals attending the orgy. He *was* able to give us the address of the flat in Hackney where the murder is alleged to have occurred. He claims to have been staying there with Joey for the past few days, but doesn't think anyone resides there on a permeant basis. Mo, whose full name is Maurice Hinkleman, was murdered at his studio the following day. Current thinking is that Warren killed him in revenge for helping Benny to rape and murder Adam. Warren denies this, claiming that the old man was already dead when he arrived at the studio. Hinkleman's flat was searched last night, but nothing of note was found."

Holland looked up from the notes he was making. "Do we believe Warren's account about Mo and Joey pinning Adam down while Benny poured sedative down his throat?"

"We do," Quinlan said, without hesitation.

"And are we happy that Adam is the boy whose body was found in Epping Forest?"

"We are," Tyler said.

"Have we established cause of death?" Holland asked.

"There's extensive bruising around the dead boy's neck and petechial haemorrhaging in his eyes, both of which are indicative of manual strangulation," Tyler said. "We'll know more tomorrow morning, when Dr Claxton carries out the SPM. Toxicology will undoubtedly show sedatives in the boy's bloodstream, but the report will take a few days to come back."

Holland noted this down in his daybook. "Have we managed to establish the dead boy's identity?" he asked, looking from Tyler to Quinlan.

"Not yet," Quinlan admitted. "A wet set of prints were taken at the scene and rushed up to NSY. Assuming Adam's in the system, we should know his full name within the next couple of hours."

"I take it that the Musgroves and the Grants have been updated that the body doesn't belong to one of their sons?" Holland asked.

"Yes, that was done late last night," Tyler confirmed.

Holland nodded, thoughtfully. "Jack, when we spoke last night, you seemed to think there's a good chance that whoever killed Adam is also involved in the abduction of our two missing boys. Do you still believe that?"

"More so than ever," Tyler assured him. Standing up, he crossed to the door, and invited the two men who were waiting in the corridor to join them. "Boss, you know Dean Fletcher, my lead researcher, and Reg Parker, my phones man. They've made some significant discoveries overnight. Once you've heard what they have to say, you'll understand why we're so convinced that everything is linked."

Holland acknowledged the newcomers with a terse nod, and gestured for them to take seats at the table.

"Who wants to go first?" Tyler asked them once they were settled.

"I'll start," Fletcher offered. He passed copies of a briefing document around the table. "The document you're looking at contains all the salient information I'm about to share with you," he told them. "If you follow that, there shouldn't be any need for you to interrupt me while I'm speaking."

That was such a typical Dean Fletcher comment, Tyler thought with a wry smile; the man was about as subtle as a brick through a window, and had no respect for the niceties of rank.

Fletcher cleared his throat, then began speaking. "Overnight, I ran all the salient information that Warren provided through the various Met databases and a number of open source sites including—"

Holland held up a hand. "Dean, as time is of the essence, would you mind confining your results to the ones that paid the greatest dividends?"

Fletcher acknowledged this with a taciturn nod. "The CRIMINT database threw up an entry timed at 06:00 hours yesterday morning, Wednesday 7$^{th}$ November. It relates to a routine stop that PCs Paxman and Alder carried out on an old Daimler Sovereign in the Epping New Road at 04:00 hours. Basically, the car pulled out of a forest clearing without any lights on so they gave it a tug. The driver and vehicle keeper details are included in the briefing document in front of you. Long story short; the Daimler was being driven by a former rent boy named Joseph Stanley McQueen."

Holland arched an eyebrow. "I'm guessing this is the same Joey that Warren told us about?"

"It is," Fletcher confirmed. "The Daimler was registered to Benny Ruben Mars, who McQueen reckoned was his uncle."

"So, now we know Benny's full name too," Holland observed. "What address is the car registered to?"

"The flat where young Warren's been staying with McQueen. It's all in here, guv," Fletcher said, irritably tapping the briefing document to make the point that the interruption had been unnecessary. "According to the database," he continued, "McQueen shares a bedsit in Holborn with another former rent boy called Aaron Remus." He glowered in Holland's direction, in anticipation of another interruption, but the DCS prudently stayed silent. "Both Remus and McQueen have petty form for soliciting, possession of cannabis, and a bit of shoplifting, but nothing heavy. Anyway, when the uniform lads stopped McQueen, they noticed that his hands and clothing were all wet and muddy. He claimed he'd pulled into the clearing to take an emergency dump because he had an upset stomach, and that he'd been caught in the downpour. After carrying out a negative breath test, they let him go."

"Didn't they search his car?" Holland asked.

"They did, guv," Fletcher confirmed, with a look of irritation. "If you read the briefing, you'll see that they found a muddy shovel and an old carpet in the boot, but they didn't think there was anything suspicious about that at the time."

"If only they'd known then what we know now," Quinlan said, shaking his head ruefully.

"Do we at least know which clearing McQueen pulled out of?" Holland asked. "It's not in the briefing document," he added, hastily.

Fletcher grinned. "No, it's not." He picked up a small bundle of A3 maps and shared them out.

"The spot marked A," Fletcher said, tapping his own map, "is where the patrol car stopped the Daimler. The spot marked B–" another tap "–represents the clearing they saw it emerge from. The spot marked C–" several taps, in quick succession to emphasis its importance "–is where the boy's body was found yesterday morning. As you can clearly see, they're all fairly close together."

"This is very impressive work," Holland said, nodding appreciatively.

Fletcher acknowledged this with a modest nod. "The PCs conducting the stop got their control room to ring Benny and confirm that McQueen was authorised to drive his car, which gave us Benny's phone number. They also had the sense to note McQueen's number, so we've got that too. Reggie will talk you through all the phone stuff in a minute."

"What do we know about this Benny Mars character?" Holland asked, glancing at his watch again.

"There are no convictions or cautions recorded against his name," Fletcher told him. "I've checked with Islington, but they don't have much on him. He runs a sex shop in Caledonian Road. It sells the usual range of pornographic magazines, imported hardcore videos from Germany and Sweden, and a few sex toys and kinky outfits. He has the requisite sex establishment licence from the local authority, and there haven't been any complaints about him."

"Is there anything else I need to be aware of?" Holland asked.

"Actually, there are a couple of things," Fletcher said. "Firstly, I ran the Daimler through the ANPR database. It was pinged in Lea Bridge Road at 02:30 hours, travelling towards Epping Forest, and again at the Waterworks roundabout at 04:20 hours, heading back towards London."

"That fits in perfectly with the times that Warren gave us for Joey being away from the flat," Quinlan interjected.

"The other thing you need to know," Fletcher continued, "is that when I ran Benny's details through HOLMES, it highlighted a very interesting piece of information." He turned to address Tyler. "Do you remember the old perv that Whitey and Kevin nicked while they were visiting local sex offenders on Monday?"

Tyler frowned, trying to recall the man's name. "Do you mean the bloke who was watching child porn when they knocked at his door?"

"Yes, him. His name's Lionel Eberhard. In interview, he claimed to have purchased the videos from a boot fair, reckoned he had no idea they contained pornographic material until he started watching one of them."

Tyler recalled that the locals had elected to bail Eberhard pending further enquiries, rather than charge him straight away, a bad decision in his opinion.

"Three child porn films were seized from his home address," Fletcher continued. "One had a tatty white business card tucked into the back cover, with a man's first name, address, and mobile telephone number scribbled on the back. Care to guess whose details they were?"

"Benny Mars?" Tyler offered.

Fletcher nodded, sagely. "Yep, so Benny boy is obviously supplying child porn to his paedophile mates."

"These people are unbelievable," Susie said, unable to remain quiet any longer. "Is there no limit to their depravity?"

"Sounds like the Obscene Publications Squad should be paying that shop a visit," Holland suggested.

"We're going to raid it later today," Tyler told him. "But Obscene Publications are welcome to tag along if they want."

Fletcher removed his glasses and leaned back in his seat. "Right, that's me finished. I'll hand you over to Reggie, so he can bore you all to death with the phone stuff."

There were muted chuckles as Parker stood up and began distributing briefing documents that were noticeably thicker than those previously circulated by Fletcher.

Flicking through his copy, Tyler groaned.

"Don't worry, boss, I'll try and keep this simple and painless," Parker promised, seeing the look of horror on his face.

"That'll be a first," Tyler mumbled under his breath.

Parker cleared his throat. "Gabriel Warren doesn't have a mobile, but Maurice Hinkleman, Benny Mars and Joey McQueen all do. While interrogating their call data, I found a number listed for Aaron Remus. You'll recall Dean telling you that he's McQueen's roommate," he quickly added when met with bemused looks. "I've been ordered, under pain of death, to restrict my input to the relevant calls this morning, but if anyone's interested, I'd be very happy to talk you through the analysis in more detail outside of this meeting."

He glanced around the room expectantly, and was genuinely disappointed that no one took him up on his offer. "Suit yourselves," he sighed, dejectedly. Turning to the first page of the report, he announced, "You can follow everything I'm saying in the handout I've just given you. If you don't," he stared pointedly at Tyler, "you'll only end up getting confused and grumpy."

Grunting a surly acknowledgement, Tyler resisted the urge to point out that confusion and grumpiness had become his default settings these days, even when he wasn't dealing with crappy call data.

"It's obvious from the amount of traffic passing between the four men that they are very close," Parker began. "I'm going to start by discussing Remus' call data. On Saturday night, between 20:00 hours and 21:30 hours, there were four calls between him and McQueen. They ranged from thirty seconds to three minutes in length. McQueen was cell sited in the West End, while Remus was pinged by the cell covering the funfair in Chingford."

That made everyone sit up and take notice.

Parker grinned. "I thought that might get your attention."

"What about Mars and Hinkleman, where were they cell sited?" Holland enquired.

"Like McQueen, Mars was cell sited in the West End, which fits in with what Warren told his interviewers. Hinkleman's handset was pinged by the cell covering his flat, so I think it's fairly safe to assume he was at home."

Susie gave a speculative shrug. "I suppose it could just be a coincidence that Remus' phone was in Chingford when the boys were abducted?"

"It could," Parker agreed, in a tone that implied it definitely wasn't. "Just as it could be a coincidence that every call he's made or received since then has been cell sited in the exact same azimuth in Leytonstone that Peter Musgrove's phone was in when the suspect listened to the boss's voicemail."

"Okay, so maybe it's not a coincidence," Susie accepted.

"Is his phone active at the moment?" Tyler asked. The two detector vans were back on standby today. Now that they knew the number for Remus' handset, he could deploy them to hunt it down if it was active.

Parker flicked through his report, consulted the relevant page. "It's been quiet overnight, but…" his voice trailed off as he ran his finger down the line of data. "Yes, as I thought. It doesn't normally become active until much later in the day."

---

Peter awoke with a start, having been disturbed by a loud clattering sound. Sitting up in the lumpy cot, he held his breath and listened attentively.

The clattering noise came again, originating from the far right corner of the room. It was metallic, like a bucket being kicked across the stone floor, and this time it was accompanied by a frustrated yell of, "Oh, bloody hell!"

"Gav, is that you?" he whispered.

"Sorry, Pete, I didn't mean to wake you. I needed a wee, but I've just knocked the pot over, and now my sock is soaked through."

Peter couldn't help but smile. That was so typical of Gavin. "You great doughnut!" he chided his accident prone friend.

Gavin started making grunting noises.

"What are you doing?" Peter asked, hoping his friend wasn't having a poo.

"Taking my sock off."

There was another groan, followed by the sound of liquid dripping onto the floor.

Peter smiled as he visualised Gavin wringing his sock out.

Leaving him to get on with it, Peter flopped down on his cot. Interlocking his fingers behind his head, he closed his eyes and waited for sleep to come.

"I'm cold, and I'm hungry," Gavin whinged, having returned to his cot. The springs were squeaking as he fidgeted, trying to get warm.

"Me too," Peter admitted.

"Do you think we'll ever get out of this place?" Gavin asked after a few moments of silence. He sounded like he was on the verge of tears.

Peter had no idea, but that wasn't what his friend needed to hear. "I'm sure we will," he said, trying to sound upbeat. "We'll find a way to outsmart that stupid soldier man. We just have to be patient."

## 32

*I'm gasping for a cuppa*

Today was the big day; the day that the two famous chickens were handed over to their new owners. Benny was feeling uncharacteristically jittery; far more so than he normally did when the wolfpack were due to make a delivery, but he told himself this was down to Mo's murder making his feel uneasy. Well, that and the fact that Adam's body had been found so soon after being buried.

Everything would go smoothly today, he assured himself. He never opened the shop on a Thursday, so at least that was one less thing to worry about. It left him free to oversee the deliveries in person; to make sure that everything went without a hitch.

Madeley planned to catch the train from St. Paul's as soon as the morning session at the Old Bailey concluded, and Benny had promised to have someone waiting outside Leytonstone station to chauffeur him to the safe house.

They were delivering the second chicken to Eberhard's house straight after lunch. Moving him in daylight was going to be slightly tricky, but they had a tried and tested method for transporting chickens from one address to another.

At eight o'clock, he strode into Remus' bedroom. The idiot was fast asleep and snoring his head off. After whipping open the curtains, Benny shook the sleeping man's shoulder.

"Get up!" he barked. "We've got things to do."

Beneath the covers, Remus groaned, then rolled over, dragging the pillow over his head to block out the light now streaming into the room. "Leave it out, Benny," he moaned, his words muffled by the pillow. "Let me have another half hour, then I'll get up."

Benny yanked the quilt back with considerable savagery. "You'll get up right now, you lazy good for nothing layabout," he growled. Bending down, he scooped up the creased pile of clothing that Remus had strewn across the floor when he'd undressed the night before, and threw them at the figure curled up in bed. "Don't make me tell you again."

Ignoring the mewling protests burbling out from beneath the pillow, he stormed out of the room and went next door to wake McQueen.

When Remus came downstairs ten minutes later, he still looked half asleep. His hair was as dishevelled as his clothing. "Is the kettle on?" he asked, leaning against the doorframe and yawning expansively. "I'm gasping for a cuppa."

He didn't get one. Instead, Benny sent him straight down to feed and toilet their prisoners. They had stopped administering the sedatives the previous day, in order to allow sufficient time for the drugs to clear their systems. This had created more work for Remus, but Benny had wanted them to be clear eyed, alert and attentive when they were handed over to their purchasers, not stumbling around like a pair of dribbling zombies.

Remus reappeared fifteen minutes later, complaining that one of the cretins had knocked the slops bucket over during the night so, in addition to feeding them and escorting them to the toilet, he had been forced to mop the floor.

Despite having hardly any sleep the previous night, Tyler felt reinvigorated as he returned to his office. They had a plan of action, and things were moving fast.

Dillon was on his way to Barking Magistrates Court to obtain search warrants for the bedsit in Holborn, the flat in Hackney and the sex shop in Caledonian Road.

A car had been sent ahead to each address, to recce it before the warrants arrived.

There had been a heated debate over how best to proceed once the search warrants were obtained. Dillon had been in favour of keeping them in their back pocket for the time being. His preference was to locate the suspects and place them under covert surveillance, in the hope that this would lead them to the children.

Susie Sergeant and Carol Keating had argued for their immediate arrest, while Quinlan had been torn, admitting there were merits and drawback for both options.

From a strategic perspective, Tyler wholeheartedly agreed with Dillon. The trouble was, unless they could categorically exclude the boys being at any of the addresses they knew about, they had no choice other than to proceed on the basis that they were inside one of them.

The final decision had been George Holland's to make, and he had ordered that the warrants were to be executed at once, and that any suspects found inside the addresses were to be arrested.

All prisoners were to be placed incommunicado, which meant that they wouldn't be able to inform anyone of their arrest or detention. Hopefully, that would prevent any suspects not yet arrested from being alerted to the fact that the police were onto them.

Imogen Askew and Bear were waiting by his office to ambush him. Following him in, Imogen treated him to her most charming smile.

Tyler responded in kind, but this was purely a mechanical reaction on his part. "I'm surprised you didn't accompany Dill to court."

"Gosh, no. That'll be terribly boring and straightforward. We want to be at the heart of the action, which is why it's imperative that we go out with one of the arrest teams."

Tyler rolled his eyes. "You know I can't allow that," he told her. Sitting behind his desk, he undid his top button and yanked his tie down as if it was a hangman's noose and he was trying to slip out of it.

Imogen wasn't going to give up that easily. "Jack," she said, stroking his name with her voice. "You're the SIO, you can do whatever you want."

Tyler ignored the aphorism.

"We won't get in the way," Bear promised, crossing his heart.

Tyler glanced at Imogen, who was now giving him big baby eyes. Lacking the energy to argue, he let out a sigh of capitulation. "Oh, alright, then."

She broke into an enormous grin. "Oh, thank you, Jack," she enthused. "I think it's probably best if we accompany the team going after Aaron Remus; that's where the boys are most likely to be found, wouldn't you agree?"

Before Tyler could express an opinion, Bear intervened. "Actually," he said, meekly. "I was going to suggest we go with the team hunting down Mars."

Imogen stared at him like he had just grown another head. "Why would we want to do that?"

"Well," Bear said, embarrassed to suddenly find himself the centre of attention. "It seems to me that he's the enabler of the group. He's the oldest, and from the little research I've done into the subject while this case has been running, he's probably the leader of their little wolfpack, which means he's the one calling the shots. We find him, we probably find the boys." He gave her a lame shrug. "It's just an idea," he said, sounding increasingly less confident. "As always, I'm happy to defer to you."

Tyler held up a hand to halt the conversation. He didn't want to be rude, but he really didn't have time for this. "Tell you what," he said, forcing a smile. "Have a word with Susie. She's coordinating the arrests. Just let her know which team you want to go with once you've made up your minds. Now, if you'll excuse me," he said, impatiently shooing them towards the door, "I've got a lot to be getting on with."

A simultaneously entry was made to all three addresses at twelve o'clock on the dot.

After smashing the door to the Holborn bedsit wide open, the burly officer wielding the battering ram stepped aside to allow the arrest team, led by DS Gary Conway, to pile into the address.

For several seconds, there were loud shouts of, "POLICE!" and "STAY WHERE YOU ARE!"

Then, there was a final shout of, "PREMISES CLEAR!" and all the yelling stopped.

"Well, this looks like a blowout," DC Andy Coltrane observed, as he undid the Velcro fastenings to his Met Vest and slipped the restrictive body armour over his head.

Conway told the rest of the arrest team to go and wait outside.

The pretty reporter and her hairy cameraman, who had followed them into the address to film the raid, lingered after the others had filed out.

"I don't suppose we could do a quick walk around and film the interior now that it's not so cluttered with people?" she asked, batting her eyelids at him like she was Marilyn Monroe.

Conway felt his knees go weak. Running a finger around the inside of his collar, which suddenly felt very restrictive, he cleared his throat. "I'm sorry, Ms Askew," he said, trying not to make it obvious that he fancied her. "I'm afraid that will have to wait until we've finished."

He ushered them out of the door, then closed it behind them.

"She's a bit of alright, isn't she?" Coltrane grinned, tracing an hour glass shape in the air with his hands.

"Can't say I'd noticed," Conway lied.

"Leave off," Coltrane chortled. "You were drooling over her."

"Rubbish," Conway snapped, conscious of the wave of heat travelling up his face. He gestured angrily at Coltrane, who was giving him a knowing look. "Come on then, soppy bollocks, let's start searching. This place is only the size of a shoebox, so it shouldn't take too long."

The main living area contained two single beds, both unmade, a couple of tatty armchairs and a coffee table littered with magazines. There was also a cheap TV cabinet containing an even cheaper TV, a video player and a metal rack that was home to a dozen VHS tapes. These would all have to be viewed on fast forward, in case they contained child porn like the ones seized from Eberhard's address.

Behind the main living room, there was a well-appointed if somewhat dated kitchen. It had been left in a right old state, with dirty plates and used cutlery in the sink. There were two boxes containing half-eaten takeaways on the side, along with a half pint of milk that had long since curdled.

Conway tutted his disgust. "It stinks in here," he complained, fanning his nose.

The final room, located just beyond the kitchen, was a poky bathroom that looked like it had been installed in the 1970s. Glancing into the toilet bowl, Conway grimaced at the brown staining.

"Dirty bastards," he growled. "Would it really hurt them to run a brush around the bog after they took a dump?"

Coltrane followed him in, slipping his hands into a pair of Nitrile gloves. "Technically speaking, this place is a studio apartment, not a bedsit," he observed, conversationally. "That's what an estate agent would market it as if it was up for sale."

Conway sighed, in no mood for small talk. "I don't care what this shithole is," he said, grumpily. "Just hurry up and start searching it while I skim through the VHS tapes. The quicker we finish, the quicker we can get back to KZ and grab some lunch."

---

Charlie White was in charge of the team raiding the sex shop in Caledonian Road. Upon gaining entry, it quickly became apparent that the place was empty, which was really annoying because, by smashing the door open, they had triggered the alarm and it was making a hell of a racket.

Apart from the shopfloor, there was a small sitting area and kitchenette at the back. There was also a damp infested toilet and a store room. The latter was locked, but one of the detectives shouldered it open with ease.

White went outside to ring Susie, who was on her way over to join them, but the alarm was so loud he could hardly hear what she was saying.

He hung up as a stocky middle-aged man, who White thought bore an uncanny resemblance to the actor Anthony Quinn, wandered out of a TV repair shop. He looked towards the sex shop and then at White, who was still wearing his Met Vest and PPE belt, and couldn't be mistaken for anything other than a police officer.

"Has there been a break in?"

The sign above his shop proclaimed the proprietor's name to be Karolos Papadopoulos, and this, presumably, was him.

White shook his head. "No," he said, raising his voice to be heard above the din. "But we need to contact the keyholder urgently, to get that bloody racket stopped. Don't suppose you know where he is, do you?"

Papadopoulos shrugged apologetically, indicating that he hadn't heard him properly, then gestured for White to follow him into his shop. Once inside, he closed the door behind them, drastically reducing the noise levels.

"That's better," White said, although his ears were still ringing. "I was asking if you knew where we could find Mr Mars?"

Papadopoulos shook his head. "No idea, the shop is always closed on a Thursday so he could be anywhere. Don't fret, though. I've got a spare set of keys. I'm always having to reset the alarm. Damn thing has a habit of going off during the night and waking the neighbours up." He gave a rumbling chuckle. "Some of them have been giving Benny a hard time over it, so much so that the council warned him that he'll be fined for causing a noise nuisance if he doesn't sort it out."

"Is Mr Mars a friend of yours?" White asked, wondering if the seemingly pleasant man was also a paedophile.

Papadopoulos shuddered. "Can't stand him, but he pays me fifty quid every time I get called out to reset his alarm." A grin spread across his unshaven face. "For that kind of money, I'm happy to be inconvenienced every now and then."

"How quickly can you reset the alarm?"

Papadopoulos motioned for him to wait where he was, then disappeared up the stairs to the flat above his shop. He returned a few minutes later carrying a small notebook.

White followed him back to Benny's shop, where Papadopoulos donned a pair of rimless reading glasses and began flicking through his notebook. Finally, he found the code and tapped it into the control panel.

"Hallelujah!" White said, when the dreadful noise had finally stopped. He patted the stocky Greek on the shoulder. "You're a lifesaver."

"My pleasure," Papadopoulos replied. "That's another fifty quid Benny owes me."

Telling the other officers to go and wait in their car, White and Murray set about checking the place out properly.

The sex shop was divided into four narrow aisles. The first was lined with erotic magazines and steamy novels, the second with raunchy video tapes. The third aisle contained sex toys of every description, along with a diverse range of blow up dolls, while the final aisle was dedicated to role play. There were PVC costumes, gimp masks, dominatrix outfits, and a mix and match section of women's lingerie, most of which was either see-through or crotchless.

The till sat upon a glass fronted counter at the far end of the shop. The shelf above it was lined with polystyrene mannequin heads, each displaying a different colour and length of wig.

Wandering up and down the aisles, Charlie White tutted with increasing disapproval. He paused when he reached the sex toys. "I dread to think what you're supposed to do with this monster?" he said, picking up a shiny black object whose label identified it as a prostate massager. It resembled a large vibrator but bent at right angles to double back on itself. He gave it a little shake and then a squeeze, then put it back where he had found it. "I suppose it takes all sorts," he declared, dubiously.

Next, the Glaswegian picked up a blow up doll that advertised having three usable orifices, and held it aloft. "Hoy, Kev! At least I know what to get you for Christmas now," he laughed. "It'll be nice for you to have a girlfriend for once, even if she is only made of plastic."

Murray looked up from the role play costumes he was rummaging through long enough to raise his middle finger.

White wandered over to the wigs, grinning mischievously when he spotted a ginger one. "Who's this remind you of?" he called, popping it onto his head.

Murray frowned, then shrugged, having no idea.

"It's Susie," White sniggered.

Murray snatched it from White's head. "I can do a much better impression than that," he grinned. Placing the wig over his genitals, he began sashaying around. "Look at me, I'm Susie Sergeant, but my friends call me the ginger minger," he cooed in a high pitched voice that was actually a passable caricature of Susie's soft Irish lilt.

White threw back his head and laughed uproariously. "Brilliant!" he said, clapping his hands.

"What's brilliant?" A stern female voice demanded from the shop's doorway.

White blanched. He spun around to face Susie Sergeant, who had entered without his noticing. "Nothing," he said quickly, knowing they must both look as guilty as sin.

Murray had whisked the wig away from his crotch, and was now concealing it behind his back.

"What was so funny that you two were in near hysterics?" Susie asked as she crossed the shop floor.

"We were just checking the inventory," White stammered, crabbing a few steps to his left to distance himself from Murray.

Susie's green eyes bored into his. "And…?"

Beads of sweat broke out on White's forehead. "I, err, I… Well, I was just telling Kev that I could buy him a blow up doll for Christmas, you know, to keep him company during those long, lonely nights."

Susie gave him a look that could have curdled milk. "Really? We're dealing with one of the most serious cases we've ever had, and you two are making smutty jokes?"

White bowed his head in shame. "Well, I–"

Susie's mobile chirped into life, sparing him a further tongue lashing.

As soon as she turned away to answer it, Murray tossed the wig over the counter.

White grabbed his arm, dragged him over to the aisle containing sex toys. "That was a close call," he whispered, "but I dinnae think she twigged we were laughing at her."

Glancing at the polystyrene mannequin head that was now minus its wig, Murray giggled.

"Stop it, you knobhead," White hissed, angrily nudging his elbow.

"Sorry." Murray took a deep breath, bit his lip, then giggled again.

"That was Jack," Susie said, making them both jump. "We've now got control of all three addresses, but none of the suspects were there, so we're at a bit of a loss as to what to do now."

That was sobering news, and it wiped the grin from Murray's face.

## 33

Alright, keep your hair on!

Frank Stebbins was feeling very pleased with himself as he barged into Craddock's office. "Boss, I've got—"

Craddock looked up from his Decision Log. "That's alright, Frank," he said, grumpily removing his reading glasses. "You just charge in here anytime you want. Don't bother knocking, it's not like you might be disturbing me or anything."

Stebbins grinned. The old man had been like a bear with a sore head all day, but he was about to change that. "Sorry, sir, but I thought you'd like to know, we've just had a DNA hit come back from the lab." He waved the docket in the air as he spoke.

Craddock frowned. "A DNA hit for who and from where?"

Stebbins opened the folder, ran his eyes down the report until he found the relevant information. "Here we are. The match is for a white male called Phillip Diggle. He's no trace on the PNC. We got his DNA from an elimination sample he provided to the

Metropolitan Police earlier this year. As to where it was found, well, that's the really interesting part."

"It probably would be if you ever got round to telling me," Craddock barked. He made an impatient motion with his hand. "Come on, man. Spit it out!"

Stebbins chuckled. He couldn't help it. "Funny you should say that, about spitting it out I mean, because the DNA is from saliva found on our victim's face."

Craddock arched an eyebrow. "Would you care to elaborate?"

"Okay, so the CSM swabbed Angus Clifford's face at the crime scene on the off chance that the suspect spat at him before killing him, or dripped beads of sweat onto his skin while tying him to the chair."

Craddock's face softened into a smile as the implications of what he'd just been told struck home. "Well, I'll be blown," he said, extending a hand for the docket.

"It's the break we've been waiting for," Stebbins said, excitedly. "The only way that DNA could have got there is if this Diggle character was with the victim at or around the time of his death."

Craddock looked up from the report. "Have you asked the researchers to start digging into Diggle's past?"

"Yes, sir, of course," Stebbins said. He had requested a full research package before bringing his boss the good news. "But I was thinking—"

Craddock winced. "Careful young Frank," he cautioned. "We all know what happened the last time you tried doing that."

"I was thinking that it might be worth me giving the Met a ring to see if they could shed any light on what the sample was provided for. There's a reference number on the report. It might speed things up."

Stebbins could see that Craddock was impressed. The boss liked it when his people used their initiative, and Stebbins had done exactly that by claiming the suggestion Yvonne Granger had made when he told her about the docket was his idea.

Benny checked his watch. It was ten past twelve. "It's time to get the chickens ready," he announced. "Aaron, bring them upstairs, one at a time. Let them shower, then get them dressed in the new clothing we've brought them."

That morning, he had dispatched McQueen to the big Woolworths in Leytonstone High Road to purchase new underwear, tracksuits and trainers for each of the boys, so that they would be presentable when they were handed over.

"Why do I always have to run around like a poxy skivvy?" Remus complained, stroppily pushing himself away from the wall he had been leaning against. "Why can't *he* sort them out for once?" he glowered at McQueen, who was slouching in a chair opposite Benny, drinking tea.

"Because you're the one who snatched them, which makes them your responsibility until they're sold on," Benny responded with such vehemence that Remus flinched.

"Alright, keep your hair on!" he mumbled, heading for the door.

"And make sure they give their teeth a good clean," Benny called after him. "I don't want their breath smelling like garbage."

"I think he's got the hump," McQueen said, as soon as Remus was out of earshot.

Benny fixed him with a cold stare. "Do I look like I give a fuck?"

Realising that he'd dropped a clanger, McQueen adopted a suitably contrite expression. "No. Sorry." He fidgeted self-consciously in his seat. Like Remus, he knew better than to get on Benny's wrong side when he was in a funny mood. "I didn't mean to annoy you, Benny. I was—"

"Shut up, Joey," Benny snapped.

McQueen opened his mouth to say something, then thought better of it.

They sat there in strained silence for the best part of a minute, then Benny took a long slurp of his tea. "Is the suitcase ready?"

"It's in the spare room. I'll bring it down as soon as the first kid goes in the shower," McQueen assured him.

"Good," Benny, said, giving McQueen a crocodile smile. He checked his watch again. "Right, make yourself scarce while I give our clients a quick call to make sure there are no last minute snags."

McQueen stood up, turned to go, then stopped. "Out of interest, will I be using the Daimler or Aaron's van to drive the chicken over to Lionel's place? Only I want to make sure there's plenty of petrol in the tank. It wouldn't do to run out of gas with a chicken in the back, would it?"

"You'll have to use Aaron's van," Benny said. "I want him to collect Madeley from the station in the Daimler. That'll make a better impression."

McQueen nodded, diffidently. "I'll have a quick word with Aaron, see where he's parked it."

Once he was alone, Benny took out his mobile and dialled Madeley's number from memory. He wasn't sure if the barrister would answer, but he did. "Good afternoon," he said cheerily. "Are you ready for the best day of your life?"

---

Parker charged into Tyler's office. "Sorry to barge in," he said, breathlessly, "but I thought you'd want to know, Benny's phone has just gone live, and it's shaking hands with a mast in Leytonstone."

Tyler's head shot up from the statement he was reading. "Would that be the same mast that Peter's phone went through when the suspect listened to my voicemail?"

"It's definitely the same mast," Parker confirmed. "But it's too early to say if it's in the same azimuth."

Tyler grabbed his phone. "How long before the TIU can say with any degree of certainty?" he asked, dialling the number for the Technical Support Unit skipper in charge of the two detector vans.

Reg's shoulders twitched. "Hopefully, not long at all."

Tyler was about to ask him another question when the ringtone he'd been half listening to was replaced by a scratchy voice with a thick Belfast accent.

"*Jerry Gallagher speaking.*"

"Jerry, it's Jack Tyler here. We've got activity on one of the suspect's phones. It's just carried out an electronic handshake with a mast over in Leytonstone."

"*Can the TIU boys narrow it down to a particular azimuth?*"

"No, not yet, but they're working on it."

"*Not to worry,*" Gallagher said. "*I'll ring the TIU directly. It'll be quicker than relying on you bouncing messages back and forth between us, so it will.*"

"I'll get the two support cars I promised you rolling, and I'll tell the DC in charge to ring you as soon as they reach Leytonstone."

Hanging up, Tyler followed Parker into the main office. "Dean, I need you to check in with the ANPR people to see if there have been any hits on Benny's car this morning."

"But they've already been told to call us straight away if—"

"Just humour me," Tyler said, cutting him off. He was about to walk away, when a thought occurred to him. "Did your research throw up anything useful on the Berlingo with no current keeper that the locals found parked up in Hampton Road yesterday afternoon, the one they didn't bother telling us about until it was too late?"

Fletcher began rummaging through the massive pile of printouts scattered across his desk. "The results from the ANPR check I ran on it came through a little while ago, but I've been so busy that I haven't had a chance to look at them yet." The rummaging grew more frantic, scattering loose sheets of paper onto the floor. "I know it looks like chaos," Fletcher admitted, checking and discarding bundles with increasing desperation, "but I know exactly where everything is."

"I can see that," Tyler said, keeping his face deadpan.

Finally, Fletcher found what he was looking for. "Aha!" he declared, triumphantly. He began flicking through the report and making rough notes on a separate sheet of paper, then he grabbed a large map of Central London and began adding crosses to it. "Okay," he said when he was finished. "There were fifteen ANPR hits on the van during the days leading up to the abduction, all occurring in Central London."

Tyler turned his nose up. "If that's the case, it's unlikely to be the vehicle we want," he said, feeling a twinge of disappointment. "It was probably just a commercial vehicle making a delivery, or a tradesman carrying out a repair, and nothing to do with Remus."

"Boss, you're missing the point," Fletcher said, holding the map he had just defaced up for Tyler to study. "Look, all these ANPR hits occurred in the vicinity of Remus and McQueen's bedsit in Holborn."

Tyler took a moment to digest the map, then nodded his agreement. "This is it, isn't it? The van we've been searching for."

"I think so."

Tyler closed his eyes, let his frustration wash over him. "If only the locals had called us when they were with the van, and not waited until the end of their shift to ring the results through."

---

It took Lionel Eberhard a few seconds to reach the ringing telephone. "Hello?" he answered cautiously. He didn't receive many calls, and those he did get tended to be from unwelcome sources, like his probation officer or the Public Protection Unit at Chingford police station, calling to check up on him and making sure that he was complying with the terms of his licence.

*"Good morning, Lionel! Today's the day the magic happens. Are you looking forward to your afternoon of fun?"*

Recognising the voice as that of a friend, Eberhard relaxed. "Hello, Benny. Yes, I'm very excited. I can't wait to receive my special delivery this afternoon." His face lit up as he thought about it, and he became conscious of a stirring in his loins.

At the other end of the line, Benny's laugh was gravelly, the result of a lifetime of chain smoking. *"Good, good, good! We're getting the merchandise ready as we speak, and I'll ring you later to let you know it's on its way. For your information, Joey will be your delivery driver today, and he'll be in a blue Berlingo van."*

"Excellent, I'll keep a look out for it."

After hanging up, Eberhard performed a one man conga

around his living room, humming the theme tune as he danced. The conga continued into the hallway and up the stairs.

Eberhard opened the door to the master bedroom and peered inside. He had changed his usual dour bedding in preparation for the chicken's arrival, replacing the grey duvet for one covered with bright cartoon superheroes. He had also put up some child friendly posters to make the boy feel more relaxed. Postman Pat, Fireman Sam, and Bob the Builder now adorned the walls. Downstairs, the fridge was stocked with cans of soda; brand names, not the cheap supermarket alternatives he usually purchased for himself. There was a large tub of Cornish ice cream in the freezer, and a dozen bags of crisps in the cupboard; he hadn't known what flavours the chicken liked, so he had purchased a selection. He desperately wanted to be a good host, and he planned to spoil his young guest rotten before taking him up to bed and ruining his life forever.

---

"Benny's phone was just active again," Parker reported as Tyler passed through the main office on his way back from the loo. "It's still in Leytonstone."

Tyler thanked him. Returning to his office, he closed the door and sat in broody silence, mulling over what he knew about the people they were dealing with.

Benny Mars, the late Maurice Hinkleman, Joey McQueen and Aaron Remus formed the backbone of a sadistic paedophilic gang who disgustingly referred to themselves as a wolfpack.

According to Gabriel Warren, they targeted vulnerable children who arrived in London from the home counties and distant shires. Initially keeping the wayward boys for their own perverse amusement, they then mercilessly pimped the abused youngsters out to all and sundry once the novelty wore off.

That had certainly been the fate of Adam Cheadle, the twelve year old found in Epping Forest the previous day. Cheadle had been reported missing from a care home in Hastings two months earlier and had no family to speak of; no one to mourn his untimely passing, no one to miss him. He had died as he had lived; lonely and alone.

Gabriel Warren would make a very credible witness, Tyler decided, having read the transcript of his interview from last night. In addition to putting Mars squarely in the frame for Adam's murder, he provided compelling evidence against McQueen and Hinkleman for imprisoning Adam against his will and administering the noxious substance that rendered him unconscious.

The fly in the ointment was that Warren was suspected of murdering Hinkleman. If he ended up being charged, it would cast massive doubts over his suitability and reliability as a prosecution witness. Would the CPS, who were very sensitive about such things, be prepared to weather the storm and rely on his testimony under those circumstances?

Tyler wasn't so sure that they would.

At least there was some corroborating evidence, which might swing things in their favour. By a stroke of good fortune, McQueen had been stopped in close proximity to Adam's deposition site at the relevant time, and this supported Warren's allegation no end.

It was a great pity that the officers conducting the stop hadn't seized the shovel and carpet from the Daimler's boot, but it was easy to say that with the benefit of hindsight. In their shoes, Tyler doubted he would have done anything differently. He allowed himself a cynical laugh as he calculated the odds of the shovel and carpet still being inside the Daimler's boot when they finally got their hands on it?

Not great, he suspected.

Grabbing the latest cluster of telephone reports, he flipped through them until he found McQueen's call log for the night that Adam's body was disposed of. Interestingly, there were six missed calls from Benny, followed by a single, very short call from McQueen to Benny.

Tyler dug out the intelligence report relating to McQueen's stop. To his surprise, McQueen had been stopped at exactly the same time as his short call to Benny concluded. Had he terminated the conversation because the uniform boys were giving him a tug?

A good barrister might be able to convince a jury that he had.

Tyler moved onto the cell site report. McQueen's phone had been stationary in Epping Forest for all six missed calls. He knew this because the azimuth hadn't changed. However, by the time McQueen called Benny back, his handset had moved to the adjacent azimuth. Benny's handset, on the other hand, had been cell sited within the same azimuth, one that covered the flat in Hackney, for all seven calls.

Tyler wondered what the calls had been about. Had Benny been checking up on McQueen to make sure the body had been buried? It would certainly make sense. If nothing else, the call data provided further corroboration for Warren's account.

Tyler thought about the flat in Hackney, where Adam had been murdered.

According to the electoral register, Benny Mars was the sole occupant. Checks with Land Registry had confirmed that he owned the property, having purchased it under the 'Right to Buy' scheme five years earlier. That tied in with the date that his car had first been registered at the address with the DVLA.

Tyler was convinced that the flat was exactly what Warren claimed it was; a staging post for the vulnerable young boys Benny's paedophile gang recruited; somewhere they could bed down for a few days until more suitable accommodation was found closer to the West End. From there, they would be put to work as rent boys and mercilessly exploited.

George Copeland had found a locked cupboard in one of the two smaller bedrooms. It had been jemmied open to reveal a stack of video recorders. There had also been three small monitors, one for each of the hidden cameras installed in the master bedroom. Upon being told about the setup, Tyler's first thought had been that Mars liked to film the homosexual orgies he held there. His second thought had been far more sinister: what if the paedophiles also took the children they snatched to the flat and filmed them being abused? What if the videos were then marketed to likeminded individuals? He had reluctantly asked Jim Stone to view the child porn found at Eberhard's house and compare the background to the master bedroom in Benny's flat.

Was it possible that the obscene video White had described to him had been filmed at the flat?

Was it equally possible that Benny Mars and a couple of his friends were the naked men who featured in it?

Inevitably, Tyler's mind returned to Peter and Gavin. Where were they? Were they even alive? Resting his elbows on his desk, he buried his face in his hands, closed his eyes.

*Hampton Road...*

The words just popped into his mind.

Local officers had spotted the Berlingo in Hampton Road.

Every call to and from Remus' handset had been pinged in the azimuth covering Hampton Road.

Peter's abductor had been within the azimuth covering Hampton Road when he listened to the voicemail message Tyler had left him.

Benny's phone was now being pinged within the azimuth covering Hampton Road.

Tyler's thoughts were interrupted by a musical rap on his door, and he opened his eyes just as Dillon entered.

"Did I wake you?" the big man asked.

Tyler smiled ruefully, then shook his head. "No, I was just running everything through my head, and it helps me to concentrate when my eyes are closed."

Dillon sat down opposite him, pulled his tie loose. "Paul Evans just rang in to say that both support cars are ground assigned. Unless one of the suspect's phones goes live and the detector vans get a lock on it, there's nothing for them to do, so I told them to start cruising the side streets in case one of the vehicles we're interested in turns up."

Tyler was tempted to send everyone to the general area; flood it with coppers in the hope of stumbling across the Daimler or the Berlingo. He weighed up the pros and cons, trying to decide if he really wanted to put all his eggs into one basket.

"Oh-oh!" Dillon said, staring at him apprehensively.

"What's the matter?" Tyler asked, snapping out of his trance.

"You're the bloody matter," Dillon told him. "You've got that worrying look in your eyes again, the one I don't like."

"What look?" Tyler demanded, wondering what his friend was rambling on about.

"*The look*! The one that says you're about to get me running around like a madman!"

Tyler smiled; he couldn't help it, for that was exactly what he was about to do.

"Dill, round up every available person you can find, and tell them to start making their way over to Leytonstone to help search for Benny's Daimler and that bloody Berlingo van. I've got a couple of quick calls to make, then I'll meet you down in the back yard. We might as well give them a hand, too, and we'll start off by checking out Hampton Road."

"See," Dillon complained, as he pushed himself out of the chair. "Shit like this always happens when you give me *the look*!"

## 34

What's your problem?

Peter removed the soft fluffy towel from around his waist and hung it on one of the hooks protruding from the bathroom door. He had to go up on tiptoe to reach it. His emaciated body was pale and pasty. He had always been thin, but when he ran a finger down his ribs, he was surprised at how much skinnier he was now than when he'd first arrived.

Peter tugged open the shower cubicle door and stepped inside. The glass sides were completely steamed up so he rubbed a little circle in one of them so that he could keep an eye on the door.

He smiled with delight as the hot water bombarded his skin, rinsing away all the dirt and grime that had accumulated while he'd been locked up in the filthy cell. His face, when he'd caught a glimpse of it in the bathroom cabinet mirror beforehand, had resembled one of the chimney sweeps from the *Mary Poppins* film.

There were bottles of shampoo and body wash in the shower tray. He squeezed a liberal amount of the former into his hand, then began working the lather into his scalp, being careful not to get any of the soapy suds in his eyes.

Dull wintery daylight filtered in through the bathroom window, but Peter had no idea whether it was morning or afternoon, having lost all track of time during his incarceration.

The soldier man hadn't spoken when he'd collected Peter from the cell a few minutes earlier. He had just marched Peter up two flights of stairs in angry silence before directing him into the bathroom. With a face like thunder, he had fiddled with the shower controls to get the temperature right, then draped a fluffy towel over the side of the bath. Speaking for the first time, the soldier man had brusquely ordered Peter to strip naked and dump all his soiled clothing into a black plastic bin liner he was holding out.

"But what will I do for clothes?" Peter had asked, worried.

"You'll be given new clothes after you've showered," his captor had snapped, glowering angrily at Peter as he spoke.

Not wanting to antagonise him, Peter had complied without further protest.

After rinsing his hair, Peter scrubbed his body with the pleasant smelling shower gel. Turning the shower off, he stepped out and wrapped the extra-large bath towel around his shoulders.

He had just finished drying himself when the door opened. Instead of the soldier man, a stooped, elderly man in a crumpled grey suit breezed in without knocking. A bundle of folded clothing was tucked under one scrawny arm.

Peter drew the towel tighter around himself, wondering who the stranger was. The elderly man had bulging eyes and a lined face. His greying hair was slicked back with gel, and he smelled strongly of cigarette smoke and body odour.

"Do you feel better for that?" he asked, smiling cheerfully.

Peter nodded, slowly, mistrustingly.

"My name's Benny," the man said, offering a claw like hand, the fingers of which were stained yellow with nicotine.

Awkwardly holding onto his towel with one hand, Peter accepted the hand with reluctance, gave it a little shake and released it as soon as he could. Hoping the man wouldn't notice, he wiped the hand he'd used on his towel.

"Now then," Benny said, handing the bundle of clothes over to Peter. "Why don't you try these on for size?"

Peter accepted the offering.

"There's a good lad," Benny beamed, staring down at him like a proud grandfather. "When you're dressed, go outside and Aaron will take you to your new bedroom."

Peter nodded, obediently, wondering who Aaron was.

When he stepped outside a few minutes later, now dressed in the clean grey tracksuit and white trainers, he found the soldier man waiting for him. "Are you Aaron?" he asked, thinking that he should probably check this in case he was supposed to wait for someone else.

"Follow me," the soldier man – who was also apparently Aaron – said, crooking a finger at him. He led Peter to the other end of the landing, stopping outside a heavy wooden door. "Right, wait in there," he ordered, standing aside to wave Peter in.

The room was lavishly decorated with velvety red wallpaper and a thick cream carpet. The king sized bed had massive pillows on it, and there were vases of fresh flowers on each of the bedside tables.

Peter was surprised to see that the entire ceiling was covered with mirrors. He couldn't figure out why anyone would do something like that, it was pointless and silly.

The room only had one window, but it was large, taking up most of the far wall. He crossed to it, intending to raise the black roller blinds and let in some daylight. Except they weren't blinds at all; the window had been boarded up and the wood had been painted black. That struck him as even odder than having mirrors on the ceiling.

Peter noticed a door to the left of the bed, but it was closed. "What's in there?" he asked, indicating the door with a little jut of his chin.

"That's the en suite," the soldier man told him. "I'll unlock it as soon as our guest arrives."

Peter frowned at that. He thought this was going to be his new room. Was he going to have to share it with someone else? If so, there was only one bed, so where would the other person sleep?

"When can I go home?" Peter asked.

"Don't worry, this will be your last day with us," the soldier man informed him, grinning in the way that people sometimes did when they knew something you didn't.

"But—"

"Shush," the soldier man cut him off. "Just so you know, this room is completely soundproofed, so you can shout and scream all you want but no one will be able to hear you. You can't open the window, so don't bother trying. If you do as you're told, and only if, you'll be allowed to go home later. If you play up, you'll be beaten until you bleed, then put back in your cell and left to rot. Do you understand what I'm saying?"

Peter did understand, but he wasn't sure he believed, at least not the bit about being allowed to go home; he had no trouble believing the other bit, about being beaten and returned to his cell.

"Yes," he said, sullenly. "I understand perfectly."

---

The tube carriage was almost empty, which was rather nice. Madeley hated travelling on the underground when it was packed, rubbing shoulders with all the dross, and having to put up with them coughing and sneezing all over him. He chose one of the bench seats. The doors slid shut with a soft hydraulic hiss, and a moment later, the eastbound Central Line train pulled out of St. Paul's station with a small jolt.

Madeley was so excited by what lay ahead that he couldn't bring himself to sit still. He crossed, then uncrossed his legs, then brushed an imaginary speck of dust from his knee. He put his leather briefcase, which had his initials neatly engraved into it, onto the seat next to him, then thought better of it and placed it on his lap.

He took a deep breath, closed his eyes and tried to relax, but that proved impossible. He couldn't believe this was really happening, that he was about to meet the boy of his dreams. He had spent the past couple of days obsessively fantasising about the child, and the thought of them finally being together brought a rush of blood to his manhood.

---

Gavin had fretted non-stop since the soldier man took Peter from their cell without an explanation. He had been convinced that something dreadful was going to happen to his best friend. Now the soldier man had returned for him.

"W–where's Peter? When's he coming back?"

"Shut up and follow me."

Gavin followed him out of the cell. Instead of turning right, towards the toilet, they went left. Gavin had never been that way before.

Upon reaching a staircase, the soldier man indicated that Gavin should go first. "Go all the way up," he ordered, giving Gavin a shove in the back.

Quivering with fear, Gavin ascended the stairs to the top floor of the house, acutely aware that his captor was right behind him. To his surprise, he was shown into a bathroom and told to remove his soiled clothes and take a shower.

"You need to make yourself presentable," the soldier man told him as he left the room. "I'll be outside when you've finished."

While he was drying himself, a stinky old man came in and gave him some new clothes to wear. There was something creepy about the man; the way he looked at Gavin made his flesh crawl.

When Gavin emerged from the bathroom, he found the soldier man waiting for him.

"Follow me," he growled, heading for the stairs.

Gavin hesitated; having seen daylight for the first time in ages, he was dreading being returned to his cell.

"Come on, Spineless," the soldier man said, impatiently.

"But–"

"Get your lardy arse over here before I lose my temper," the soldier man snapped.

Tears prickled at Gavin's eyes, but he did as he was told.

Instead of taking him back down to his cell, the soldier man led him through to the ground floor kitchen at the back of the house. Two men were sitting there; the old man who had given him new clothes, and another who seemed to be about the same age as the soldier man.

Gavin eyed them warily.

The old man had a cigarette on the go. He stood up as soon as Gavin entered, and shuffled forward to greet him. "I didn't introduce myself upstairs, but my name's Benny." He placed a blotchy hand on Gavin's shoulder and gave it a little squeeze, then nodded towards the seated figure. "And this is Joey."

Gavin tried to back away, but Benny dug his fingers deeper into his shoulder, halting him.

Gavin winced. "You're hurting me."

Joey laughed at his discomfort. "Don't be such a pathetic little wimp," he mocked.

Benny returned to his seat. "Don't be so hard on the boy, he's got a busy day ahead of him."

Both men laughed, as if sharing a private joke.

As Gavin massaged his aching shoulder, he noticed a large polycarbonate suitcase lying in the middle of the floor. "What's that for?" he asked, staring down at it.

"We're going to give your parents a big surprise," Benny told him. "You like surprises, don't you?"

Gavin nodded, cautiously.

"Good! Here's what's going to happen. You're going to get inside the case, and then me and Joey will drive you back to your parents' house. Imagine the look on their faces when they open it and find you inside?"

Gavin swallowed hard. He liked the idea of surprising his parents, but he wasn't good with enclosed spaces, and the thought of being stuck inside the suitcase made him feel very panicky.

He shook his head.

"What's the matter?" Benny's voice had hardened, become accusatory. "Don't you want to make your parents happy?"

Gavin was becoming flustered. "I–"

"For fuck's sake," Joey said, levering himself out of the spindle backed chair. "You're going in that case whether you like it or not, so stop snivelling and get on with it."

Gavin looked down at the empty case, blanching. "But I won't be able to breathe in there," he protested.

Benny came over and knelt beside the case, wincing as his ageing knees cracked loudly. "Yes, you will," he said, firmly but kindly. "Look, we've drilled loads of air holes in it for you," he pointed to them with a bony forefinger. "And you'll only have to stay inside the case for a few minutes at a time, first while we carry it from here to the van, and then again when we reach your parents' address."

"I don't want to," Gavin whined.

Reaching out, Benny tenderly ran his fingers through Gavin's tousled hair. Then, quick as a flash, he grabbed his chin, forcing the startled boy to look directly at him. "You wouldn't want to disappoint your parents, would you?"

Tears rolled down Gavin's cheeks. "No," he murmured.

"Good lad," Benny said, releasing Gavin's chin.

Benny reached into his suit jacket. His hand reappeared a moment later, holding a big bar of chocolate, which he dangled in front of Gavin's face.

Gavin's eyes widened with desire. He hadn't been given any treats since he'd been kidnapped. Without thinking, he reached out for the bar, then hesitated, his fingers stopping millimetres away.

"Go on," Benny enticed.

As Gavin grabbed for the chocolate, Benny snatched his hand back out of reach.

Joey laughed.

Gavin's face fell, and he looked questioningly at the old man, as if to say, 'but you told me I could have it!'

Benny grinned. "Don't worry, it's all yours," he assured the boy. "But only if you agree to get into the case for us."

Gavin looked up at him, then at the bar of chocolate, then down at the case. He frowned for a moment, his tormented expression reflecting his inner dilemma, then he nodded and grabbed the chocolate.

---

Lionel Eberhard examined his reflection in the bathroom mirror. He tugged at his freshly shaven jowls, then at the loose skin beneath his eyes. There was no doubt about it, he was starting to get a little saggy in places. Perhaps he should consider a little nip and tuck procedure, to make himself look younger? He had watched a programme on plastic surgery the previous evening, and had been amazed by the transformations it could achieve.

Humming to himself, he removed a bottle of Dior Fahrenheit from the bathroom cabinet and splashed a liberal amount over his face. As an afterthought, he also put a dab behind each ear and a little splash on his wrists. Sniffing the air around him, he smiled approvingly.

Returning to his bedroom, Eberhard examined the red velvet smoking jacket and white silk scarf he had laid out on the bed, confident that he would look resplendent in the suave, stylish outfit.

On checking his watch, he saw that time was getting away from him. His very special guest would be arriving within the hour, and he still had so much to do before then. Grabbing a pair of black formal trousers from their hanger on the wardrobe door, he struggled into them. They seemed much tighter than the last time he had worn them, and he vowed to go on a diet after tonight's indulgence.

---

McQueen parked the van with both nearside wheels up on the pavement. Turning his hazard lights on, he checked that the rear wheels were clear of the zebra crossing's zig-zag lines, then jogged back to the house. It was a very busy road, and he was keen to get the chicken away before a passing lorry sideswiped the van, or worse, a passing police patrol stopped to ticket it.

Inside the kitchen, Benny was down on his knees, zipping the case up. The chicken's muffled mewling could be heard from inside.

"Just take deep breaths and relax," Benny soothed the panicked boy. "You won't be in there for long. Joey's just got back with the van, and we're going to carry you straight out to it. Once you're inside, I'll let you out until we reach your parents' house."

As he spoke, he looked up at Joey and rolled his eyes.

They worked together to stand the suitcase up, then carried it between them along the hall, out of the front door and along the street to the van.

The chicken started whinging that the swinging motion was making him feel sick. Luckily, there was so much road noise from passing traffic that the chances of anyone hearing the boy were negligible.

McQueen opened the van's back doors, and they tossed the case into the back, ignoring the chicken's cries of pain. Sweating profusely from the exertion, Benny awkwardly climbed into the back with him, assisted in by McQueen.

As McQueen pulled away, the driver of a beat-up box van travelling in the opposite direction gave him a funny look.

Had the idiot thought McQueen was going to cut him up?

Probably.

## 35

*That was then and this is now*

Behind the wheel of the TSU detector van, DS Jerry Gallagher's jaw dropped as he read the registration number of the blue Citroen van that had just pulled away from the opposite kerb. The sighting was so unexpected that it took him a moment to process the information, and by then, it had driven past him.

"Fuck!" he cursed, snapping out of his stupor and looking for somewhere to spin around in. A junction was coming up on his left so he indicated to turn into it, then saw it was a no entry. "Fuck," he cursed again, louder this time.

"What's the matter?" his engineer called from the back, where he was monitoring all the electrical equipment.

Gallagher briefly considered stopping dead and performing a three-point-turn, before realising that the lumbering lorry sitting on his tailpipe would probably plough straight into the back of him if he tried doing that.

With a sinking feeling, Gallagher caught a last fleeting glance of the Berlingo in his wing mirror as it disappeared around a bend in the road.

"FUCK!" he yelled a final time, thumping the steering wheel in frustration.

"Are you gonna tell me what's going on or not?" an agitated plea from his engineer, who hated being left out of anything.

There was another junction coming up. Gallagher signalled left and stood on the brakes. Behind him, the lorry driver leaned heavily on his horn.

The sharp left turn sent his faithful engineer, Stan, toppling sideways out of his seat. "Bloody Nora!" he shouted, hanging on to the worktop for dear life. "Where did you get your bleeding driving licence, Jerry, out of a cornflakes box?"

By the time Gallagher had circled the block, the Berlingo was long gone. Cursing under his breath, he scooped up his radio and toggled the mic. "All units from DS Gallagher, we've just sighted the Berlingo heading west along Grove Green Road towards Leyton High Road. The driver's an IC1 male, and I'm almost certain it's Joey McQueen."

The radio squawked into life almost immediately. "*Jerry, have you still got it in sight?*" The voice belonged to DCI Tyler, and he was having to shout to make himself heard above his vehicle's siren.

"No, negative," Gallagher said. "We were travelling in the other direction, and by the time I turned around, it was long gone."

"*Received.*" That was Tyler again, sounding miffed. "*All units from DCI Tyler, make your way towards Leyton High Road to start searching for it.*"

---

Sitting uncomfortably on a vibrating wheel arch, Benny wedged his body against the side of the van and placed a foot on top of the suitcase to prevent it from sliding around. "Turn the heating up," he shouted to McQueen. "It's bloody freezing back here."

Inside the suitcase, the chicken was becoming increasingly vocal, crying out every time they went over a bump or down a pothole.

"Quiet!" Benny barked, whacking the case with the heel of his shoe.

There was a frightened whimper from within, followed by the sound of very quiet sobbing.

Benny pulled his mobile phone from his overcoat pocket and dialled Eberhard's number to let him know that his special delivery was on its way.

---

Remus felt aggrieved as he climbed the stairs to the first floor landing. He could put up with Benny ordering him to shave the bumfluff from his face and tie his hair back into a ponytail, but the old man was taking liberties by making him wear the cheap, ill-fitting grey suit he had acquired from one of the many charity shops dotted along Leytonstone High Road. The garment hung listlessly on his slim frame. It was far too wide in the body, and an inch too short in both the sleeves and the trousers. Without the belt he was wearing, the trousers would have slid straight down to his ankles. Remus felt stupid, and it angered him that Benny was willing to humiliate him by making him dress like a chauffeur, just to impress a client.

Unlocking the door to the master bedroom, he found Troublemaker slouching on the massive bed. Startled by his sudden appearance, the boy sat bolt upright in alarm.

"Come over here," Remus ordered, beckoning for him to get off the bed.

Troublemaker stood up, approached with great reluctance. "What are you going to do to me?" he demanded, in that feisty manner of his.

"Hold out your hands," Remus instructed, extending his own in front of his chest, with the wrists close together, to demonstrate the exact position he wanted the boy to adopt.

With a frown, Troublemaker did as he'd been told.

Remus thought it was the first time the brat had ever complied with an order without questioning it. He produced a pair of padded handcuffs, then threaded the short chain linking them through a D shaped holding bar that protruded from the wall. It was a good inch thick, made from solid steel, and secured by large bolts. "Put your hands in these."

"But—"

"Just do it!" Remus snapped, annoyed that the boy's compliance without questioning routine hadn't lasted very long.

Giving him a hateful glare, Troublemaker held out his left wrist, then his right while Remus clamped the handcuffs around them. He checked to make sure they were nice and tight, but not so tight as to cut off the chicken's circulation.

"Right," Remus said, staring at the now shackled boy with a malicious smile. "Sit down and behave yourself till I get back. And remember, not only is this room soundproofed, but the door and windows are securely bolted, so don't waste your time and energy by trying to escape or calling for help."

"Where exactly am I supposed to sit?" Troublemaker asked, as objectionable as ever. He was too far away from the bed to sit on that, and there were no chairs in the room.

Remus grinned. "On the floor."

Troublemaker sat down, but with his hands cuffed to the holding bar, this required him to keep his arms extended high over his head. "This is really uncomfortable," he complained. "Why can't you just get me chair to sit on?"

"Because I don't want to," Remus replied, with a sadistic smile.

Locking the door behind him, Remus descended the stairs, where he shrugged himself into the drab overcoat that Benny had also provided for him. It was old and mottled, and it smelled of mothballs, but it was far too cold to forego wearing a coat, so it would have to do.

Remus grabbed the Daimler's keys from the sideboard and stormed out of the house, slamming the street door behind him.

"Jerry, one of the phones just went live," Stan called from the back of the detector van.

"Which one?" Gallagher asked, excitedly.

"Benny Mars," Stan shouted back. "It's pinging in Leyton High Road. Looks like it's travelling around the one-way system by Church Road and heading towards the Bakers Arms."

Having started his career as a PC at Leyton, Gallagher knew the area reasonably well. He set a course for the Bakers Arms. "How far ahead of us would you say the handset is?"

"Hard to say," Stan replied, not wanting to commit himself. "And the call's just been terminated, which means I can't zero in on its location anymore."

Gallagher vented his frustration in a lengthy sigh. Stan was a top rate engineer, but he had an annoying habit of sitting on the fence when you needed him to give a firm opinion. "I promise I won't berate you *too* much if you're wrong."

Stan chuckled. "In that case, I reckon it was about half a mile ahead of us, but that was then and this is now."

"Meaning?"

"Meaning it could have turned off by now, and be heading in a completely different direction."

"Bloody hell, Stan! Why do you always have to be so negative?"

"I'm cautious, not negative," Stan corrected him.

"How fast was the signal moving?"

Stan responded with an overly theatrical sigh. "Jerry, I'm tracking its satellite signal when it makes and receives calls, not using a radar gun to work out its sodding speed!"

Gallagher dragged a hand across his face. This was like getting blood from a stone. "I just need to know whether the handset was moving fast, like its owner was in a vehicle, or slow, like its owner was on foot."

Stan considered this. "Well, it could have been in a slow moving vehicle or in the pocket of someone who walks really, really fast," he cogitated.

There. Clear as mud!

"Well, this is like Groundhog Day," Dillon complained as he guided the BMW along Grove Green Road. They had driven the length of Hampton Road first, hoping to spot the Daimler, but there had been no sign of it, so they were now checking the surrounding streets. They sat in comfortable silence for a few seconds, then Dillon sighed thoughtfully. "Do you think we'll find those kids alive, Jack?"

"I honestly don't know, Dill," Tyler confessed, wishing that he felt more optimistic. "We finally know who we're looking for, and I'm confident that we'll catch them before too long, but will we be in time to save those poor kids?" He performed a heavy shrug. "I really wish I knew."

---

Benny had been forced to cut short his call to Eberhard because the chicken was having a panic attack, and his caterwauling had drowned out their conversation.

Pocketing his phone, Benny gave in and he unzipped the case.

The boy sprang up like a Jack-in-the-Box, trying to scrabble free, but Benny was too quick for him. He grabbed the chicken's collar and yanked him back down into a sitting position.

The boy raised his hands in subjugation, wailing, "Please don't hurt me."

His face was flushed; tears streamed from his puffy eyes, and yellow snot leaked from both nostrils.

"For fuck's sake," Benny snarled. "What's the client going to think if you turn up looking like that?" He took a deep breath, forcing himself to calm down. "Look, I'm sorry you were left in the suitcase for so long, but you're out now so let's get you cleaned up."

The boy was still sobbing, but at least he had stopped struggling.

Benny reached into his pocket and withdrew a packet of tissues. "Blow your nose and wipe your eyes," he instructed, tossing them onto the boy's lap. "You can stay out of the case till we get there, as long as you behave."

Benny's phone rang.

It was Madeley, calling with the news that he was one stop away from Leytonstone. Benny assured him that his limo would be waiting for him, and hung up.

The chicken had blown his nose and wiped his eyes, and was looking slightly more presentable.

"What do you want me to do with these?" he asked, holding the soiled tissues up for Benny's inspection.

Benny hated stupid questions. "Just toss them in the case," he said with forced civility. Turning his back on the child, he dialled Remus' number. "Aaron, it's me. Where are you?"

"*I'm parked outside the tube station.*"

"Which one?" Benny asked. He wouldn't have put it past the idiot to go to the wrong one.

"*Leytonstone, obviously!*" Remus said, performing the verbal equivalent of an eye roll.

"Well, don't just sit there, you moron," Benny snapped. "Go inside and meet Mr Madeley."

"*But I don't know what he looks like,*" Remus protested.

Benny pinched the bridge of his nose. "He's a sixty something year old barrister with silver hair. He's posh, so he'll probably be wearing a bowler hat and pinstripe suit, carrying a briefcase and an umbrella. How many people like that do you think will be getting off the train at bloody Leytonstone?"

There was a moment's silence, before Remus said, "*Could be loads,*" with no conviction whatsoever.

"Christ!" The word exploded from Benny's mouth. "Sometimes, you can be as thick as shit, Aaron! It's a wonder you can even manage to get dressed on your own! Go and find Madeley and ring me back when you've got him."

He hung up, shaking his head in despair.

The chicken was watching him, fearfully.

"What do you think you're looking at?" he barked, causing the boy to flinch.

Up front, McQueen had just switched the radio on, and Benny instantly recognised the catchy intro from *Getting Away With It*.

"Turn the volume up," he shouted forward. "I like this one."

McQueen obliged, and Benny allowed himself a contented smile as he hummed along.

This song could have been his anthem, he decided. He had been getting away with it all his life. He was still getting away with it, and he didn't intend for that trend to change any time soon.

## 36

Please don't say that

Tyler's mobile chirped into life. The call was from a withheld number, which probably meant it was someone at the office. "DCI Tyler."

"*Boss, it's Reggie. The TIU have just called me to report a little flurry of activity on Benny's phone.*"

Sitting bolt upright, Tyler flipped open the daybook on his lap. "Tell me everything," he demanded.

The tension in his voice alerted Dillon, who gave him a sideways look of anticipation.

Tyler mouthed, "Benny's phone has been active."

He put the call on speaker, so that Dillon could follow it.

"*Over the past few minutes, Benny's received one call and made two of his own,*" Parker told him. "*He's just come off the phone to Remus. The other calls, one outgoing and one incoming, connected to the two numbers he was in contact with earlier in the day. I'm still waiting for the subscriber check results to come back on them.*"

"Where does the cell siting place the handsets?" Tyler asked.

"*It looks like Benny's handset is moving towards Walthamstow,*" Parker said. "*Interestingly, one of the two unknown numbers it's been in contact with was bouncing off a mast covering part of Walthamstow, so I wonder if Benny's heading over to meet the owner? The other phone is…*" There was a pause while Parker consulted the printout. "*Oh, this is interesting. At the start of the call, the handset was pinged by a mast in Stratford, but by the time it finished, the handset had moved to the next mast along, which is in Leyton.*"

"What about Remus?" Tyler asked. "Is his handset in its usual location?"

Parker flicked through more papers, muttering away to himself. "*Yes, it looks like it's within the same azimuth it's always pinged in.*"

An unpleasant idea had started to germinate in Tyler's mind. "Reg, let me run a scenario by you. A little while ago, Jerry Gallagher spotted McQueen driving the Berlingo along Grove Green Road towards Leyton. There was no one in the front with him, so we all assumed he was alone, but what if he wasn't? What if Benny was in the back of the van?"

"*Why would Benny travel in the back of the van when he could sit up front with McQueen?*" Parker asked, sounding dubious.

Tyler could feel a headache coming on. He really didn't want to be right about this, but the more he thought about it, the more convinced he became that he was onto something. "Well, the obvious reason is that the bastards are taking one or both of the kids to a client."

Parker considered this. "*It's possible,*" he conceded. "*I mean, if Benny and McQueen are on their way to drop one of the kids off, it would make sense for Remus to remain at the house with the other one.*"

"In which case, the other unknown number could belong to a different client who's making his way to the house in Leytonstone in order to collect the second boy."

Parker groaned, despairingly. "*Bloody hell, guv. Please don't say that.*"

Tyler dry washed his face. "Reg, get onto the TIU. Explain our fears to them, and make sure they understand that we need those subscriber results urgently. Ring me the second you hear anything."

"That didn't sound good," Dillon said as Tyler hung up. "If you're right, there's no way we'll be able to find those boys in time."

---

Gallagher had almost reached the Bakers Arms junction when Stan shouted that Benny's handset was active again.

"Where is it now?" Gallagher yelled, tightening his grip on the steering wheel.

"Looks like it's in Hoe Street, up near Walthamstow Central."

"Who's he calling?"

There was a brief pause while Stan checked. "He's the one being called, and it's the number attributed to Aaron Remus."

Up ahead, the traffic lights turned red. Like falling dominos, the brake lights of the cars in front of them came on one after the other.

The phasing of the Bakers Arms lights was notoriously slow, and Gallagher was acutely aware that, if he waited for them to cycle back to green, they might lose contact with Benny's phone.

Hoping it wouldn't end in disaster, he dropped a gear and floored the accelerator.

"What are you doing?" Stan's worried voice called from the back.

Gallagher ignored him. Steering the van onto the wrong side of the road, he accelerated past the now stationary row of cars. Ignoring the red light, he drove straight through the busy four way junction, half expecting to be T-boned before he reached the other side.

The blaring of horns came from every direction.

A car coming from his right broadsided to avoid smashing into the side of the van. Luckily, it stopped without hitting anything, as did the cars following behind it.

"Sorry!" Gallagher called out, knowing he wouldn't be heard but feeling obliged to make the apology.

"You bleeding maniac!" Stan yelled from behind.

A moment later, they were hurtling along Hoe Street. "Where's Benny's handset now?" Gallagher demanded.

"It's passing the turning for the High Street... No, cancel that! It's just turned right into Church Hill."

They made good progress until they reached Queens Road, at which point they hit a solid wall of traffic. Gallagher's heart sank; without blues and twos, there was no way he could forge a path through that lot.

There was a sanctimonious snort from behind. "Tell me, Jerry. Was it really worth driving like a maniac, and risking both our lives back there, just to end up in a traffic jam thirty seconds later?"

Gritting his teeth to avoid saying something he might later regret, Gallagher grabbed his mobile phone from the dash and dialled Tyler's number.

---

McQueen pulled up outside the client's house. No sooner had he stopped than the street door opened and Eberhard appeared, wringing his hands together in anticipation and hopping excitedly from foot to foot like a child at Christmas. He was wearing a red velvet smoking jacket, and had a white silk scarf tied around his neck.

"Bloody hell, look at him," McQueen scoffed as he opened the rear doors to let Benny out. "The silly fucker thinks he's Noel Coward."

"I'm surprised you even know who that is," Benny said as he helped McQueen remove the case.

McQueen was offended. "He's the posh bloke who plays Mr Bridger in *The Italian Job*. It's one of my favourite films." Clearing his throat, he treated Benny to a woeful Michael Caine impression. "You were only supposed to blow the bloody doors off!"

"Shut up, and give me a hand to get this case into Lionel's gaff before the chicken kicks off again."

Between them, they lugged the case along the garden path and through the street door.

"Where do you want it?" Benny asked, puffing from the effort.

"In the living room would be perfect," Eberhard told them, leading the way.

After they lowered the case to the floor, Benny stood up, massaging the crick in his back. "I'm definitely getting too old for all this shit."

Eberhard was leaning over the case, rubbing his hands together in anticipation. He seemed excited by the muffled cries from inside.

"Would you like to do the honours, and open it up?" Benny asked.

Eberhard's face lit up. "Oh yes, that would be wonderful." He set about adjusting his jacket and scarf until they were just right. "How do I look?" he asked the others. "I don't want to disappoint him."

"You look great," Benny assured him.

Eberhard beamed at the compliment. "I'm a little nervous," he confided.

"Perfectly understandable," Benny said, wishing he would hurry up and release the chicken so that he and McQueen could leave.

Bending down, Eberhard grabbed the zipper. Looking up at the two men, he licked his lips nervously, then took a deep breath. "Here goes."

As soon as he peeled the lid back, the boy sat up, rubbing tears from his eyes.

"Oh my," Eberhard said, placing a hand across his heart. "He's beautiful."

The boy was crestfallen to see Eberhard staring down at him, and not his parents. "He's not my daddy," he muttered in a tiny, quivering voice.

Eberhard placed two fingers under his chin and gently tilted his head upwards to get a better look at his face. He didn't seem to notice when the boy recoiled from the contact. "I can be whoever you want me to be," he whispered, lustfully.

"Can I take your coat?" Remus offered, after ushering Madeley into the safe house.

The barrister unbuttoned his expensive overcoat and allowed Remus to assist him out of it. Adjusting his shirt cuffs while the younger man hung it up for him, he surveyed his surroundings with disdain. "Where's Benny?" he enquired. "I was told he'd be here to greet me."

Remus adopted what he hoped was a suitably apologetic expression. "He'll be here shortly," he promised. "He's asked me to take care of you until he arrives."

"And the chicken?" Madeley asked, glancing up the stairs. "I presume he's waiting for me up there?"

"That's right, sir."

"I'd like to see him," Madeley said, taking a step towards the stairs. "Would you be kind enough to show me the way?"

Remus moved to block his path. "Begging your pardon, sir, but I'll need to you take a seat in the lounge for a few minutes, while I pop upstairs and make sure that everything's prepared to your satisfaction." He smiled ingratiatingly, to defuse the man's disappointment. "I assure you it won't take long."

Reluctantly, Madeley allowed himself to be guided into the downstairs sitting room.

"Can I get you something to drink while you're waiting?" Remus offered.

"No, thank you," Madeley replied, curtly.

Remus went through to the kitchen. Removing a very expensive bottle of Dom Perignon from the fridge, he plonked it down on a serving tray. Next, he added a long stemmed crystal glass, a box of Belgian chocolates, and a large Cuban cigar. Apparently, it was Madeley's favourite brand.

Remembering that he was to provide a soft drink for the chicken, he grabbed a bottle of pop from the fridge and a plastic cup from the sideboard. Lastly, he added a single red rose, which Benny thought showed a touch of class but Remus thought was laughable.

"Won't be long now, Mr Madeley," he called as he breezed past the lounge on his way to the stairs.

---

Peter's ears pricked up when he heard the street door slam shut downstairs. That meant that the soldier man was back.

A few minutes later, the door to the bedroom opened inwards and the soldier man strode in carrying a silver tray. There was a bottle of wine on it, along with some cola, a massive cigar, some chocolates and, of all things, a red flower.

The soldier man seemed to be in a rush. As soon as he put the tray down, he came over and jabbed Peter in the chest with a bony finger. "Right, you listen here," he growled in his usual threatening manner. "Mr Madeley is a very important man, and he's paid a lot of money to spend time with you, so you make sure you're on your best behaviour and don't do anything to displease him. If you do, you horrible little toad, I'll beat you black and blue, and you won't *ever* be allowed to go home to your parents. Do you understand?"

Peter nodded, fearfully.

Removing a key from his pocket, the soldier man unlocked the padded handcuffs.

Peter rubbed his wrists. They were a little sore, but there were no marks there.

The soldier man barked out an order for Peter to sit on the bed, warning him not move until he returned with their guest, then he left the room, locking the door behind him.

---

"Put your foot down," Benny ordered. "I want to make sure that Mr Madeley's being properly looked after."

"I don't see what you're so worried about," McQueen said. "Not if Aaron's there with him."

"I'm worried *because* Aaron's there with him, you idiot," Benny snapped. "He might be good at disposing of bodies and keeping the rent boys in check, but he can't be trusted to look after an important client like Madeley." He sat there in agitated silence for a few seconds, then pulled out his phone. "Perhaps I should give him a quick call, just to make sure that everything's okay."

---

Tyler's phone rang. It was Gallagher again. "*Guv, we've just pinged Benny's phone in The Drive in Upper Walthamstow. Looks like it's heading towards Shernhall Street. We're stuck in traffic, so can't get near it. I don't suppose you've got any units in the area?*"

Tyler experienced a frisson of excitement. "As it happens, we're not too far from there ourselves," he said, urgently motioning for Dillon to make a right at the lights they were approaching.

---

All the other cars had been called away to search for the Berlingo in Walthamstow, but Tyler had asked Debbie and Kelly to remain in the vicinity of Grove Green Road to assist the second TSU detector van, should it pick anything up from Remus.

Debbie was fine with this, but Kelly, who suspected that Tyler was deliberately trying to keep her away from the action because she was pregnant, had the raging hump about it.

With Kelly stewing in silence beside her, Debbie listened to Magic radio. She was gently strumming the wheel with her fingers and singing along to Kylie Minogue's *Can't Get You Out of My Head*.

When she reached Hampton Road, she turned left rather than continue straight ahead for no other reason other than the turning was there. A few seconds later, they were approaching the junction with Grove Green Road when Kelly stiffened and shouted, "Look, there!"

The Daimler was parked up on their left, no more than ten yards ahead of them.

"Well that definitely wasn't there the last time we drove down this road," Debbie said, drawing level with it.

Kelly was out of the car in an instant, rushing over to the bonnet and placing a hand on it. "It's still warm," she said, excitedly. "It can't have been here very long."

"I'll pull over," Debbie said, "and we'll start knocking on doors to see if we can track down the owner."

## 37

Damn and buggeration!

The Berlingo was trapped in a long line of slow moving vehicles on the approach to the traffic lights at the top of Forest Road. "These poxy lights are a joke," Benny complained, fidgeting restlessly in his seat. The lights changed, and they edged closer to the line.

"With any luck, we should get through next time," McQueen said, trying to mollify him.

Benny stubbed out a cigarette and immediately lit a new one, then blew a thick plume of smoke from the side of his mouth. With the windows wound up to keep out the cold, the cabin was thick with it. "Tell me, why is it that only two or three cars are getting through when we've got a green, but about twenty of the buggers fly past us every time the lights are red against us?" he demanded, as if this were McQueen's fault.

McQueen shrugged, stoically. "There's nothing we can do about it, so I don't see any point in getting stressed."

Benny cuffed him smartly around the head. "Who do you think

you're talking to?" he castigated his bewildered driver, who was giving him the hurt look of someone who doesn't know what they've done wrong. "Tell you what, Joey, when you're running this wolf-pack, you can decide when to and when not to get stressed. Until then, do yourself a favour and shut the fuck up."

The lights changed, and this time they got through.

---

Evans suddenly sat up straight. He pointed at a blue van that had slipped through the lights on amber, and was now turning right into Woodford New Road. "Bloody heck! That's the Berlingo we've all been searching for."

"Are you sure?" Stone asked, craning his neck to get a better view. The van was ten or twelve vehicles ahead of them.

Evans unclipped the mic from its clip on the dashboard. "It'll be miles away by the time we get through these lights. I'll see if anyone else can intercept it."

"We can't just let it go," Stone said, setting his jaw determinedly.

"What else can we do?" Evans snorted. "We're in an unmarked car with no blues and twos."

Switching the headlights on, Stone edged the pool car out of the now stationary line of traffic and started driving along the wrong side of the road towards the traffic lights. He was flashing his headlights and sounding his horn in a steady rhythm to warn oncoming cars of his approach.

"Not sure this is a good idea," Evans said, instinctively reaching for the grab rail above his head.

"You just concentrate on getting us some backup, and let me worry about the driving," Stone retorted.

As he picked up speed, an oncoming car, whose driver had obviously only just noticed them, swerved violently to the nearside.

"Bit of an overreaction, wasn't it?" Stone observed, calmly.

Evans wasn't so sure that it was.

As a punishment for clowning around, Susie Sergeant had lumbered White and Murray with waiting at Benny's shop for the boarding up service. It had taken ages to arrive, and they were only now making their way back to Hertford House. To add insult to injury, they now found themselves stuck in a traffic jam halfway along Lea Bridge Road.

"Well, this hasnae turned out to be the exciting day I was hoping for," White said. Slouched against the passenger window, he was struggling to keep his eyes open.

"It's been a complete blow out so far," Murray agreed.

There was a crackle of static from the radio, then Paul Evans' voice, taut with excitement, burst over the airwaves.

"*All units, we've just spotted the Berlingo. It's turning right, right, right into Woodford New Road from Forest Road.*" In the background, a car horn was tooting away, sending out short, sharp blasts. "*It's heading towards Whipps Cross roundabout. We've managed to get through the lights after it, but it's a long way ahead of us. Is anyone near Whipps Cross to intercept it?*"

Tyler's voice followed almost immediately, all but drowned out by a wailing siren. "*Paul, we're in Forest Road, not far behind you. Keep the commentary going as best you can until we reach you.*"

Another transmission, this one from Dean Fletcher. "*Guv, me and Colin are already at Whipps Cross roundabout, waiting for it.*"

White and Murray exchanged mystified looks. Had they missed an important development while they had been stuck at the sex shop?

"How far away from Whipps Cross are we?" White asked, hoping to get involved.

"Too far," Murray told him, firmly.

White sagged back in his seat, bitterly disappointed. "Damn and buggeration! Why do we always miss out on all the fun?"

---

Dillon was driving the BMW with a ferocity that Tyler hadn't seen before. He was used to Steve Bull driving like Stirling Moss, but the big man was normally far more reserved.

Shooting down the wrong side of the road, forcing oncoming cars to give way, they made rapid progress, and within two minutes of Evans putting up the sighting, they were turning right into Woodford New Road.

"*The van's just passing the turnoff for Snaresbrook,*" Evans issued an update. "*Continuing straight on towards Whipps Cross roundabout…*"

"*We're parked up by the roundabout,*" Fletcher chimed in. "*Stand by, stand by… I've got sight of the van. It's two up. Looks like McQueen's driving, with Mars as his front passenger. We're pulling out directly behind the van… It's turning left, left, left into Whipps Cross Road, travelling towards the Green Man roundabout, current speed twenty-five miles-per-hour.*"

"Looks like you were right about Benny being in the back, earlier," Dillon said, grimly.

Tyler nodded, wishing he hadn't been.

"*Guv, we're only six vehicles behind Dean,*" Evans transmitted. "*Do you want us to try and stop the van?*"

Tyler was about to say yes, when a thought struck him. "Dean, are the suspects aware you're behind them?"

"*I don't think so,*" Fletcher replied, a moment later.

The BMW was almost at the roundabout. "Kill the lights and siren," Tyler instructed.

"Do what?" Dillon asked, shooting him an incredulous look.

"Just do it, Dill!" Tyler ordered. He squeezed the transmit button. "Dean, do not stop them. I repeat, do NOT stop the van. Let's just see where it takes us. With any luck, they'll lead us straight to the house in Leytonstone where the other kid is being held."

Having killed the noise and lights, Dillon slotted seamlessly into the line of traffic. He was giving Tyler an uneasy look. "I hope you know what you're doing, Jack."

"So do I," Tyler confessed.

---

"What are you suddenly so interested in?" Benny asked as McQueen studied his side mirrors intently.

"It might be nothing," McQueen said, still gazing into the mirror.

"What might be nothing?" Benny demanded, irritably. He didn't like his employees being cagey. "Spit it out."

"Well, there was an Astra parked up by the roundabout, which I thought was a bit odd, but then it pulled out directly behind us…"

Benny shrugged. "So?"

"So, it cut another car up to do so, and the two blokes in it look very much like Old Bill to me."

Benny peered into the nearside wing mirror, trying to spot the car McQueen had described. Sure enough, there was an Astra immediately behind them, and it contained two suited men, one white, the other black, but that didn't mean they were… The white male raised a radio to his lips and began speaking into it.

Benny felt his blood run cold. "Pull into the layby with the burger van," he instructed, pointing at the little clearing by Hollow Ponds that was coming up on their left.

McQueen glanced sideways; the order having taken him by surprise. "But–"

"Just do it," Benny snarled. Reaching over, he grabbed the steering wheel and wrenched it to his left.

The back end drifted out as the van swung into the layby, kicking up a spray of loose dirt as it left the road. McQueen stamped on the brakes, and the Berlingo bounced across the uneven earth, suspension protesting, before coming to rest between two parked cars.

"Bloody hell, Benny! You could have killed us." McQueen fumed.

"But I didn't, did I?" Benny said, watching the police Astra pull in after them.

Instead of approaching them, it drove to the other end of the clearing and stopped.

"What now?" McQueen asked, edgily.

"Now, we wait and see what they do," Benny said, staring at the unmarked car.

They sat there for the best part of five minutes, saying nothing.

"I don't like this," Benny eventually said, breaking the strained silence. "Why haven't they given us a tug? They've had plenty of time."

McQueen fidgeted uncomfortably, and it was obvious to Benny that something was weighing heavily on his mind. "Spit it out, then," he instructed. "What's bothering you?"

McQueen shrugged, then fidgeted some more. "I've got a nasty feeling that it's me they're after," he finally confessed.

Benny looked at him, frowning. "What do you mean, Joey? Why would they be interested in you?"

All the colour had drained from McQueen's face. "Maybe they've linked me to Adam's death," he said with a pitiful shrug. "The Old Bill stopped me just after I left the clearing, remember?"

Benny was about to ridicule him for being paranoid when it occurred to him that what McQueen was suggesting actually made a lot of sense. If the police really were looking for McQueen, and they had done their homework properly, they would have worked out that Aaron Remus was his flatmate and that he owned a Berlingo.

"Joey, you *were* careful not to leave any incriminating evidence at the scene, weren't you?" Benny asked casually, so as not to spook McQueen.

McQueen hesitated a moment too long, before nodding without any real conviction.

Benny was suddenly overcome by a powerful urge to distance himself from his lieutenant. "Right, here's what we're going to do," he said, reaching for the door handle. "I'm going to get out and walk away. As soon as I do, I want you to drive off."

"Where to?" McQueen asked, staring at him gormlessly.

"Pop over to the flat in Hackney and stay there until you hear from me."

"But how will you get back if I do that?" McQueen asked, starting to panic at the prospect of being abandoned.

"Don't worry about me," Benny said, dismissing his concern. "I'll get the bus back to Leytonstone and make sure that everything goes smoothly for Madeley, then I'll ring you in a couple of hours to see how you're getting on."

"What about retrieving the chicken from Eberhard's place?" McQueen fretted. "Won't you need the van, and the suitcase?"

"Stop worrying," Benny said, patting his knee. "We're not picking the brat up until late this evening, and with any luck, all the fuss will have blown over by then."

If not, they would purchase another suitcase and take the Daimler.

---

Stebbins made a point of knocking loudly on Craddock's door this time, and then stubbornly waited outside until he was called in.

Craddock looked up from the forensic statement he was engrossed in and frowned at him. "Well, don't just stand there, Frank. Come in, come in," he said, impatiently beckoning his subordinate into the room.

Stebbins inwardly rolled his eyes, thinking that his boss was probably the most contrary person he had ever met. But he was also, without doubt, the best detective that Stebbins had ever known, and that more than made up for his faults.

"I just received the information I requested about Phillip Diggle back from the Met," he said, sliding into the seat Craddock had indicated he should take.

"Have you now, young Frank?" Craddock beamed. He held out an expectant hand.

Stebbins blushed. "I, err, I haven't actually brought my notes in with me," he said, inwardly cursing himself for the oversight.

Craddock's giant eyebrows began undulating, a sure sign of his displeasure. "And why on earth not?" he demanded, shaking his big head in disappointment.

Feeling incredibly stupid, Stebbins wished the ground would open up and swallow him.

"Never mind," Craddock, huffed. "Just tell me the gist of what you've found out about him. You can remember, I take it?"

Cringing with embarrassment, Stebbins nodded. "He's a white male, born in 1965, which makes him…" his voice tailed off as he attempted the mental arithmetic.

"Thirty-six," Craddock said, rolling his eyes at the pitiful sight of his bag man counting with his fingers. "It makes him thirty-six, Frank."

"Yes, thirty-six," Stebbins agreed, sheepishly. "He's never been in trouble with the police, not so much as a parking ticket. I managed to find out his home address, which is in Kent, and his employer details. He works for a company based in London. I managed to get his mobile telephone number from his employers, and I've asked Yvonne to submit a subscriber check. I figured we could get his call history and cell site data for the date of Angus Clifford's murder, and that might place him in Caister."

Craddock gave him a nod of approval. "Well done, young Frank. That was good thinking."

"Do you want me to assemble a team to arrest him?" Stebbins asked, eagerly. He was hoping to get his name down on the charge sheet for this one. It would look good on his résumé.

"Go and get me your notes first," Craddock instructed. "I'd like to see those first. Then I'll be better placed to decide whether we should nab him at work or wait for him to return home."

---

Eberhard stared at the nervous boy sitting across the kitchen table from him. The little gannet had already consumed a large glass of cola and two bags of crisps. Despite his obvious unease at being there, the boy was very well behaved.

For his part, Eberhard was enjoying a glass of wine, to help him relax. "Would you like to take a nice hot bath?"

The chicken shook his head. "No, thank you. I had a shower this morning."

Eberhard frowned. "Are you sure? I always find a nice soak in the bath, with lots of bubbles and a couple of scented candles on the go, very relaxing." He lowered his voice to a conspiratorial whisper. "We could have a bath together, if you'd like? That would be fun."

The boy's expression told him that it really wouldn't.

Eberhard sighed. "Perhaps later, after we've become better acquainted."

"Can I have some more crisps?" the chicken asked, scrunching up the second empty bag.

---

Gareth Madeley was full of nervous anticipation as Remus unlocked the door to the master bedroom and ushered him inside.

The boy was sitting on the bed, but he stood up as soon as the door opened. He was even more beautiful in person than in his photographs, and the sight of the wide-eyed angel standing there, staring up at him imploringly, took the barrister's breath away.

"Can you help me?" the chicken asked, in a voice that made Madeley's knees go weak with desire. "I want to go home to my mum and dad."

Madeley glanced sideways at Remus, who gave him a knowing smile. "I'll leave you two to get better acquainted," he said. "I'll be downstairs if you need me. Remember, the room's soundproofed, so you'll have to ring me on this number." He handed the barrister a plain business card with his name and mobile number scrawled on it.

Mesmerised by the chicken, Madeley took it without looking. A moment later, he heard the door being locked from outside.

"What's your name?" he asked as soon as they were alone. Benny had advised him that it was always better not to know, not to form an attachment, but he couldn't help it. He wanted to know everything about this child before they became intimate.

After a pause, the boy responded, "Peter."

Madeley sat down on the bed, patted the mattress to indicate that Peter should sit next to him.

Peter remained where he was, but when Madeley patted the mattress a second time, more insistently, he reluctantly complied.

"Now," Madeley said, in his most charming voice. "Tell me all about yourself."

---

Debbie and Kelly were actively knocking on doors along Hampton Road, trying to trace the Daimler's owner. Very few people had answered, and they had been met by vacant looks and disinterested shrugs from those who had.

Kelly rapped on the next door she came to.

"Hang on, I'm coming," a female voice called from within. A few seconds later, a middle-aged white woman, with curlers in her hair and a fag hanging from the corner of her mouth, opened the door a crack, and peered out suspiciously. "Whatever you're selling, I'm not interested," she said in a thick Liverpudlian accent.

She made to close the door, but Kelly quickly jammed her foot into the gap, preventing her from doing so. Kelly held up her warrant card for inspection. "I'm a police officer and I'm trying to find out which house that Daimler over there belongs to."

The woman inspected her ID closely, then opened the door to take a look at the car. "I think I've seen it around here a few times before," she said, "but I haven't got a Scooby which house the owner goes to."

Thanking the woman, Kelly met up with Debbie on the pavement outside.

"Any joy?" Debbie asked.

Kelly shook her head, feeling deflated. Pulling out her phone, she rang Tyler. "Jack, I know you're tied up following the Berlingo, but you need to know we've found the Daimler. It's parked up in Hampton Road, near the junction with Grove Green Road."

"*Is anyone with it?*"

"No, but the engine's still warm, so it's not been here long. We've started knocking on doors, but we're having no luck. Is there anyone left at the office who could come down and give us a hand?"

"*I'm sorry, Kelly. The cupboard's empty. Apart from you and Debs, everyone's either tied up with searches or down here with me and Dill.*"

Kelly took a moment to digest that. "Okay, we'll carry on making enquiries here. If we get any leads, we'll radio the locals for backup. What's happening with the two you've got under surveillance?"

"*Not a lot at the moment. They're parked up outside a burger van in Whipps Cross Road. Dean and Colin have eyeball on them. Me and Dill are parked up nearby, as are Jim and Paul. We're hoping they'll lead us back to the house in Leytonstone when they move off. If that's looking likely, you'll have to make yourselves scarce so you don't spook them when they arrive.*"

"Do you want us to back off now, in case Remus sees us and rings them?"

Tyler pondered this for a moment. "*No. Crack on unless you hear otherwise from me.*"

"Will do, but I wish we had a couple of extra people to help out."

"*Jerry Gallagher's on his way back to you. When he gets there, we'll ask the TIU to ping Remus' phone with a fake text. That might help the detector vans to pinpoint the house we want*"

"I'll give him a call, see how long–"

"*Kelly, I've got to go,*" Tyler cut in. "*It's just come over the radio that Mars has got out of the van, and now the bloody thing is driving off without him.*" With that, he hung up on her.

---

Fletcher watched as Benny Mars walked away from the Berlingo, which was already reversing out of its parking space and manoeuvring to turn around. Benny was wearing a Crombie overcoat and an old Trilby hat, and a cigarette was hanging from the side of his mouth in a way that seemed to defy gravity.

"He looks like a shady second hand car salesman," Fletcher scoffed, then reminding himself that Benny traded in young flesh not worn out jalopies, he pressed the transmit button. "Guv, the van is doing a right, right, right into Whipps Cross Road. Do you want us to go after it or stay with Benny?"

377

"*You stay with Mars,*" Tyler instructed. "*We're parked up in St. James Lane, by the ambulance station. We'll pick the van up when it drives past.*"

"*We're parked up in the bus stop at Whipps Cross roundabout,*" Evans transmitted. "*It'll have to go straight past us.*"

Fletcher grabbed his coat from the back seat. "I'll go after chummy on foot," he told Franklin. "You stay in the car. I'll leave the radio here with you, and we'll keep in contact by phone."

"I've got a bad feeling about this," Franklin said.

"Bad feeling or not, we're committed now," Fletcher said, slamming the door shut. He jogged a few yards to regain sight of Benny, then fell into step behind him.

---

"Shit!" Benny hissed under his breath.

He had just clocked one of the policemen getting out of the Astra to follow him. "Shit! Shit! Shit!" he repeated, with increasing savagery.

He had banked on them sticking with McQueen, but it seemed they were interested in him, too. Benny knew he was too old and unfit to make a run for it, so he would have to lose his tail by guile, instead. As he entered the grounds of Whipps Cross Hospital, he calculated that the detective was about a hundred yards behind him. If he could just maintain that distance until he reached the main building, he would be able to lose himself amongst the maze of corridors and nip out of a different exit.

---

As soon as the Berlingo drove past them, Dillon nudged the selector into drive and released the handbrake. They had to wait for another car to pass the junction before pulling into Whipps Cross Road, but that was a good thing as it gave them a little cover.

"The target van's just entering the roundabout," Tyler transmitted a few seconds later. Almost at once, he spotted the Job Astra parked in the bus layby, its left hand indicator flashing. He raised the mic to his lips. "Paul, the Berlingo's passing your car now and it's going left, left, left into Lea Bridge Road towards Hackney."

"*Received...*"

Looking in the wing mirror, Tyler saw the Astra pull out behind them.

The vehicle that was sandwiched between their BMW and the Berlingo signalled right and pulled into the filter lane to turn into Wood Street.

"We're directly behind the target, with no vehicles for cover," Tyler transmitted.

"*Received,*" Evans responded. "*We're two cars behind you.*"

"Try not to get too close to him," Tyler told Dillon. "I don't want him getting spooked."

## 38

Contact! Contact! Contact!

Charlie White grinned manically at Murray. They were almost at the Bakers Arms, having finally made a little progress through the slow moving traffic. "Pull over," he said, excitedly. "It sounds like they're coming straight towards us."

It looked like they were going to get involved in the fun after all, he thought, rubbing his hands together in glee.

McQueen had clocked the silver BMW parked in the James Lane turning as he'd driven by it. The two men inside looked very similar to the two in the Astra. Short hair, stern faces, wearing suits; they just had to be cops. He had watched it pull out and follow him with a sinking heart.

Unless he was being completely paranoid, the Astra that was parked by the bus stop at the roundabout was also an unmarked police car. Like the BMW, it had pulled out as soon as he had driven past it.

There could no longer be any doubt; the police had somehow discovered his involvement in Adam's murder.

But how?

His eyes flickered to the bandage on his left hand and wrist. Had they found his blood at the scene? Had that generated a DNA profile that their computers had matched to him?

As he drove past the Army Cadet Force headquarters on his left, he glanced in the mirror. Sure enough, the BMW was immediately behind him, and the Astra was two cars behind that.

"I've got to lose them," he whispered. "I can't go to prison."

McQueen was fast approaching a set of temporary traffic lights at the start of a contraflow system that had been put in place while emergency gas repairs were completed along this section of Lea Bridge Road, but he was so preoccupied with watching the two police cars in his rear view mirror that he didn't notice they had turned red until the very last second.

Stamping on the brakes, he brought the van to a juddering halt.

The BMW cruised to a stop behind him.

McQueen nervously checked his mirrors again. He fully expected the BMW's doors to fly open and the detectives to run over and drag him from the van.

To his surprise, they didn't.

They just sat there, waiting.

Waiting for what, though?

---

Madeley poured the chicken a second glass of cola.

"Thank you," Peter said, accepting it gratefully.

He was a very polite boy, Madeley thought. He took a sip of his champagne, nodded his approval, then offered the boy a chocolate, which he refused.

Standing up, the barrister removed his suit jacket, then his tie. "Shall we get ready for bed?" he suggested, as he hung them up.

Peter looked up at him, frowning. "But I'm not sleepy," he said, not understanding what the man wanted of him.

"Neither am I," Madeley told him, unbuttoning his shirt.

---

In the kitchen, downstairs, Remus was making himself a cup of tea when his phone rang. His first thought was that the client either wanted something brought up or was calling to complain about Troublemaker's stroppy attitude. Then he saw the caller ID and rolled his eyes. It was Benny, no doubt calling to check up on him.

"Everything's fine," he said, as soon as he answered the phone.

"*No, Aaron. It bloody well isn't!*" Benny sounded out of breath, like he was running, and there was an awful lot of road noise in the background.

Why wasn't he in the van, with Joey?

"Where are you, Benny? I thought you—"

"*Shut up and listen to me,*" Benny cut him off. "*The Old Bill are following us, so we've had to split up. I'm just walking into Whipps Cross Hospital. I'll get a cab back as soon as I've lost my tail. Joey's driving over to the flat in Hackney. I don't know what they want with us, but stay there until I get back.*"

A knot formed in Remus' stomach, like indigestion but worse. "Do you think they know we're responsible for snatching the chickens?"

There was a moment's hesitation, filled by the old man panting. "*It might be linked to something else, something that involves me and Joey,*" he said, guardedly. "*I'll tell you all about it when I get back.*"

"Do you think they know about this place?" Remus asked, fighting the urge to run to the window and look out into the street.

"*Don't be stupid,*" Benny snapped. "*How could they?*"

---

The second detector van was driving along Grove Green Road when the technician picked up the signal. "The mobiles assigned to

Mars and Remus are talking to each other," he called out to his driver, a bald DC in his late forties called Percy Atkins. "The one attributed to Remus is static in a cluster of houses up near the railway bridge. I can't be any more specific than that without the other van to help us triangulate it."

Before the engineer had even finished speaking, Atkins was ringing Gallagher, and demanding to know how quickly he could join them.

---

Fletcher was certain that Mars had cottoned onto him. The slimy old git was talking to someone on the phone, but he kept firing shifty glances over his shoulder. How ironic it would be, Fletcher found himself thinking, if Mars had dialled 999 to report the suspicious looking character who was following him. Of course, it was far more likely that he was speaking to one of the other suspects. He hoped it was Remus, because that would help the TSU detector vans to zone in on him.

Fletcher raised his phone to his ear. "I think we're blown," he told Franklin. "I think he's trying to shake me, so I'm gonna call the boss, tell him I think we should nick him."

"You do that," Franklin told him. "I'll drive into the hospital grounds via the front entrance. Hopefully, we'll trap him in the middle."

"As long as I don't lose him first," Fletcher said, as Mars entered the main building by a side entrance and disappeared from view.

---

The silver haired man had stripped down to his vest, underpants and socks, which were being held up by silly little suspender things. Peter thought they looked ridiculous and wondered why anyone would even bother with such things.

Turning to face Peter, the man clasped his hands behind his back and thrust his chin forward, the way his headmaster did whenever he made an important announcement during school assembly. "Now then, Peter. I want you to stand up and take your clothes off for me," he stated, firmly.

Sitting on the bed, Peter tensed. He might only be young, but he instinctively understood that he was being asked to do something that wasn't right. "I need to use the toilet first," he said, stalling for time.

Eyeing him cynically, the man placed his hands on his hips. "Really? Didn't you go before you came upstairs?"

Peter shook his head, his face a picture of innocence. "I haven't been for ages, and I really need a wee."

With an impatient sigh, the old man waved him up. "Oh, very well. There's an en suite through that door," he said, pointing to it. "Be as quick as you can."

Peter was up in an instant, heading towards the en suite. Closing the door behind him, he checked for a lock, and was hugely relieved to find a fairly substantial looking bolt. Clearing his throat to cover any sound that it might make, he carefully slid it across.

He felt a lot safer with a locked door between him and the old man, but he knew it was only a temporary reprieve. He needed to find a way out of there, and fast.

The en suite was tiny, no more than a metre wide, with a toilet and shower cubicle at either end and a small wash basin in the middle. Above this, there was a frosted, double glazed window. Hoping he would be able to climb out of it, Peter climbed onto the window sill. His hopes were dashed when he saw there was only a small vertical opener at the top. Opening this as far as it would go, he peered into the busy road below.

---

"Are you sure, Deano?" Tyler asked, miffed that Fletcher had given himself away.

A pause. *"Positive, boss."*

"Very well. Arrest him and give me a call once he's in custody."

Killing the call, he turned to Dillon. "That's not ideal," he said, miserably.

"I take it that Benny's clocked them?"

A sullen nod. "Looks like it. They're moving in to arrest him now."

After what seemed like an age, the lights turned green, but the Berlingo didn't move.

"Come on," Dillon sighed, rolling his eyes heavenward.

The car immediately behind them honked its horn impatiently. Before long, others joined in. Still the Berlingo didn't move.

"Do you think he's okay in there?" Tyler asked.

The lights changed to amber.

Then red.

"What's the numpty playing at?" Dillon asked, spreading his hands in frustration.

A line of cars was driving towards them through the contraflow.

Tyler reached for the door handle. "Maybe something's happened?" he said, pushing it open. As soon as his foot touched concrete, and he started to lever himself out of the BMW, the Berlingo took off like a rocket.

Turning right, it narrowly avoided a head on collision with a saloon coming the other way.

"Get after him!" Tyler snapped, throwing himself back into the car.

"I'm trying," Dillon insisted, activating the blue lights and siren.

Grabbing the radio, Tyler pressed the transmit button. "The Berlingo's just jumped the lights in Lea Bridge Road. It's turning right, right, right into Eastern Road. We're blocked by oncoming traffic and can't go after it."

It finally dawned on an oncoming driver that the police car that was trying to turn right had its blue lights flashing and siren wailing because it was on an urgent call, and not making a doughnut run, and they stopped to let it go.

There was no sign of the van as they pulled into Eastern Road.

With a curse, Dillon floored the gas pedal, and the BMW surged forward like the finely tuned machine it was.

Tyler glanced behind to see if Jim Stone had dared to follow them through, but he and Evans were still stuck in the line of traffic, and would no doubt remain so until the lights changed to green.

---

After jumping the lights and losing his tail, McQueen took the first left turn he came to, even though there were NO ENTRY signs, and it meant he would be driving the wrong way down a one way street. Luckily, there was nothing coming the other way. At the end of the road, he stamped on the brakes. Smoke billowed from the rear wheels as the van slewed into Western Road and drove the short distance back to Lea Bridge Road.

Stopping at the junction, he found himself at the other end of the contraflow system. He waited for the lights to change in his favour, then turned right into Lea Bridge Road and headed towards Leyton Green.

With an effort, he forced himself to relax. The hairy manoeuvre he'd just pulled off could so easily have ended in disaster, but the risk had paid off and he had lost the police. That was all that mattered.

---

Unaware that the van had made a sneaky left turn, Dillon guided the BMW along Eastern Road at warp speed, believing it to have gone that way. "I don't understand it," he said through gritted teeth. "The van wasn't *that* far ahead of us, and we should have reacquired it again by now."

"I think he must've turned off, Dill," Tyler said, as they took a bend so fast that his stomach dropped. "I think we need to turn around."

Cursing under his breath, Dillon found a junction that was wide enough to swing the car around in, and floored the gas pedal, taking them back the way they had just come.

When the lights finally changed to green, Jim Stone pulled away at a sedate speed, continuing along Lea Bridge Road while keeping one eye peeled for a layby or other suitable spot to pull into while they waited for an update from Tyler.

As they reached the end of the contraflow, a small blue van pulled out of the side road on their right, slotting neatly into the traffic flow ahead of them.

Stone didn't pay too much attention to it at first, but then he noticed the GB sticker and read the registration number.

"You're not gonna believe this," he said, nudging Evans' elbow with his own. "Look what's just pulled out in front of us."

Evans looked up, did a double take, and broke into a wide grin.

"You're right, I don't believe it."

Shaking his head in incredulity, Evans raised his radio to his lips and pressed the transmit button.

"Contact! Contact! Contact! We've just reacquired the Berlingo. It's back on Lea Bridge Road and heading towards Leyton Green."

# 39

His heart missed a beat

"How long are you going to be in there?" Madeley demanded, thumping the door.

"Not long," Peter called back.

With a sigh of impatience, Madeley rested his forehead against the door, wondering what the boy could possibly have been doing in there for the past ten minutes. Then it occurred to him that he might be having a bowel movement, and that he was taking so long because he had a dicky stomach?

He grimaced at the thought.

Returning to the bed, he poured himself another glass of bubbly and told himself to relax. There was no rush. They had all afternoon.

Jerry Gallagher acknowledged Kelly and Debs with a wave. They were standing by an old Daimler, but there was nowhere to park near it, so he continued up to the junction with Grove Green Road. Activating his hazard lights, he jumped out and jogged back to them.

"Any luck finding the right address?"

Kelly shook her head. "None. One resident thought she recognised the car, but didn't know which house it was associated with."

"Have you tried knocking on any of the houses in Grove Green Road?"

Kelly seemed surprised by the question. "No, not yet. Why?"

Gallagher shrugged. "When I saw the Berlingo earlier, it was parked in Grove Green Road, which makes me wonder if the Daimler's only parked here because they can't leave it in the main road."

"I guess that would make sense," Kelly agreed. "Show us where you saw the Berlingo."

Gallagher led them back to Grove Green Road and pointed twenty yards to his right, where zig-zag lines of a pedestrian crossing ended. "It was parked just over there, about a car's length beyond the zig-zags."

Kelly stared at the houses opposite. Could Remus be holding the boys in one of those? "When I spoke to Jack, he mentioned something about getting the TIU to send a fake text message to Remus' phone," she said. "If we did that, could your vans pinpoint which house his phone is in?"

"Potentially," Gallagher allowed with some reservation, "but it's a tactic that has to be used very sparingly to prevent it from being blown, so you would only get one go at it. How sure are you that Remus is actually in the same house as the kids?"

Kelly shrugged. "We think Mars and McQueen took one of the kids to a client's house in Walthamstow, leaving Remus here to guard the other one."

Gallagher was warming to the idea. "Then it could work."

"Is that something you could arrange for us, or should I ring the office and speak to Reg?"

Gallagher winked at her. "Leave it with me."

Peter knew he couldn't stall for much longer.

There was another bang on the door. "Good grief, boy! How much longer are you going to be?" The impatience in the well-spoken man's voice was turning to anger.

"Not long," Peter replied quickly. Climbing back onto the window sill, he peered out of the window again. The first time he'd looked, there hadn't been a single person in the street below, so his heart jumped with joy when he spotted two women and a man standing on the other side of the road.

Peter was about to shout out for help when there was another series of bangs on the door.

"I've had enough of this. Open the door," the man demanded.

Peter hesitated.

Thud! Thud! Thud!

"If you don't open this door immediately, I'll be forced to break it down."

Peter knew he had to do something, and fast. He thrust his face into the opening and screamed at the top of his voice.

"HELP ME! I'M UP HERE! PLEASE, HELP ME!"

---

When Madeley heard the boy's cries, he froze, not knowing what to do. Then he began banging on the door in panic. "Stop that racket at once!" he snarled. The chauffeur had assured him that the bedroom was soundproofed, but could the same be said for the bathroom?

On the other side of the door, the boy's yelling continued, growing more frantic by the second. "HELP ME! I'M UP HERE. I'M TRAPPED IN THE BATHROOM!"

Madeley tried to shoulder the door open, but it held firm. He barged into it a second time, putting all his weight into it. The door frame rattled, but the lock held.

"HELP ME!"

"Shut up, you wretched boy!" Madeley barked.

Terrified that someone in the street below would hear, he grabbed his mobile and dialled in the number on the card he'd been given. "Come up here now!" he ordered as soon as the call was answered. "The chicken's locked himself in the bathroom, and he's calling out to passers-by for help."

---

"What was that?" Debbie Brown asked, tilting her head sideways. They were standing beside the detector van, waiting for Gallagher to get a decision about the fake text message from the TIU supervisor he was on the phone to.

"What was what?" Kelly queried. All she could hear was the loud clunking of the detector van's diesel engine, and the constant traffic noise.

"I didn't hear anything either," Gallagher said.

"Kill the engine," Debbie demanded, then when he didn't do it quickly enough for her liking, she snapped. "Kill the bloody engine, now!"

Reaching into the van, Gallagher removed the key from the ignition.

They all stood statue still, straining their ears.

A bus trundled by, followed by a lorry and two large vans.

"The traffic noise is drowning everything else out," Kelly complained.

Debbie raised a finger to her lips.

Another lorry shot by, followed by several cars, and then there was a brief gap in the traffic, during which a faint voice reached their ears. It seemed to be coming from one of the properties across the road.

"Is that someone calling for help?" Gallagher asked, cupping a hand to his ear.

"Yes, and I'm fairly sure it was a kid's voice," Kelly said, looking at Debbie for confirmation.

But Debbie was no longer there; she was rushing across the road, staring up at an open window a little way off to their right.

---

Benny hated everything about hospitals, from the sound of the lino squeaking underfoot to the ever present smell of disinfectant mixed with cabbage and the maudlin expressions on everyone's faces. His progress was being impeded by a porter who was pushing a gurney along the corridor with painstaking slowness. As soon as the man veered off towards the X-ray department, Benny broke into a waddling run, negotiating a left hand bend, followed almost instantly by a right hand bend. And suddenly, there it was: the main entrance and freedom.

Once outside, he scuttled along the building line towards the exit. Shooting a final backwards glance over his shoulder, he ran across the service road, intending to cut through the trees on the other side and emerge into Whipps Cross Road.

Luckily for him, the driver of the slow moving ambulance he ran straight in front of saw him in time to slam on the brakes. Even so, the grill came to a halt two inches shy of Benny's thigh.

"Watch out!" the startled driver shouted, shaking his head in dismay.

"Up yours!" Benny retorted, giving him the finger.

The two cars following the ambulance had no choice but to stop behind it. As Benny drew level with the first one, the driver's door opened violently, slamming into him and sending him sprawling backwards onto the tarmac. Landing heavily on his rump, he sat there in stunned silence, wincing at the throbbing pain in his bruised bottom.

A good looking black man in his late twenties leisurely extracted himself from the driver's seat and ambled over to where Benny was vigorously rubbing one buttock.

He just stood there, hands on hips, grinning down at him.

"It's not bloody funny," Benny snapped. "You could've crippled me, doing that." Had he not been so desperate to get away, he would have feigned serious injury, with a view to making an insurance claim against the man.

The ambulance driver wandered over. "I think he must be drunk," he opined. "The silly sod ran out in front of me a second ago."

"Get up," the black man ordered.

Benny held out his hand, expecting to be pulled up. The hand hung in the air for a couple of seconds before he realised that no one was going to assist him.

"You're lucky I don't call the police and get you done for assault," he snarled as he struggled to his feet, still rubbing his bruised backside.

"You don't need to call the police," the black man said, holding his warrant card out for inspection. "I'm already here."

Benny felt the colour drain from his face.

"You are Benny Mars, aren't you?" the detective enquired, pocketing his ID.

Dusting himself down, Benny shook his head, vigorously. "Nah, mate. I'm not. You're obviously mistaking me for someone else."

He started to limp off, but the detective grabbed him by his arm and yanked him back. "Nice try, Benny," he said, unimpressed. "I'm DC Franklin, and I'm arresting you on suspicion of murdering Adam Cheadle at your flat in Hackney on or before Wednesday 7th November this year. You don't have to say anything but – ouch!"

Benny had just kicked him hard in the ankle.

A look of shock and pain appeared on Franklin's face, but he didn't surrender his grip of Benny's arm, so Benny kicked him again.

"Argh! Stop it, you little shit!" Franklin growled, hopping in pain. "Stop it or I'll – OUCH!"

People were stopping to watch the commotion.

"I think he's drunk," the ambulance driver told them, and mimed taking a drink to get his point home.

"Help! He's mugging me!" Benny called out, still trying to kick the detective's shins.

"I'm a poli– OUCH!"

Benny had just kicked him again, this time in the knee.

As Benny drew his leg back to deliver another kick, Franklin punched him squarely on the nose, flooring him for a second time.

Curling into a foetal position, Benny lay writhing on the floor, clutching at his nose, which was now bleeding profusely.

The white cop that Benny had given the slip inside the hospital came running over. "What the fuck's going on?"

"After I arrested him, the little swine started kicking me," Franklin said, indignantly.

"I think he's drunk," the ambulance driver added.

By now, the queue of stationary vehicles trapped behind the ambulance stretched all the way back to the hospital entrance, and someone from security came running over to see what was causing the hold-up.

Still breathing hard, the white cop grabbed Benny by the scruff of the neck and hauled him to his feet. He leaned in close, so no one else would be able to hear. "I'm not as nice as my colleague. If you kick me, or give me any shit whatsoever, I *will* knock you out. Savvy?"

Benny had been around the block enough times to know that he wasn't bluffing. In fact, the angry detective looked like he would relish any excuse to hit him.

Still pinching his nose to stem the blood flow, Benny nodded meekly and said, "Alright, guv. I'll come quietly."

---

The man in the red velvet jacket had forced Gavin to accompany him upstairs while he ran a hot bath. With the door shut, the room quickly filled with steam, but he appeared not to notice. He was humming to himself as he poured the luxury bubble bath mix into the running water.

"This is going to be *sooo* much fun," he announced, joyously.

Sitting on the floor in the corner, where he had been ordered to wait, Gavin said nothing; he was too terrified to speak. Red jacket man reeked of a sickly mixture of aftershave and alcohol, and he kept looking at Gavin strangely, like he wanted to eat him. For some reason, he kept stroking Gavin's face and arms, like he was a pet kitten or something. It was creepy, and it made him feel very uncomfortable.

With the sleeves of his smoking jacket rolled up just beneath the elbows, he was bending over the bath, swishing the water around to generate more bubbles.

"When can I go home?" Gavin asked.

Red jacket man sighed, as if Gavin had just said something in very poor taste, then removed his dripping hand from the water. "I'm getting fed up with you keep asking me that," he said, crossly. "You're here to have fun with me, so stop spoiling my very special day." He tugged at Gavin's grey sweat top. "You can start by taking that off."

Gavin swallowed, hard. "But—"

"JUST DO IT!" red jacket man suddenly shrieked, slamming the side of the bath with his hand.

Gavin recoiled in fear, banging the back of his head against the bottom of the sink. Cradling his head, he burst into tears.

"Turn around and let me take a look," red jacket man ordered, sounding genuinely concerned. He spun Gavin around and began prodding his skull. "Hmmm, well, it's not bleeding and there are no bumps, so I think you'll probably live," he declared, trying to make light of the situation. "Now, why don't you be a very good boy for me and get undressed, hmm?"

Gavin shrank away from him.

Red jacket man sighed, clearly vexed by his reaction. He reached for the bottom of Gavin's sweatshirt. "Fine, I'll take them off for you," he muttered under his breath.

He had left his mobile phone on top of the toilet lid. As he began tugging Gavin's top upwards, Gavin leaned over and snatched up the Nokia, then tossed it straight into the running bath. It floated there for a split second, then vanished beneath the bubbles, coming to rest on the bottom with a soft plop.

Red jacket man was horrified; his hands flew to his mouth, and a little squeal of alarm escaped his fleshy lips. "Argh! What have you done, you dreadful little boy?"

Pushing Gavin roughly aside, he thrust his arm deep into the water and began groping beneath the suds for his phone.

With his captor momentarily distracted, Gavin sprinted out of the bathroom and slammed the door shut behind him.

There was a bellow of rage, followed by, "Come back here!"

Gavin ran full pelt down the stairs, clinging to the bannister to avoid tripping over his own legs and tumbling down them.

---

Murray was driving the pool car as quickly as he dared without the safeguard of blues and twos.

There was a squelch of static, and then Evans was transmitting his latest update. "*All units, the target vehicle's now approaching the junction with Leyton Green. The lights have just turned red, and the target vehicle is held at the junction with Leyton Green. Looks like he's planning to go straight on, towards the Bakers Arms. This is a perfect spot for a containment if you can all get here before he moves off.*"

White snatched up the radio. "Paul, we're thirty seconds away, coming towards you from the Bakers Arms. We'll block him in from the front as soon as you give the word."

"*Paul, we're only a few cars behind you now.*" That was Tyler. "*We've got the traffic lights in sight, so we're ready to go when you are. If Whitey and Kevin can block him in from the front, we'll pull alongside him and box him in.*"

They were now close enough for White to see into the Berlingo, and it was obvious from the way McQueen was impatiently drumming the steering wheel that he was eager to get going. He squeezed the transmit button. "Boys, if we're going to do this, we need to act now, before the lights change." He glanced sideways at Murray, and gave him an impish wink. "I'm going to enjoy this," he said, undoing his seatbelt in preparation for a rapid exit.

Fletcher searched Benny, then handcuffed him and placed him in the rear of the pool car. Franklin joined them a moment later. "Benny, where are Peter Musgrove and Gavin Grant?" he asked as soon as he was behind the wheel.

Benny's eyes hooded, became unreadable. "I don't know what you're talking about," he said, defiantly.

"Benny," Franklin said, turning in his seat to look the prisoner square in the eye. "We know you and your mates abducted those boys. The game's up, and I need you to tell me where they are right now, so we can get them safely back to their parents. It will look much better at court if you cooperate."

Benny's eyes were full of hatred as he met Franklin's gaze. "Go fuck yourself."

# 40

Air holes

McQueen's day turned to rat shit in the blink of an eye. One second, all was right with the world; the next, his van was being blocked in by the two cars that screeched to a halt in front and beside him. Angry men were piling out, running towards him, yelling commands.

"What the fu—"

He was cut off mid-sentence as a baton crashed through his window, sending shards of glass flying into his face.

"POLICE!"

"TAKE YOUR HANDS OFF THE WHEEL!"

"STAY STILL!"

"DON'T MOVE!"

"SHOW ME YOUR HANDS!"

They were all shouting at the same time, their words cancelling each other out. Suddenly, his door was violently yanked open and a fierce looking man who was built like a tank reached in and dragged him from the driving seat. McQueen's feet barely touched the floor as he was spun around and slammed face first into the side of the van. The gorilla holding onto him twisted his arm so far up his back that he felt sure it would snap.

McQueen was screaming in pain, but they ignored him.

Within seconds, he had been handcuffed and was being thoroughly searched. When all the shouting died down, the gorilla manhandled him into the back of an old Astra. As he sat there, disorientated, gasping for breath, he feared that his world would never be the same again.

The gorilla knelt down and flashed his warrant card in his face. "Joey McQueen. I'm DI Dillon from the Homicide Command, and I'm arresting you on suspicion of being concerned in the murder of Adam Cheadle and the subsequent disposal of his body."

He rattled off the caution, but McQueen was no longer listening. All he could think about was the bite mark on the heel of his hand. How was he going to explain that away?

Closing his eyes, McQueen let his head sag forwards until his chin rested on his chest. He had a horrible feeling that he was well and truly screwed.

---

As soon as McQueen was under control, Tyler ran to the back of the van. Pulling the doors wide open, he prayed that he'd find one of the children inside.

It was full of clutter, but there were no kids.

That meant they were too late; that Benny and McQueen had already dropped the boy off.

Cursing under his breath, Tyler strode over to the Astra McQueen was sitting in. Pushing Dillon aside, he leaned in and locked eyes with the prisoner. "Where are the kids?"

McQueen blanched. "I don't know what you're talking about."

"Don't lie to me," Tyler snapped, baring his teeth in anger. "Where are Peter Musgrove and Gavin Grant?"

McQueen swallowed hard. "I want my lawyer."

Tyler felt white hot anger erupt inside his chest. He wanted to drag this worthless excuse for a man from the car and beat the truth out of him. Somehow controlling his rage, he said, "Tell me where those kids are now, and it will help you further down the line."

McQueen opened his mouth, closed it again. With a stubborn shake of his head, he stared down at his shoes.

Returning to the van, Tyler donned the Nitrile gloves that Kevin Murray was holding out for him.

"I don't suppose he told us where they are?" Murray asked.

Tyler shook his head, too angry to speak.

The van's cargo area contained a large carbon fibre suitcase, some old rugs and a couple of hessian sacks. There was also a grime covered sleeping bag and some loose strands of rope.

"Why are there so many holes in that case?" Murray wondered aloud.

"Huh?"

Murray pointed at the suitcase. There were numerous holes, neat and circular, as if they had been drilled. He unzipped it and probed a couple with his finger. "If you wanted to smuggle a child into an address without being seen, this suitcase would make an ideal delivery system."

"Are those used tissues?" Tyler asked, pointing at the two crumpled objects snagged in the lining.

Murray peered in, frowning. "It certainly looks like it."

"They still look wet," Tyler observed.

Murray produced an exhibits bag and a pair of tweezers. "Best I bag them for the lab to examine."

At that point, Tyler's mobile rang. He keyed the green button, not an easy thing to do when you're wearing Nitrile gloves. "DCI Tyler speaking."

"*Boss, it's Reg. Are you free to speak?*"

"Unless it's really urgent, Reg, I'm a bit busy," Tyler responded, which was an understatement.

"*I think it might be,*" Parker said. "*I've just had the subscriber checks back on the two numbers Benny was calling earlier today. One belongs to a bloke called Gareth Madeley, who's no trace on any of our systems. The other's regis-*

tered to Lionel Eberhard. He's the old nonce that Charlie and Kev nicked for possessing child porn."

Tyler's face darkened. "I remember Eberhard."

Beside him, Murray stiffened at the mention of the paedophile's name.

"Well, Eberhard lives in Upper Walthamstow."

"Are you suggesting they took the kid to Eberhard?" Tyler asked.

"It all fits," Parker said.

Tyler agreed; it did.

"Boss...What do you think?" Parker enquired, still waiting for answer.

"What I think, Reg, is that you're a genius!"

Tyler turned to Murray, who was looking at him expectantly. "Do you know how to get to Eberhard's house from here?"

"Of course."

Tyler patted him on the shoulder. "Good, because we need to get around there as quickly as possible."

---

Remus burst into the master bedroom to find Madeley banging ineffectually on the en suite door.

"Do something!" the barrister pleaded. "He's locked himself in there, and he's calling for help."

Crossing the room at a run, Remus delivered a hard kick to the lock. His foot bounced off it, but a crack appeared in the frame. With a savage curse, he kicked it again, and again. On his third attempt, it exploded inwards to reveal Troublemaker up on the toilet cistern, his right arm pushed all the way through the window's top opener as he called for help.

---

"Up there!" Debbie Brown was pointing up at a small frosted window, from which a small arm protruded.

"HELP!" its owner shouted through the narrow top opener, waving frantically to get their attention.

Kelly's heart leapt into her mouth as she shouted. "What's your name?"

"Peter!" a boy's voice called back, hoarse from shouting.

Beside her, Debbie gasped, then muttered, "Oh, thank God."

"Please help me before the—"

The boy's words were drowned out by the crashing sound of a door being forced open. There was a blur of movement behind the frosted glass, and then a larger figure grabbed Peter and dragged him away.

---

"You little shit," Remus raged, grabbing Troublemaker by his hair and pulling him away from the window. Wrapping an arm around his torso, he carried the boy, kicking and screaming all the way, back to the bedroom and threw him onto the bed. Telling Madeley to keep an eye on him, he ran back to the en suite and peered out of the top opener, praying that no one had heard anything.

Closing the window, he returned to the bedroom, panting from his exertions.

Troublemaker cowered away from him, pressing his back into the headboard, yet there was a glint of defiance in his eyes that made Remus want to break every bone in his body.

"Did anyone see you?" Remus demanded.

Troublemaker shook his head.

"Are you sure?" Remus pressed, fists clenching and unclenching.

"Yes, I'm sure. Nobody saw me."

The two men exchanged nervous glances. "What do you want to do?" Remus asked the client.

Madeley hesitated, unsure. "I–I don't know."

The doorbell rang.

Madeley gasped, eyes widening in fear.

Troublemaker smiled.

The caller kept their finger pressed against the buzzer, making it very clear that they weren't going away.

"Oh, fuck," Remus said, as his heart sank.

---

Gavin stumbled down the last few stairs, twisting his ankle on the bottom one. If he hadn't been holding onto the bannister, he would have faceplanted on the floor, but somehow, he managed to remain upright.

Behind him, the angry footfall of his captor's descent was deafening. "Stop right there, you beastly boy!" he panted.

Gavin's outstretched hand found the door handle. He turned it, but nothing happened. It was locked; he was trapped inside.

He spun to face his angry pursuer, who had reached the bottom of the stairs.

Pressing his back into the door, Gavin braced himself for the blow that must surely come. Red jacket man stopped a few steps short of him. Placing his hands on his knees, he struggled for breath. Sweat was dripping from his face, which was almost the same colour as his velvet jacket.

"Did you… did you really think I would be so naïve as to leave the door unlocked?" he mocked. Straightening up, he produced a set of keys and jangled them in front of Gavin's nose.

Gavin dropped to his knees and began sobbing.

"Oh, stop being such a prima donna all the time," red jacket man ridiculed him.

Grabbing Gavin's upper arm, he began dragging him back towards the stairs.

Gavin tried to pull free, but that just earned him a cuff around the ear.

"I really wanted to make this a pleasant experience for you," red jacket man said, tartly. "But as you've been such an ungrateful brat, I don't see why I should bother being nice to you anymore."

---

The caller had given up on the bell and was now pounding the door with their fists.

"Who could it be?" Madeley asked, stupidly.

"Well, it's not Santa Claus, is it?" Remus snapped.

Creeping onto the landing, he cautiously peered down the stairs.

He could see blurred shapes through the frosted glass in the street door.

There were at least three of them.

Hugging the wall to avoid being seen, he tiptoed down the stairs.

"Where are you going?" Madeley hissed.

Remus raised a finger to his lips. If it was just nosy neighbours, he might be able to placate their concerns with some bullshit story.

"OPEN UP! IT'S THE POLICE!" A woman's voice, strong and very determined.

Remus felt his legs turn to jelly.

What was he going to do now?

He glanced back up the stairs, saw the barrister standing there in his underwear. Their eyes met briefly, and Remus saw his own fear reflected in Madeley's.

"POLICE! OPEN UP!" A man's voice this time, Northern Irish from the sound of it.

Remus decided that the game was up; it was now every man for himself.

"I'm going make a run for it along the railway lines at the back of the house," he whispered. "If you've got any sense, you'll do the same."

With that, he fled down the hallway towards the rear of the house with only one thought in his mind: escape.

---

While Debbie and Jerry Gallagher were busy trying to gain entry, Kelly radioed for assistance.

The response was immediate. "*SCD unit requiring assistance from Juliet Lima, what have you got, over?*"

Juliet Lima was the phonetic code for Leyton division.

As soon as Kelly mentioned Peter Musgrove's name, the controller pushed the panic button, and the JL radio network was instantly linked to the Force Main Set, which effectively meant that every mobile unit in North East London would be listening.

The airwaves quickly became clogged by units offering to assist. In the end, the MP operator got so miffed that he told them all to shut up and just make their way.

India 99 had also responded. It was travelling from nearby Hackney, and would be with them within a couple of minutes. That was good news. The eye in the sky would be able to keep the rear of the property under observation until ground units got there to secure it.

"Why don't you try shouldering the door open," Kelly suggested to Gallagher.

He gave her a surly look. "I tried that while you were on the radio," he informed her, rubbing his right shoulder. "It didn't budge an inch."

Kelly wasn't surprised. The TSU skipper was a nice bloke, but he was hardly the manliest specimen she had ever worked with. Raising the radio to her lips, she asked, "Can anyone bring an Enforcer down to Grove Green Road? I think we're going to need one."

"*SCD unit from Trojan 502, we're nearby and we've got one on board,*" an Armed Response Vehicle eagerly offered up. "*Our ETA is three minutes.*"

As Kelly thanked them, she heard the distinctive whump-whump-whumping of the helicopter's approaching rotors.

## 41

Kick it in

Dillon screeched to a halt outside the terraced house in Upper Walthamstow.

"This is the place," Murray said, taking the lead as the four detectives alighted the car. "Watch out for all the shit along the path," he shouted as they ran towards the pebbledashed house.

Tyler hammered on the door. "POLICE! OPEN UP!"

Dillon peered through the bay window, but the curtains were drawn. "Is there a way in around the back?" he asked, addressing the question to White.

White shrugged. "Dunno, we went in through the front last time."

Tyler gave up on knocking. "Kick it in," he told Dillon, stepping aside to give the big man room.

"My pleasure," Dillon said, rolling his neck muscles.

Madeley hurriedly pulled his shirt on. He did up a couple of buttons, mismatching them to the holes they were meant to go through. The chicken was sitting on the bed with his knees pulled up to his chest, watching him through hate filled eyes.

Well, fuck him, Madeley thought! All that mattered was getting out of the house before the police gained entry. He shimmied into his trousers, but didn't waste time tucking his shirt in. Ramming his feet into his expensive shoes, he shrugged his arms into his suit jacket.

Grabbing his overcoat and briefcase, Madeley descended the stairs two at a time. He fired a nervous glance at the blurry shapes on the other side the frosted glass as he shuffled past the street door, then he was running along the hall, towards the back of the house.

"Hoy, you!" the Irish cop yelled, having detected movement inside. "Open this bloody door right now!"

Ignoring him, Madeley ran through the kitchen and into the garden beyond. In the distance, he caught a fleeting glance of the chauffeur disappearing over the high fence at the rear; a rat deserting a sinking ship.

Clutching his overcoat and briefcase to his chest, Madeley ran along the stone path that led to the rear of the garden, recalling the chauffeur's advice about making his escape along the railway lines.

---

Eberhard had just dragged the screaming boy into his bedroom when the thumping on his street door began. The noise was completely unexpected, and it startled him. Pushing the boy onto the bed, he raised a finger to his lips, then crept back onto the landing to listen.

The banging grew louder. It was angry, insistent, and it screamed 'visit from the police'.

"POLICE! OPEN UP!"

Eberhard's heart sunk. How was he going to explain the child's presence?

"HELP!" the chicken suddenly screamed.

Horrified by this, Eberhard ran back into the room.

"HE—"

Eberhard clamped a hand across the boy's mouth, cutting short his cry for help. "Shut up," he hissed, digging his fingers into the boy's soft flesh and making him squirm with pain.

Outside, the shouting stopped.

Had they heard the boy's cries?

Suddenly, the street door shuddered violently as something smashed into it with enough force to make the walls vibrate.

"Oh my!" Eberhard murmured, poking his head into the hallway.

There was an even louder impact, and Eberhard's PVC door exploded inwards with an almighty bang, slamming into the wall.

"POLICE!" the word came out as a roar.

A Scottish voice bellowed, "EBERHARD, WHERE ARE YOU, YOU WEE SHITE?"

Heavy footsteps thundered up the stairs.

A moment later, a detective whose face Eberhard instantly recognised from the televised appeals burst into the master bedroom. He took one look at the boy cowering on the bed, and his face transformed into a mask of fury. He advanced on Eberhard like an apex predator, fists clenched, teeth barred in a snarl.

"Don't hurt me!" Eberhard begged, shrinking away until he had backed himself into a corner.

Another man appeared behind the first detective, so big that his massive shoulders filled the doorway. "Jack," the newcomer warned, placing a restraining hand on his companion's shoulder.

The first detective stopped, his face inches away from Eberhard's.

"I can explain," Eberhard said quickly, although, of course, he couldn't.

The detective called Jack grabbed the ends of Eberhard's scarf and spun him around, so that he toppled into his colleague's waiting arms.

"Dill, take care of this piece of human flotsam," he ordered, his voice quivering with barely controlled rage.

---

There was a crackle of static from the handheld radio in Debbie's hand.

*"Ground units from India 99, be advised we've got two runners in the back garden. Both are IC1 males… The first is late 20s or early 30s. His hair's tied back in a ponytail, and he's wearing a suit. The second looks to be early to mid 60s, silver haired, also suited. Looks like he's carrying a briefcase and a coat."*

Leyton's area car screeched to a halt, and two uniformed officers ran over to join them.

Kelly flashed her warrant card. "I'm DC Flowers from the murder squad. We've got reason to believe Peter Musgrove's being held captive in there and we need to force entry to arrest the scumbags who snatched them."

One of the officers removed his ASP, racked it in one flowing movement, and stepped forward. "Mind your faces," he cautioned, placing his free hand in front of his own to shield it from flying glass fragments.

It took several strikes to smash through the reinforced glass.

As soon as there was a big enough gap, the constable slid his arm through and undid the latch. Pushing the door wide open, he stepped aside to let the detectives in first.

Kelly's priority was finding Peter, so she ran straight up the stairs, leaving Debbie to search the rooms on the ground floor.

Gallagher, closely followed by the two uniforms, made straight for the garden.

"PETER!" Kelly called at the top of her voice. "IT'S THE POLICE. YOU'RE SAFE NOW."

"I'm in here," a timid voice announced from the front of the house.

Kelly's heart leapt with joy as she ran towards the bedroom the sound had come from.

The relief she experienced, when she first laid eyes on him, was simply indescribable. As he ran towards her, she spread her arms wide to receive him, enveloping him in a big hug the moment he reached her.

"You're safe now," she promised.

---

Now in handcuffs, Eberhard was frogmarched to the BMW and placed in the rear seat.

"Where's the other boy?" Dillon asked. "Where's Peter?"

Eberhard shrugged. "How would I know?" he demanded, truculently. "I was never in the market for that one."

Leaving White to guard him, Dillon returned to the kitchen, where Tyler was sitting at the small dining table with the rescued child. The boy was drinking cola, and working his way through a packet of crisps. He looked pale and exhausted, but his appetite obviously hadn't been affected by the harrowing ordeal.

"I want to see my mum and dad," Gavin said.

Tyler nodded, then smiled. He leaned forward to ruffle Gavin's hair, but stopped when the boy recoiled in fear. "Don't be afraid," he said, softly. "You're completely safe now. We're going to take you to the police station so that a doctor can examine you. By the time that's done, your mum and dad will be there, and you can tell them what an incredibly brave boy you've been."

Gavin looked like he was about to burst into tears. "Peter's the brave one," he said, bottom lip quivering. "Not me."

"Well, I think you're both *very* brave," Tyler said.

The boy considered this, nodded reluctantly.

Tyler phrased his next question carefully. "Gavin, can you tell us where the bad men are holding Peter?"

Gavin shook his head, forlornly. "We were in an old house, in a damp, smelly room with a red light, but I don't know where it is." There was a short pause then, "I hope Pete's alright."

Gareth Madeley's shoes were caked in mud, and his dark suit was covered with moss and algae from where he had unsuccessfully tried to scale the five foot high fence.

The problem was, he didn't have the strength in his arms to haul himself up and over. Looking around for something to use as a step up, he spotted a large wooden crate amongst the bushes off to his right. It was a good two feet high and would provide the step-up he needed. Dragging it over, he gingerly stepped onto it. It creaked and wobbled alarmingly, but then settled.

Madeley cocked one leg over the panel. As he straddled the fence, putting all his weight on it, it began rocking dangerously. For all of two seconds, he rode it like a cowboy on a bucking bronco, but then he lost his balance and toppled back into the garden. As he fell, a protruding shard of wood impaled his right trouser leg, gouging his calf from knee to ankle.

As Madeley lay on his back, clutching his leg and screaming in agony, a man in workman's overalls burst into the rear garden, closely followed by two burly uniformed constables.

They sprinted towards him, but slowed to a walk when they realised Madeley was going nowhere.

One of the uniforms was grinning at the barrister as he held his injured leg.

The man wearing overalls walked up to the fence, peered over the top, then said something into the radio he was holding.

Above them, the noise of an approaching helicopter reached Madeley's ears. A moment later, the machine appeared above them, hovering majestically.

The man in overalls was looking up at the helicopter, talking animatedly into his radio and pointing to his right.

"Don't just stand there, call me an ambulance!" Madeley yelled.

The two uniformed constables looked at each other, then grinned. "You're an ambulance," one of them said.

"Help the old codger up," the man in overalls ordered. He was obviously an undercover detective, and from the way he addressed them, senior in rank.

The constables duly obliged by grabbing an arm each, and hauling Madeley to his feet.

"There you go, mate," one of them said. It was the same one who had made the crass joke.

"Take it easy," Madeley snapped, his features twisted with pain. "Can't you see I'm badly injured?"

The constable made a big show of looking down at his cut leg, then shook his head in bemusement, as if he couldn't see what all the fuss was about. "It's just a scratch, mate. It's not even bleeding that much."

"I've had worse from shaving," his colleague chipped in.

Seeing as the man had a beard, Madeley seriously doubted that.

The officers assisted him back into the kitchen, and one of them dragged over a chair for him to sit on.

"Thank you,' he said, begrudgingly.

A female detective wandered in to join them. She gave Madeley a poisonous look, then turned to the Irishman. "Where's the other one?"

He shrugged. "Did a runner along the railway tracks. India 99's directing units to intercept him. Don't worry, he won't get far."

The female detective had a homely but not unattractive face. Pulling out her warrant card, she held it out for Madeley to see. "I'm DC Brown from the Met's Homicide Command, and I'm arresting you on suspicion of being involved in the kidnapping and false imprisonment of Peter Musgrove and Gavin Grant."

"This whole thing is a complete misunderstanding, and you have no right to treat me in such an appalling manner," Madeley complained. "Look!" he said, pointing to his leg. "I'm injured. I need medical assistance."

Instead of answering him, the detective cupped a hand to her ear, listened intently.

Madeley looked at her as though she had completely lost the plot. "What on earth are you doing?" he spluttered.

"Did you hear that faint gargling noise?" she asked him.

He listened carefully, frowned at her and shook his head. "No. What was it?"

She smiled sweetly. "It was the sound of any sympathy I might have had for your injured leg going down the drain."

---

"I hope Gavin's okay," Peter said as Kelly led him down the stairs.

Considering what he had been through, he seemed in remarkably good spirits, and she was enormously impressed by his resilience. "As soon as we get back to the police station, we'll get you checked over by a police doctor, and then you can go home with your mum and dad. They've been so worried about you."

Peter nodded, solemnly. "I'd like that very much." An awkward pause, then, "Were they very angry with us for wandering off from the fairground?"

The question surprised Kelly. Placing her hands on his shoulders, she stared down into his eyes. "Angry? No, of course not? Why would they be angry?"

"Mum's always telling me not to go off with strangers, but I did it anyway."

Kneeling down, Kelly pulled him in close, wrapping him in her arms. "Trust me, your parents aren't in the slightest bit angry with you. Nor are Gavin's. No one thinks any of this is yours or Gavin's fault, I can promise you that." She smiled as she released him, then crossed her heart to make it official.

Peter returned her smile, but she could see he was fighting back tears.

"My mum tries to hide it, but I know she worries a lot about me," he confessed. "And I've been very worried about her, too."

Kelly nodded her understanding. "I know you have, but you'll be back with her soon, and everything will be fine." She led him outside, where she counted six patrol cars parked up, all with blue lights strobing.

"Wow! Did all these police cars come here to help me?" Peter asked, staring at them in awe.

Kelly grinned. "Yep, and there were lots more too, but they've gone now."

The driver of an Armed Response Vehicle stuck his head out of the window as she walked by. "I take it you won't be needing our Enforcer now?" he asked with a grin.

"No, but thank you for offering."

He pointed up to the helicopter, which was hovering a little to their right. "In that case, we'll be off to try and catch the suspect who's still adrift." Waving to Peter, he gunned the accelerator and the Omega shot off.

Kelly led Peter across the road and into Hampton Road, where their pool car was parked. "I've just got to make a quick call, and then you'll have my undivided attention," she promised when they were sitting comfortably together in the back.

"It's not as nice as the patrol car we just saw," he said, turning his nose up at the rather bland interior.

"It's not as fast either," she confessed, ruffling his hair.

"I've decided I'm going to be a policeman and help people when I grow up," he told her. "But only if I can drive one of the big fast cars."

Kelly laughed, thinking boys and their toys! She dialled Tyler's number, wishing she could see the look on his face when she broke the good news to him.

---

Following the instructions from the helicopter circling high overhead, PC Colin Samuels drove the dog van into Connaught Road. In the back, Fluffy, his long haired German Shepherd, was barking excitedly. The dog had an uncanny knack for knowing when they were on a call, and he was becoming increasingly desperate to be released.

"*Dog van, if you follow the road all the way round to the right, you'll come to the railway bridge. Stop there,*" a tinny voice instructed. The rotors could clearly be heard in the background, whirling away. "*The suspect's just coming up to that location now.*"

Samuels did as he'd been told, gliding to a halt by a pedestrianised walkway that ran beneath the railway bridge and linked Connaught Road to Madeira Road on the other side.

*"Dog van from India 99, the suspect has stopped on the bridge directly above you, and he appears to be looking for a way to climb down."*

Samuels wound down his window and poked his head out. There was no sign of anyone moving about above, so he figured the suspect had to be on the other side of the bridge, in Madeira Road.

*"Dog van, from India 99, the suspect's going over the wall... he's lowering himself onto a ledge halfway down. Now he's getting ready to drop the rest of the way down."*

Samuels jumped out, ran to the back and opened the doors. Fluffy bounded out an instant later, straining at the leash. Quivering with anticipation, his eyes were wide and feral, and his lips were drawn back in a fearsome snarl as he strained at his leash.

"Come on, boy," Samuels encouraged his mutt. "Let's get him."

---

As Remus dropped, he kept his feet together and his knees slightly bent, but he still landed hard. The jarring impact compressed his spine and knocked the wind out of him. Tottering backwards, arms flailing, he landed flat on his backside. He wriggled his toes and flexed his ankles; thankfully, nothing felt broken. He rolled onto his knees, tearing the cheap material of his suit trousers, before staggering to his feet.

Wincing from the pain in his feet, which felt as though a thousand needles were being stuck in them, he set off along Madeira Road, half jogging, half hobbling.

He had travelled no more than ten yards when he heard the savage snarling behind him, and a harsh male voice shouted, "Stop, or I'll release the dog!"

---

Alison Musgrove was preparing the evening meal when the telephone sounded in the hall. Her mother was peeling potatoes beside her, and they glanced expectedly at each other, each waiting to see if the other was going to volunteer. In the end, Alison pushed herself away from the counter with a resigned sigh. "Fine, I'll get it," she said, wiping her hands on a dishcloth as she set off for the hall.

"Well, it is your house, after all," Marjorie pointed out.

Rushing into the hall, Alison scooped up the receiver. The familiar sense of dread that had become synonymous with answering the telephone washed over her.

"Hello…?"

*"Alison, it's Kelly. I've got some very important news for you."*

Alison felt an icy hand reach into her chest and squeeze her heart. "Oh, God, no," she moaned, fearing the worst. Leaning against the hall table, she squeezed her eyes tightly shut. The detective was still speaking, but Alison had stopped listening.

Had they found another body?

Was it Peter's this time?

When the news had reached them, late the previous evening, that the body found in Epping Forest belonged to a rent boy, and not Peter or Gavin, Alison's relief had been indescribable; she and Ciaron had just stood there for ages, hugging each other and sobbing. He had never cried in front of her before, not even during Andrew's stillbirth, or at Luke's funeral, and it had felt like a groundbreaking moment in their relationship.

*"Alison…? Alison, are you there…?"*

"What…? Sorry…" Blinking back tears, Alison ran a shaking hand over her face. "You said something about having some news for us?" The apprehension in her voice was unmistakable.

*"Alison, we've found them! We've found both of the boys!"* Kelly announced, her voice joyous with excitement. *"We're taking them to Chingford police station to be examined by a doctor, but they're safe and well. Alison, did you hear me…?"*

Alison had heard the words, but she was struggling to process them. Her mouth opened and closed several times but she was unable to form any cohesive sounds. "Can you… can you say that again?" she eventually managed, swatting away the tears streaming down her face.

"*We've found Peter and Gavin,*" Kelly repeated, this time speaking more slowly, more deliberately. "*They're both safe and well, and we're taking them to Chingford police station to be checked out by a police doctor. I'm sending a car to pick you up as we speak.*"

Alison's hand flew to her mouth, smothering a gasp. Her knees buckled, and she crumpled into a heap on the floor. "Ciaron," she called out, or tried to. The noise she made was little more than a rasp. "Ciaron," she tried again, a little louder. "CIARON!" She screamed when she finally found her voice. "CIARON! MUM! THEY'VE FOUND THE BOYS!"

She was laughing now, crying and laughing at the same time. Her little boy was safe! He would be coming home soon. This was the most wonderful, incredible news; so good in fact that she could barely allow herself to believe it.

Behind her, the lounge door was thrown open and Ciaron ran into the hall, his face flushed, his eyes wide. "They've found them?" he asked, shell-shocked.

Alison nodded, meekly at first but then with increasing vigour. Through her tears, she gave him a watery smile.

Ciaron bent down, scooped her up into his arms and held her so tight that she could feel her ribs being crushed. He was unashamedly crying, she realised. For the second time in as many days, he was actually crying!

Marjorie appeared from the kitchen, dabbing the moisture from her eyes with a tissue. "Is it really true?" she sobbed.

Ciaron surprised Alison for a second time by spreading an arm wide and inviting Marjorie into the hug they were sharing.

"Yes, it's true," Alison said, smiling through her tears. She suddenly remembered that Kelly was still on the phone. Wiping her eyes on her sleeve, she cradled the receiver to her ear. "How did you find them? When did you find them? Where were they being kept?" The questions flew off her tongue so quickly that they all seemed to merge into one long word.

"*I'll explain everything in great detail when I see you at the station,*" Kelly promised. "*For now, all you need to know is that they're safe and well.*"

"What about Tom and Margo, do they know yet?" Alison asked

next.

"Debbie's on the phone to them as we speak," Kelly assured her, with a smile in her voice. "We're sending a car for them, too."

"Would it be possible for me to speak to Peter?" Alison asked, clutching the receiver so tight that the whites of her knuckles showed through.

"*I'm not with him at the moment,*" Kelly said, "*but you'll see him soon, and you can speak to him then.*"

## 42

## FRIDAY 9TH NOVEMBER 2001

*You need to bring your A-games today*

Susie Sergeant took the last remaining seat at the table, inserting herself between the two experts that Holland had insisted on drafting in from the National Police Improvement Agency.

They were in the meeting room on the second floor of Stoke Newington police station, and she had been given the unpleasant task of introducing the experts to the interviewers, none of whom were remotely happy to have them there.

"Morning all," Susie said, trying to inject some enthusiasm into her voice. "Time's slipping away from us, so let's whizz through the introductions." She decided to work her way around the table from left to right. "This is Colin Franklin and Dick Jarvis." She pointed to each officer in turn. "They are going to interview Benny Mars."

Franklin responded with what Susie felt was a resentful nod, while Jarvis gave them a polite, if not exactly friendly, smile.

"The two dodgy looking characters next to them are Charlie

White and Kevin Murray," Susie continued. "They'll be interviewing Joey McQueen."

White reluctantly raised a hand in acknowledgement, while Murray made a point of staring up at the ceiling and ignoring them.

Susie moved quickly on. "Lastly, we've got Paul Evans and Gurjit Singh, who will be interviewing Aaron Remus."

The two men nodded in tandem, their faces showing no expression whatsoever.

"As you know," Susie said, addressing the assembled officers, "our guests are experts in their respective fields. They'll be remotely monitoring the interviews with me, and if they have any suggestions, I'll communicate these to you via text message, so one of you needs to keep an eye on your phones."

Silence.

There were no acknowledgements, and none of the customary jokes.

All that was missing was tumbleweed blowing across the room.

Inwardly cringing, Susie gave each of the experts a little smile of encouragement. "Perhaps you'd be kind enough to introduce yourselves and say a little something about your particular skillset?"

The woman sitting to Susie's left cleared her throat, signalling her intention to go first.

"My name's Judith Sinclair, and I specialise in evaluating emotional intelligence, which in layman's terms means that I'm trained to look at the words spoken and identify any hidden meanings concealed within them." Her voice was confident; her pronunciation crisp, without any obvious traces of an accent. "Likewise, I analyse body language to establish the emotional content of a subject's micro expressions, which helps me to decipher what he or she is really thinking and feeling below the surface."

Kevin Murray covered his mouth and coughed loudly, simultaneously saying, "Bullshit!"

There were a few sniggers.

Susie felt her heckles rise. Whatever the detectives thought of the two academics, there was no justification for being disrespectful.

"That's enough of that," she snapped, her nostrils flaring in anger. "I'm sorry," she said, turning to Sinclair.

"It's fine," Sinclair responded, seemingly unoffended. She smiled at the officers. "Look, I know it all sounds a bit pompous and far-fetched, but the science behind this works, and hopefully we'll be able to give you some relevant insights as the day progresses."

Thanking her, Susie turned to the man sitting to her right, who was a good decade older than Sinclair. His thinning brown hair was swept back in a futile effort to mask the bald spot starting to develop on his crown, and he was dressed in a tweed jacket with leather elbow patches, a check shirt, and corduroy trousers.

He looked every inch the career academic.

"My name's Jarrod Hawkins, and I'm a professor of linguistics." He flashed them an anxious smile, as if beseeching them to go easy on him. "My role is to listen to what a subject says and how they say it, and then decipher what's genuine and what's fabricated."

He spoke with a Mancunian accent, and Susie idly wondered whether he supported City or United.

"Like Judith," Hawkins continued, "I'm trained to look for hidden meanings. These are clues that inadvertently slip out during a sentence or a phrase that the subject doesn't want us to know about."

His words were met by stony silence, and even stonier faces.

"Right," Susie said, giving each of the specialists a pitying look. "Why don't you two pop down to the canteen and grab yourselves a coffee? I'll send someone to collect you as soon as we're ready to start."

Susie waited until they had left the room, then whirled to face the assembled group. "You ignorant bunch of tossers," she snarled, slapping the table with her palm. "How dare you be so rude! Like it or not, these people are our guests, and I expect you to behave professionally and treat them with respect. Do you understand?"

There were sheepish mutterings of apology, but none were terribly convincing; even Dick Jarvis gave the impression of merely going through the motions.

Susie slapped the table again, even harder this time. "I asked you a question. Do. You. Understand?"

"Yes, ma'am," they chorused. Even White and Murray, who normally called her by her given name, responded with the formality that her seniority in rank deserved.

Still seething, Susie took a deep breath. "I need you to bring your A-games today. You can't afford to say or do anything that would give the slimy barristers representing these monsters an excuse to argue that the interviews should be excluded, or any reason to criticise the way their precious clients were treated whilst in custody." Her voice mellowed. "Okay, the lecture's over. I'll climb down from my high horse now and let you get on with the job in hand. Good luck, and remember to be nice to the experts."

---

The ABE suite at Stoke Newington police station was located on the ground floor of the old section house building in the rear yard. It had been designed to be a comfortable, non-threatening environment, and resembled a brightly painted, cosy living room.

Both the Achieving Best Evidence in Criminal Proceedings guidance and the Youth Justice and Criminal Evidence Act of 1999 stipulated that all children under the age of seventeen, along with other vulnerable witnesses or victims, should be allowed to provide their evidence-in-chief in the form of a video recorded interview. However, these interviews had to follow a defined structure and be conducted by specially trained officers, which both Debbie and Kelly were.

"Are you ready?" Kelly asked them as soon as they were all settled on the sofa. Debbie was sitting in the adjacent room, monitoring the interview remotely and acting as controller.

Alison and Peter shared a loving look, then nodded in tandem.

"Yes," Alison said. "I think we are."

Kelly was struck by the remarkable difference in Alison's appearance today; she was like a totally different person. The colour was back in her skin, the bounce was back in her step, the bags had disappeared from under her eyes, which were no longer red rimmed from crying, and she looked ten years younger. But it was more than that; her whole aura was different. The heavy cloud of hopelessness and despair that had shrouded Alison since Kelly first met her had completely evaporated, and she was positively glowing with love, hope and happiness.

"Good. In that case, let's make a start."

---

Over at Chingford, Steve Bull was beginning to wonder if Eberhard had somehow found God overnight, because he was hellbent on confessing all. His solicitor had interrupted several times already, to remind his client of his advice to make no comment, but it was as if a dam had burst inside the paedophile, and nothing could prevent the outpouring of his many sins.

Eberhard had just finished explaining how the bidding process worked for Benny's clients, and how he had succeeded in purchasing Gavin Grant, even though his final bid had technically been submitted after the official closing date expired.

"Your colleagues cost me a lot of money when they arrested me the other day," Eberhard complained, resentfully. "If I hadn't been stuck in a cell all night, my initial bid would have been submitted in time, and I would have saved myself twenty-five grand."

"I'll be sure to pass on your displeasure," Bull assured him.

"Yes, please do," Eberhard said, seemingly unaware that Bull was being facetious.

Eberhard went on to explain how Benny Mars and Joey McQueen had dropped the child off less than an hour before he had been arrested, with an agreement in place that they would collect the boy later that night for disposal.

"What do you mean by disposal?" Bull asked, keeping his voice non-judgemental, some might even say friendly; not an easy thing to do when the person you were talking to made your skin crawl.

The truth was, Bull had been dreading this interview since Susie had asked him to conduct it the previous evening. He had lain awake for much of the night, tortured by the thought of spending the following day talking about children being abused. Bull was the proud father of two young boys. They were his world; he would kill any man who harmed them and damn the consequences. Yet here he was, having a pleasant conversation with a sadistic predator who had fully intended to rape Gavin Grant before handing him over to Mars and McQueen for disposal.

*Disposal!*

Eberhard shrugged. "Well, obviously, Benny would have killed him and buried the body," he explained with a casualness that Bull found staggering.

"And you know this because…?"

Eberhard licked his lips, looked from one interviewer to the other as if considering how much to reveal.

Inside, Bull's emotions were in turmoil, but outwardly he was Cool Hand Luke. He leaned back in his chair, studied his fingernails, content to let the silence build.

Finally, Eberhard spoke. "I was arrested a few days ago, because two of your colleagues found me watching a film when they called at my house."

"Yes, I know," Bull said, forcing a smile. "Being stuck in a cell overnight cost you an extra twenty-five grand."

"Yes, that's right," Eberhard agreed. "Look, because I like you, I'm going to share a secret with you."

His solicitor groaned, shot him a warning look.

"Go on then," Bull said. "You have my undivided attention."

Eberhard leaned forward, lowered his voice conspiratorially. "You know the film they caught me watching? Well, I was one of the three men in it." He giggled naughtily, as if he were merely confessing to placing a whoopie cushion under his teacher's seat. "Benny and Mo Hinkleman, God rest his soul, were the other two."

A shiver ran down Bull's spine.

Had Eberhard really just admitted to being one of the three men who had raped the unconscious boy in that dreadful film?

Had he really just implicated Mars and Hinkleman as being the other two?

Bull hadn't seen the footage himself, but White's graphic description had been enough to induce nightmares.

"The boy in the video, what was his name?"

Eberhard shrugged disapprovingly, as if to imply it simply wasn't the done thing to ask questions like that. He adopted an aloof pose. "I don't know. I find it's always best not to know their names."

Bull swallowed down his anger. He wasn't a violent man, but he could have quite happily throttled the man sitting opposite him.

Unaware that Bull loathed him, the paedophile was smiling at the detective like they were the best of friends.

Taking a deep breath, Bull forced himself to continue. "Was he drugged?"

Eberhard nodded, enthusiastically. "Oh, yes. The Cola that we gave him was laced with a very strong sedative."

"Was the boy scared?" Somehow, Bull managed to keep his voice even.

Eberhard nodded. "Benny was holding his hand. The chicken was trying to pull away, asking to go home." His voice trembled, and his eyes seemed to cloud over with nostalgia. "Even after the drugs kicked in, and he started getting sleepy, he was still asking for his mum."

Bull wanted to throw up. "Did you all rape him?"

Eberhard smiled, wistfully. "We took turns. I was the last to have a go, because I was lower down the pecking order than the other two. I wore a condom, because I didn't want their cum touching my dick, or any of his blood for that matter."

"His blood?" Bull queried, fighting a losing battle to keep the horror from his voice.

Eberhard pulled a face, mistaking Bull's disgust for something else. "I know. I was horrified, too. The chicken was bleeding quite badly by the time I got to ride him, and you never know if these boys are carrying infectious diseases."

Bull just about suppressed a shudder as a line of sweat trickled down his back. "Was he still conscious at that point?"

Eberhard shook his head. "No, he had passed out by the time I got to him."

Was it Bull's imagination, or had Eberhard actually sounded disappointed?

Even the solicitor representing Eberhard was starting to look a little green around the gills.

Bull forced himself not to dwell on what was being said. He was afraid that, if he thought too deeply about the disgusting things he was being told, he might go insane.

"Who actually killed him?"

"Benny," Eberhard said, softly.

"How?"

"He put a hand over the boy's mouth and nose, then placed his other forearm across his throat and pressed down. The boy squirmed and struggled, but not for very long. He was only small, you see."

## 43

The penis isn't a vital organ

So much had happened during the preceding twenty four hours that Tyler had struggled to keep up with all the developments.

All five members of the paedophile gang had been arrested.

Peter and Gavin had been reunited with their respective parents. Miraculously, apart from being slightly malnourished and nursing a few minor scrapes and bruises, both were physically fine. To everyone's great relief, the doctor's examination had failed to unearth any signs of sexual assault. Emotionally, it was another matter entirely, and Tyler suspected it would take a considerable amount of time and professional counselling to help the two families move beyond the terrible mental and emotional trauma of the past few days.

The media was having a field day milking the good news for all it was worth, and Tyler was happy to let them get on with it. He and his colleagues were the heroes of the hour; one newspaper had even described them as the Met's finest detectives. The praise made a welcome change from having the press breathing down their necks and the top brass screaming for results.

Imogen Askew, having been granted an access to all areas pass while filming the fly-on-the-wall documentary series, suddenly found herself in great demand. Dillon had informed Tyler that her bosses had offered her the opportunity to co-present the season finale with Terri Miller. The extended episode would focus on Peter and Gavin's abduction, and the sinister paedophile ring that had been unearthed during the subsequent investigation. There was no doubt that the on-screen exposure she received when it was aired would see her stock as an investigative journalist soar.

Tyler genuinely could not have been any happier for her.

Following their arrests, Mars, McQueen and Remus had been taken to Stoke Newington, while Eberhard had been driven to Chingford and Madeley had been shipped off to Leyton.

It was yet to leak out that Madeley was a senior barrister and part-time Crown Court judge. When it did, there would undoubtably be some very uncomfortable questions to be answered about the judicial vetting system, but thankfully not by Tyler.

Every distinguishing mark, scar and tattoo on the paedophiles' bodies had been mapped by a doctor and photographed by Ned Saunders from SO3. The child porn that Eberhard had been watching at the time of his arrest was being reviewed, to see if any of the prisoners' marks or scars matched those on the hooded men in the video.

It was getting on for two o'clock when Tyler sat down with Dillon, Quinlan and Keating to apprise them of the findings of Adam Cheadle's post mortem, which he had just returned from.

"Old Creepy confirmed that the cause of death was manual strangulation," he began. "In addition to the extensive bruising to the neck and petechia in the eyes we already knew about, the hyoid bone had been snapped." The hyoid was a U shaped bone located in the throat, and it was often fractured when death was inflicted by strangulation. "He found skin cell fragments under Adam's fingernails, from where he tried to fight his killer off." As he spoke, he removed three ten by eight colour photos from the folder on his lap.

"These are photographs of Joey McQueen's left arm, taken upon his arrival in custody yesterday."

"They definitely look like scratch marks," Keating said, leaning in for a closer examination.

"The DNA from the skin fragments under Adam's fingernails will almost certainly match Joey's profile," Tyler predicted. "In addition, Claxton found traces of blood in Adam's mouth, although there was no sign of gum disease and no cuts."

"What was Claxton's theory for it getting there?" Dillon asked.

"He thinks Adam took a bite out of his attacker during the struggle. The mouth swabs George Copeland took are being sent straight up to the lab for analysis. With any luck, we'll get the results back by close of play tomorrow." Tyler removed two more stills from the envelope and passed them around. "These are photographs of an infected bite wound on the heel of Joey McQueen's left hand," he informed them. "Which means, he's the one that Adam bit."

Quinlan whistled. "Well, well, well. It looks like Joey played a much bigger role in Adam's murder than we initially thought."

"Had the poor boy been raped?" Dillon asked.

Tyler shook his head. "Thankfully, no. Although there was clear evidence that Adam had previously engaged in anal sex, there was no sign of intercourse, consensual or otherwise, having occurred immediately prior to his murder."

"That's one small mercy, I suppose," Quinlan said, shaking his head sadly.

Tyler turned to Keating. "While we're here, what was the outcome from Hinkleman's SPM?"

Keating had attended that one the previous afternoon, but with all the madness that had been going on, this was the first opportunity that Tyler had had to ask her how it went.

She shuddered at the recollection. "Well, the bruising to Hinkleman's wrists, from where he was tied to his chair, occurred ante-mortem. There's also some ante-mortem bruising to his jawline, which suggests the killer punched him to subdue him. Hinkleman was still very much alive when the killer chopped his wedding tackle off and stuck it in his gob. Why he felt the need to do that is beyond me. For his pièce de résistance, the killer slashed Hinkleman's throat and left him to bleed out."

"You mean for his penis de résistance," Dillon corrected her with a devilish chuckle.

"Do you think his genitals were cut off to make him reveal where the cash box was hidden?" Tyler asked, ignoring Dillon's childish remark.

Keating could only shrug. "Jack, Hinkleman kept the cash box in the bottom drawer of his desk, which wasn't locked. It would have been one of the first places that anyone searching the place would have looked in, so I seriously doubt it."

"I take it the throat slashing—" Tyler mimed slitting his throat with a forefinger "—was the official cause of death?"

"Technically speaking, exsanguination is the official cause of death, but that only happened because his jugular and carotid arteries were severed, so yes."

"Out of interest," Dillon asked. "Would Hinkleman have bled to death anyway, after his genitalia were removed?"

Keating scrunched her face up. "According to Creepy Claxton, the penis isn't a vital organ. There are no main arteries passing through it, so while a man might pass out from the pain and shock of having it chopped off, he would almost certainly survive the ordeal unless he had some other underlying condition." She looked at each man in turn, openly smirking at their pained expressions. "I'd be willing to bet a month's wages there's not one man on this command would agree with Old Creepy about his dick not being a vital organ."

Tyler grimaced. "Well, I certainly consider mine to be pretty vital, so I think it's safe to say you would win that bet."

"Me too," Dillon agreed, subconsciously placing a hand over his private parts.

Quinlan refrained from passing comment; he could be quite prudish about such things.

"Did you notice any unusual marks, scars or tattoos on Hinkleman's body?" Tyler asked.

Keating considered this for a moment, then nodded. "As a matter of fact, there were a couple of things. The most obvious was a large, ungainly scar from an old appendicectomy operation. There was also a—"

"Sorry, can you describe the scar?" Tyler interrupted.

Keating shrugged. "Well, the suturing was a bit crude, leaving a very visible indentation. Old Creepy was very critical of the surgeon's workmanship, reckoned the operation could have been carried out abroad."

Tyler made a hurried note in his daybook. "What else?"

"The only other thing was a small tattoo of a wolf's head, howling up at the moon, on his left buttock. It was only about this big." Keating raised her left hand, joining the tips of her thumb and forefinger together to make a circle.

Tyler removed another photograph from his folder. This one showed a man's saggy bottom. A small tattoo was visible on the left cheek. It was identical to the one that Keating had just described, and it had a single word written beneath it.

Keating leaned in, squinted, then shook her head in defeat. "What does it say? I can't tell without my glasses."

"Alpha," Tyler informed her.

"Alpha? As in Alpha male?" Quinlan queried.

"That's my take on it," Tyler confirmed.

"All Hinkleman's marks and scars were photographed by the SO3 snapper in attendance," Keating told them. "I've got the disc on my desk. I'll get the photos of the scar and tattoo printed up for you."

Tyler smiled his gratitude. "That would be most helpful." At that moment, his mobile chirped into life. "Excuse me," he said, standing up and walking a few steps away from the others to take the call.

*"Boss, it's Jim. I've just finished viewing the porn film Eberhard was watching when he was arrested."* The former para's voice sounded strained, as if the experience had been quite an ordeal. *"I think I've worked out where it was shot, and who one of the men in it is."*

"I'll be right along," Tyler told him.

The viewing room was small, with a single window overlooking the parking area at the back of the building. There were two desks, one with a TV-video combo set up on it, the other with a number of notes and photographs splayed out across it.

An image was frozen on the screen, from where Stone had paused the video he was playing.

"Watching this has been one of the worst things I've had to do since joining The Job," he confessed, nodding grimly toward the screen. "It's made me feel physically sick." He was trembling with anger as he said this.

"I'm grateful, Jim," Tyler said, placing a hand on his colleague's shoulder and giving it a gentle squeeze. "Hopefully your efforts here will help us to put these monsters away for the rest of their natural lives. So, who is it you think you've identified?"

Stone shook himself like a dog, then sat down in front of the TV and motioned for Tyler to join him.

Pulling a chair over, Tyler stared at the screen with a sense of trepidation, wondering how much of this awful footage he would be required to watch.

"I've identified Benny Mars," Stone said, leaning forward to press the play button.

A small white male with a stoop, middle-aged and flabby around the middle despite his spindly arms and legs, strode past the camera in a state of arousal. As he turned to face the unconscious boy lying on the bed, Stone pressed the pause button. "There," he said, triumphantly.

"What exactly am I looking at?" Tyler asked, squinting at the flickering freeze-frame image.

"His arse, guv," Stone said, tapping the screen with the nib of his biro. "Look, there's a tattoo of a howling wolf's head on the left cheek. And can you see here?" he tapped the image again. "There's a word written beneath it. It says, Alpha."

Tyler moved closer to the screen, trying to focus his eyes on the smudge of a word. "How can you possibly read that?" he demanded, sceptically. "It's just a blur."

"It is there," Stone admitted. "But further into the film, when he's... when he's penetrating the child, there's a close up of his backside, allowing you to read the word perfectly."

Tyler screwed his face up in disgust.

"I'll fast forward the film to that point if you really want me to," Stone offered. "But, trust me, after seeing it, you'll wish you hadn't."

Tyler hesitated. He really didn't want to see it, but how could he bottle out when he had made Stone view it? "Show me," he said, his voice brittle.

Stone gave him a dubious look, then nodded. He fast forwarded the footage to the relevant scene, then pressed play.

Tyler noticed the detective averted his eyes while the footage was playing.

Tyler watched the clip, feeling increasingly sick. Beneath the table, he was clenching his fists so tightly that his nails cut into his palms. The room suddenly felt stiflingly hot and oppressive, and he wanted to run out.

"That's enough," he said, a few seconds later, when he was satisfied that the image on the screen matched the photograph of Benny's tattoo in his folder.

Stone quickly turned the video off. "I'll get some stills printed, and you'll be able to read the word clearly in those."

Tyler stood up, anxious to be gone. "Did you say that you'd managed to identify where this filth was shot?"

Stone crossed to the next desk along and picked up one of the many stills scattered across its surface. "This is a shot of the master bedroom in the house in Grove Green Road, the room that Peter Musgrove was rescued from," he said, handing it to Tyler.

"You think the video was filmed there?"

"I'm positive it was," Stone assured him. "The size, shape, and layout are all exactly the same. Even the décor is identical."

Tyler thanked him. As he turned to leave, a question popped into his mind. "I take it neither of the other men in the video had any distinguishing marks, scars or tattoos?"

"Actually, one of them had a similar tattoo, minus the inscription, on his left buttock," Stone said. He checked his viewing log. "I've noted it here, along with the fact that he had a nasty scar on his right side."

"Show me," Tyler said, rushing back to the chair he had just vacated.

Stone spent a few seconds winding the tape forward, then paused the picture. "There you go."

Tyler studied the image for several seconds, then pulled out his mobile and dialled Keating's number. "Carol, it's Jack. How quickly can you print off those stills of Hinkleman's tattoo and appendix scar? You're doing it now? Good. I'll come and collect them."

## 44

I don't stand a chance!

The interviews at Stoke Newington had been paused in order for the mobile identification team to complete the video captures of Mars, McQueen and Remus.

"This is dog shit," Remus complained to his solicitor when it was his turn to be led to the room being used for the recordings. His nerves were shot to pieces and he was shaking like a leaf. "Those kids are going to pick me out, no trouble. And so will any other witnesses that the Rozzers dig up, seeing as the E-fit of my face has been plastered all over the TV and newspapers. I don't stand a chance!"

"That's something we can argue at court, if the case gets that far," his solicitor, a podgy man in his fifties with a lined face and a bad case of dandruff, assured him.

"What if I refuse?" Remus asked. "They can't make me do it, can they?"

The solicitor sighed. This was the third time that his client had posed that particular question. "As I've already told you, there's no point in refusing. If you do, they will just use footage from the custody office CCTV, and it will look very bad for you at court."

---

Quinlan's phone rang. It was Sam Calvin, the Crime Scene Examiner. "*Andy, I'm up at the lab with the blood pattern analyst, and we've just been examining Gabriel Warren's clothing, only two items of which have Hinkleman's blood on them. The first is his denim jacket, which has two big smears down the front. We're happy these are transfer stains, caused by Warren wiping his bloody hands on them, and not by the victim bleeding directly onto him. The second is his shoes. Both soles are covered with the victim's blood, and we think that got there when he trod in the puddle of blood that had formed on the floor after Hinkleman was castrated. The interesting thing is, there's no trace of any arterial spray on any of Warren's clothing, and no passive blood stains from where the victim's blood dripped onto them while the genital injuries were being inflicted. Realistically, there should have been something.*"

Quinlan sat up, reached for a pen and pad to make some notes. "Surely, if the boy was standing behind Hinkleman when he slit his throat, that would explain why there's no arterial bleed on his clothing?"

"*Yes, of course.*"

"There you are then!" Quinlan said, latching onto this.

"*You're missing the point,*" Calvin said, as though lecturing a rather dim pupil. "*Before slitting Hinkleman's throat, the killer castrated him and stuffed his genitalia into his mouth. Trust me, hacking his gonads off with a blunt kitchen knife, like the one Warren chucked, would have been hard work and extremely messy, and there's no conceivable way that Warren could have done that without getting Hinkleman's blood all over him.*"

Quinlan let out a weary sigh. "I don't think I like where this is heading."

"*I'm sorry, Andy, but based on the notable lack of blood on Warren's clothing, I think it's looking highly unlikely that he's your killer. In fact, I'd go as far as to say the trail of bloody footprints we found at the scene corroborates the account he gave in interview.*"

"In what way…?"

"*Have you got the crime scene photos to hand?*" Calvin asked. "*It'll make it easier to explain if you're looking at them.*"

Quinlan told him to wait while he dug them out. Returning to his desk a few seconds later, he spread them out in front of him. "Okay," he said, breathlessly. "Which one should I look at first?"

"*Shot four,*" Calvin said without hesitation. "*It's taken from the doorway and shows the victim sitting in the centre of the room. There's a puddle of blood between his legs and a number of footprints leading away from it.*"

Quinlan plucked the relevant photo from the rest. "Yep, looking at it now."

"*We found two distinct sets of footprints in the blood. The first belongs to Warren; the second to PC Vickers. They both follow a similar path to begin with. Upon entering the room, they step through some arterial spray on the carpet as they make their way over to the body. When they reach Hinkleman, they both stand in the puddle of blood caused by his castration, presumably checking the victim for signs of life. After that, the footprints diverge. Vickers takes a reciprocal route to the hallway, whereas young Warren detours over to the desk, presumably to steal the cash box from the drawer, before exiting the room. The footprints tell us that Warren didn't get Hinkleman's blood on his shoes until after he was dead.*"

Quinlan sighed. "Surely, that doesn't automatically exclude him from being the killer, does it?"

"*I think it probably does,*" Calvin said, almost apologetically.

Quinlan hung up feeling frustrated and annoyed. He had been hoping the blood pattern analysis would convict Warren, not exonerate him. It was the second setback he had received that day, the first being that there was no CCTV coverage of the studio entrance. It was Sod's Law; The Narrow Way was literally peppered with CCTV cameras, but the entrance to Hinkleman's studio was located in one of the few blind spots.

The Police and Criminal Evidence Act allowed for a suspect to be held for up to twenty-four hours, without charge. A superintendent could authorise an additional twelve hours if their continued detention was necessary in order to secure or preserve evidence. Detention beyond thirty-six hours could only be authorised by a

Magistrates' Court, and only in the case of a serious arrestable offence.

At six o'clock the previous evening, Quinlan had successfully applied for a warrant of further detention, and had been granted an additional thirty hours, which meant he had to either charge or release Warren by midnight tonight.

In light of everything that Quinlan now knew, it was obvious that Warren hadn't murdered Hinkleman, so there was no point in holding onto him any longer.

He rang Zoe Sanders over at Shoreditch and gave her the BPA update from the lab. "In light of that, you might as well NFA Warren regarding the murder right now."

"*What do you want to do about the kitchen knife he lobbed while being chased, and the cashbox he nicked from Hinkleman's studio?*"

Quinlan sighed. "He's of previous good character, so caution him for both offences and get rid of him."

"*Wouldn't it be better to bail him over the murder, just until we receive the formal report from the BPA scientist?*"

"No point," Quinlan said. "I've had verbal confirmation, and Sam's e-mailing me an interim report this afternoon."

"*In that case, I'll sort out getting him cautioned and released,*" Sanders said.

"Have his parents arrived yet?" Quinlan asked.

"*Yes, they're sitting in the waiting area outside the front office,*" Sanders told him. "*I was gobsmacked when I saw his dad was a vicar. Between me and you, he's a pious so-and-so, and I can see why he and Gabe fell out.*"

"Once he's NFA'd, take a key witness statement from him about Adam's murder. Don't let him leave without providing that."

Hanging up, Quinlan consoled himself with the knowledge that, with Warren in the clear for Hinkleman's murder, Jack would be free to use him as a witness against Benny Mars and his repulsive cohorts. That was a good result for Jack, but it still left him without a suspect for the elderly photographer's murder.

People often lied during police interviews. That was a fact of life. The trick was learning how to identify when they were doing this and how to use it against them. Franklin had a natural gift for reading body language and picking up on micro expressions, and he resented having Sinclair and Hawkins scrutinise his interrogation technique via the video link.

They had already sent him two text messages. The first had pointed out that whenever Benny was faced with a difficult question, he rotated his head almost ninety degrees to the right. The second had been to make Franklin aware that Benny was prone to dramatically slapping the table whenever he wanted to make a point, but the slapping motion was always out of sync, in that he executed it on a different word to the one he was trying to emphasise. That, they had condescendingly pointed out, was a classic tell that the paedophile was lying.

Franklin had picked up on both of these traits long before the texts arrived.

Benny's eyes were watchful, calculating, constantly jumping from one detective to the other. Even when answering simple questions, the old man had deliberately been vague, using one or two sentences to give as obscure an answer as possible so he couldn't be pulled up for providing wrong information later on. Franklin was surprised one of the experts hadn't messaged him to point this out, too.

"I'm not too sure," Benny said to the latest question. Glancing from one officer to the other, he shrugged apologetically. "Sorry, I'd like to help but I just can't remember."

They were almost forty minutes into the current interview, and since breaking for the video capture, Benny's body language was rich with contradiction. He was doing his best to come across as relaxed and unconcerned, but he couldn't completely mask his stress and anxiety.

Franklin smiled inwardly. "Oh, I think you remember perfectly, Benny," he countered smoothly. "You just don't want to tell us."

Benny wiped his sweaty palms on his legs. He had done this several times during the past few minutes, and Franklin knew it was a sure sign that he was feeling the pressure. He felt a petty stab of satisfaction that the experts had missed this, too.

"No, I definitely can't remember," Benny said, mustering a fake smile.

The mobile phone in Franklin's hand buzzed, heralding another message from Susie. He casually glanced down at the screen, fully expecting it to be another unhelpful insight from one of the experts. Perhaps they had finally picked up on the sweaty palms?

He raised an eyebrow as he read it; for once, the message was helpful.

*'Lionel Eberhard is singing like a canary. Take a break as soon as the tape ends so I can brief you properly.'*

Franklin smiled, pocketed his phone. The 45 minute long tape would end in a couple of minutes anyway, so this was perfect timing.

"Are you sure you don't want to unburden yourself, Benny?" Franklin asked, casually leaning back in his seat and clasping his hands across his stomach, deliberately giving the impression of a man who was totally in control of the situation and held all the aces.

Benny was eyeing him with increased suspicion. He obviously realised that Franklin had just received some interesting news.

"You might as well," Franklin said with a knowing smile. "It's all coming out anyway."

Benny stiffened. "What's that supposed to mean?" he demanded, leaning forward to peer intently at his interviewer.

Franklin spread his arms. "I just mean that it might be better if you gave us your account willingly, rather than leaving it to other people to tell us what you've been getting up to."

Benny's right eye twitched, and his lips compressed into a cruel, thin line. The implications were obvious; someone was talking. Maybe more than one?

"You're trying to make me think that someone's grassed me up," he said, clearly rattled. "But I don't believe you. You're just trying to play mind games with me."

The tape machine made a loud buzzing noise, signalling that the tapes needed to be changed.

Franklin glanced at his watch. "That noise signifies that the tapes are coming to an end, and I think this is a good time to take a short break so that you can consult with your legal advisor and I can speak to my colleagues." The smile he gave Benny, as he removed the master and working copy tapes from the machine, was one of a cat toying with a mouse before finally putting it out of its misery.

"You lot think you're so clever," Benny snarled as he stood up to accompany his solicitor out of the room, "but I'm not beaten yet."

## 45

Slag! Tart! Jezebel!

Leaving the gaoler to escort McQueen back to his cell, Murray walked his sour faced solicitor to the front counter. "If you'd like to wait here, Mr Grealish, I'll give you a shout when we're ready to continue."

"When exactly do you think that's likely to be?" Grealish asked, sounding peeved.

Murray shrugged. "No idea." He didn't like the man, and was sick of seeing him toady up to his loathsome client.

"That's not very helpful," Grealish, objected.

Murray shrugged again, belligerently this time. "Not my job to be helpful," he informed the solicitor.

"In that case, I'll pop out and get my client some decent food. I think he's a bit sick of the slop you lot serve in here."

Murray didn't do sympathy, empathy, patience or kindness at the best of times. He knew he had an unfortunate gift for saying the wrong thing at the wrong time, and an uncanny ability to upset almost everyone he spoke to without even trying. The thing was, he really didn't care. He had been called sexist, homophobic, racist, a misogynist and much more besides, but he didn't consider himself to be any of these things. He just spoke his mind, and if that offended people, it was their problem, not his.

"Really?" he said, shaking his head in bewilderment. "You're going to spend your own money on a sub-human scumbag like Joey McQueen?"

"My client is not sub-human," Grealish objected, as if he felt morally obliged to take offence on McQueen's behalf.

Murray snorted. "If you believe that, then you're even more stupid than you look, which I wouldn't have believed possible until you said that."

"How dare you!" The solicitor spluttered. His face had turned the colour of puce.

"No!" Murray growled, slamming his hand down on the station office counter with such force that Grealish recoiled. "How dare you! Have you ever lost a loved one? Have you ever had to sit down and listen to a police officer tell you that your nine year old son has been abducted, beaten, raped and then strangled?"

The vehemence in Murray's voice took Grealish totally by surprise, and he responded with an infinitesimal shake of his head.

"I didn't think so," Murray spat, his voice trembling with anger. "Because if you or someone you cared about had, you wouldn't be spouting that shit. This is all a game to you; a big case that will earn your company lots of money and raise its profile, but it's real life for the poor victims and their families. You make me sick."

Dick Jarvis and Gurjit Singh appeared, having heard the commotion as they made their way over to the canteen.

"Everything okay?" Singh asked, looking with concern from the detective to the solicitor and back again.

"Everything's fine," Murray growled. "Mr Grealish and I were just having a friendly disagreement."

"Where's the weirdest place you've ever had sex?" Murray asked. He was sitting in the canteen with Dick Jarvis and Gurjit Singh, and had calmed down considerably since his earlier outburst in the station office.

The three men had adjourned for a quick cuppa while Susie briefed their lead interviewers, Franklin, White and Evans, regarding Eberhard's confession.

"That's an odd question," Jarvis said, clearly uncomfortable with the topic.

"Go on, tell me," Murray insisted. "You're amongst friends here, so don't be shy."

Jarvis shifted uneasily. "Well, it's not something I feel comfortable discussing, to tell you the truth."

Murray rolled his eyes. "Look, I'll start. I had sex in a graveyard once."

"I hope you put the corpse back afterwards," Gurjit Singh tittered.

"Oh, very funny," Murray said, clapping his hands in sardonic applause.

It was Jarvis' turn to laugh, and Murray's to feel uncomfortable. Emboldened by Singh's comments, he said, "Was she as much fun as the blow up dolls you usually have sex with?"

"We're not judging you, Kev," Gurjit persisted, struggling to keep a straight face. "There's nothing wrong with necrophilia, as long as it's consensual."

"I think I preferred talking to that wanker of a solicitor than to you two." Murray snapped, wishing he'd never started the conversation.

---

Two rowdy female prisoners were shouting at each other in the caged area outside the custody office. They would have tried to gouge each other's eyes out had they not been handcuffed. Ignoring the arresting officer's pleas to calm down, they continued to hurl obscenities at each other.

"Slag! Tart! Jezebel!"

"Frigid cow!"

"Home wrecker!"

"Yeah, well, perhaps if you'd been able to satisfy him, he wouldn't have felt the need to stray…"

"You no-good conniving bitch! Everyone knows you're happy to spread your legs for anything with a pulse."

"Yeah, well, he reckons having sex with you was like doing it with a dead fish, or was it that your fanny smells like a dead fish? I can't remember now."

And so, it continued.

One of them spat at the other, who retaliated by trying to kick her.

"Break it up, ladies," one of the officers yelled as he and his partner pulled them apart.

The two sergeants performing custody duty were struggling to make themselves heard above the din. "God, can you imagine what it must be like, living with them?" one of them remarked to his opposite number.

"I'd rather stick toothpicks in my eyeballs," came the weary reply.

Both men laughed.

"You'd better bring them in," the first sergeant called out to the officers in the cage. "The quicker we get these two charmers into cells, the better."

Dillon had been standing up on the podium while all this was going on, briefing the PACE inspector on the investigation's progress. On his way out, he caught sight of Imogen and Bear standing by the entrance to the cell passage. Her face lit up when she saw him, and she eagerly beckoned him over.

"How's the filming going?" he asked, trying to make himself heard over the shouting.

Imogen shrugged, pointed at her ears and shook her head.

Dillon ushered her into the nearby fingerprint room, which was empty, and closed the door behind them. "It's like a bloody zoo out there," he complained, wondering how the custody sergeants put up with dealing with crap like that on a daily basis. "I asked you how the filming was going?"

Instead of answering him, she reached up, wrapped her arms tightly around his neck and drew him in for a kiss.

"What was that for?" he asked, when she allowed him up for air.

"No reason," she said, eyeing him coquettishly. "I just enjoy being spontaneous every now and then."

Dillon nodded, approvingly. "Me too."

Imogen sidled up to him. "Are *you* up for a bit more spontaneity?" she enquired, stroking his arm suggestively.

With an alluring smile, she went up on tiptoes intending to kiss him again, but he placed a hand on each shoulder to keep her at bay.

"I thought you enjoyed a little spontaneity?" she asked, giving him an injured pout.

Dillon smiled, mischievously. "I do. If you'd care to let me know the day, date, time and place you want me to be spontaneous, I'll make a note in my diary!"

She punched his shoulder. "Very funny."

His mobile started ringing. "See, we would have been interrupted anyway," he said, feeling vindicated. Pressing the green button, he took the call. "Hello...?" A huge grin lit up his face as he recognised the caller's voice. "Barty Craddock, you wily old rascal! To what do I owe this unexpected pleasure?"

The two detectives had met earlier in the year, when their respective cases overlapped, and they had kept in touch ever since.

Returning Imogen's wave as she slipped out of the room, Dillon listened intently to what the Norfolk detective had to say. The smile quickly evaporated, replaced by worry lines that seemed to deepen with every passing second. "Are you absolutely sure, Barty?" he asked with a heavy heart, after Craddock had finished speaking.

---

No one noticed as Phillip Diggle wandered down the cell passageway. As a civilian, he wasn't allowed down there without an escort, but with both custody sergeants distracted by the two gobby prisoners, and the poor stressed gaoler running around like a headless chicken, it had been easy to slip away. When he reached the cell that Benny Mars was being held in, he lowered the wicket and peered in.

"What do you want?" Benny demanded, looking up sullenly from the cot he was sitting on.

Diggle said nothing. His expression remained calm and relaxed, almost serene, revealing nothing of the hatred that raged within him.

Diggle knew the police had more than enough evidence to charge Mars, and that he would spend the rest of his life in a cell, but he still wanted him dead. No doubt, someone in prison would eventually do the job for him. Diggle knew how the system worked; Mars would be subjected to prison rule 43, which meant he would be housed on a vulnerable person's unit with all the other paedophiles and rapists, but there would inevitably come a time when a lifer with nothing to lose found a way to get at him.

With any luck, one of them would stab or bludgeon Mars to death, or squeeze the life out of him with their bare hands. When they did, Diggle would send them a letter of gratitude.

In the meantime, there were plenty of other monsters who deserved Diggle's particular brand of summary justice, and with the three men responsible for Robbie's death finally out of circulation, he could turn his attention to them.

"Are you just going to stare at me, or what?" Mars said, standing up and walking over to the open wicket.

Diggle took a half step backwards, said nothing.

Mars leered at him, then thrust his face through the gap. "Who are you anyway?" he asked. "You ain't a cop."

For a moment, Diggle considered punching him, sending his fist through the aperture to devastate the old man's face, but that would be hard to explain away, so he merely closed the wicket instead.

As he turned away, intending to return to the custody office, he was surprised to see Dillon leaning against the wall, arms folded, one ankle crossed over the other, watching him thoughtfully.

"What are you doing down here?" Dillon asked. There was an edge to his voice that Diggle had never heard before. It made him wary.

He mustered a smile, gave a self-deprecating shrug. "Sorry, I was looking for the loo and took a wrong turn, ended up down here by mistake." He made to walk off, but Dillon blocked his path.

"It's funny," the detective said, grim-faced. "I've known you for a little while now, yet until a few minutes ago, I never knew your real name. It's Phillip Diggle, isn't it?"

"I prefer Bear," Diggle said.

"It's a good name, suits you down to the ground," Dillon acknowledged with a sad smile.

Diggle stared at the detective for a long moment, realising that the big man knew his secret. "How did you find out?"

"One of the prerequisites to you and Imogen filming your show was that you both provided elimination samples of your fingerprints and DNA," Dillon explained. "It transpires that your DNA matches a sample that the killer left at a house in Caister when he murdered a paedophile named Angus Clifford."

Diggle winced. "That was clumsy, wasn't it?"

Dillon shrugged. "These things happen, that's why people rarely get away with murder."

"So, what happens now?" Diggle asked, seemingly resigned to his fate.

"I'm sorry, Bear, but I'm arresting you on suspicion of the murders of Keith Smithers in February of this year, Michael Krebs in August of this year, Angus Clifford in October of this year, and Maurice Hinkleman, who was killed at his photographic studio in Hackney, yesterday."

He formally cautioned Diggle.

Diggle frowned. "I take it you found more DNA at the other scenes?"

"I can't discuss the evidence before interview," Dillon told him. "It's for your protection as much as mine."

Diggle nodded. "I understand, and to tell you the truth, I felt guilty about that Warren boy getting the blame for something he didn't do, so maybe it's a good thing."

Dillon placed a hand on his arm to guide him back to the custody office. "Imogen's going to be devastated when she finds out."

Diggle nodded, feeling a lump form in his throat. "I love that sweet girl. She's like the kid sister I never had." He could feel tears welling in his eyes, and he blinked them away, not wanting to appear weak. "I hope she won't judge me too harshly," he said, in a voice that was suddenly thick with emotion.

## 46

*I have an official announcement to make*

Tyler was just about to pop down to the canteen when his landline rang. It was Mel Howarth, calling from Chingford with an interesting update.

"Good afternoon, boss," she said, sounding very chipper. "*I was just talking to Steve Bull down in custody, and he tells me that Lionel Eberhard is talking so much, he can hardly get a word in edgeways.*"

Tyler smiled. "Yes, it's as if Eberhard suddenly feels the need to confess every transgression that he's ever committed, and he's chosen to unburden himself on poor Stevie."

Howarth chuckled. "*I still can't believe that you guys rescued those kids unharmed. It's such a brilliant result. Well done!*"

"We couldn't have asked for a better outcome," Tyler admitted, feeling a huge surge of pride over the effort his team had put in.

"*Anyway, the reason I called was to let you know that we've found a witness who saw the suspect ushering the kids into the back of his van at the fairground on Saturday night.*"

"Oh, who?"

"*I don't know if you recall, but that night, a number of cars were broken into at the fairground. Luckily for us, the suspect cut his hand on one of them, and our Crime Squad arrested him this morning when his blood came back as a match on a DNA docket. His name's Sean Murphy, and he's a well-known local toerag. He put his hands up to screwing all the cars, which is great for our clear-up rate, but he also admitted to seeing a white male usher two children into the back of a van and drive off. He claims he called the Incident Room, but wouldn't give his name for fear of us linking him to the car crimes. Anyway, now he's been caught for those, he's willing to attend an ID parade, to see if he can pick out the suspect.*"

Tyler recalled the call he'd fielded while covering for Gurjit Singh on Monday afternoon. "I think I was the one who took his call," he told Howarth.

"*Really? Small world. I'll e-mail his details over to the MIR so they can arrange the viewing.*"

---

Imogen was still waiting in the custody area when Dillon escorted Bear out of the cell passage. She was chatting to Kevin Murray, Dick Jarvis and Gurjit Singh, who had recently returned from the canteen and were patiently waiting for the custody sergeants to finish processing the two objectionable women so that they could book their prisoners back out to continue the interviews.

She smiled at Dillon, but her expression quickly morphed into a frown when she saw he was holding her cameraman's arm.

That was strange.

Dillon gave her a troubled look, while Bear avoided looking at her at all.

Instead of joining them, Dillon led Bear over to the fingerprint room, beckoning for the gaoler to join them. The three men disappeared into the room, and Dillon closed the door behind them.

That was even stranger.

The journalist in Imogen instinctively knew that something was amiss. Excusing herself from the others, she set off for the fingerprint room, being careful to give the two, still arguing, women a wide berth.

Imogen was just about to knock on the door when it opened, and Dillon emerged. He reacted guiltily, as if she had just caught him doing something he shouldn't.

"Oh, hello," he said, being uncharacteristically awkward with her.

"What's going on?" she asked, locking eyes with him.

Unable to hold her gaze, he looked away. "Look, Imogen, I can't tell you right now, so you'll just have to trust me when I say that I'm not being cagey."

His words stung. When they had decided to commit to each other, they had discussed the potential trust issues that might arise when their professions created conflicts of interest, and they had sworn never to jeopardise their relationship by breeching a confidence that the other one had shared with them.

"Okay," she responded, frostily. "If you're going to be like that, I'll just wait in there with Bear until you're ready to trust me with whatever secret it is that you're hiding." As she spoke, she attempted to step past him and enter the room.

He moved sideways, blocking her path. "I'm sorry," he said, awkwardly, "I can't let you see Bear at the moment."

She frowned at him, then laughed at the ridiculousness of the statement. "Why? It's not like he's under arrest, is it?" She had meant this as a throw away comment, but his reaction startled her.

It was as if she had guessed his guilty secret.

Folding her arms across her chest, Imogen gave him a mutinous look. "Tony, what are you playing at?"

Dillon was squirming. If she hadn't been so angry with him, she might have been amused that this behemoth of a man was so easily intimidated by little old her.

"Tony..." The word came out from behind gritted teeth, sounding very much like a growl. "What's going on?"

Fletcher rapped on Tyler's door and entered without knocking. "Apologies, guv, but I've been working my way through the list of boys who went missing from the Dover area in July of 1992. There were only three, and I think I've found a match for the boy Eberhard's been telling Steve about."

Tyler gestured for him to take a seat.

Fletcher was obviously very excited. Sitting down, he slid three A4 documents across the desk for Tyler's perusal.

"The first is a copy of the missing person report, the second is a copy of the photograph the care home provided, and the last one is a still from the porn video we recovered from Eberhard's house, which Jim printed off for me a few minutes ago."

Tyler scooped them up. "Clive Walker, aged ten when he disappeared. Last seen at a travelling fairground in Dover," he said when he'd finished reading the missing person report. "Why do you think it's him?"

"Walker was a street urchin, well known to the local constabulary for committing petty crimes. He had no family to speak of, and had been in local authority care for several years by the time he vanished. He was a regular absconder, so they weren't too worried at first. He had been AWOL from the care home for three days when he was sighted at the fairground by his social worker, who was there for a night out with her own kids. He was talking to two men when she approached him, but as soon as he saw her, the little sod ran off. Anyway, the local plod followed up the lead she'd given them, and spoke to the men before the fairground moved on. Care to hazard a guess as to what their names were?"

Tyler shrugged, in no mood to play games.

"Well, the first one was called Angus Clifford, and he was working at the fairground as a rigger."

Tyler shrugged; the name meant nothing to him.

"The second was his mate, Benny Mars, who was staying with him for the weekend."

Tyler leaned back in his chair and began stroking his bristled chin, deep in contemplation. He could easily envisage how things had played out: Clive Walker had returned to the fairground at some point over the weekend. Young and impressionable, deeply unhappy with his current life, he would have been highly susceptible to the alluring offer that Mars made him of a new life in London. Beguiled by promises of money and excitement, he would have accompanied the paedophile there willingly, unwittingly placing himself at the monster's mercy by doing so.

Tyler shuddered at the thought. "This is outstanding work," he said. "I've no doubt that you're right, but I don't know how we can prove it."

"But we *can* prove that Mars was one of the men who raped the boy in the video," Fletcher persisted.

"Yes," Tyler allowed.

"So, surely, as long as we prove Clive Walker was the boy being raped, and we carry out proof of life checks to establish he hasn't been seen or heard from since, we can at least invite a jury to believe that Mars murdered him, especially as Eberhard confirms this?"

Tyler sighed. If only it were that easy. Eberhard was claiming that Mars killed the boy in the video, and Tyler believed him. But he didn't know the child's name, so without a body, how could they prove the rape victim was murdered? It might be different if they could conclusively establish that the boy being raped was Walker. Then, they could do as Fletcher had suggested, and carry out extensive proof of life checks. The CPS might be willing to charge Benny with murder on that basis.

But they couldn't.

"Dean, at this point, we can prove that Mars was one of the three men who raped the hooded boy in the porn video, and we *will* charge him with that, but we can't prove the victim was Clive Walker."

"Well, with all due respect, I beg to differ," Fletcher argued. "I think we *can* prove it was him."

Tyler spread his hands in exasperation. "How? If you can pull that one off, you're a better detective than me."

Fletcher flashed him a triumphant smile. "Then I'm a better detective than you," he said, snatching up the missing person report and photograph that Jim Stone had printed off. He held the photo out for Tyler to take.

"I've already looked at it," Tyler said, making no move to accept the offering.

"Look again," Fletcher implored him.

Tyler took it, ran his eyes over the hooded figure lying on the bed, then made to return the photograph.

It was Fletcher's turn to decline. "Look at his right foot," he told his boss.

Tyler could feel his patience evaporating. "Dean," he cautioned.

"Look at his right foot," Fletcher insisted.

Tyler shot him a warning look to let him know he was pushing his luck, then did as he'd been asked. It was a child's foot, nothing more; nothing less. "Whatever it is you want me to notice, I don't see it," he said, testily.

"Count his toes," Fletcher instructed.

"Count his...?" Tyler was beginning to wonder if Fletcher was losing the plot. Nonetheless, he obliged. There were five. No, wait, there were four. The little toe was missing. He looked up at Fletcher, his eyes questioning.

His lead researcher was holding out Clive Walker's missing person report. "Read the section on marks and scars."

Tyler snatched it from his hand. His eyes scanned the report until they found the relevant entry. His lips moved quickly but silently as he read the contents to himself. He glanced up at Fletcher, and their eyes met. "Well, I'll be damned," he said, as a smile stretched across his face.

"See, I told you we could prove that the boy in the video was Clive Walker," Fletcher said, triumphantly.

Tyler stood up, walked over to the door. "Follow me," he ordered, striding into the main office. With five prisoners being interviewed, two crime scenes being processed, and the ABE interviews underway, there was hardly anyone there, but Tyler clapped his hands to get the attention of those who were. "I have an official announcement to make," he told them, wrapping an arm around

Fletcher's shoulders as he spoke. "I want you all to know that, without doubt, Deano is a much better detective than I am."

Ignoring the questioning looks his seemingly random statement had evoked, he returned to his office, a very happy man.

---

"I just don't believe it," Imogen said, shaking her head in denial. "Bear would never do something like *that*. He's far too nice."

Having asked Singh to wait in the fingerprint room with Bear until he returned, Dillon had marched Imogen out of the custody suite in order to speak to her in private.

"I'm so sorry, Imogen," he said, softly. Discovering that Bear, a man she trusted implicitly, was a serial killer had hit her hard. He could see that she was in a state of profound shock, and struggling to process the news. "I know how close you two are. I like him, too."

He stepped forward, intending to embrace her, but she retreated, swatting his hands away.

"Why would he do it?" she demanded, running her hands through her hair in agitation.

"I don't know," he confessed, "but I'm afraid there's no doubt that he did."

Imogen looked like she wanted to cry. "Four men! You're seriously telling me that Bear, a man who wouldn't say boo to a goose, murdered four men? That he tied them up and cold bloodedly cut off their manhood? That he sliced their throats open and left them to bleed out?" Her voice grew louder as she spoke, becoming increasingly manic.

Dillon raised a finger to his lips, afraid that someone passing by the room they were in would overhear their conversation.

"Don't you *dare* shush me," she snapped, stamping her foot in anger.

He raised his hands, placatingly. "I'm sorry, but I shouldn't even be discussing this with you, so I need to you keep the noise down."

She started pacing up and down. "Are you really sure?" she

demanded, stopping to face him again. "Is there any way this could all be a big mistake?"

The desperation in her voice brought a lump to his throat. He shook his head, sadly. "No. There's no mistake. His DNA was found at a murder scene in Caister, and on top of that, he admitted the murders to me when I arrested him."

Imogen's face crumpled. Her entire body seemed to deflate as she stood there, arms by her sides, looking very much like a lost child.

This time, when Dillon moved forward to take her in her arms, she didn't resist.

He held her tight, wishing there was something he could say to ease her pain. Knowing there wasn't, he just stood there in silence, stroking her hair while she cried.

## 47

# SATURDAY 10TH NOVEMBER 2001

I've been doing this since I was a teenager

After an unbelievably manic week, and a case that had really looked like getting the better of them right up to the bitter end, everything was finally coming together. For days on end, they had struggled to gather any evidence at all, yet now they were drowning in it.

At five o'clock, Holland summoned Tyler, Dillon, Susie Sergeant, Andy Quinlan and Carol Keating down to the meeting room in the Command Corridor so that they could review the evidence and agree the specific charges to be laid against each prisoner.

Holland's bagman, DS Derek Peterson, had kindly laid on tea, coffee and biscuits for them, and as they took their seats around the table, the atmosphere was a lot less stressful than it had been during their previous meeting.

"Now then," Holland said, kicking off the meeting with a contented smile. "For the moment, I want to leave out anything to do with Hinkleman's murder because, as we all now know, that forms part of a separate series that Andy is running in conjunction with DCI Craddock from Norfolk Constabulary. Instead, I want to focus on the evidence relating to the murders of Adam Cheadle and Clive Walker, and the evidence relating to the abduction of Peter Musgrove and Gavin Grant. Jack, why don't you start by talking us through the forensics? The rest of you, please feel free to chip in as and when."

Tyler cleared his throat. There was a lot to get through. "Let's start with Benny's flat in Hackney. Hair follicles belonging to Adam Cheadle were found in the bedroom Warren claims he was strangled in. Additionally, we recovered an unwashed glass that had been kicked under the bed. This had Benny and McQueen's fingerprints on it. There was some sediment in the bottom of the glass, which contained traces of Temazepam and Diazepam. We fully expect to find a considerable amount of both drugs in Adam's blood when the toxicology results come back, but that won't be for another week. Oh, and there was a big lip shaped smudge around the rim of the glass. The saliva on it matches Adam's DNA profile."

"That's excellent news," Holland said, approvingly. "It corroborates Gabriel Warren's account very nicely." A frown creased his brow. "I take it that he's been key-witness interviewed now that he's no longer a suspect?"

Tyler glanced at Quinlan for clarification.

"Zoe Sanders conducted a key-witness interview with Warren immediately after his release," Quinlan confirmed. "His mum sat in as appropriate adult, and she got through the best part of a box of tissues while listening to the poor boy's account. By the way, he had no trouble picking Mars and McQueen out from the ID parades."

"By making enquiries with the local authority, we identified a garage that came with the flat," Tyler said, resuming his narrative. "When we searched this, we found the roll of carpet they wrapped Adam's body in to transport it to the forest, along with the shovel McQueen used to dig the grave. Several strands of hair were snagged in the carpet fibres. There were also mud splodges and some blood smears. As expected, the hair follicles matched Adam's DNA profile and the blood matched McQueen's. We haven't had the results back for the mud yet, but we're supremely confident it will match the soil samples taken from the forest."

"Excellent, excellent," Holland beamed, making neat little notes in his daybook.

"As we've touched on the body deposition site, I'll deal with what was found there next," Tyler informed them. "Firstly, George Copeland spotted a tiny droplet of blood on one of the thickets surrounding the grave. Tests have matched it to McQueen's DNA profile. Secondly, there were some muddy footprints around the grave. Naturally, the CSM took plaster casts, and these matched the soles of a muddy pair of size nine training shoes that were found at the flat in Hackney. No doubt, we'll get Joey's wearer DNA from them."

"The lab results for the skin cells found under Adam's fingernails and the blood found in his mouth came in this morning," Dillon chipped in. "Both are 100% matches for Joey McQueen's DNA profile."

"Anything else?" Holland enquired. His jaunty tone suggested that it would be superfluous.

"One last thing," Dillon said. "The FME examining McQueen's hand injury said it was a bite mark. A forensic odontologist has viewed the photographed and concurs. Sam Calvin's made arrangements for a cast to be taken of Adam's teeth, so that a true comparison can be made."

"That's more than enough evidence to charge Mars and McQueen with Adam's murder," Holland said, allowing himself a little chortle of satisfaction. "And to think that, at one point, the Senior Command Team at The Yard were worried this case was going to be a sticker," he said, giving the impression that he had never harboured any such doubts himself.

Tyler, like everyone else in the room, laughed politely, knowing full well that he had.

Franklin sat down opposite Benny and his solicitor for what he hoped would be the final interview. The process had been a gruelling one. It had taken a lot out him, but it had also taken its toll on Benny. When the interviews commenced the previous morning, Benny had sauntered into the room with the confidence of the Alpha male he clearly envisioned himself to be. Franklin had gradually chipped away at his arrogance, eroding his confidence a little with each new revelation. Now, Benny seemed like a frail old man, and looking at him in that context, it would have been oh so easy to forget that he was a dangerous predator who had ruined countless lives.

Benny knew that he was beaten; Franklin could see it in his eyes. Yet, the ageing paedophile was still putting up a fight.

Franklin nodded to Jarvis, who dutifully pressed the button to start the recording device. When the buzzing stopped, Franklin plodded through the usual opening spiel, introducing everyone present, stating the day, date, time and place.

Then he cautioned Benny.

"Before we took a short break for you to consult your legal advisor, I played you a pornographic video that was seized from the house of Lionel Eberhard earlier in the week. The tape featured three hooded men taking turns to rape an unconscious boy. I pointed out that the first man to rape the boy had a distinctive tattoo of a howling wolf's head on his left buttock. The word 'Alpha' was written beneath it in gothic script. I then pointed out that the second man to rape the boy had an identical wolf's head tattoo on his left buttock, although his one didn't have any writing beneath it. He did, however, have a nasty appendix scar to the right of his navel. Do you accept that I showed you the video and pointed these things out to you?"

Benny sneered at him. "Fuck off."

"Afterwards," Franklin continued, completely unfazed by Benny's response, "I showed you a copy of exhibit NS/30. That's a photograph of the wolf's head tattoo on your left buttock. It was taken by a police photographer when you arrived at the station after your arrest. It is identical in every respect to the tattoo on the first man to rape the child. Do you accept that?"

Benny glared at him but said nothing.

Franklin shrugged. "I then showed you copies of exhibits NS/100 and NS/101. These were two photographs taken at the post mortem examination of Maurice Hinkleman. NS/100 shows a wolf's head tattoo, minus any writing, on Hinkleman's left buttock. NS/101 shows an appendicectomy scar on his right side. They match the tattoo and scar on the second man to rape the child. Do you accept this?"

Benny looked down at the floor, said nothing.

"Benny, will you answer the que—"

"Fuck off!" Benny snapped. He rested his elbows on the table and buried his head in his hands, staring miserably into his lap. "I've had enough of this bullshit."

"Do you deny being the first rapist?" Franklin persisted.

"Are you deaf? I told you to fuck off," Benny snarled, growing increasingly angry.

"Do you deny that Hinkleman was the second rapist?"

Benny looked up suddenly, his eyes full of hatred.

Franklin smiled at him. "Will you tell us who the third rapist was?"

Benny opened his mouth, presumably to swear, then thought better of it and said nothing.

Franklin paused a breath, letting the tension between them build. "I also showed you a copy of a business card that was found at Eberhard's house. It was tucked into the sleeve of the video tape we showed you. It had your name, mobile telephone number and business address scribbled on the back. Do you recall being shown that card?"

Benny fidgeted in his seat, and Franklin sensed that he was wrestling with himself, that his temper was gradually getting the better of him, and that he was on the verge of saying something incriminating.

Franklin just needed to push him a little further. "Your fingerprints have been found on that card, Benny," he said, conversationally. "How do you explain that?"

Benny looked up, his face registering surprise. "Bollocks! You can't get fingerprints from paper."

Franklin had to stop himself from smiling. This was the first time that Benny had responded with anything other than 'no comment' or a variant of 'fuck you' all day.

"Oh, but you can," Franklin took pleasure in telling him. "There's a chemical called Ninhydrin that can recover fingerprints from paper and cardboard, and the scientists used it on your business card. I thought *everyone* knew that."

Benny sat up a little straighter, his lips compressing into a thin cruel line. "If my card was in with his video, he must have put it there, not me. I give those cards out to anyone who comes into my sex shop, which is a totally legitimate business by the way."

"No, you don't," Franklin told him, firmly. "The business cards you hand out at the shop are professionally printed, and they contain your business landline, not the number for your private mobile. And as I've already said, the card we found in the video was handwritten by you, not printed."

"How do you know it was my handwriting?" Benny challenged. "Lionel could have written that."

"That's a feeble attempt at an excuse," Franklin goaded, shaking his head in mock disappointment. "I would have expected better from you."

Benny was staring at him with utter loathing.

"We've had the card examined by a handwriting expert, who compared it to various documents we seized from your shop. It's your handwriting, Benny." A pause; then, "And Lionel Eberhard confirms it."

Benny reacted as though he'd been slapped. "There's no fucking way he would do that."

"Ah, but he did," Franklin assured him. "He also told us that you were the first man to rape the boy, that Maurice Hinkleman was the second, and that he was the third. What do you say to that?"

Benny didn't say anything. His mouth sagged open, flapped several times, then clamped itself shut.

"What's more," Franklin continued, taking a perverse pleasure from turning the screw. "He says that he was there when you subsequently murdered the boy."

"This is a fit up," Benny said, springing halfway out of his chair. "No way would he drop me in it like that, or himself for that matter." For all his bluster, there was fear in his eyes, and his face had taken on a haunted look.

Benny's solicitor placed a restraining hand on his arm and gently pushed his client back into his seat.

"I assure you I'm not fitting you up," Franklin said. "The boy's name was Clive Walker, and he was ten years old when you met him at a fairground in Dover one Friday night in late July 1992. Do you remember that night, Benny?"

Benny shrugged. "I worked for a travelling fair for years. I used to speak to young boys all the time, you can't avoid it when you're working the rides."

"True," Franklin acknowledged. "But you had stopped working as a ride attendant and rigger by then. You were visiting your buddy, Angus Clifford."

Benny's face paled.

Franklin could almost hear the cogs turning as the old man tried to second guess how much the detective actually knew.

"Well, maybe he was talking to Angus, and I just happened to be standing next to him," Benny said.

Franklin smiled. He had the paedophile on the back foot now. "No, that's not the case at all. We have a witness who saw you speaking to Clive on your own. You had your arm around him."

"Your witness must be mistaken. Perhaps it was another boy talking to another man. It certainly wasn't me."

"The witness was Clive's social worker. She knew him well. When she approached the two of you, Clive ran off. And we know it was you, because the local police questioned you about it afterwards and you admitted that you'd spoken to the boy."

Benny was reeling. He knew he had made a big mistake by

putting himself at the fair. "The boy in that video had a canvas hood over his head, so how do you even know it was the same boy I was supposedly talking to?" he objected.

"Well, for starters, Eberhard told us it was the same boy," Franklin said, and let Benny think about that for a couple of seconds before continuing. "Eberhard told us how you boasted about picking him up in Dover and bringing him back to London for your own amusement."

"He's lying. It's his word against mine."

Franklin raised an eyebrow. "We've got video footage of you raping Clive. Granted, we can't identify his face or yours because everyone's wearing a hood, but I don't think that matters anymore. I think your distinctive tattoo will convince a jury that the rapist couldn't be anyone other than you. I think they'll be equally convinced that the second rapist couldn't be anyone other than Hinkleman, thanks to his tattoo and scar." He raised an eyebrow, inviting Benny to pass comment, but the old man just crossed his arms and huffed loudly.

Franklin withdrew four A4 sheets of paper from a folder by his foot. "Likewise, I believe they will accept that the boy in the video is Clive because of the documents I'm about to show you." He placed the first one on the table between them, tapped it with his finger. "This is a copy of exhibit JS/15. It's a blow up of an image taken from the rape video, and it shows Clive's right foot. Look closely and you will see that he only has four toes."

Benny made a big show of squinting at the photograph, as though the image wasn't at all clear.

"The print's a bit grainy," Franklin conceded, "but there's no mistaking the fact that there are only four toes on the boy's right foot." When it became apparent that Benny wasn't going to say anything, Franklin laid the next document down. "This is a copy of exhibit DJ/20. It's a heavily redacted copy of the Kent Constabulary missing person report for Clive Walker, and it's dated Wednesday 22$^{nd}$ July 1992. Can you see the section listing marks and scars? It's about halfway down on the right."

Benny ran his eyes down the report until he found it, then nodded. "Yeah, so what?"

"Would you care to read it out for me?" Franklin asked.

"No, I would not care to do that."

"I'll paraphrase it for you then," Franklin offered. "It states that Clive Walker was born with only four toes on his right foot."

When Franklin laid the third sheet down, Benny groaned. "Now what?"

"This is a copy of exhibit DJ/101, which is the photograph Kent police were given of Clive following his disappearance." He placed the final sheet beside it. "And this is a copy of exhibit GC/100, which is a Polaroid photograph that was found in a shoebox full of similar photographs. The shoe box was in one of the filing cabinets in the basement of your house in Grove Green Road. It shows you standing next to Clive Walker in the master bedroom of the very same house. If you compare the bedroom in the photo of you and Clive to the bedroom in the rape video, you can easily see that they are one and the same place." Franklin touched the Polaroid. "Who's this man standing way over to your right, towards the edge of the photograph?"

Benny looked at the image, then shook his head. "Dunno."

"You do know," Franklin told him. "That man is Lionel Eberhard. For the record, he's been shown a copy of this photograph and has confirmed it's him. The date, Saturday 1$^{st}$ August, is helpfully written on the back of the photograph. To jog your memory, that's the weekend after you visited Angus Clifford in Dover." Franklin angrily jabbed each of the photographs in turn. "Now tell me you didn't know Clive Walker; that you didn't rape him; that you didn't murder him?" Franklin dared him, finally letting all the anger and disgust he had bottled up during the previous interviews show itself.

Benny sat there in brooding silence looking down at the photographs for a very long time. To Franklin's surprise, when he finally looked up, he was smiling. Then he started to giggle, and the giggle quickly turned into a manic laugh.

Franklin and Jarvis exchanged uneasy glances. This wasn't the reaction they had been expecting. Benny's eyes burned with a fervour that Franklin found slightly unnerving.

"You lot think you're oh so fucking clever, don't you?" Benny sneered, his words dripping with contempt. "Okay, so you've got me for snuffing out a couple of worthless chickens. I'll give you that, but so fucking what?" Spreading his arms wide, he shrugged ruthlessly. "I've had a good run. I'm sixty-seven years old now, and I've been doing this since I was a teenager. I've enjoyed more chickens than you've had hot dinners."

Franklin sat there in stunned silence. The paedophile was actually boasting about his exploits; he was proud of what he was and what he had done.

"What?" Benny demanded, sneering at him. "Did you expect me to break down and cry?" he seemed amused by the shock and revulsion that had appeared on the detectives' faces. "I'll let you into a little secret; I was fucking little boys like them before you were even born." He grinned broadly, then winked at them. "Killing them too." With that, Benny tilted his head back and started laughing again.

Franklin stared disbelievingly at the man seated opposite him, convinced that he was in the presence of pure evil.

## 48

*This is beyond terrible*

"So, in relation to the abduction and child trafficking offences, what have we got?" Holland asked.

"All the ID showings have been completed," Tyler said. "Peter and Gavin picked Remus out as the man who abducted them. They both identified Benny as one of the other men from the house they were kept prisoner in. Gavin picked out Joey, but Peter didn't. Gavin identified Eberhard as the man he was delivered to, and Peter identified Madeley. Sean Murphy had no trouble picking Remus out as the man he saw ushering the kids into the Berlingo, but the fairground worker failed to pick Remus out as the man he had seen the boys following into the trees."

"What about the Berlingo, did we get anything useful from that?" Holland asked next.

"We did," Tyler confirmed, happily. He opened a slim manila docket and read from it. "Hair follicles belonging to Gavin were recovered from inside the suitcase. The two snotty tissues snagged in the lining also matched Gavin's DNA profile. Joey McQueen left us a beautiful thumb print on the suitcase handle, and there were a couple of prints belonging to Benny Mars on the exterior." He closed the docket. "The van's still being examined over at Charlton car pound, so there's a strong likelihood we'll find more over the next couple of days."

"What about forensics from the house in Grove Green Road?" Holland enquired.

Tyler picked up a second docket. "It'll take several days to process that place properly. The CSM reckons it's a gold mine of forensic evidence. We found two black bin liners in a wheelie bin in the back garden. The first contained all the clothing the kids were wearing when they were abducted. We've arranged for the FLOs to show the items to the boys and their mums later today, and we'll take statements from them, identifying what belongs to who. Naturally, we'll back that up by obtaining wearer DNA. The second bag contained men's clothing. Amongst other things, there was a camouflaged jacket and a pair of army khakis."

"I take it that's what Remus was wearing on the night he abducted the kids?" Keating asked.

Tyler nodded. "We'll get wearer DNA from it in due course, but yeah, that's our thinking."

"What about inside the house?" That question had come from Quinlan.

"What an insidious place that is," Tyler said, suppressing a shudder. "As you all know, we found a room in the cellar that had been converted into a holding cell. There were two metal cots in it. We've seized all the bedding, and expect to find the boys' DNA over everything."

"I take it we can link the suspects to the house just as easily?" Holland queried.

"We can," Tyler assured him. "Their dabs are all over the place. We recovered Peter's mobile phone from a rucksack we think belongs to Remus. It was in the bedroom he was sleeping in. Remus' fingerprints were all over the handset. We're confident we'll get his

DNA from the bedding to prove he was staying there, but that hasn't been submitted to the lab yet."

"Let's talk about Clive Walker," Holland said, working his way down his list.

"Clive Walker's murder will be slightly more problematic to prove," Tyler admitted, "but I'm confident we'll get there in the end. Susie's been coordinating our efforts so perhaps she's best placed to fill us in."

Susie cleared her throat. "Eberhard tells us that in 1992 he was invited to join Benny and Hinkleman in making a child porn movie featuring a boy that Benny abducted from Dover the week before. The boy was drugged before being raped by all three men. On the day of the filming, Benny collected Eberhard from his house in Upper Walthamstow. Eberhard doesn't know where he was taken, because Benny insisted on blindfolding him on the way there and on the way back, but it was only a fifteen minute drive. After the filming finished, Benny killed the boy in front of the others. Eberhard doesn't know where the body was disposed of, because he was taken home before that was done."

"This is beyond terrible," Keating said, the colour draining from her face.

"Dean managed to identify the boy in the video as Clive Walker, who was last seen alive at a fairground in Dover on 24$^{th}$ July 1992. He obtained copies of the missing person report, and the photograph of Walker that Kent police were given by the care home. Arrangements are currently being made for statements to be taken from everyone involved in the missing person enquiry, including the social worker who saw him at the fairground and the two officers who spoke to Benny and his mate, Angus Clifford, afterwards."

"Are we looking at arresting this Clifford chap, too?" Holland asked. His tone implied that they ought to be.

"Clifford's dead, murdered by Phillip Diggle. His decomposing body was discovered at his cottage in Caister on 31$^{st}$ October," Dillon interjected.

Holland frowned. "So, Clive Walker's case is indirectly linked to the four murder's that Andy's team are jointly investigating with DCI Craddock?"

Dillon nodded. "I think it's fair to say that, one way or another, everything we've discussed today is linked."

"Zoe Sander and a chap called Stebbins from Norfolk Constabulary are interviewing Diggle as we speak," Quinlan informed them. "He's being very cooperative and hiding nothing. From what I can gather, apart from his propensity to commit rather gruesome murders, he's quite a decent chap."

"In fairness, he only kills sadistic predatory paedophiles," Dillon said, defensively, as if that made it okay.

"All of his victims were predatory paedophiles," Quinlan agreed. "Keith Smithers, his first victim, was murdered in Wales in February of this year. Smithers raped a number of children over the years. Michael Krebs, Diggle's second victim, was killed in Northumberland. He was an even worse offender than Smithers. Angus Clifford, Diggle's third victim, was murdered in Caister last month, and Hinkleman, his fourth victim, was—"

"I'm sorry, Andy, but can we stop referring to these men as victims," Dillon interrupted, angrily. "They were monsters."

"They were," Quinlan conceded. "But that didn't entitle Diggle to murder them."

Dillon opened his mouth to argue, but Tyler placed a restraining hand on his friend's arm.

"Diggle kept detailed files on all his targets," Quinlan continued. "These were recovered from his hotel room. Diggle claims that Mars, Hinkleman and Clifford were responsible for abducting his twin brother, Robbie, back in the summer of 1976. The investigation was documented on paper, so there was nothing about it on our computer records when we ran background checks on Diggle. We've pulled the file from General Registry and it makes for a gruesome read. Robbie was never found, and it was obvious to everyone involved in the investigation that he had been murdered, but the suspects were never identified. When the police failed him, Diggle took the law into his own hands, tracked them down and killed them. He openly admits that he was planning to dispose of Benny in an identical fashion to the others."

"We seem to have strayed off topic, and I'd like to get back to the Clive Walker investigation," Holland said.

He gestured for Susie to resume her narrative.

"We found some Polaroids in a filing cabinet in the basement of the Grove Green Road house. One featured Benny with an arm around Clive Walker's shoulder. They were standing upstairs, in the master bedroom, where the rape was filmed."

Keating raised a hand to her throat. "Isn't that the same room that Peter Musgrove was found in?"

Susie nodded. "We think he had a very lucky escape."

"My understanding is that everyone in that dreadful video wore hoods, so how can we possibly hope to identify anyone in it?" Holland asked.

Susie smiled reassuringly. "Putting Eberhard's confession aside, we can prove Benny's one of the rapists because we can clearly see his wolf's head tattoo. Likewise, we can prove Clive's the victim because we can see there are only four toes on his right foot, which is a birth defect and not the result of an accident or operation. Once we've obtained their medical records, and carried out the requisite proof of life checks on Clive, we should be able to present the CPS with a compelling argument to charge Mars and Eberhard with Clive's murder, even without a body."

Holland was chewing the end of his biro thoughtfully. "I take it there's no way we can charge them tonight?"

Susie shook her head. "We could probably charge Eberhard, but Benny? I don't think so. The plan is to grant technical bail in relation to Clive Walker's rape and murder, but we'll throw the book at them over everything else."

"I've had a preliminary discussion with the CPS," Tyler told them. "They are very much on board with that."

"Well, that all sounds—" Holland was interrupted by the sound of Susie's mobile phone ringing.

She looked at the caller ID, then grimaced. "Sorry, I need to take this."

She left the room for a couple of minutes.

When she returned, she was smiling broadly. "That was Colin Franklin. Benny's only gone and admitted to killing Adam and Clive in interview! Apparently, he lost his rag and just blurted it all out." She glanced hopefully at Tyler. "In light of that, maybe you should talk to the CPS again, to see if they will authorise charging him and Eberhard with Clive's murder tonight?"

---

It was getting on for nine p.m. when Benny Mars was brought before the custody sergeant to be formally charged. Escorted by the gaoler, with his solicitor by his side, he shuffled in, looking ten years older than when he'd arrived on Thursday afternoon.

Because of the intense media interest that the case continued to generate, the charge room had been cleared of all non-essential personnel beforehand.

Remus and McQueen had already been charged with abduction, false imprisonment, child trafficking and multiple counts of making, possessing and distributing indecent images of children. McQueen had also been charged with Adam Cheadle's murder.

Neither man had said anything in relation to any of the charges. They had simply stood there, staring down at the floor, resigned to their fate.

As Benny entered, he glanced at the small crowd of detectives who had gathered to watch the proceedings. Tyler and Dillon were amongst them. Imogen was there too, accompanied by the replacement videographer the production company had rushed over following Bear's arrest.

When Benny saw that he had an audience, his mouth twisted downwards into a sneer of defiance, and he glared hatefully at them. "You should've sold tickets."

Tyler stared back, unblinking. He saw through the paedophile's act of bravado, and wasn't impressed.

"Benny Mars, there are a number of charges against you, this evening," the custody sergeant announced with the solemnity of a hanging judge.

Apart from the hum of the air conditioner, the room had gone completely silent. No one moved. They hardly even breathed.

"The first charge is that on Wednesday 7th November 2001, within the jurisdiction of The Central Criminal Court, you did attempt to murder Adam Cheadle. This offence is contrary to the Criminal Attempts Act 1981."

Benny smirked at him, but said nothing.

The custody officer then charged Benny with Clive Walker's abduction, false imprisonment and rape, before concluding with the most serious of all: his murder.

When he finished, Benny placed a hand to his mouth, yawned theatrically.

The next set of charges to be read aloud related to the false imprisonment and child trafficking of Peter Musgrove and Gavin Grant, but by this stage, Benny had completely lost interest and was looking down at the floor.

"Are we going to be much longer?" he interrupted halfway through. "Only this is taking forever, and I want to grab some shuteye."

"It will take as long as it takes," the angry custody sergeant told him. To prove his point, he went into slow motion mode, deliberately dragging the process out. The last round of charges related to Benny making, possessing and distributing indecent images of children.

When he had finally finished, the custody officer paused for breath, then formally cautioned Benny. "Mr Mars, in relation to these charges, you do not have to say anything, but if you fail to mention now anything you subsequently rely on in court, a jury may draw an inference from your silence. Anything you do say may be given in evidence."

Benny considered his reply carefully, making a show of stroking his stubbled chin in a thoughtful manner. Then he smiled up at the custody officer and said, "Fuck you."

Tyler had spoken to DCI Barty Craddock over the telephone a couple of times earlier in the year, but this was the first time they had actually met. His Norfolk counterpart was a large, imposing man whose craggy face was dominated by a bulbous nose and a pair of bushy eyebrows that seemed to have a mind of their own. Tyler was instantly reminded of Denis Healey, the Labour Party politician who had served as Chancellor of the Exchequer during the 1970s, and whose trademark eyebrows had been similarly huge.

They were seated around the small coffee table in Tyler's office. Tyler was just waiting for Kelly to return from informing Peter and Gavin's family about the charges, and then he intended to head off home.

For his part, Craddock was working his way through a packet of chocolate digestives that Dillon had pilfered from Gurjit Singh's desk.

"Well, Barty, it's nice to finally be able to put a face to the name," Tyler said, smiling warmly at his guest.

Craddock chuckled, sucked chocolate from his thumb and forefinger, then took a sip of coffee. "That's what my wife said the other night, when I got home," he declared in his thick country burr. "It was her subtle way of telling me that I've been spending too much time at work lately."

"How much longer do you think you'll be staying in London with us?" Tyler asked.

Craddock shrugged, giving the matter some thought. "Another couple of nights at least, I should imagine. Mr Diggle's being very cooperative, but with four murders from four different parts of the country to put to him, there's an awful lot of evidence to get through. We'll be applying for a warrant of further detention first thing tomorrow morning. Frank's sorting out the paperwork as we speak."

"Frank?" Tyler asked. The name was unfamiliar to him.

"Frank Stebbins, my bag man."

"Ah, I see," Tyler said.

"He's a good lad, bit slow off the mark but his heart is in the right place."

"Tell me, Barty," Dillon asked. "Do you think Bear was working alone?" It was a question that Imogen had posed to him earlier in the day.

Craddock's eyebrows undulated as he considered this. "I do. We found all his research in his hotel room. I must say, it was very extensive." He sounded genuinely impressed. "There were detailed dossiers on the four paedophiles he's already killed, and a half dozen more on what I can only assume were future targets."

Every time that Craddock spoke, Tyler battled the irrational urge to burst into a chorus of *I've Got A Brand New Combine Harvester* by The Wurzels. Maybe the sleep deprivation was catching up with him, playing tricks with his mind?

"I hear the house in Grove Green Road yielded some very interesting evidence," Craddock observed, with a twinkle in his eye.

"That's the understatement of the year," Tyler said.

It would take a forensic accountant weeks to muddle through all the paperwork that had been seized, which included extensive mail order lists, detailed bank records listing financial transactions from all over the country, and a Rolodex containing the names, addresses and payment details of every client that Benny had supplied pornographic material to over the past ten years.

If Tyler's suspicions were correct, the information contained within Benny's secret files would identify numerous active paedophiles across the UK.

"Thankfully, the powers that be have decided my team's involvement will be confined to investigating the murders of Adam Cheadle and Clive Walker, and the abduction of Peter Musgrove and Gavin Grant," Tyler said, unable to keep the relief from his voice. "Everything else is to be handed over to a joint task force comprised of officers from obscene publications, child protection and child exploitation."

"Perhaps, before you head back to Norfolk, we could all go out for a celebratory drink?" Dillon suggested.

Craddock's face lit up. "That's the best offer I've had all bloody week," he said with a smile.

---

It was very late. Craddock had gone back to his hotel. Tyler and Kelly had gone home. The few stragglers who remained in the office were getting ready to do likewise.

Steve Bull, looking fit to drop, was shrugging himself into his overcoat.

"How did you get on with charging Eberhard?" Dillon asked him.

Bull managed a weary smile. "We charged him with the rape and murder of Clive Walker, the false imprisonment and trafficking of Gavin Grant, and the three counts of possessing indecent images of children. I was expecting him to be gutted, but he had a spring in his step when he was taken back to his cell, like he was relieved to finally get it all off his chest." He shrugged to show he didn't understand the man at all.

"Not like Madeley then," Dillon snorted. "Apparently, he made no comment throughout interview, and didn't bat an eyelid when he was charged. Hopefully, he'll bump into some of the cons he's sentenced while he's on remand, and they'll kick the living shit out of him."

Imogen entered the office, looking very subdued. She hesitated when she saw Dillon talking to Bull, then went into his office to wait for him.

"I'd better go," Dillon said, patting Bull on the shoulder.

Grabbing his coat, he walked Imogen down to his car, which was parked out the front of the building. She didn't say a word all the way down.

"How do you feel?" he asked, unlocking the car. It was a stupid thing to come out with, but he felt compelled to say something.

"Okay," she said, sounding anything but.

"How did the production company react when you broke the news about Bear?"

She waited until they were inside before answering. "They were stunned, Tony. Bear was universally liked, if not loved. No one can believe it." She let out a long sigh, and her body seemed to deflate. "I hope he's alright," she said, miserably.

Dillon leaned over and squeezed her leg. "I promise he's being well treated. I spoke to Zoe Sanders, who's conducting the interviews with some DS from Norfolk. I've told her to make sure he's okay. From what I've been told by Barty Craddock this evening, Bear's talking very openly about what he did and why he did it."

She nodded, forlornly. "Thank you for keeping an eye on him, and for making sure he's looked after. I really do appreciate that."

Dillon started the engine. "What about the new girl, Molly? Holly? Polly? How's she getting on?"

Polly Bradshaw was the replacement videographer.

Imogen shrugged. "It's Polly, and she seems okay. She's very professional, but a bit too talkative for my liking."

"To be fair, it can't be easy for her, stepping in to replace Bear in circumstances like this."

"No, you're right," Imogen conceded. "I'll give her a chance before I start judging her too harshly."

They drove along Hertford Road in silence.

"What will happen to Bear?" Imogen asked, as they joined the A406.

Dillon had been expecting this question, and he really wished he could give her a better answer. "They're going to get a warrant of further detention in the morning, because they need more time to question him about all four murders. At the end, he'll be charged and remanded in custody pending trial."

Imogen was picking at a jagged fingernail. "I've decided that I'm going to visit him in prison," she said, warily, as if she was afraid that Dillon would object.

"You should," he told her. "You're his friend, and from what I gather, he doesn't have many of those. I'll come with you, if you like."

She glanced sideways, surprised by the offer. "Really?"

Dillon smiled "Of course. His brother was murdered by

paedophiles when he was nine years old. The bastards tried to kill Bear in the process. After going through that, it's no wonder he's done the things he has. I can't condone murder, but I completely understand what drove him to commit it."

"Wouldn't it be frowned upon, you visiting him, what with you being a DI and all?"

Dillon responded with a carefree shrug. "I don't see why it should be a problem. It's not my case, and I won't be talking to him about it, so if you want me to come with you, I will."

She was quiet for a while, thinking about his offer. In the end she said, "I can't tell you how much it means to me that you offered, but I think it would probably be for the best if I went alone, at least for the first few times."

Nodding his understanding, Dillon said nothing. He loved Imogen and would do anything for her but, in truth, he suspected that his visiting a man remanded for murder would be frowned upon by the establishment.

"I love you, Dill."

He shot her a quizzical look. "Dill?"

She had never called him that before; no one had, apart from Tyler.

She gave him a sassy smile. "I like it. And I've decided that, if it's good enough for Jack to use, it's good enough for me."

Dillon grinned back. That was more like the Imogen of old.

"I love you too," he told her.

# EPILOGUE

Three months later...

Every UK prison has a healthcare centre where inmates can be seen by a doctor, nurse or dentist, and where they can be given access to prescribed medication. Healthcare centres are invariably very busy places, with every available appointment taken up on most days. Prisoners with mental health issues and chemical dependencies account for the majority of patients, but there are also those in need of medicine for general ailments or treatment for minor injuries.

Few prisons have dedicated hospital wings, but most have infirmaries with a limited number of in-patient beds. These were always at a premium, so the recent norovirus outbreak had pushed the healthcare team to breaking point.

That night, there were five patients staying in the infirmary; four suffering from the winter vomiting bug and one with a minor concussion, caused by him slipping in the shower and bashing his head. Three of the patients with sickness and diarrhoea were scheduled to be released back to their wings the following morning, but one, an elderly man who was still badly dehydrated, was likely to need another day or two.

It was the middle of the night. The duty nurse had just returned to her cubicle after completing her hourly rounds. Sitting with her back to the patients, she didn't see the man who had been admitted with concussion slip out of his bed and tiptoe across the room to the far end, where the elderly man slept.

The nasty bump on Phillip Diggle's forehead, which was easily the size of a golf ball and had required three stitches, had been caused by him deliberately headbutting one of the tiled walls in the showers. The thumping headache he had given himself was real enough, but the concussion had been faked in order to fool the medical team into admitting him to the infirmary for overnight observations.

He had come up with the idea after overhearing two screws discussing the recent outbreak of norovirus. One of them had mentioned that the new celebrity prisoner from the Vulnerable Persons Unit had been carted off to the infirmary with it the previous night, and they had both commented that he deserved a lot worse than a stomach bug.

Diggle stood over Benny Mars for a few seconds, watching him sleep, then he placed a hand over the old man's mouth and nose and clamped down hard, cutting off his air supply.

Almost at once, Benny's eyes opened wide in alarm. He tried to call out, but was unable to draw breath. He attempted to wriggle free, but he was far too weak from his illness, and Diggle was a massive man, not just heavy but strong with it. Climbing on top of Benny, he pinned him to the bed, crushing him with the weight of his body.

"If you move or make a noise," he hissed in the old man's ear, "I'll snap your neck. Blink twice if you understand."

After a moment's hesitation, Benny blinked twice in rapid succession.

"Good," Diggle said, relaxing his grip enough for the old man to take a breath.

"Do you know who I am?" Diggle asked, staring into the old paedophile's terrified eyes.

Benny tried to move his head, but Diggle's hand was clamped around his jaw, preventing him from moving. "Blink once for no, twice for yes. Do you know who I am?"

One blink.

No.

"Do you know the name Robbie Diggle?"

A frown, then one blink.

No.

"Robbie was my twin brother," Diggle explained, his voice as cold as steel. "You, Mo Hinkleman and Angus Clifford raped and murdered him back in the summer of 1976. Do you remember that?"

The eyes went wide with fear.

Then one blink, slow and deliberate.

No.

"Liar."

Robbie's disappearance had attracted as much media attention in its day as Peter Musgrove and Gavin Grant's had the previous November.

Diggle clamped his hand over Benny's mouth and nose again, cutting off his air supply.

He waited until the old man was on the verge of passing out before allowing him to take a breath.

Benny gulped down air, taking several breaths in quick succession.

Diggle could feel the old man's heart; it was beating like a triphammer.

"Do you remember now?" Diggle hissed, baring his teeth in a snarl.

Benny swallowed, stalling for time.

Diggle reached into the top pocket of his pyjama top and pulled out a dog-eared photograph of him and Robbie at the campsite in Norfolk. The two boys were standing outside their newly erected tent, laughing at their mother as she took the snap of them.

"Look," he hissed, ramming it into Benny's face. "That's Robbie, on the left. Look how happy he was."

Benny's eyes were darting all around the room, looking anywhere but at the photo. Diggle realised that he was hoping one of the other patients would see what was going on and call for help. Two of the other inmates, woken by the commotion, were propping themselves up on their elbows, watching in silence. Diggle wasn't worried; everyone in the infirmary knew who Benny was, and what he had done, and none of them would lift a finger to help him.

"Don't expect anyone here to come to your rescue," he whispered, tightening his grip over Benny's mouth and nose. "No one likes a nonce, and they all want to see you get what you deserve."

Unable to breathe, Benny started thrashing around again. His legs began cycling, and he tried to free his arms, but they were pinned to his sides by the bigger man's bulk.

Diggle said nothing. The time for talking had passed. His face impassive, he yanked the pillow out from beneath Benny's head and placed it over the old man's face. Then he pressed down hard, leaning all his weight on it.

It took Benny longer to die than Diggle had anticipated, but eventually the old man stopped moving. Just to be sure, Diggle continued applying pressure for another minute.

As a means of execution, suffocation wasn't anywhere near as gratifying as cutting Benny's shrivelled manhood off and then slitting his throat would have been, but under the circumstances, Diggle decided that it would have to do.

Checking for a pulse and finding none, Diggle carefully replaced the pillow under Benny's head. He tucked the old man in and made him look comfortable. By the time he was finished, there were no signs that a struggle had occurred.

Diggle shot a quick glimpse at the nurse's station, to make sure that she hadn't noticed anything, then crept back to his own bed.

One of the other patients was smiling at him. Another gave him a thumbs up sign. He acknowledged each of them with a taciturn nod, confident that neither man would grass him up when the body was discovered in the morning. Even if they did, Diggle thought stoically, he was already facing a life sentence for the four murders he had admitted, so what did it matter if they charged him with another?

Closing his eyes, Diggle smiled contentedly. Wherever he was, he hoped that Robbie would finally be able to rest in peace, safe in the knowledge that the three men who had so cruelly ended his life all those years ago had now been punished, and that his untimely death had been properly avenged.

"Sleep well, my beloved brother," he whispered.

## TURF WAR

May 1999.

An out of town contract killer is drafted in to carry out a hit on an Albanian crime boss.

That same evening, in another part of town, four Turkish racketeers are ruthlessly gunned down while extorting protection money from local businessmen.

As the dust settles, it becomes apparent to DCI Jack Tyler that the two investigations are inexorably linked, and that someone is trying to orchestrate a gangland war that will tear the city apart.

But who? And why?

The pressure is on. can Tyler can find a way to stem the killings and restore order to the streets, or will this be the case that destroys his career?

---

## JACK'S BACK

October 1999.

When a horribly mutilated body is discovered lying beneath a taunting message written in its own blood, it quickly becomes apparent to DCI Jack Tyler that he's witnessing the birth of a terrifying new serial killer.

With the relentless media coverage causing panic on the streets of Whitechapel, Tyler is put under increasing pressure to bring the case to a rapid conclusion, but the murderer is scarily smart; a ghost who always seems to be one step ahead of the police.

Tyler knows that this case could make or break his career, but he doesn't care about the bad press, or the internal politics; all he's interested in is finding a way to stop the killer before he strikes again…

But what if he can't…?

## THE HUNT FOR CHEN

November 1999.

Exhausted from having just dealt with a series of gruesome murders in Whitechapel, DCI Jack Tyler and his team of homicide detectives are hoping for a quiet run in to Christmas.

Things are looking promising until the London Fire Brigade are called down to a house fire in East London and discover a charred body that has been wrapped in a carpet and set alight.

Attending the scene, Tyler and his partner, DI Tony Dillon, immediately realise that they are dealing with a brutal murder.

A witness comes forward who saw the victim locked in a heated argument with an Oriental male just before the fire started, but nothing is known about this mysterious man other than he drives a white van and his name might be Chen.

Armed with this frugal information, Tyler launches a murder investigation, and the hunt to find the unknown killer begins.

## UNLAWFULLY AT LARGE

January 2000.

When DCI Jack Tyler put Claude Winston behind bars, he was convinced the psychotic killer would never breathe fresh air again. Then the unthinkable happened and Winston escaped, leaving behind a trail of death and destruction.

Recapturing Winston won't be easy. He'll be better prepared this time around and, due to the bad blood that exists between them, he'll be itching for another chance to see Tyler lined up in the crosshairs of his gun.

Tyler doesn't care. With a colleague dead, this case has become personal, and he'll do whatever it takes to see justice done, even if that means putting his reputation and his life on the line.

## THE CANDY KILLER

July 2001.

When DCI Jack Tyler is called upon to investigate the murder of a man killed while trying to protect a girl from an aggressive drunk, he thinks the case is going to be fairly straightforward. He should have known better.

Recently released from prison, a convicted rapist is desperate to track down the love of his life and rekindle their relationship, but she has very different ideas, and would rather die than have him come anywhere near her.

When a kidnap plan goes wrong, those involved begin to turn on each other.

As their fates become increasingly entwined, not everyone will survive the fallout.

## DIAMONDS AND DEATH

October 2001.

When an ex-squaddie who's struggling to keep his failing business afloat discovers that a local thug has been entrusted to look after a small fortune in diamonds, he senses an opportunity to get rich quick. But there's a snag. The gems belong to a notorious East London gangster, and he's not a man you steal from if you want to continue breathing.

When an unidentified body is found floating in Regent's Canal, DCI Jack Tyler is tasked with solving the sinister mystery. A difficult and frustrating case from the start, it doesn't help that he's been saddled with a TV crew who are making a documentary about homicide investigations.

It hasn't been a great start to the week, and things are about to get a whole lot worse…

# ACKNOWLEDGMENTS

Edited by Yvonne Goldsworthy

Cover design by Darren Howell

As always, I'd like to say a very special thank you to my brilliant team of Beta Readers, not only for taking the time to read the first draft of the manuscript, but also for all the fantastic feedback they provided. They are: Clare R, Danny A, Cathie A, and Darren H.

# GLOSSARY OF TERMS

AC – Assistant Commissioner
ACPO – Association of Chief Police Officers
AFO – Authorised Firearms Officer
AIDS – Acquired Immune Deficiency Syndrome
AMIP – Area Major Investigation Pool (Predecessor to the Homicide Command)
ANPR – Automatic Number Plate Recognition
ARV – Armed Response Vehicle
ASU – Air Support Unit
ATC – Air Traffic Control
ATS – Automatic Traffic Signal
Azimuth – The coverage from each mobile phone telephone mast is split into three 120-degree arcs called azimuths
Bacon – derogatory slang expression for a police officer
Bandit – the driver of a stolen car or other vehicle failing to stop for police
BIU – Borough Intelligence Unit
BPA – Blood Pattern Analysis
BTP – British Transport Police
C11 – Criminal Intelligence / surveillance

*Glossary of terms*

CAD – Computer Aided Dispatch
CCTV – Closed Circuit Television
Chicken – A child who willingly or unwillingly engages in homosexual sex with a paedophile
CIB – Complaints Investigation Bureau
CID – Criminal Investigation Department
CIPP – Crime Investigation Priority Project
County Mounties – a phrase used by Met officers to describe police officers from the Constabularies
Cozzers – Police Officers
CJPU – Criminal Justice Protection Unit (witness protection)
CRIMINT – Criminal Intelligence
CPS – Crown Prosecution Service
CSM – Crime Scene Manager
(The) Craft – the study of magic
CRIS – Crime Reporting Information System
DNA – Deoxyribonucleic Acid
DC – Detective Constable
DS – Detective Sergeant
DI – Detective Inspector
DCI – Detective Chief Inspector
DSU – Detective Superintendent
DCS – Detective Chief Superintendent
DPG – Diplomatic Protection Group
DVLA – Driver and Vehicle Licensing Agency
ECHR – European Court of Human Rights
Enforcer – a heavy metal battering ram used to force open doors
ESDA – Electrostatic Detection Apparatus (sometimes called an EDD or Electrostatic Detection Device)
ETA – Expected Time of Arrival
(The) Factory – Police jargon for their base.
FLO – Family Liaison Officer
FME – Force Medical Examiner
Foxtrot Oscar – Police jargon for 'fuck off'
FSS – Forensic Science Service
GP – General Practitioner

*Glossary of terms*

GMC – General Medical Council
GMP – Greater Manchester Police
GSR – Gun Shot Residue
HA – Arbour Square police station
HAT – Homicide Assessment Team
HEMS – Helicopter Emergency Medical Service
HIV – Human Immunodeficiency Virus
HOLMES – Home Office Large Major Enquiry System
HP – High Priority
HR – Human Resources
HT – Whitechapel borough / Whitechapel police station
IC1 – PNC code for a white European
IC2 – PNC code for a dark skinned European
IC3 – PNC code for an Afro Caribbean
IC4 – PNC code for an Asian
IC5 – PNC code for an Oriental
IC6 – PNC code for an Arab
ICU – Intensive Care Unit
IFR – Instrument Flight Rules are used by pilots when visibility is not good enough to fly by visual flight rules
IO – Investigating Officer
IPCC – Independent Police Complaints Commission
IR – Information Room
IRV – Immediate Response Vehicle
JL – Leyton police station
JS – Leytonstone police station
KF – Forest Gate police station
KZ – Hertford House, East London base of the Homicide Command, also known as SO1(3)
Kiting checks – trying to purchase goods or obtain cash with stolen / fraudulent checks
LAG – Lay Advisory Group
LAS – London Ambulance Service
LFB – London Fire Brigade
Lid – uniformed police officer
LOS – Lost or Stolen vehicle

*Glossary of terms*

MIR – Major Incident Room
MIT – Major Investigation Team
MP – Radio call sign for Information Room at NSY
MPH – Miles Per Hour
MICH/ACH (Modular Integrated Communications Helmet / Advanced Ballistic Combat Helmet)
MPS – Metropolitan Police Service
MSS – Message Switching System
NABIS – National Ballistics Intelligence Service
NADAC – National ANPR Data Centre
NFA – No Further Action
NHS – National Health Service
Nondy – Nondescript vehicle, typically an observation van
NOTAR – No Tail Rotor system technology
NPIA – National Police Improvement Agency
NSY – New Scotland Yard
OCG – Organised Crime Group
OH – Occupational Health
Old Bill – the police
OM – Office Manager
OP – Observation Post
P9 – MPS Level 1/P9 Surveillance Trained
PACE – Police and Criminal Evidence Act 1984
PC – Police Constable
PCMH – Plea and Case Management Hearing
Pig – Derogatory slang expression for a police officer
PIP – Post Incident Procedure
PLO – Press Liaison Officer
Plod – Slang expression for a police officer, usually a uniformed officer on beat patrol
PM – Post Mortem
PNC – Police National Computer
POLACC – Police Accident
PR – Personal Radio
PS – Police Sergeant

*Glossary of terms*

PTT – Press to Talk
RCJ – Royal Courts of Justice
RCS – Regional Crime Squad
Rent boy – a male prostitute, often under the age of legal consent
Ringer – stolen car on false number plates
RLH – Royal London Hospital
Rozzers – the police
RTA – Road traffic Accident
RT car – Radio Telephone car, nowadays known as a Pursuit Vehicle
QC – Queen's Counsel (a very senior barrister)
Rubber Heelers – Police officers attached to Complaints Investigation Bureau
SCG – Serious Crime Group
Scruffs – Dressing down in casual clothes in order for a detective to blend in with his / her surroundings
SFO – Specialist Firearms Officer
SIO – Senior Investigating Officer
Sheep – followers of Christ; the masses
SIDS – Sudden Infant Death Syndrome, commonly referred to as cot death
Skipper - Sergeant
SNT – Safer Neighbourhood Team
SO – Specialist Operations
SO1 – Homicide Command
SO8 – The Flying Squad
SO11 – Criminal Intelligence / surveillance (formerly C11)
SO19 – Met Police Firearms Unit
SOCO – Scene of Crime Officer
SOIT – Sexual Offences Investigative Technique
SPM – Special Post Mortem
SPOC – Single Point of Contact
Stinger – a hollow spiked tyre deflation device
Tango – Target
TDA – Taking and Driving Away
TDC – Trainee Detective Constable

*Glossary of terms*

TIE – Trace, Interview, Eliminate
TPAC – Tactical Pursuit and containment
Trident – Operation Trident is the Met unit investigating 'black on black' gun crime
TSG – Territorial Support Group
TSU – Technical Support Unit
Tyvek suit – The all-in-one zip up forensic barrier suits that are worn at crime scenes
VODS – Vehicle On-line Descriptive Searching
Walkers – officers on foot patrol
Trumpton – the Fire Brigade
VFR – Visual Flight Rules are regulations under which a pilot operates an aircraft in good visual conditions
Wolfpack – a name historically used by predatory paedophilic gangs to describe themselves

# AUTHOR'S NOTE

Wolfpack is the seventh story I've penned in the DCI Tyler Thrillers, and because of the highly emotive subject matter it deals with, it has been by far the most difficult to write. In fact, if I'm being completely honest, there were a number of times during the research phase when I genuinely considered giving up on it and writing a different story instead.

According to the missing person statistics set out within the National Crime Agency report 2021 - 2022, someone is reported missing every 90 seconds in the UK. Of the 170,000 people reported missing each year, 70,000 are children. Many of the children who are reported missing are vulnerable and or at risk; a large percentage are repeat absconders. Seven out of ten children who have been sexually exploited have also been reported missing at some point.

Fortunately, less than 2% of children remain missing for more than one week.

Missing persons are reported to the Police National Missing Persons Bureau (PNMPB) after they have been missing for 14 days or more. During the 2001 – 2002 reporting period, which is when

## Author's note

this story is set, 1,034 children under the age of 18 were reported missing to the PNMPB.

In 2001, the majority of the UK's runaway teenagers gravitated towards London before disappearing into the ether. Every other coach pulling into Victoria deposited more vulnerable kids onto the streets. Naturally, many of the new arrivals gravitated towards the West End, attracted by the glitz and the glamour. The bright lights, buzzing atmosphere and numerous amusement arcades drew impressionable teenagers like Gabriel Warren like moths to a flame. It was an exciting place to be at first, but then the cold, thirst, hunger, depression and loneliness set in, and a grim realisation dawned upon them that the streets of London were most definitely not paved with gold.

The urgent need for easily acquired cash forced many of them down a well-trodden path to self-destruction. Sexual predators like Benny Mars, Aaron Remus and Joey McQueen were aware of this, and they flocked to the area to stalk their vulnerable prey. It was almost like shooting fish in a barrel. All they had to do was wait for the youngsters to show up and offer them kindness. The predators would befriend them, carefully groom them, and then corrupt and abuse them. When they were no longer of any use, the children were discarded like rubbish and new sex slaves were recruited to take their place. The police officers working clubs and vice knew what was going on, but with the limited resources available to them, trying to stop it was like trying to plug a sieve.

In the late eighties and early nineties, a number of predatory paedophilic wolfpacks like the one described in this book operated in London. The Dirty Dozen, led by the infamous Sidney Cooke, is perhaps the most famous, but there were others who were equally deplorable.

Although this book is entirely a work of fiction, and the paedophiles who feature in it are made up, it is a sad fact of life that loathsome creatures like Mars, Hinkleman, Remus, McQueen, Eberhard and Madeley did and do exist. Grotesque films of children being abused, like the one that Eberhard was arrested for watching, were – and probably still are – made and distributed to

*Author's note*

likeminded individuals by evil men who are happy to profit from the suffering of innocents

The police and other law enforcement agencies continue to wage a never ending war against those responsible for these hideous crimes, and I wish them every success.

Thank you for reading Wolfpack. If you've enjoyed it, please, consider leaving a quick review on Amazon for me. It really doesn't have to be anything fancy; just a couple of lines to say whether you enjoyed the book and would recommend it to others. I can't stress how helpful feedback like this is for indie authors like me. Apart from influencing the book's visibility, your reviews will help people who haven't read my work yet to decide whether it's right for them.

If you haven't read it yet it, pop over to my website, www.markromain.com, and grab yourself a free copy of The Hunt For Chen.

Right, it's time for me to get cracking on Tyler's next big case! The next book will feature some very nasty Russian mobsters!

Best wishes,

Mark.

# ABOUT THE AUTHOR

Mark Romain is a retired Metropolitan Police officer, having joined the Service in the mid-eighties. His career included two homicide postings, and during that time he was fortunate enough to work on a number of very challenging high-profile cases.

Mark lives in Essex with his wife, Clare. They have two grown-up children and one grandchild. Between them, the family has three English Bull Terriers and a very bossy Dachshund called Weenie!

Mark is a lifelong Arsenal fan and an avid skier. He also enjoys going to the theatre, weightlifting and kick-boxing, a sport he got into during his misbegotten youth!

You can find out more about Mark's books or contact him via his website www.markromain.com or Facebook page:

Printed in Great Britain
by Amazon